THE LOST CHILD

Also available from Millennium

Moths to a Flame
Songspinners

·The Lost Child·

SARAH ASH

MILLENNIUM
An Orion Book
LONDON

Copyright © Sarah Ash 1998
All rights reserved

The right of Sarah Ash to be identified as the author of this
work has been asserted by her in accordance with
the Copyright, Designs and Patents Act 1988.

This edition first published
in 1998 by Millennium
An imprint of Orion Books Ltd
Orion House, 5 Upper St Martin's Lane
London WC2H 9EA

A CIP catalogue record for this book is available
from the British Library

Typeset at Spartan Press Ltd
Lymington, Hants

Printed and bound in Great Britain by
Clays Ltd, St Ives plc

To my sister, Jessica

Acknowledgements

To my editor Caroline Oakley, with my thanks for her insight, patience and literary intuition – and to Mike for his support and cups of tea!

Blue petals, blue as the cloudless sky above, drift down from open windows on to the procession passing below.

It is the first day of spring, Lady Day, in the city of Arcassanne. Led by Prieur Maugis, the followers of the Lady process with Her statue through the streets of the city. Girls strew Her path with blue flowers, the colour of Her gown, the colour of redemption. Choirs of little children sing the Lady's song in high, piping voices, clear as a chorus of skylarks. It is a day of happiness for the city, this first day of spring, the day when the Lady's statue is taken to each well on Her way, to bless and purify the waters for the year to come.

The procession approaches the archway that leads to the dark, narrow streets of the Tsiyonim Quarter. By order of the Comtes of the city of Arcassanne, the Tsiyonim are allowed to practise their religion without interference or persecution. The Lady passes on by.

In the *shul* the little congregation of Tsiyonim have gathered together. The Elders take dust from the floor and smear it on their foreheads. The dust is stained with their tears. Oblivious to the sounds of rejoicing in the city, they listen to the words of the Book of Alevi and mourn the loss of their own holy city, Tsiyon, as they have done on this day for years without number. The day of joy for the followers of the Lady is their day of sorrow and bitter regret.

Rebh Jehiel intones the ancient prayer, the prayer that they may one day return to Tsiyon and rebuild the holy city, that they may one day put right the mistake their forefathers made, the one terrible mistake that cost them their land and their holy city.

1

PROLOGUE

Watchfires glowed, casting scorched shadows on the moonlit dunes. Captain Jaufré d'Orbiel sat in his tent, writing by the wavering light of a single lantern, finishing the last dispatches to be sent back to Arcassanne.

The night was so still that Jaufré could hear the distant slow tread of the nightwatch patrolling the perimeters of the camp. A gust of dry wind stirred the lantern-flame, exuding a faint breath of desert fragrance: spikenard and balsam, sweetly bitter as burning incense.

Jaufré sighed as he dipped his pen into the ink.

He had lost too many men. Six dead, seven wounded and three unaccounted for. A heavy toll for what should have been a simple task for his company, the Hawks, escorting Comte Aymon's diplomatic mission to the Potentate of Djihan-Djihar with the aim of establishing a new trade route to the coast.

With a heavy heart he inscribed the name 'Alois Guisbourg' at the end of the list, adding, 'Missing, presumed dead.' Alois, his boyhood friend and companion-in-arms. Alois, with his eager, lop-sided grin, his untidy shock of barley-fair hair, his bantering good humour ... The last time anyone recalled seeing Alois was in the shabby little town of Ilh-djor where the detachment had stopped to buy provisions. Pedlars and traders had rushed up to sell their wares and in the confusion, Alois had just ... disappeared.

Jaufré was weary of soldiering, weary of writing reports, dispatches. In Arcassanne, he was better known as a poet than a soldier ... though when had poetry ever earned a man enough to live on?

He paused, breathing in the hot, scented air. There was a kind of poetry in the harsh heat of the desert, he supposed, but thus far it had eluded him. The aridity of the wastes of Djihan-Djihar had parched his imagination as surely as it had dried the ink in the ink-well.

He began to wonder if he would ever write a poem again . . .

A gust of dust-dry wind shivered through the camp. Jaufré glanced up –

And saw that he was no longer alone. A man stood in front of him, swathed in faded ochre robes and burnous.

Assassin. Snake Warrior. Jaufré reached for his sword.

'Captain. Wait.' The figure drew back the concealing head-dress to reveal a shrunken, emaciated face beneath, a hideous mummified face, burned to the texture of old leather. Jaufré stared, the sword half-drawn from its sheath, into eyes that burned dark with the dying fire of fever.

'Who the hell –'

'Jaufré . . .' The stranger gripped his arm with spindle fingers. His breath was foul, rank with the taint of decay. Jaufré made to break away, but the man clung to him as if he were drowning. 'Don't you know me?' His words came haltingly yet with no trace of a Djihari accent. 'Am I so changed? It's me. Alois.'

Jaufré forced himself to gaze into the sun-seared face.

'Alois?' he said slowly, disbelievingly. 'But – we thought you were dead.'

The cracked lips twisted into a grimace, revealing blackened gums.

'Dead. Better dead than – than this life in death. Help me, Jaufré. Help me to put an end to it.'

'How – how can I help you?' Mesmerised by Alois's staring eyes, Jaufré did not dare to conjecture what had transformed the confident, handsome young soldier he remembered into this shambling, diseased shadow.

'W-water –' Alois's claw hands stretched out tremblingly towards Jaufré's flask which stood beside the half-written dispatch.

'Here.' Jaufré put the flask in his hands. 'Drink.'

Alois raised the flask to his mouth and gulped greedily as the water came pouring out; spilling down his chin. But after a few mouthfuls, he began to retch, dropping the flask, clutching at his throat, his sunken belly. 'Ahh. It burns. It burns.'

Jaufré let the flask lie where it had fallen; he had no wish to drink again now that Alois's diseased lips had touched it.

Alois dropped to his knees; he slowly raised his withered head until Jaufré could see that a dark, blood-stained slime hung in trails from his mouth.

'In God's name, Alois, what has happened to you?' Jaufré said in a whisper. 'Shall I fetch a doctor?'

Alois shook his head.

'No point . . .'

'A priest, then?'

Alois's hunched shoulders began to heave, to shake convulsively. Jaufré took a tentative step forwards, wondering if the young man had begun to weep. But then he realised that Alois was laughing, a gasping, shuddering laugh that it hurt Jaufré's ears to listen to.

'A priest? I am beyond the help of our faith, my friend. So far beyond that you would not –' The laughter broke off suddenly as a spasm gripped Alois and he rolled over, writhing as if in unendurable agony.

Jaufré knelt down by him and, steeling himself to overcome his revulsion, put his hands on Alois's shoulders, holding him down until the spasm calmed.

'Only you can help me, Jaufré . . .' The dark eyes were filmed, cloudy with pain, yet a fevered flame still burned faintly in the hollow eye-sockets.

'How?'

'You must . . . take it, give it back . . .' Alois's voice was growing fainter.

Jaufré leaned closer, trying not to breathe in the mephitic stench exuding from the wasted body.

'Give what back?'

The twisted fingers reached up, scrabbling to pull something from under the filthy rags that had once been a Hawks tunic.

'This . . .'

Jaufré stared. Against Alois's dirt-caked, burned skin, it gleamed like the sun breaking through stormclouds. An enamelled disc of beaten metals, it portrayed a winged figure, arms outstretched, wings widespread, each black pinion outlined in crimson, vermilion and copper. The beauty of the artistry, the skill of the crafting took his breath away. He could feel the itch in his fingers, longing to reach out, to touch the precious object –

'What is it?' Jaufré breathed.

'You must give it back to them . . .' Alois was becoming agitated again; his fingers plucked at Jaufré's sleeve. 'Promise me, Jaufré. Promise me you'll give it back.'

Jaufré stared at the disc, mesmerised.

4

'How did you come by it?'

'I – I bought it. The trader – said it would bring – good luck. Good luck!' Another shudder of dry laughter convulsed Alois's frame. 'I didn't know then – what it is or – where it came from –'

'What is it, man?' demanded Jaufré. 'And who wants it back? Was it stolen?'

'It – is Tsiyonim.' The words came out on a trail of blood-tinged spittle. 'Part of – an amulet. An – ancient amulet of power. There is – a curse on it –'

'An amulet?' Jaufré could not disguise his scepticism. 'Don't tell me you fell for that old Djihari trick, Alois!'

'You must believe me –'

'I warned you all at the start of the campaign, didn't I? The Snake Tribe are lethal enemies. There's no magical power in this amulet . . . but I'll lay bets the trader who sold you this impregnated it with venom. Your good-luck charm has lain next to your skin, leaching its poison into your body –'

'No . . .' Alois's fingers fumbled at Jaufré's collar. 'It came from . . . the Temple ruins in Tsiyon . . . It must be given back to the Tsiyonim. It is . . . too powerful . . .'

'Powerful?' It was certainly an exquisite piece of craftsmanship. Jaufré could not take his eyes off it; it seemed to radiate a dull, burnished lustre as if a flame burned at the heart of the metal. 'What d'you mean – powerful?'

Alois's grip tightened on his collar, dragging Jaufré's head closer to his own.

'Don't let yourself be seduced.' Alois's ribs heaved as he struggled for breath. 'Get rid of it – before it starts to work its mischief on you.'

'Mischief?'

'It was never meant for us . . . it works through us, it seeks the others . . .'

'Others? What others?' Jaufré caught hold of Alois by the shoulders, shaking him in his frustration.

'There were four . . . one to guard each corner of the Temple . . .' Alois seemed not to hear Jaufré's question. His eyes had begun to slide upwards. The rasping breath became a rattle. A death rattle.

'Alois! Alois!' Jaufré cried, shaking him.

'Give it back to the Tsiyonim . . . promise me you will give it back . . .'

'I . . . I will give it back.' Even as he spoke the words, Jaufré's fingers were stealing out to touch the dark lustre of the gleaming amulet. 'I give you my word, Alois.'

The wheezing rattle was slowing, fading to silence.

He felt Alois's head slump sideways against his arm. The life had seeped out of the emaciated body, which now lay limp and still.

Jaufré gently eased Alois down on to the ground and closed the sunken, staring eyes. Then he sat back on his heels, still staring at the dead man.

Alois Guisbourg had been twenty-four years old when he set sail for Djihan-Djihar. The body that lay on the sandy ground was the body of an ancient man, sucked dry of youth and life.

Give it back . . .

Give it back – but to whom? Djihan-Djihar had once belonged to the Tsiyonim – until the Djihari tribesmen had swept down from the mountains, burned their Temple and razed the great city of Tsiyon to the ground, claiming the land for their god Ilh-Alh. The few surviving Tsiyonim tribes had been driven out, scattered to the four corners of the world.

There were Tsiyonim in Arcassanne. He would take the amulet back with him and give it into the safe-keeping of the Elders of the community.

Jaufré reached out to touch the amulet – and then checked himself. Suppose he had been right – and the gleaming disc was tainted with one of the lethal Djihari desert poisons? He drew his handkerchief from his pocket and wrapped his hand in it before leaning over to take the amulet from the dead man's hand.

The twisted claw-fingers still clutched the treasure tightly and he had to prise them apart to ease the amulet free, swallowing back his revulsion. As he took the amulet into his own hand, a sudden gush of black, viscous liquid issued from the corpse's mouth, seeping into the sand. Jaufré drew back in disgust. He was not squeamish, but there was something about this sudden leaking of dark, noisome fluid from the ravaged insides of a body not yet cold and stiff that turned his stomach. It was almost as if his removing of the amulet had caused the noxious expulsion, as if some concentration of evil substances had left the body, like lice seeking the warmth of a new, living host. Now Alois's wasted, sun-seared shell lay relaxed, empty.

Jaufré gazed down at the ancient amulet which lay, protected by his linen handkerchief, in his cupped hands. Now that he

6

could see it more clearly, it was evident that it was incomplete, a part of a whole. Was that what Alois had meant when he had babbled about the Temple? Was it a part of the fabled lost treasure of the Temple at Tsiyon?

In the wavering lanternlight, Jaufré could just make out what looked like characters in the corona surrounding the winged figure's upraised head. Was it a name . . . or a word of power? He had reacted with his habitual scepticism when Alois had called the amulet powerful. How could a piece of crafted metal be powerful? But now that he held it, he felt a faint thrill of sensation, a visceral stir of excitement.

Give it back . . .

He glanced guiltily at Alois's still body. It seemed indecent to be so obsessed with the amulet when there was the news to be broken to the company and a burial to be organised. And . . . how to explain Alois's deterioration and death when he did not begin to understand it himself? He must not under any circumstances mention the amulet. He would report the cause of death as exposure and dysentery.

He stood up and went to open his writing chest in which he kept his pens and inks, placing the wrapped amulet carefully inside and locking the chest with the key he kept on a chain around his neck.

In the adjoining tent, his lieutenant, Berengar de Belcastel, lay asleep, wrapped in his cloak. Jaufré knelt down and shook him by the shoulder.

'Wh-what?' Berengar struggled up, half-dazed with sleep. 'Attack?'

'I want you to organise a burial.'

'B-but who –'

'Alois. Crawled back here to die. Poor wretch – out there in the desert, he didn't stand a chance.'

CHAPTER 1

Jaufré d'Orbiel stood at the open window of his high turret room, watching the summer storm raging over the walled city of Arcassanne.

On his desk lay a clean sheet of vellum, untouched. Beside it, his pen, the nib dry.

For weeks now since his return from the campaign in Djihan-Djihar he had been afflicted with this terrible lassitude, this deep, dragging sense of . . .

Futility.

Nothing excited him any longer. Nothing inspired him, not even the white thighs of Grazide, the Lily of Arcassanne.

His songs were flat, stale, derivative.

The fire of love that had once inflamed him had died to cold ashes.

Grazide had been so much more desirable whilst she was Comte Aymon's mistress. He had called her a frost-lily, a flower of ice . . . The more she disdained his advances, the more he burned with desire, his words smouldering with unfulfilled passion, his melodies throbbing with the obsessive patterns of despair.

But since the night the flower of ice had melted in his arms, he had lost interest in her caresses. This dragging malaise had infected his soul.

His hands strayed to his writing chest, unlocking it, pushing up the lid.

There it lay, gleaming amongst the ink-phials and pens, enamelled bronze, crimson and glossy black, colours of night and sunset.

The Tsiyonim amulet.

It was the only thing in his life which still had the power to excite some dull stirring of interest.

He knew he should have given it into the keeping of the Tsiyonim community in Arcassanne. He had made that promise

8

to Alois as he lay dying, that hot, spice-scented night in Djihan-Djihar.

And he would fulfil that promise . . . in his own good time.

He just needed to conduct a little research into the origins of the amulet before he handed it back to the Tsiyonim. Any scholar would have done the same. He was not going to keep it, he was merely investigating it.

His investigations had led him into sordid back streets of Arcassanne to the apothecaries and alchemists who sold illicit love philtres and sleep draughts.

Lightning lit the turret room. Thunder rolled from the distant mountains.

The book of Tsiyonim magic lay open on the writing desk. The alchemist who had sold it to him claimed it was bound in human skin and written in human blood. Jaufré did not for one moment believe the claim – yet he was intrigued enough not to argue too much over the exorbitant price. The book had piqued his curiosity.

It gave him a certain perverse pleasure to handle it, to wonder if his fingers were caressing dead skin . . . and if so, how it had been removed . . . Had the skin been flayed off a living man . . . or woman? The thought always aroused a delicious shiver of disgust.

The text purported to be translated from the *Sefer Rhaziel* and contained – in Jaufré's sceptical opinion – all manner of nonsense. Fragments of mystical texts were mingled with meaningless mumbo-jumbo.

There came another flash of lightning, its white flare illuminating the worn pages.

Jaufré stared.

Between the diagrams of circles and pentagrams, the occult symbols and spells of summoning, the lightning had revealed other, hidden words, written in invisible ink. In the lightning's brief flare Jaufré identified luminous characters, glimmering like phosphorus.

He seized his pen and, dipping it in the ink, feverishly began to trace over the fast-fading lightning-letters.

The Tsiyonim knew ancient, arcane secrets. They knew how to harness the power of the lightning to their will. And he sensed that the key to their secret knowledge – and the key to the secret of the amulet – was concealed somewhere within these faded, stained pages.

'Yet let he who summons Them beware. Let him remember the fate of Ithamar and all his Tribe.

'Barakiel, Wielder of Heavenly Fire, shall come from the East; from the North, cold Shalgiel with snow-feathered wings; the earth shakes at the tread of Rashiel. The last of these is Lailahel, Bringer of Eternal Night.'

'Four,' Jaufré murmured. What had Alois said as he lay dying? *'Four . . . to guard each corner of the Temple . . .'*

'They will seek the blood of the pure, blood of the innocent. To that blood They will cleave . . .'

Lightning and thunder converged overhead in one dazzling, ear-splitting explosion. The stones of the Orbiel Tower shuddered.

Jaufré flung up one arm to protect his eyes from the blinding brightness.

'Jaufré . . .'

As he lowered his arm he glimpsed a figure silhouetted against the window, a shadowfigure that dwindled even as his dazzled eyes focused upon it.

'You gave me your promise, Jaufré . . .'

'Alois?' Jaufré cried.

'Remember. Remember what became of me . . .'

But the storm was already passing on overhead, and when the lightning shivered through the chamber again, Jaufré saw that he was alone.

The narrow lanes of the Tsiyonim Quarter of Arcassanne were dark and dank, even in the pitiless heat of an Arcassanne summer when the sun's intense light dazzled off the white walls and watchtowers of the city. But the houses of the Tsiyonim huddled close together as if seeking shelter from a hostile world.

Jaufré walked swiftly through the gathering dusk, one hand on the hilt of his sword. He was aware that he was being watched; aware that there were wary eyes staring behind iron grilles and patterned shutters. But no one challenged him – and the few Tsiyonim he passed vanished into doorways or alleyways at his approach. No one made any overt gesture of hostility, but he could sense he was not welcome.

The most learned man in the community, he had been told, was the scholar, Rebh Jehiel. Jehiel's house was in the heart of the community, next to the *shul*, the house of worship. Who

10

better to return the amulet to but the only Tsiyonim priest and scholar in Arcassanne?

He had promised Alois he would give the amulet back to the Tsiyonim. But now that the lightning had revealed the hidden text in the Sefer Rhaziel, he knew he could not relinquish it without first uncovering its secret.

Besides . . . he had to be certain that this Jehiel was worthy to take the amulet. He could not bear to think that it would pass to a man who did not appreciate its archaic beauty – or its peerless craftsmanship. To that end he had brought the *Sefer Rhaziel* with him, concealed beneath his jacket.

The lane in which the *shul* stood was overhung with gnarled mulberry trees and vines. Jehiel's cottage nestled in the shadow of the *shul*, a modest little house built of weathered Arcassanne stone.

Squaring his shoulders, Jaufré went up the path that led to the front door and knocked. No one answered.

Perhaps Jehiel was at his prayers and did not wish to be disturbed?

Jaufré knocked again. Still no reply.

He was on the point of turning away when he heard hesitant footsteps approaching within, and the door opened. To his surprise, a grey cat came whisking out between his legs, disappearing into the shadows like a ghost.

'Yes? How can I help you?'

A white-haired old man stood on the doorstep, blinking up at Jaufré through a pair of ill-balanced pebble pince-nez spectacles.

'You are Jehiel the scholar, archivist of the community?' Jaufré asked.

'That is my name.' Jehiel took off the spectacles and narrowed his eyes as he scrutinised Jaufré. 'But you have me at a disadvantage, messire –'

'I need your help in a matter of scholarship.' Jaufré did not wish to give his name.

'A Gentile wanting help from a Tsiyonim?' The scholar's pale eyes narrowed a little as he gazed at Jaufré. 'Perhaps you had better come in.'

The desk in Jehiel's study was spilling over with books, scrolls and documents. As they entered, a second grey cat arose from the desk and leapt down with a soft thud of paws.

'Mischkin, Mischkin,' chided Jehiel, 'sitting on the Holy Laws again . . .'

11

Jaufré caught a glint of slanting eyes, yellow as amber, as Mischkin slunk out with an offended swish of his grey-silk tail.

'So how may I help you?' Jehiel said, sweeping up an armful of parchments to make a space on the desk.

Jaufré cleared his throat.

'Does a book called the *Sefer Rhaziel* mean anything to you?'

'I've heard that certain men calling themselves alchemists sell what they claim to be translations of the *Sefer Rhaziel*. I assure you, sieur, they are all fakes.'

'Even this one?' Jaufré removed the book from where he held it concealed within his jacket and placed it on the desk.

'Assuredly, that one too.'

'So it's a fake?' Jaufré opened the book at the place he had marked and began to read. '"Barakiel, Wielder of Heavenly Fire, shall come from the East . . ."'

Jehiel dropped the parchments he was holding.

'God preserve us.'

Jaufré had not expected the scholar to react so dramatically. And then a slow burn of excitement began to spread through his body as he realised that Jehiel recognised the words he was reading – and knew what they meant. 'I hoped you might be able to shed some light on the meaning of the passage. Is it a metaphor? Has it some religious significance?'

'But what possible interest could it hold for you, a Gentile?'

'I have not long returned from Djihan-Djihar,' Jaufré said.

'Ahhh.' Jehiel let out a sigh heavy with longing . . . and despair. 'I know I must call it by that other name . . . but to me and my people, it will always be the Land of Tsiyon. Never Djihan-Djihar.'

'"They will seek the blood of the pure, blood of the innocent. To that blood They will cleave,"' read Jaufré. 'What does that mean?'

Rebh Jehiel was staring at him with a stricken expression on his face.

'It would take you years of study, messire, to begin to gain some understanding of our sacred texts,' he said stiltedly.

'Then let me be your student. Teach me.'

'You are asking something of me which I cannot do.'

'Cannot?' Jaufré said, angered. 'Or will not?'

'Don't you understand? The meaning is hidden; it is not revealed because it is not meant to be revealed.'

12

'Or not revealed to the uninitiate?' Jaufré had not expected to encounter such inflexibility. Perhaps he had unwittingly offended the scholar by not offering payment for his skills? 'I've gold in my purse – and I can bring more.'

'All the gold in Arcassanne would not make me change my mind.'

Jehiel brusquely handed the *Sefer Rhaziel* back to him and marched to the study door, holding it open. Jaufré realised he was being dismissed – with all the courtesy afforded to an unruly schoolboy.

'So you refuse.'

'I am not fit to undertake this – this instruction. That path is reserved for the very few. The chosen.'

Damn all the Tsiyonim and their precious secrets to Hell!

Still stinging from Jehiel's abrupt dismissal, Jaufré unlocked the chest in which the amulet lay concealed and pulled back the fine layers of linen in which he had wrapped it.

Bronze pinions, flame-tipped, glimmered against the liquid black of the enamelled sky.

Jaufré's fingers itched to touch it. If there were any poison on the enamel, it must by now have seeped into the folds of linen . . . and there was not a trace of a stain on the white cloth.

He had reached in, lifting it out, before he became fully aware of what he was doing, gloating that the treasure was now *his*, not the crusty old scholar's.

Now that he held it close he could see that the winged figure was a man, dark-skinned as night, his streaming locks of black hair lit with fire.

'Angel . . .' he whispered.

But who now would reveal the name of the fiery angel? Who would tell him its significance? Jehiel, the only scholar of repute in the whole city, had shut the door in his face.

There must be some way to unlock its secrets . . .

He uncorked the phial of Arkendym sleep draught on his desk and swallowed down a mouthful, grimacing at the bitter taste. It was concocted from the juice of the rare moonblue poppy which grew, so the apothecary assured him, below the snowfields of the Mountains of Mynezhil . . .

When he slept, his dreams were filled with the beat of night-feathered wings.

*

13

Jaufré gazed down from the open window of his high turret room and saw an angel in the street below.

Halo of sunglints in wild, wind-tangled hair . . .

He shaded his dazzled eyes against the summer sun's fierce glare and saw his angel was only a boy, a ragged street child, playing alone in the gutter. He seemed utterly unselfconscious, absorbed in his game, spinning a coin high into the air and catching it. He was seven, maybe eight years old . . .

'Blood of the pure, blood of the innocent . . .'

Jaufré leaned out over the sill – and whistled.

Startled, the child looked round and the coin fell into the gutter. Cursing, he began to scrabble with his fingers, searching. When his efforts seemed to prove fruitless, he turned, shaking his fist up at Jaufré.

'I was given that at Schimeon the Tailor's. You owe me.'

Jaufré beckoned, smiling.

'Want to earn ten times as much?'

The boy hesitated; he seemed sceptical rather than wary.

'Show me.'

'And supper. Cassoulet. As much as you can eat.'

A thin, fine cloud, filmy as gauze, moved across the sun. The dazzling light dimmed a little and Jaufré saw that his angel was dirty, the halo-bright hair tarnished by neglect and poverty.

Turn away. Toss him a coin and go back to your desk, there's still time . . .

'Supper?' Angel-blue eyes widened with hunger. 'I'm *starving*.'

The knowledge that he might be on the brink of a revelation intoxicated Jaufré. He made an effort to control his excitement.

'Wait there. I'll let you in.'

Jaufré was certain no one had seen him beckon the boy down into the wine cellar. He had laced the servants' wine with the same poppy juice he had slipped into the boy's food; the strong spices in the cassoulet had concealed its distinctive bitter taint.

Now the child had slipped forwards against the wine cask Jaufré had used as a makeshift table, his golden head resting on his arm, curls spilling into the gravy stains on his empty plate. The other hand still clutched a half-eaten chunk of bread.

Jaufré stood silently, gazing down at him. He could feel the pulse of blood in his own temples, a dull, persistent throb. The boy slept silently except for the occasional heaving sigh. Poppy

14

juice provoked troubled dreams, as Jaufré knew only too well. When the child woke, his head would ache, he would vomit up the remains of his dinner . . . he would remember nothing of the night.

'"Blood of the pure, blood of the innocent . . ."'

Jaufré murmured the words as he slowly traced out the signs of power in the dust on the cellar floor. The beeswax candles gave off a thick, yellowing smoke redolent of old, musty temple vaults. He lit a cone of green incense to sweeten the frowsty air of the cellar; thin wisps, resinously aromatic, twisted upwards into the smoky darkness.

'"And King Sulaimon drew a circle – as the angiel Rhaziel instructed him."' Jaufré's voice sank to a whisper. '"And within the circle he inscribed the signs of summoning."'

He glanced up at the sleeping boy, whose breathing was now deep and regular. He would not feel the sting of the blade.

Jaufré drew the keen-sharpened knife from his belt. He had bought it in Monlaures from a merchant used to trading with the Tsiyonim; their butchers used such knives to slit and drain the slaughtered meat carcasses of blood.

Jaufré stood over the boy.

The child's lashes, gold lashes, fluttered – but did not open. His prey lay still sleeping, unaware.

Jaufré felt a sudden tightening in his chest, a sudden, intense stab of pain.

A pang of some long-forgotten, long-submerged emotion twisted his heart.

Compassion.

This was a child, a living child –

And then cold reason reasserted itself, cold as the steel blade he gripped.

Compassion was for the weak. The strong had no need of compassion to survive. The man who gave way to such feelings became vulnerable. Jaufré had long ago taken care to armour himself securely against pity, compassion . . . love.

He knelt. Took hold of the loosely dangling arm gently – so gently that the boy did not even stir.

He moved the little enamel dish to catch the drops of blood.

His fingers moved over the dirt-engrained skin, searching for a vein. He raised the knife.

His hand trembled.

Why hesitate? He wasn't about to slit the child's throat!

15

And yet . . . the Book said that the instant warm blood dripped into the dish, its allure would draw from the darkness spirits that would do his bidding, spirits that could be compelled to reveal the secrets of the amulet.

Or . . . would nothing happen at all? Would he find himself staring at the ultimate irony?

Was there nothing beyond the shadows? No guardian spirits, be they angels or daemons?

He had to know. He had to make sense of it, this tedious, nonsensical existence.

He gripped the knife and made a cut in the boy's arm; a small, neat incision, clean and quick.

The child let out a soft moan and shifted his position, swatting his hand feebly as though batting away a flea or a mosquito.

Blood welled, dark against the dirty skin, and slid in a thin trickle down his arm, dripping into the dish.

Jaufré, breath choked in his throat, watched, counting the drops.

Snatching the dish up, he placed it in the centre of the smoke-filled circle.

Then he laid the amulet beside it and began to recite the invocation, his voice low, stumbling over the arcane language.

The thick, drifting candlesmoke gusted, billowing up in his face.

Through watering eyes, he thought he could see the dark smoke gathering itself, darkest at the heart of the circle. The shadowform wavered, a windblown candleflame . . .

Jaufré bit his lip to stop himself from crying out aloud.

A deep sound began to issue from the smoke, the slow, dull throb as of a single string vibrating. On it thrummed until the whole cellar seemed to vibrate with its dark shimmer and Jaufré felt as if his temples must burst with the pressure.

Now. He must speak to it now or it would overwhelm him.

'Daemon, I – I adjure thee –' Jaufré's voice faltered; his mind was filled with swirling smoke, his thoughts, faint sparks in the obscurity, were extinguished one by one. He fought – in vain – to keep control.

'Reveal to me – the Guardian of this amulet –'

The throbbing became the pounding of storm waves. Smoky water boiled up around him. He was drowning, drowning in a sea of darkness. Flailing, choking, he swayed, trying to stay conscious.

'N-no –'

Jaufré's knees gave way. He had lost all control. Darkness and chaos filled the cellar. A black shadowtide swept over him, dragged him down into oblivion . . .

Jaufré opened his eyes. He was lying beached on the floor of the cellar, where the shadowflood had flung him.

A single candleflame still guttered in its source.

How long had he been unconscious?

Slowly, shakily, he forced himself to his feet. The presence had fled; all that remained was the chaos of its passing.

Dark liquid pooled on the floor at his feet. Bottles of red wine must have shattered, disgorging their contents on to the flagstones.

In the last candle's dying light, he walked unsteadily to where the boy lay sleeping.

He bent to touch his cheek.

The boy did not stir.

Jaufré touched him again, more roughly this time, took him by the shoulder, shook him. Still no response.

The child's skin was pale beneath the film of dirt, pale as church candles.

'Dear God,' whispered Jaufré aloud. He looked down at the floor. The rich red wine pooling around his feet . . . it exuded a strange, metallic tang, a tang he remembered only too well from the field of battle.

Blood.

He had not properly staunched the incision he had made in the vein. The trail of blood led from the loose-dangling arm down the side of the cask in runnels on to the floor.

The boy's life had slowly bled away as he lay deep in drugged sleep.

The angel-child was dead.

Jaufré opened his eyes. He was still kneeling beside the dead child. He had no idea what hour of the night it was, whether minutes had passed or hours since he made the terrible discovery.

How could it have gone so badly wrong?

Voices whispered in his head, reasoning, arguing . . .

He's only a street child, no one will come looking for him. Dump the body in the river. The current will carry it downstream.

17

Too far to carry it to the river. Guards to be bribed at the River Gate.

The cellar stank of candle fumes, tainted with an underlying reek of stale blood.

Must get rid of the body.

He pulled out an old sack and spread it on the cold flagstone floor. Then he went to lift the body and wrap it in the sacking.

He shuddered, looking down at his hands.

Child-killer.

And somewhere in the back of his mind he heard an echo of that dry shadowlaughter, mocking him.

Why so squeamish, Jaufré? Haven't you seen worse, done worse in the heat of battle?

The little body was light now that the animating spirit had fled, as light as a faun, all bones. As he laid it down on the sacking, something rolled out, glinting in the last of the candlelight.

A little copper coin, a half-obole.

'*I was given that at Schimeon the Tailor's . . .*'

Of course. The child had run errands for the Tsiyonim tailor.

The dry laughter began again, dry, abrasive laughter. But this time it was not in his mind.

And where was the child last seen? On an errand for Schimeon the Tailor? It was the perfect solution. He could exonerate himself from all guilt . . . and implicate the Tsiyonim, all by the careful placing of one little body. After all, it was the power of their amulet that had caused the boy to die; he had only been its agent, hadn't he? And then he would have a rack on which to twist the Tsiyonim until one of them broke – and told him how to find what he so desperately craved to possess.

He knelt on the floor, doubled up, still laughing that dry, mirthless laughter until his throat burned and his eyes wept salt tears.

CHAPTER 2

Schimeon the Tailor's workroom was hot with the steam of pressing irons heating on the fire.

Rahab set down his heavy bundle of swatches and peeled off his jacket.

'Ouf,' he said, wiping his face on his sleeve.

'So?' Schimeon said, looking up at his apprentice from the cutting bench. 'Did Sieur Berengar give us the wedding contract?'

'The wedding is in six weeks' time. We're to start straight away.'

Schimeon set down his shears and beamed at him.

'Excellent! And did he approve the velvets I sent?'

Rahab hesitated. 'There was a little ... um ... disagreement between Sieur Berengar and his betrothed as to the colours. I am to return in two days' time.'

There came a stifled giggle from the corner where Michal, Schimeon's eldest daughter, sat waxing lengths of button thread with a lump of hardened yellow beeswax. But when Rahab turned round, she looked away. She was always glancing at him these days; at sixteen, she was no longer the pigtailed little girl he had played catchball with. Brown-skinned as a hedgerow berry, with autumn eyes black as sloes, there was no denying that Michal had grown into a handsome young woman.

Rahab opened the fabric chest and carefully laid the swatches inside, hiding beneath the heavy lid of beaten metal from Michal's provocative gaze.

'Press that surcoat for me, will you, Rahab?' Schimeon said, face shiny with perspiration as he bent over his cutting.

Rahab rolled up his shirtsleeves and lifted a heavy iron from the grate, taking care not to touch the sizzling metal. With slow, careful strokes, he began to press the fresh-sewn seams of the surcoat. The hot-lint stink of iron on cloth filled his nostrils.

'So? What was she like? The Lord Berengar's betrothed?' Michal's questions pricked as sharply as the needles she was threading. Rahab looked up to see her dark eyes sparkling with malicious amusement through the haze of steam. 'You're very quiet, Rahab. Why aren't you regaling us with amusing tales about the Gentiles? Was the girl pretty? Skinny . . . or well-endowed?' Michal mimed extravagantly ample bosoms. 'Did Lord Berengar let you take her measurements? Or was he hovering jealously, making sure you laid not a finger on her? You know what they say, even the touch of one of the Tsiyonim can sully a girl's reputation . . .'

Rahab hefted the iron back on to the grate to reheat.

'Well?' Michal insisted.

'Let the boy get on with his work,' said Schimeon, pausing to mop the sheen of sweat from his broad forehead. 'You're distracting him. I don't want any burns on that cloth.'

'I think the girl must be very pretty. I think Rahab is too embarrassed to tell us.'

Pretty? Rahab had been so concerned to carry out his instructions correctly that he had not really thought about Damoiselle Maury until now.

'Have you finished waxing that length of black button thread, girl?' Schimeon said in a warning rumble.

'Here you are, Father,' Michal said, twirling the waxed thread in front of his nose.

'Then go make yourself useful to your mother in the kitchen.'

'You said I could finish the buttonholes today,' Michal pouted. 'You promised.'

'Then do them and do them quietly.' Schimeon raised his eyes to heaven, mouthing the word 'Daughters . . .' to Rahab.

Rahab, honoured to be included in the master's confidence, grinned. The long years of apprenticeship were nearly over; sometimes he dared to hope that Schimeon might make him a partner. Though the price of partnership would be – he suspected – to become family, to marry Michal. Schimeon and Chadassah had no sons to inherit the business. This time it was Rahab who glanced up from his work to look at Michal; her glossy dark head was dutifully bent over the lengths of thread she was measuring.

Well, there could be worse futures . . .

For a moment he let his thoughts wander. He saw himself working in his own cutting room, Michal in the kitchen kneading the dough for poppyseed *challah*; he could almost smell the new bread baking . . .

'Rahab!'

Not bread baking – but hot fabric beginning to singe –

Alarmed, he jerked the heavy iron off, seeing the telltale brown stain smirching the white pressing cloth. He unpeeled the cloth . . . but too late; the fine Arcassanne woollen beneath, dyed a delicate yellow, had turned a darker shade.

'Daydreaming again!' Schimeon shook his head, clicking his tonge. 'And that was my last length of Golden Cloud.'

'I'm sorry, master.'

Rahab heard a smothered snort and saw Michal trying to stifle her laughter behind one hand.

'You'd better go straight to the clothier's and buy a new bolt. And that surcoat is to be delivered tomorrow – even if it means you stay up working on it all night.'

Clouds covered the crescent moon. In the narrow, winding streets of the Tsiyonim Quarter of Arcassanne, the shutters were tightly barred, the doors double-locked against the night . . . and the darker shadows who stalked the night.

Rahab was still working on the surcoat of Golden Cloud in his garret, bending close over his work by the light of one oil-lamp.

What was that noise outside?

Startled, he pricked his finger. Casting down the work so that he should not stain it with his blood, he paused, listening.

The night's silence hurt his straining ears.

He went to the casement window and threw it open, gazing down into the dark three storeys below.

'Who's there?' he shouted.

There was a shudder of movement.

Someone – or something – had slipped out of the shadows and was running away.

'*Stop!*' Rahab's voice echoed, reverberating in the narrow alley. Shutters opened, heads leaned out into the night.

Rahab went hurtling down the rickety stairs and out into the street. He almost fell headlong over the bundle left lying on the doorstep.

Picking himself up, he bent to see what had tripped him.

A large heap of old clothes dumped outside –

Whose idea of a joke was it, to leave stinking rags outside the tailor's?

21

Clouds scudded away from the moon.

In the moonlight Rahab caught sight of the hand protruding from the bundle. A little hand. A child's hand.

He drew back, not wanting to unwrap the bundle any further.

Behind him, he heard other doors opening cautiously, heard the murmur of voices.

'What is it, Rahab? someone called. The sound of his own name jolted him back. He looked down at his hands. They were shaking.

'Trouble,' he said. 'Bad trouble.'

'Bring a lantern.'

Lights appeared at doorways. The onlookers ventured closer.

'Well? It's just a bundle of old clothes.' It was Schimeon, tetchy after being disturbed from sleep. 'Take it away. Burn it.'

'Wait.' Tobiah the Notary stepped in and with a flick of the wrist pulled the coverings open.

Rahab closed his eyes.

No. Don't look. You don't want to look.

He heard the cry of dismay and disbelief.

'A child. How could anyone do such a thing? Such a terrible thing?'

A child.

'Someone should call the Watch.'

There was silence. No one moved.

Rahab opened one eye.

The child's face lay exposed to the moon, bleached white by the light. A boy, curls tousled . . .

He knew him. With a sickening jolt of recognition he saw that it was the little errand boy who had brought him a spool of golden thread earlier today. The boy to whom he had given a half-obole because he had reminded him of . . . Shaoni.

'If we call the Watch it'll bring suspicion on the community.'

'If we don't call the Watch it'll look even worse. It'll look as if we've something to hide.'

About seven or eight years of age, the same age as Shaoni. Lost Shaoni . . .

Rahab's hand crept out and brushed the boy's open lids shut. The soft skin was still warm, though rapidly chilling. And at that touch, he found himself hurtled back into the past, reliving memories he had tried to forget . . .

Fires light the sky. Everywhere smoke, choking smoke and the acrid smell of burning. Heat sears the smoky air.

22

The boy grabs his little brother's hand. The child pulls away.

'Mama. I want Mama.'

People fighting, pushing, stampeding to get out. A floodtide of people breaks, the force pulling them, tugging them apart.

'No!' the boy cries, trying to hold on.

'Mama!' The little one twists and cries, panicked. 'Where are you, Mama?' His thin voice, reedy with fear, pipes out amidst the crack and hiss of burning timbers. Rooftiles crash into the street. A woman is hit on the head; she buckles, falling at their feet, her bundle of possessions spilling open. Blood from her broken head spatters their clothes, glistens on the cobbles.

'Stay with me,' the boy insists fiercely. Buffeted, he almost loses hold. 'Mama said stay with me.'

The little one starts to cry. The boy wants to cry too but he cannot, he must not, he is the one in charge, he is no longer a child.

'Not that way!' a man shouts to him. 'They're coming!'

The boy blinks, catching the glint of drawn blades through the smoke.

'To the river!' someone cries in the confusion.

The floodtide turns, sweeping them back towards the flaming ghetto.

Now he sees them. The persecutors. The Gentiles.

Men bearing down on them, men carrying torches whose flames light eyes that are glazed with the lust for blood.

'Mama!'

The little one jerks his hand out of his – and the floodtide sweeps him away. Dazed, the boy can only stand and gaze numbly at his empty hand.

'This way, boy! D'you want to be killed?' A woman catches hold of him, points him in another direction. 'Run!'

'Shaoni!' he cries as he runs. Now he is crying and he doesn't care. Tears spurt from his eyes, streak his cheeks. They taste salt and bitter in his mouth, more bitter than the acrid smoke. 'SHAONI!'

'None of us would do such a terrible thing.'

'But they'll blame us anyway.'

The hushed voices jolted Rahab back to the moonlit street. Tears pricked his eyes. *Shaoni. Little brother. Where are you?*

'Of course they'll blame us.' There was anger in Schimeon's voice. 'Look at the child. Is he one of ours?'

Even in the fading moonlight the child's hair glinted, angel-fair.

'He's not Tsiyonim. He's a Gentile.'

*

23

Rahab stood with the other Tsiyonim men in a chamber of the Tour de la Justice. The men of the Watch lined the walls, arms folded, watching them. They wore a new uniform, black tabards, embroidered in silver thread with the emblem of a hawk in flight. Rahab eyed the Hawks with suspicion. Comte Aymon had pensioned off the old watchmen and recruited younger men, trained soldiers from his bodyguard returned from campaigns overseas.

'You can't hold us.' Tobiah the Notary had volunteered to speak on behalf of the community. 'You have no proof.'

'We found a body, that was all,' put in Schimeon.

'A child's body.' A voice rang out across the chamber, a voice that resonated with the brazen timbre of beaten metal. 'Ritually murdered. With a Tsiyonim butchering knife.'

'That proves nothing,' Tobiah said calmly. 'Anyone can steal a Tsiyonim knife.'

Rahab gazed uneasily around the chamber to see if he could identify the speaker.

'Approach the dais, Captain d'Orbiel,' ordered the clerk of the court.

Orbiel. Jaufré d'Orbiel. Rahab craned his neck to see as the Captain made his way up to the dais: a tall, lean, sunburned man, whose hooded eyes swept across the huddle of Tsiyonim with a look of such contempt that Rahab wanted to shrink into the shadows.

'Is that Orbiel the poet?' Rahab whispered to Rebh Jehiel, who stood beside him.

Jehiel seemed not to hear him; when Rahab looked at the elderly scholar he noticed that he seemed mesmerised by the sight of the Captain.

'The child is not Tsiyonim. I suggest the words "ritually sacrificed" be written in the records,' Jaufré said to the magistrate.

'What kind of poisonous allegation is this?' Tobiah cried.

'Ritually sacrificed . . .' murmured Jehiel under his breath.

'It's written in your scriptures,' Jaufré said. His intelligent, cultured tones lent the wild allegations an air of veracity. 'Shall I quote you the passage?'

'You have no need to quote our scriptures to me,' Tobiah said quietly. 'And I take objection to your linking the work of a deranged killer to our holy texts. I say look for the man who molests children. The man who watches little ones at play, who

24

waits in dark alleys for the unsuspecting child. Do not blame us. We do not make blood sacrifices.'

'Not to summon dark forces?' Jaufré said. 'Not even to create a *golem*?'

There was a silence in the chamber.

'Captain Orbiel, I have always taken you to be an intelligent man. A learned man.' Tobiah's voice was dry. 'Surely you do not believe those old legends? Next you'll be asking us to believe that there are Rocs in the mountains, laying jewelled eggs in their nests.'

Rahab held his breath. Tobiah was leading them along a narrow ledge; in deriding Jaufré's accusations, he risked sending them over the edge.

'If you have proof that one of our community has committed this atrocity – then we shall hand him over to the justice of the city, we shall not protect him. But until you can furnish proof, you cannot hold us here.'

'Oh, I shall furnish proof, never fear,' Jaufré d'Orbiel said, turning to the huddled Tsiyonim with a cold smile. 'Already I have the sworn testimony of Sorel the Silk Merchant, confirming that he sent the boy with a spool of Golden Cloud thread to Schimeon the Tailor. If Sorel can make a positive identification . . .'

'Now it begins again,' whispered Mandel the Shoemaker. 'And I had thought we were safe here in Arcassanne.'

'We shall never be safe. Not until we can go home,' said Rebh Jehiel sadly, shaking his white head. 'Home to Tsiyon.'

Every night before he slept, Rahab still repeated the prayer his mother Ariel had taught him, the prayer every Tsiyonim child learned.

'And bring us safely home to Tsiyon . . .'

Tsiyon.

To a child, the name had evoked visions of a golden city dreaming under a blue sky, a city filled with green gardens and orchards, clearwater streams and playing fountains. In spring the orchard trees were white with blossom; in autumn, the boughs hung heavy with ripe fruit: sweet, crisp apples, fragrant blush-peaches, juicy pomegranates.

In Tsiyon, no one went hungry, no one was cold or afraid. In Tsiyon the children played outside in the streets and gardens. The adults smiled, laughed, sang songs . . . At dusk there was no curfew, the streets were filled with people strolling in the warm night air, visiting friends, dancing . . .

The memory was all he had left to remember his mother by. He no longer believed that he would ever return to Tsiyon; the Tsiyonim had been cast out of their homeland centuries ago. But he repeated the words because it brought her back to him, because every time he said them he was back in his home and she was bending over his bed, tucking him in . . . and he felt safe, so safe as she smiled down at him . . .

For all the years since he had seen her, he had preserved that memory, a sacred memory, untouched by the horrors that had sundered them. For all the years that he had wandered, searching for lost Shaoni, he had never forgotten to repeat the evening prayer.

Now, as he lay on his pallet in the stuffy garret room, his window open to the stars, he could not sleep. Every time he closed his eyes, he saw the child again, the pale, dead eyes staring at him, accusing –

Fear fouled his mouth with a dry, sour taste.

Rahab rolled off the pallet and went to the crock to gulp down a mouthful of water. The foul taste in his mouth remained. He glanced around uneasily. His garret seemed peopled with milling shadows, shadows from the past.

Here in Arcassanne he had felt safe. But tonight he had looked into the eyes of Jaufré d'Orbiel and seen hatred, a lucid, fanatical hatred.

The feeling of safety had been an illusion.

Nowhere was safe for the Tsiyonim.

CHAPTER 3

Lia Maury slowly opened her eyes, luxuriating in the wash of golden light that lapped her sheets. She was floating in a sea of sunlight, idly soaking in the summer's warmth.

It was going to be hot today.

For a moment she let herself drift in the warm sun, eyes closed, thinking of nothing in particular.

And then her hand crept to her throat, feeling for the fine golden chain –

Yes, it was still there, where he had placed it last night, threading it around her neck, parting the hair at the nape of her neck with gentle fingers.

His betrothal gift.

She stared at it, hardly daring to breathe lest the costly emerald, delicately cut in the form of a leaf, melt away.

'Berengar.' She breathed his name into the sunlight – and then fell back on the bed, hugging herself. 'Berengar. My *betrothed*.' Then she began to giggle, for 'my betrothed' sounded so ridiculously formal. Hadn't she known him all her life? In distant childhood days Alissende's older brother had kept himself aloof, too busy with his companions to bother with little girls. But when he and Jaufré d'Orbiel had returned from the Comte's campaign to Djihan-Djihar, their friendship had begun anew, and friendship had soon led to a more formal arrangement . . .

Opening the shutters, she gazed out over the ramparts of the walled city. Doves arose in a flutter of wings from the dovecote in the courtyard garden below and wheeled over whitewashed stone and red-tiled roofs. From the pepper-pot watchtowers along the walls, pigeons flew out to join them, circling overhead. Far away, out in the green plain, she could just glimpse the masts and bright sails of merchant ships on the river Aude, sailing slowly, steadily towards the sea.

'Safe journey, dear Papa,' she whispered. He had delayed his argosy for the betrothal ceremony – and then set sail before dawn. He would not be back for two months, maybe three.

She could just see her mother at the far end of the garden, head shaded from the heat of the sun by a broad-brimmed straw hat. Zillaïs could be found tending her beloved garden in all weathers, pruning and weeding, taking cuttings and collecting seeds. As far back in her childhood as Lia could remember, Zillaïs had devoted her time to her herbs and her flowers, making simples and tisanes. Her remedies had gained her a certain reputation in the neighbourhood as a healer but she had always refused payment of any kind.

Lia stared at her mother's distant figure, inelegantly bent over as she strained to pull out chickweed from amongst the strawberry plants. Lia felt she would never fully understand her mother's obsession with the garden. Other wealthy bourgeoises of Arcassanne liked to spend their leisure time visiting each other and indulging in gossip; Zillaïs preferred to be alone with her plants.

At least there would still be flowers in plenty for the wedding crowns . . . though by autumn, the striped roses that now bloomed so profusely, scenting the garden with their clove-sweet musk, would be finished.

One part white wine to five parts thrice-boiled water, left to cool . . .

Lia placed a square of muslin over the neck of the pitcher and slowly, dreamily, poured in the angelica water.

'Two handfuls of angelica and three sprigs of borage . . . or is it the other way round . . . ?'

Bees droned outside in the lavender . . . the garden drowsed in the sun . . .

'Lia! *Lia!*'

Lia looked up, hearing Alissende's voice. Setting the pitcher down, she ran to let her and her chaperon in.

'I've just made some angelica water.'

'How delicious!' Alissende waved her hand to her chaperon, as though shooing away a troublesome lapdog. 'Wait in the courtyard. I may be a little while.'

'Well?' Lia took her friend's arm and led her inside. 'Where's Berengar? What's the news?'

'Haven't you heard?'

'Heard what?'

'They found a body,' Alissende said in a whisper. 'A child. In the Tsiyonim quarter.'

28

Lia felt cold, as if a cloud had covered the sun. She did not want any unpleasant news to spoil her happiness. She looked at her arms and saw they were covered in goosebumps.

'Jaufré showed Berengar the body. He said it was . . . horrible.'

'A Tsiyon child?'

'No, no, not one of their own. A laundress's boy from the river quarter. No one knows how he had come to stray so far from home, unless *they* enticed him with sweetmeats . . .'

'*They* enticed him?' Lia's mother stood in the doorway, carrying a trowel and pruning knife. She was frowning. 'Are you accusing the Tsiyonim of the murder?'

'Oh no, Dame Zillaïs.' Alissende had blushed bright red.

'That's how rumours spread. Idle chatter, thoughtless chatter.' The expression on Zillaïs's face was cold, forbidding.

'Well . . . I'd better be on my way.' Alissende hurried towards the door. 'I have other visits to make.'

'But what about the angelica water? It must be ready to drink.' Lia followed her friend to the door. *Mother's in one of her moods again, take no notice*, she signalled to Alissende. 'Do stay.'

Alissende shook her head and slipped swiftly out into the courtyard where her chaperon was patiently waiting for her.

Lia glared at her mother. This was not the first time Zillaïs had openly rebuked Alissende; her manner made Lia deeply uncomfortable. She could take offence at the most trivial, inoffensive remark.

'Alissende is a sweet-natured girl but her head is full of air. Sometimes she talks a great deal of nonsense.' Zillaïs's words seemed to make light of the incident, but Lia saw that her expression was still unforgiving.

'So? What's the harm?'

'The harm?' Her mother's dark eyes glittered. 'She is the daughter of one of the oldest families in Arcassanne. She has *influence*. She should learn to curb her tongue.'

Lia opened her mouth to retort – but her mother turned on her heel and went out of the kitchen before she could speak. Lia went to go after her – and then checked herself. This was an argument she would not win.

'Well, thank you, Mother, that's my morning ruined!'

She went over to the jug of steeping angelica water and poured herself a glass of the fragrant liquid. Then she sat in the window seat, kicking her heels rhythmically against the limewashed stone, gazing out over the courtyard garden.

Why was Zillaïs so sensitive? Lia had hoped the news of her betrothal to Berengar would please her mother. Such an auspicious match! Surely most mothers would have been bubbling with excitement at the prospect of making preparations for the wedding?

The morning sun burned down on to the pots of herbs and striped gillyflowers from a cloudless sky; clove perfume spiced the hot air. Lia could see her mother bending down to snip the dry seed-heads from the early-flowering pinks. Maybe it was the fierce summer's heat that made Zillaïs so ill-tempered?

Lia sipped the angelica water. It was cool and refreshing, infused with the green sweetness of the steeped herbs. But it would have tasted even better if shared with Alissende.

She cast a resentful glance at her mother's bent figure. She had been looking forward to a delightful morning of self-indulgence; planning clothes for the marriage ceremony with Alissende, gossiping and giggling together over the guest list. It was too bad that her mother had spoiled their plans.

Losing a daughter, gaining a son . . .

Perhaps Zillaïs did not approve the match? Lia thought, scooping out a candied fragment of angelica from the bottom of the glass and thoughtfully sucking it. Whenever Berengar was visiting, she became reserved, aloof, replying in clipped phrases to his questions. Was she overawed by his lineage, his position in the city? Was she afraid her daughter was not a good enough match?

Bees buzzed amongst the dark-striped gillyflowers; in the acacia tree, a cicada began to whirr.

Or was it Alissende's story that had upset Zillaïs? The murdered child? Lia felt again the frisson that had chilled her on first hearing the news. Even here, in the safety of the walled garden, it sickened her. Who could have done such a terrible thing?

As the afternoon sun seared the river plain, Lia left the baking heat of the courtyard garden and busied herself helping Emmenza make paste from the tomatoes they had been drying on the roof.

It was too hot to concentrate and her mind kept wandering to other matters . . . a silly game she and Alissende had been playing the other day, likening their friends to birds and beasts . . . Plump Emmenza, Lia's childhood nurse, could be a corn-fed woodpigeon, they decided, with her waddling gait. Jaufré, Lia had declared, was a mountain eagle, with his aristocratic aquiline nose and hooded eyes . . .

'Is the Damoiselle at home?'

Lia went to the window, throwing wide the shutters, leaning out.

'Berengar!' she called, waving.

Evening sunlight glinted in the dark gold of his hair as he shaded his eyes, gazing up at her.

A lion, Lia thought proudly. Yes, he's a lion, with his golden mane of hair and his leonine features.

'Wait! I'm coming down!' she called, and flew out into the courtyard. She went to fling her arms around him – but stopped on seeing her mother watching from the arbour.

'Dame Maury.' Berengar had also seen her; with his customary courtesy, he turned to bow to Zillaïs before greeting Lia.

Zillaïs glanced up from her tapestry.

'Sieur Berengar.' She inclined her head in a gesture of acknowledgement; she did not smile nor move forwards to welcome him.

Mother! Lia winced at her mother's coldness. Even now her attitude could drive Berengar away; who would want to be saddled with such a sour-tempered mother-in-law as Zillaïs?

'Ouf.' Berengar tugged open his collar. 'It's hot.'

'Come inside,' Lia said, drawing him towards the house. 'It's much cooler in the solar.'

Zillaïs set her tapestry aside and rose to her feet. She spoke.

'That's a magnificent tunic you are wearing, sieur. Is it new?'

'I – I'm glad you like it, Dame Maury.' Berengar seemed momentarily caught off-guard. 'It was made for me by a very skilful tailor. The same tailor I have commissioned to make our wedding clothes.'

Lia smiled warmly up at him.

'That device.' Zillaïs came closer, pointing to the embroidered badge. 'I have seen other young men wearing it around the city. What does it signify?'

To other ears, the question would have sounded innocent enough. But Lia heard an underlying tension colouring her mother's voice.

'It's a hawk, Dame Maury,' Berengar answered, easily enough. 'It is the badge of the new evening watch, the Night-hawks. Jaufré d'Orbiel is our Captain.'

31

'So you follow Jaufré d'Orbiel?' Zillaïs said.

Lia began to feel uneasy; there was a distinct edge to her mother's voice which grated.

'I am honoured to be one of his company, yes.'

'And what precisely do you do in this evening watch?'

'We patrol the streets and keep the peace.'

'So the city watch do not provide adequate protection for the citizens?'

'Mother!' Lia whispered. This was beginning to sound like an interrogation.

'Many of them are old veteran soldiers, Dame Maury. Comte Aymon was pleased to use younger, more able men – and they were glad to be relieved of their nocturnal duties.'

Zillaïs put her arm around Lia's shoulders.

'I have only my daughter's best interests at heart, you understand. I trust you will not be leaving her on her own every night!'

A sudden hot breath of wind stirred the vines overhead. Lia shivered, looking up at the sky. Her skin felt damp, clammy.

'Perhaps we shall have a storm?'

'Not till the harvest is in,' Berengar said.

'But it's stiflingly hot. It would clear the air.'

'And flatten the ripening corn on my estates. My farms are still recovering from last year's poor harvest.'

'So, Sieur Berengar,' said Zillaïs, 'to what do we owe the pleasure of this unannounced visit?'

Lia winced; her mother could be so withering at times.

'There was one thing,' Berengar cleared his throat, 'a trivial thing which was overlooked at the betrothal ceremony.' He seemed suddenly ill at ease.

'Overlooked?' Zillaïs repeated.

'The notary brought it to my attention this morning. It's only a formality. I would have approached your husband . . . but as he won't be back for a while, I have to ask you.'

'Lia,' Zillaïs said sharply, 'You have not offered Sieur Berengar any refreshment. Go inside and get Emmenza to draw some ale from the cellar.'

A formality. Lia looked questioningly at her mother but Zillaïs's unblinking stare said only, *Do as you are bidden.* She turned on her heel and flounced into the house.

'Ale, Emmenza!' she called loudly.

The voices carried faintly in from the courtyard garden. She

32

crept back to the window, straining to hear what Berengar was saying.

'The notary needs further documentation. It's for the marriage contract, you understand, Dame Zillaïs. When you join a family as old and as eminent as mine –'

'I thought my husband's notary had delivered all the necessary papers.' Her mother's voice sounded taut, strained.

Berengar hesitated.

'It appears he has nothing from your side, Dame Zillaïs.'

There was a silence. Lia heard the cicadas start to whirr in the acacia tree.

'Perhaps you have forgotten,' Zillaïs said in clipped tones, 'that I lost everything – family, documents, jewels – in a shipwreck.'

'There must surely have been some records of your birth in your home city . . . Tolonada, wasn't it?'

Emmenza appeared, bearing a full jug of ale, puffing with the exertion of having climbed the steep cellar stair.

Lia, startled from her eavesdropping, jumped back from the window just in time as Zillaïs swept into the kitchen, Berengar following.

'Emmenza – stay with our two young people, will you? I have matters to attend to.' She walked straight past Lia without even glancing at her.

Emmenza eased herself into the wooden armchair by the fireside.

Lia picked up the heavy pottery jug and poured ale for Berengar.

He seemed distracted, slowly turning the cup round and round in his hands.

Lia stood watching him awhile. Maybe she had better change the subject.

'Alissende says the Watch found a child. Dead.'

He nodded.

'That must have been – horrible.'

He looked up from the cup. His eyes were haunted, reflecting the night-shadows from the darkening garden.

'Jaufré has a theory he was killed by one of the Tsiyonim.'

The sky outside was growing rapidly darker; it had become almost too dark to see Berengar's face.

'Why would the Tsiyonim want to kill a child?' Lia struck a tinder-flame and lit the candles in the alcove. 'They're just different from us. They have different customs, different beliefs –'

'Different.' Berengar swallowed down a mouthful of ale. 'Jaufré claims he has heard of these Tsiyonim practices before. Last time it was across the mountains, in Galicys. About ten years ago.'

'But there's never been anything like that in Arcassanne!'

Berengar shrugged.

'You know how it is with poets . . . Jaufré reads too much, his head is stuffed full of strange fantasies.' He drained the last of his ale in one draught.

'But . . . in the circumstances . . . maybe we should cancel the contract with Schimeon for the wedding clothes,' Lia ventured.

'Why? Schimeon's the best tailor in Arcassanne. No one can cut a jacket as well as he can – and if he was good enough for my father, he's good enough for me.'

Berengar sounded so like his late father that Lia had to stifle a giggle; for a moment she saw him, thirty years on, Lord of his Demesne, holding forth on his favourite topic . . .

'I'm damned if I'll let a few foolish rumours spoil our wedding –'

A distant rumble cut across his words. He looked up. Drops of rain spattered against the shutters.

'I'd best be getting back.'

'You could shelter here –'

Berengar opened the door and looked out. Rain was dripping through the curtain of vine leaves. 'I would not want to put your mother to any inconvenience.'

'You're family now!' Lia moved closer.

He turned up his collar. 'But we wouldn't want to cause public censure so close to our wedding, would we?'

'Oh, wouldn't we?' Lia said teasingly, raising her hand to pull up a corner of his collar that he had overlooked, letting her fingers brush against his throat –

Emmenza gave a sudden snore and shifted her bulk in the fireside chair.

Berengar kissed the top of Lia's head and went out into the rain.

She stood watching him dodge the puddles until he had disappeared into the night.

*

Raindrops began to spatter the dusty street as Jaufré d'Orbiel made his way home from the Tour de la Justice. A thin, warm wind whined fitfully about the rooftops. It set Jaufré's jangled nerves even more on edge.

Far away, above the mountains, lightning flickered, an eerie corona, pallid against the louring night sky.

He had intended to go straight to his chamber and to bed. But now he found himself taking out the key to the cellar, thrusting it into the lock, turning it, going in . . .

Jaufré closed the heavy clove-nailed door and leaned back against it, eyes closed. He was tired, achingly tired. He had not slept since – since the catastrophe. He wanted to sleep now, wanted sleep more than anything. So what had driven him back to the cellar? Remorse? It was too late for that now. The boy was dead; remorse would not bring him back.

Eyes still closed, he sensed a sudden stir in the subterranean air, slight, like a sigh –

'Who's there?' He held his lantern high, straining to see beyond the dark-shrouded wine casks.

Jaufré was not easily unnerved. He had stood watch when the camp was stalked by the Snake Warriors of Djihan-Djihar – veiled assassins who crept up on their enemies and stifled them with poison-impregnated scarves. But there was an unwholesome taint to the air in the cellar that made the hairs rise on the back of his neck.

He had scrubbed and scrubbed the dark stains where the child's blood and the spilt wine had mingled, until the stones were clean . . . but now it looked as if the stain was still there.

Impossible!

His lantern cast a pool of light on to the flagstoned floor as he set it down to look more closely.

The faint, telltale stain of brown accused him.

He had tampered with unseen forces, he had bared his soul to the dangers of occult influences – and all for nothing.

'Jaufré . . .'

He started, almost knocking over the lantern. someone had whispered his name in the darkness, he was certain of it.

'Who – who's there?' His hand slid to the hilt of his sword.

'Jaufré . . . ' He felt the breath of a sigh at the back of his neck.

Panicked, he found himself scrambling up the stairs, slamming the door shut, locking it.

Sleep. He was sleep-starved, he was hallucinating, he must rest –

In his turret chamber he fumbled with trembling hands for the phial of Arkendym sleep draught, tipping the last drops of the precious liquid into his mouth.

The cold bitterness of the draught salved his mouth and throat; a creeping calm slowly began to numb his fevered mind, as if the chill of the distant snowfields where the poppies grew were embalming his whole body.

With a sigh he sank down on his bed . . . and let the poppy's spell lull him into oblivion . . .

In his garret, Rahab, half-drowned in sleep, heard the rain drumming on the roof: heavy thunder drops, spattered with hail.

Rain.

He opened one eye – and a cold splash of water fell on to his face. And then another – and another –

'Why doesn't Schimeon get someone to mend this leaky roof?'

Grumbling, he rolled out of bed and began to drag his bedding to the other side of the garret. He placed a saucer beneath the leak; a monotonous drip-drip-drip began instantly. Bleary-eyed, he wrapped himself in his blanket and turned on his side to face the wall.

Drip-drip-drip.

Ignore it.

Lightning scored the sky.

He pulled the covers over his head.

Rain battered the shutters; the wind shrieked around the rooftops.

Sheet lightning, blue-white, irradiated Rahab's garret – and in the shriek of the wind, he heard a shrill, high voice calling, a child's voice.

It must be Iudith or Thirzah, frightened by the thunder. How could a child be out, alone, in this storm?

A blade of blue light clove the darkness; against the thunder's crash, Rahab heard the child's cry again.

Clumsy with sleep, he stumbled to the window, unlatched one shutter. The wind's force blew it inwards, banging the carved wood against the wall.

Rainspray drenched Rahab's face as he peered out into the storm.

36

In the rainswept street below, a young boy gazed up at him, arms raised imploringly.

The street below ran with a torrent of water.

'Don't be afraid!' Rahab called, his voice half-drowned by the tumult of the fast-falling rain. 'I'm coming down!'

He hurried down the three flights of stairs and unbolted the front door. Rain sprayed inwards from an empty street.

There was no one there.

A faint, high cry pierced Jaufré's drugged sleep.

He woke to the drumming of thunder.

Another summer storm had boiled up in the sultry air and come rolling down from the mountains.

Lightning flickered around the walls of the turret room; thunder rumbled, loud as the din of Djihari war-drums.

Jaufré turned on his side, trying to block the din of the thunder with his pillow.

'Jaufré . . .'

Someone was calling his name in a thin, shrill voice. A child's voice.

No. He must be imagining it. It must be the wind.

A window blew inwards, one pane of coloured glass smashing to fragments.

'Jaufré . . .'

Jaufré forced himself out of bed, staggering across to try to close the banging window.

In the rainswept street below, a young boy gazed up at him, arms raised imploringly.

'No . . .' Jaufré whispered. 'Not you. You're . . .'

The night sky split open.

Riven with lightning, hair crackling with whitefire, the boy rose up into the air. He was naked. Blue wounds scarred his luminous body; from his outstretched fingertips lightning sizzled.

The house shook with thunder.

Jaufré, sight seared by the brightness, turned away, shielding his face with his arm.

When he opened his dazzled eyes again, the street was empty.

CHAPTER 4

Rahab set down his heavy bag of swatches and mopped his face. The fierce sun had turned last night's storm-rain into hazy humidity. The climb was long and steep from the narrow streets of the Tsiyonim Quarter to the cooler heights where the Belcastle mansion overlooked the sweltering city. He had no wish to appear hot and sticky before Schimeon's most illustrious clients. He had gone to the baths early this morning, but the heat of high summer and the weight of the bag had sent sweat trickling down his body, undoing his efforts.

After Jaufré d'Orbiel's public accusation, Schimeon had fully expected Lord Berengar to cancel the wedding contract – yet that very morning, a message had arrived confirming the afternoon's appointment.

A servitor led Rahab through a hall hung with tapestries, shields and antlered hunting trophies to a door which led out into a terraced garden.

Two young women were sitting in an arbour heavy with creamy honeysuckle, sipping wine from goblets of fine, translucent glass; Lord Berengar was leaning over them. They were laughing together.

Rahab paused a moment, entranced by this summer idyll. They seemed so idle, so carefree, the girls in their loose silks, pale as marguerites, their chatter floating like distant music into the cicada-whirring air.

Then Lord Berengar glanced up and saw him.

'Good-day to you, Rahab.'

Rahab bowed his head in greeting but kept his eyes on the terrace paving, studying a crack through which a creeping plant had emerged. Always be polite, Schimeon had advised him – but never obsequious or fawning. Maintain your dignity – but remember your place.

'Lia and I couldn't agree on the materials for our wedding

clothes, Alissende,' said Lord Berengar, 'so you must act as arbiter.'

'Bring him to the solar!' cried Lady Alissende, leaping up. 'He can spread the materials out on the big table.'

To Rahab's relief, the solar was cool after the intense heat of the sunlit garden. He began to unwrap his bundle and shook out square after square of fabrics: brocades, velvets, silks.

'What a rich shade . . .'

'Tawny, like a fox.'

The girls eagerly picked up each swatch in turn, exclaiming over the dyes, whilst Berengar stood, arms folded, slightly aloof from their deliberations as though it were beneath his dignity to involve himself in women's matters.

'What about this pearl silk?' Alissende handed it to Lia.

Lia stroked the silk against her cheek. 'It feels so light. Like thistledown.'

'Might I suggest matching the pearl with an overskirt of the gold-threaded lily brocade?' Rahab placed the two fabrics in her hand and laid a third, a velvet of pale gold, beside them.

'Oh, *yes*. Look, Berengar. What do you think of these?' She held them up so that he could see the colours against her skin.

'Mmm. But maybe the velvet is too heavy?'

Rahab cleared his throat. 'I understand the marriage is to take place in the autumn. The winds can blow cold across the mountains.'

'You see?' Lia said. 'Your tailor thinks of everything.'

'And for you, sieur, this darker velvet, honey and burnt umber . . . or the new shade they are calling Dragon's Blood?'

Rahab drew out another two swatches to set against the ones Lia had chosen, displaying his wares with the flourish of a marketplace conjuror.

'These richer shades will complement the colour of your hair, sieur.'

Berengar frowned, flicking critically between the two swatches.

'Which do you prefer, Lia?'

'I think he's right,' Lia said, smiling up at him. 'The darker colours suit you very well.'

'If the sieur would be so good as to let me assist him in removing his tunic, I'll take some preliminary measurements . . .'

Rahab expertly eased the tunic from Berengar's shoulders,

and unwinding a length of notched string from his pocket, stretched it from the nape of Berengar's neck to his waist, from shoulder to wrist, counting notches under his breath and making notes with a piece of chalk.

'Hola!' A voice rang out in the courtyard below. 'Is the Sieur de Belcastel at home?'

Rahab started and dropped his chalk; he recognised that voice with its strong singer's resonance: Jaufré d'Orbiel.

Berengar flung open the window and called down into the courtyard.

'Here, Jaufré! We're choosing our wedding clothes. Come up and help us in our choice!'

Alissende flew to the window and cried out, 'Yes, *do* come up and help us!'

Rahab shrank back into the shadows. The last person in all Arcassanne he wanted to meet this afternoon was Jaufré d'Orbiel.

'Comte Aymon has summoned us,' Jaufré called. 'Be at the Palace within the hour.'

Berengar closed the window and turned back to Lia. 'Did you hear? The Comte himself! It must be a matter of some importance.'

'More important than our wedding plans?' Lia said acidly.

Why was Aymon summoning the Hawks? Had they discovered new evidence to incriminate the Tsiyonim? Rahab, flustered, could no longer concentrate on the wedding clothes; his thoughts kept straying.

'Hurry with those last measurements, will you, Rahab?' Berengar said.

Rahab lifted his measuring tape. But where before his movements had been quick and deft, now he became clumsy, fumbling in his haste to get things finished.

Berengar began to tap one foot on the floor impatiently.

'This is taking too long.'

'I can complete the other measurements later, if the sieur so desires —'

'I do so desire.' Berengar seized his tunic.

'You seem very eager to be on your way,' Lia said, offended.

'Duty calls, *ma mie*.' He grabbed her hand and brushed it with his lips, a perfunctory farewell.

'Don't call me that, you know I hate it.' She snatched her hand away. 'Alissende and I will choose what you wear, then? Yellow and red stripes maybe? Jongleur's colours?'

'Fine!' He was already out of sight, carelessly flinging the last word back.

Rahab sensed he was *de trop*. Hastily he rolled his swatches up into a bundle and, nodding a quick bow to the damoiselles, backed towards the door and scurried away.

'Murderers!'

Rahab heard the shouting as he approached the gate to the Tsiyonim Quarter. He hesitated, uncertain whether to go any further.

'Tsiyonim filth!'

Edging warily to the end of the street, he peered around and saw a group of men and women gathered together, angrily haranguing a thin, stooped figure.

'No – no – my good people – you're mistaken –'

Rahab recognised the mild tones of Rebh Jehiel.

'Liar!'

A man stooped to gather up a handful of mud and lobbed it at the scholar, covering his worn coat in dirt. Others followed suit.

Rahab heard a voice shouting out, 'Let him be! He's just an old man.' To his horror he realised as they turned around that it had been his voice. Whatever had possessed him to be so stupid?

Well, he had started this, he would somehow have to brazen it out.

He began to walk forwards towards Jehiel, forcing himself to keep his pace unhurried. He sensed their hostility as he approached; he could almost smell it in the air. And who were they? Just ordinary people, housewives, tradesmen.

He reached Jehiel, who was cowering on his knees, his arms covering his head. Bending down, he whispered, 'Are you hurt?'

The old man shook his head; he seemed too shocked to speak.

'Child-killers!' cried a woman, her voice shrill with hysteria.

'Come,' Rahab said, hooking his arm around Jehiel's shoulders, trying to pull him up to his feet. 'Take no notice.'

Something whizzed through the air and struck the gate above Rahab's head. A large pebble. Dear God, they were going to stone them to death.

'Quickly!' urged Rahab, stumbling forwards, dragging Jehiel with him.

A hail of stones followed. One hit Rahab on the back of the head – but he kept dragging the old scholar onwards.

'Break it up! Break it up!'

Stones no longer cracked on to the cobbles. Rahab propped Jehiel against a doorway and dared to look back over his shoulder.

Beyond the gateway they stood, still staring at him with hostility. But a man had placed himself between them, a richly dressed young man, with a mane of fair hair.

'Did you hear me? Go about your business. It's over.'

The crowd lingered a moment or two longer . . . then, one by one, moved away. The young man stood his ground until they had all gone. Then he turned – and Rahab recognised Berengar, Lord of Belcastel.

'Are you all right?' Berengar asked, coming towards him.

Rahab put his hand to the back of his head and winced.

'Thank you, sieur. Just a bruise.' He turned to Jehiel but the old man was still winded and could only clasp his hands together in a gesture of thanks. Shutters began to open on either side of the street; curious faces appeared, wide-eyed.

'Good.' Berengar nodded. He turned back towards the gate.

'Thank you, thank you, sieur –'

Berengar raised his hand to silence Rahab.

'Just be sure you make a good job of my wedding clothes, tailor.'

'I don't want to put you to any trouble, Schimeon . . .' protested Jehiel.

'No, no, Rahab was right to bring you here.' Schimeon took the old scholar's arm and drew him into the house. 'You're in no fit state to return home alone. I'm going to summon the Elders. Sit down in the cool and rest.'

'Let me fetch you something to drink, Rebh Jehiel,' Chadassah said, easing him into the most comfortable chair.

'Look at the mud on your coat!' exclaimed Schimeon. 'Rahab, take Rebh Jehiel's coat. He'll clean and mend it for you, won't you, Rahab?'

'Rahab will do nothing of the sort!' Chadassah said. 'Can't you see? He's bleeding.'

'Am I?' Rahab, surprised, put one hand to the soreness at the back of his head; his fingers came away smeared with blood. Now that the excitement was over, he suddenly felt rather weak.

42

'I'll clean that up for you. Now, Rebh Jehiel, how about a cup of camomile tea? That's good to calm the nerves.'

'Mama! *Mama!*'

Schimeon's little daughters, Thirzah and Iudith, came running in.

'What's happening?'

'How did Rahab hurt his head?'

'Let's go find Mama's magic medicine for bumped heads.' Chadassah shooed them out.

'Tsk, tsk!' Schimeon was examining Jehiel's coat. 'These sleeves are worn through at the elbow. And the cuffs . . . Rebh Jehiel, do me a favour, accept a new coat. It will be my pleasure to make you one.'

Jehiel held up his hand.

'My dear wife Miriam, may she rest in peace, gave me that coat. I would not dream of throwing it away.'

'Your wife Miriam was a good woman. Would she want to see her husband dressed in rags? I've just finished a fine coat. Arcassanne wool, light and soft. Dark blue, lined with silk. I'd like you to have it. Don't offend me, Jehiel, by refusing it.'

'I'm very fond of my old coat, Schimeon. It's like . . . a part of me. It has memories. Besides . . . I'm not so fond of blue.'

'At least wear the blue coat home tonight. For the sake of my business. I can just hear the rumours: "Did you see that? Rebh Jehiel left Schimeon's in his shirtsleeves! What kind of a tailor sends his customers home without a coat on their backs!" Rahab can bring you your old coat when he's mended it.'

'You're a very persuasive man, Schimeon,' Jehiel said, capitulating.

'Rahab's not mending anything until I've bathed his head.' Chadassah came back bearing a cup of fragrant camomile tea for Rebh Jehiel and a basin of hot water. 'Now, let's take a look . . .'

Rahab felt her fingers gently lifting and parting the hair at the back of his head. He winced.

'Hold still,' she chided, dipping a clean rag in the hot salt water and starting to dab at the wound.

Rahab's eyes began to water as the salt sank into the abrasions.

'Does it hurt?' enquired a solemn voice, and he saw that the little girls were watching him with great interest.

'Yes,' he said.

'It hurt when I fell over and cut my knee,' Thirzah announced to Rebh Jehiel, lifting her skirt to show the scar, 'but I didn't cry.'

'Yes you did.'

'Didn't!'

'I'll have to cut some of your hair.' Chadassah reached for her scissors. 'Behind the ear . . .'

'Cut away,' Rahab said resignedly, wishing that Iudith and Thirzah would not argue so loudly when his head was throbbing. He heard the snip of Chadassah's scissors, felt the tug of the blades against the matted strands of hair, then the soft pressure of the damp cloth, wiping away the last of the dried blood.

'What's this?' She paused in her dabbing. 'Some kind of . . . birthmark?' She peered more closely. 'It looks like a . . . a tattoo.'

Rebh Jehiel looked up from his camomile tea.

'Let me see.' He came over and peered at Rahab's scalp whilst Chadassah held back the hair.

'Tattoo?' Rahab said, irritated at being prodded and examined. 'What do you mean?'

'You didn't know you had this mark?'

'No!'

'Ahh,' said Jehiel, nodding, going back to his chair.

'Well?' Chadassah began to apply her witchhazel salve. 'Do you know what it is, Rebh Jehiel? Have you ever seen anything like it before?'

Jehiel shook his head. He seemed absorbed in drinking his tea.

The salve had begun to work its soothing cool on Rahab's bruised head; he stood up, looking around for a mirror. Chadassah unhooked her little hand-mirror from the chain around her waist and handed it to him. Standing in front of the full-length mirror in the workroom, he tried to angle the hand-mirror so that he could reflect the back of his head.

There *was* something there . . . smudged blue and red tattoo-marks in a whorl-pattern that was too regular to be a birthmark. But who had put it there? And when? He had no memory of any such operation being performed on him . . . but then he had tried to obliterate all memories of Galicys, as if he had sealed his life there in a chest and thrown away the key.

Did Jehiel know what the whorl pattern meant?

Rahab's head throbbed with the effort of thinking.

He would ask him . . . later . . . when this pounding headache

44

had calmed. Now all he wanted was a quiet, dark room . . . and another soothing poultice.

The Elders gathered at Schimeon's house. Chadassah went amongst them, offering cinnamon cakes and raisin wine. Rahab, head still aching, hovered on the edge of the circle, neither invited in nor excluded.

'The way I see it,' Schimeon said, 'is that we are no longer welcome in Arcassanne. We must start to make plans.'

'I'm not leaving!' cried a voice. Rahab recognised the querulous tones of the Eldest, Baruch. 'I secured us a safe haven here. Fifty years ago the people of this city agreed to let us live and practise our beliefs in Arcassanne undisturbed. They signed a contract. Comte Aymon's father – may he rest in peace –'

'Contracts can be torn up, burned,' Schimeon said, shrugging. 'A great deal can happen in fifty years. Aymon is not the man his father was.'

'I'm too old to make another move. Arcassanne is my home,' grumbled Baruch.

'According to their reasoning, good fortune will not return to Arcassanne until the boy's killer is brought to justice,' said Mandel the Shoemaker, shaking his head. 'All the ill luck that befalls the city will be blamed on us. Take last night's storm –'

'And that's the fault of the Tsiyonim? Yes, yes, we've heard it all before, haven't we? In Galicys – and in Tolonada – and before that in Ebora. When there's sickness, they blame us. When the harvest fails, they blame us. What possible reason could we have for wanting to spoil the corn? If there's not enough corn to go round, we starve too.' Baruch held out his glass for Chadassah to refill. 'Excellent raisin wine, my dear, I can almost taste the sun ripening the grapes on the vine.'

'But where could we go?' persisted Mandel. 'Where is safe?'

'The mountains,' Schimeon said. 'Tifereth.'

Tifereth. Rahab glanced up. Tifereth, high in the mountains, far away from the distractions of everyday life. Tifereth, the house of learning and prayer, college of the students of the Sacred Laws, renowned for their scholarship and wisdom. Once he had been destined for a life of study . . .

'You won't catch me climbing mountains.' Baruch took a noisy sip of his wine. 'Not at my age! I'm staying here. Let the young ones go if they wish, let them leave the sick and the old to fend for themselves . . .'

45

Rahab silently took the glass of raisin wine Chadassah offered him. She shook her head at him, whispering in his ear, 'Old men. All talk.'

'We have to make plans. Each time in the past we've said, "Let's weather the storm, sit it out." And what's happened? Torches in the night.'

Rahab stared into the dark wine in his cup, seeing florets of candlelight reflected in the liquid, like distant torches. He shuddered.

'It'll be talk of poison in the wells next, you mark my words,' Schimeon was saying.

'The only poison in Arcassanne comes from the ideas spread by Jaufré d'Orbiel.' Baruch wiped the sticky drops of wine from his curling white beard. 'Do we not honour and obey our Sacred Laws? Why should we want to sacrifice a child? The death of a child – that is the most terrible thing.'

'Can we be certain it was not one of us?' Mandel said. 'Maybe we have to hold our own investigation.' His words were almost smothered in an outburst of protests.

'But why leave the body on my doorstep?' Schimeon asked.

'Do you know of anyone who might harbour a grudge against you, against your family?'

'Fe!' Mandel said dismissively. 'It could have been anyone's doorstep – as long as they were Tsiyonim.'

'Schimeon's right. It might be a clue to the killer's identity –'

'I say you're wasting your time trying to find out who did it,' Schimeon said. 'Start to pack your valuables and board up your shops. If we leave for Tifereth now, we'll make it before the first winter snows.'

Rahab saw Chadassah raise her apron to her mouth to stifle a cry.

'And if we run, they'll say it's as good as an admission of guilt. Don't you want to clear your name, Schimeon?'

'Rebh Jehiel – what do *you* advise?' Schimeon turned to the old scholar who till that moment had been listening, taking no part in the argument.

'Yes, Jehiel, tell us,' Baruch said. 'What should we do?'

There was a long pause, in which Jehiel seemed to be pondering what had been said before.

'My dear friends,' he said eventually, 'you must make up your own minds on the matter. I am too old to go to Tifereth. Arcassanne has been my home for the past fifty years. All my memories are here. I shall stay – and weather the storm.'

The light was slowly fading from Rahab's garret; Rahab still sat sewing, determined to finish mending Rebh Jehiel's coat before nightfall. But although his hand moved rhythmically, mechanically, pushing the needle in and out of the worn cloth, his thoughts kept returning to what had been said at last night's Council of Elders.

What was he still doing here in Arcassanne? Why was he sitting cross-legged, pushing a needle and thread, when he should be searching for his brother?

So many years had passed. He was a grown man, not the frightened starving child who had made the arduous journey to the haven of Arcassanne. How could he have broken his contract with Schimeon before the appointed time? Schimeon and Chadassah were all the family he had now; they had taken him in, fed and clothed him, trained him –

He *owed* them.

This time it would not be the same as it was in Tolonada, in Galicys.

He jabbed the needle viciously into the cloth.

He would not let it happen again. Iudith and little Thirzah would not be caught up in the same terror that had split him from Shaoni, from his own parents.

Shaoni . . .

The dreams had begun again. For the last year or so they had ceased and he had found a kind of peace, an acceptance. But now the dead child had conjured them back. Last night he had awoken sweating, staring into the darkness, seeing nothing but flame-lit faces, distorted by fear – and Shaoni.

He had sat hunched in his garret, gazing out at the ramshackle rooftops and chimneys, unable, unwilling to sleep, going over the fragmented memories of that distant night, tormenting himself with thoughts of what he should have done. If only he'd run this way, not down that alley, if only he'd tied Shaoni's wrist to his own, if only he'd hidden in the cellar, waited till the mob went past . . .

Now a new, grim determination had formed in his mind.

He had not been able to save Shaoni . . . but he would give his life's blood to save the Tsiyonim children of Arcassanne from the hatred stirred up by Jaufré d'Orbiel.

*

47

The rough stones of the city walls had trapped the day's heat in the lanes, and there was a taste of dust on the air that dried the mouth and made the eyes sting. Rahab walked slowly, relishing the first stir of the evening breeze. The sweet, powdery scent of tamarisks drifted across the lane from a neighbouring garden. Rahab sniffed the breeze; he could smell cooking. His mouth watered at the enticing aroma of tomatoes seething with basil and garlic coming from Baruch's kitchen.

Rebh Jehiel's house was the last at the end of the lane. Since the death of Jehiel's wife Miriam three summers ago, the old scholar had lived on in the house alone, surrounded by his books and his cats, politely but stubbornly refusing all offers of more comfortable accommodation. The children of the community who attended his classes usually paid with gifts of food – and tonight, honouring the old custom, Rahab had brought a cake from Chadassah.

Mischkin, one of Jehiel's grey cats, leapt silently down from the windowsill and came to wind himself about Rahab's leg, purring ingratiatingly.

Rahab scratched the cat's ear.

Jehiel opened the door a crack, peering warily out into the twilight.

'Good evening!' Rahab said.

'Oh, it's you, Rahab, come in, come in!' Rebh Jehiel hurriedly ushered him in, shutting the door behind him and standing with his back against it, as though to prevent anyone else entering.

'Are you feeling all right, Rebh Jehiel?'

Jehiel had drawn out a handkerchief and was mopping his face with it; short, sharp dabs. Rahab saw that his hand was shaking.

'Yes, yes. I'm fine.'

Rahab hesitated; should he probe any further? 'I've brought your coat,' he said lamely, holding out his handiwork. 'And a caraway cake from Chadassah.'

Jehiel shook the folds out of the coat and pulled it on.

'Good as new,' he said, smiling at Rahab. 'Maybe better.'

'It's not too tight under the arms?' Rahab cast a critical glance at the fit of the new sleeves.

'Well, maybe just a little . . .'

Rahab had started forwards to test his handiwork when he saw that the scholar's face had crinkled into a smile: Jehiel was teasing him.

'You're a good boy, Rahab. Schimeon's a lucky man to have such a gifted apprentice. Now tell me,' and the smile faded from Jehiel's face, 'are you sure you weren't followed here?'

'Me? Followed?' The thought had never occurred to Rahab. In the confines of the Quarter he felt safe; he didn't look behind him.

'No one saw you?'

Rahab saw the anxiety in Jehiel's eyes.

'I saw no one. It's supper-time.'

Jehiel glanced around nervously, as though still not sure they were alone.

'You told me once at scripture class that your family name was Chazhael.'

'That's what my father told me.'

'Chazhael is an ancient tribe name. And you have been marked with the sign of that ancient tribe, marked not long after birth, I would guess.'

Rahab shrugged, wondering what Jehiel was leading up to.

'I'm going to ask a favour of you, Rahab ben Chazhael.'

'Ask,' Rahab said, still puzzled.

Jehiel went into the hall and took down the shell prayer-case that hung outside the study door.

'If anything should happen to me,' he said, 'I want you to take this to Tifereth.'

'T-Tifereth?' Rahab took a step back.

'To the scholars. We were not blessed with children, Miriam and I, so I have no one else to leave it to.'

'Leave it to – ? Are you sure you're feeling all right?' Rahab glanced anxiously at the old scholar, wondering if he were about to collapse; in the twilight, his skin looked as thin and translucent as fine vellum. 'Shall I call a physician?'

'No need, no need. But in taking this to Tifereth, you will put my mind at rest.' Jehiel pressed the prayer-case into Rahab's hands. 'It's been in my family for . . . for years without number. And now you come along, the right man at just the right time. Who'd have thought it, mm?' He gave a dry little chuckle. 'Who'd have thought that we were tribe-brothers?'

'You?' Rahab was becoming increasingly confused. 'And I? How can that be?'

'See. Here.' Jehiel lifted up his thinning grey locks, revealing a faded pattern tattooed into the skin; a whorl of blue and red, very like the one Chadassah had discovered earlier. 'The tribe of

49

Chazhael was scattered to the four corners of the world when Tsiyon fell. All that we have left to us is this shell . . . and the mark given to us at birth. It seems meet and just to me that another of our tribe should carry this to Tifereth.'

'I'd have to ask Schimeon –'

'No!' Jehiel said sharply. Then his tone softened. 'Don't tell anyone about this. Not even Schimeon. This is just between you and me, Rahab. And above all –' his voice dropped to a whisper, '– don't let it fall into Gentile hands.'

'Gentile? What would the Gentiles want with –'

Rahab broke off. Something was scratching at the front door.

Jehiel raised his finger to his lips, signalling silence. He went out into the hall and opened the door a crack.

The grey shadowcat squeezed in and darted down the passageway, its silky tail waving like a pennant.

'Mischkin! That confounded cat!' the scholar said, although Rahab could sense the relief in his voice.

'Would you like to come back with me? I'm sure Chadassah would be pleased for you to share our supper.' Rahab was not at all sure how Chadassah would react but he felt he should make the offer.

'I'd be delighted but I'm in the middle of a singularly fascinating piece of textual interpretation: an alternative reading of the chariot rider verses in the Book of Zhekiel. I'd like to make sense of it by tomorrow. Please – thank her for the cake. She knows I'm very partial to caraway . . .'

Jehiel glanced warily up and down the twilit lane before opening the door wide enough for Rahab to go through.

'Take care, my boy. I can't tell you what a relief it is to know *it* is safe.'

Behind him Rahab heard the clank of heavy chains and the squeal of rusty bolts as Jehiel barred and double-locked the door.

CHAPTER 5

Rahab is dreaming. In his dreams he is walking across a wide, empty sea-strand at low tide. The sand feels deliciously warm beneath his bare toes, sun-parched, soft . . . until his foot stubs against a sharp object.

'Ouch. Ouch!'

He stumbles, cursing, as he tries to nurse his throbbing foot, sinking down into the sand to take a closer look.

A drop of blood oozes from the cut as he brushes away the clinging sand particles. What has he cut his foot on: broken glass, a jagged rock hidden in the sand? He sifts through the sand and uncovers . . .

A shell.

A twirling curlicue of a shell, as long as his middle finger, pink and cream and brown.

Far away the tideline shimmers, a slick of silver on the distant horizon. Only a high spring tide could have deposited such a treasure so far ashore.

A faint tremor begins within his hand. Maybe some sea creature is trapped inside –

He raises the shell to take a closer look.

The vibration becomes a sound. A humming buzz.

Tentatively he shakes it, holds it to his ear.

And hears

The distant murmur of voices, many voices, rising like a distant stormwind . . .

A fine smoke slowly begins to emanate from the shell, curling out, unravelling in whorls.

He cries out and hurls the shell away from him, as far as his strength will carry it.

The smoke continues to unravel, filling the sky with cloud until the sun-warmed beach is dark with the shadow of imminent storm.

*

Rahab woke with a start. He was sitting bolt upright, staring blindly into nothingness. His eyes felt grittily sore, as if he'd been up half the night sewing.

The shell. *The shell?*

His hands fumbled beneath his bolster where he had hidden Jehiel's prayer-case and brought it out into the dawn light.

Its sharp corners must have protruded through the thin stuffing of the bolster and penetrated his dreams. It was that – or he had eaten too many of Chadassah's cream cheese pancakes for supper. Didn't they say that cheese gave you bad dreams?

He wasn't taking any chances.

He rolled off on to the floor and lifted his mattress, stuffing the prayer-case beneath.

'One disturbed night I can cope with. Two – and I start sewing sleeves together.'

'Make the rabbits again, Rahab,' begged Iudith.

'Yes, make the rabbits!' lisped Thirzah.

Rahab glanced around; Schimeon was in the workroom cutting out velvet – a tricky operation which always made him bad-tempered – Michal had been sent to the market to buy aubergines and Chadassah was busy in the kitchen. If anyone complained, he would protest he was merely amusing the little girls to keep them out of their parents' way.

With a solemn face he delved first one hand and then the other into his bag of threads. He kept two pockets of discarded felt inside, one brown, one red; in a rare moment of idleness he had embroidered eyes, nose and whiskers with ends of leftover thread. The girls had been enchanted with them, naming them rabbits for reasons he could not quite understand . . .

He popped one gloved hand out of the bag – and then the other, making little whiffling noises. Almost instantly Thirzah began to giggle.

'Hé, you, sieur! Yes, you, sieur! You stole my carrot!'

'I never touched your carrot –'

Iudith's lips began to twitch. As Rahab made his rabbits bump into each other, the girls subsided into helpless laughter.

'Oh, stop, stop –' begged Iudith, holding her sides. 'I'm – aching –'

'No, don't stop!' Thirzah cried. *'More!'*

'Stay out of my burrow or I'll –'

'Papa, *Papa!*'

Michal's voice, shrill and breathless, made Rahab break off in mid-stream. Forgetting the puppets were still on his hands, he hurried to the door, followed by Iudith and Thirzah.

Michal's face was flushed, her headscarf had come undone and her hair was loose about her shoulders.

'What's wrong?' Schimeon appeared at the door of the workroom, shears in hand. 'Why is your head uncovered, girl?'

'Jehiel – arrested.' Michal could hardly speak; she clutched at her side as if she had a stitch from running.

'Arrested?' Schimeon repeated. 'But – why?' His eyes met Rahab's over Michal's dishevelled head; Rahab stared back, aghast.

Thirzah tugged at Rahab's jacket.

'More rabbits, Rahab,' she pleaded.

Rahab rested one gloved hand on her shoulder, hoping to distract her for long enough to hear Michal's news.

'Comte Aymon – ordered it.'

'In connection with the boy's death?'

Michal nodded.

'Where have they taken him?' Rahab asked.

'To – the Tour d'Orbiel.'

'What?' Schimeon bellowed. 'Why not to the Tour de la Justice?'

Rahab felt Iudith shrink against him, frightened by her father's outburst. He looked down; she was sucking her thumb, a baby habit she reverted to when tired or miserable.

'Captain Orbiel is to interrogate him.'

'Oh, so now Captain Orbiel has become the city inquisitor?'

'They say the Comte has authorised him to arrest and question anyone he wants until he finds the murderer.'

'I must go tell the Elders,' Schimeon said. 'Rahab – keep shop till I'm back.' He went out at once, still brandishing his shears, his measuring string dangling around his neck.

'Be careful, Schimeon!' cried Chadassah as the door slammed behind him.

The others stood in silence, staring at each other. Then Thirzah began to grizzle.

'More rabbits . . .'

'Rahab's got to keep shop now,' Rahab said.

'Yes, Rahab's busy.' Chadassah took each little girl by the hand and bustled them into the kitchen, Thirzah's long, thin wail of protest trailing behind her like a streamer.

53

'And you're going to serve customers like that?' Michal said with a glint of her customary teasing.

Rahab hastily pulled off the glove-puppets and, red-faced, threw them back into his thread-bag.

Up in the attic, Rahab took Rebh Jehiel's prayer-case from beneath his mattress.

What should he do?

'If anything should happen to me . . .'

He had understood Jehiel's concerns; without children to succeed him, it was only natural that he wanted to bequeath his family prayer-case to his fellow scholars. It was a way of ensuring continuance – of a kind.

But he had never for one moment imagined that anything like this would happen.

Had Jehiel foreseen his arrest?

The facts of the matter did not add up. Jehiel a child-murderer? The very thought seemed ridiculous. Besides, even if the elderly scholar had killed the little boy, it was hardly likely that he would have had the strength to drag the lifeless body to Schimeon's doorstep and then run away. And who-ever had dumped the body on the doorstep had run away – fast.

'Don't let it fall into Gentile hands.'

Rahab frowned down at the shell of ivory. It was plain and yellowed with age; not as ornately carved as the prayer-cases that hung outside the Tsiyonim houses in Arcassanne. Only a single character had been etched on the ivory and that was so worn that Rahab could not make out whether it was a letter of the ancient alphabet or some other arcane character.

What would any Gentile want with such an old, chipped relic?

Rahab began to wrap the case in an offcut of fine wool he had saved from the workroom; as he turned it, he heard something rattle inside. He shook the shell. Whatever it was, it did not sound like a scrap of parchment.

Curiosity overcame him; he reached for a pair of embroidery scissors and levered with the fine blades. The shell had been sealed with a hard, yellow wax which chipped away in fragments.

He worked on until he was able to slip the scissor blade into the crack, prise it open and tip the contents into his palm.

The enamelled metal of the half-disc glinted in the evening light: gold inlaid with lapis lazuli, malachite and amethyst.

'Ahhh . . .' Rahab whispered into the dusk. 'An amulet . . .' He brought it closer, trying to make out what the pattern was. Were those pinions, wing feathers, etched into the jewelled enamel?

His hands began to shake as he realised what he had found. His father had told him of just such a sacred talisman; he had read to him from the Book of the Covenant. Every Tsiyonim child learned that passage by heart:

'And Ithamar the Smith did as the Lord commanded. He took the precious metals to the forge and wrought the amulets, each one inlaid with costly jewels.

'Then the Lord breathed into the heat of the furnace and the breath of the Lord forged the amulets.

'And the Lord spake unto Ithamar, saying, "Receive these four amulets as tokens of the Sacred Covenant which is between us."'

'A G-Guardian Amulet.'

He knelt on the floor of his garret room, holding the precious fragment of amulet cupped in his shaking hands, exhilarated – and terrified.

He held the proof of the ancient sacred covenant, the birthright of his people.

' "But let not these Four be divided. They shall abide in Tsiyon and where They abide, there shall I abide too."'

' "Let not these Four be divided",' murmured Rahab. In those simple words lay the root of the sadness that shadowed the Tsiyonim's long years of wandering. In Tsiyon, they had disobeyed that one command, they had divided the amulets. And in dividing them, they had sundered the divine powers, the Winged Guardians that protected them – and the city had fallen. Rahab had heard tales, rumours that fragments were still treasured in distant, scattered Tsiyonim communities. But until this moment, he had never imagined that he would see one, hold one, let alone be made its caretaker.

The weight of responsibility made his shoulders buckle. He cowered in the twilight, paralysed with fear.

'I want you to take this to Tifereth . . .'

'And how shall I get it to Tifereth?' Rahab asked the absent Jehiel. 'Do you suppose Schimeon's going to give his apprentice a whole week's holiday to go walking in the mountains?'

Now he understood why Jehiel had made him promise to tell

no one; the knowledge was dangerous. And now Jehiel had been arrested –

'Orbiel!' Rahab said aloud. The sudden moment of clarity chilled him to the bone in spite of the stuffy heat trapped beneath the eaves.

Suppose the investigation into the child's murder was no more than a blind, an excuse to cover a very different quest? Orbiel was a soldier – but he was also a poet, a scholar, an intellectual. It was not difficult to imagine how alluring the legend of the Guardian Amulets would be to a dilettante like Orbiel . . .

The methods of questioning employed by the Watch were known to be crude – and effective. How long would Jehiel's courage support him? How long would it be before the Watch were breaking down Schimeon's door, looking for Rahab the tailor?

He carefully laid the broken amulet down on the woollen cloth.

Seal it up again in the prayer-case. Hide it.

He looked around in a panic for a candle to melt to re-seal the treasure inside the shell. But to save money, the household economised on candles in summer and Rahab had given his last stump of candle to Chadassah to melt down to make new ones. Beeswax, then, the hard lumps of wax they used to wax button thread . . .

He fetched his thread bag and pulled out the worn lump of beeswax. One of the glove puppets fell out on to the floor. He picked the red felt rabbit up, weighing it in his hand. Its embroidered mouth grinned lop-sidedly back at him.

Who would think to look in a child's puppet?

He sealed the amulet back in its case with melted beeswax and then tucked the shell inside the rabbit, stitching it in place.

Then he eased his hand inside the puppet, taking care not to strain the stitches. He waggled the rabbit to and fro a few times, making the ears waggle.

No one would ever guess . . . or so he hoped.

Lia gazed down at the Belcastel family archives. They were meticulously-penned genealogical documents with each badge and escutcheon painted on yellowing vellum. Each new bride or groom's family tree was carefully delineated with names and dates . . .

She slowly traced Berengar's lineage until her fingertip rested against his name – and the gap beside it where her name and parentage should be. She glanced up at Berengar.

'But you know my mother was shipwrecked, you know she lost everything –'

Berengar shrugged and replaced the precious documents in the great iron chest, locking it with an ornate key.

'Why does it matter so much? If we love each other, surely that is enough?'

Berengar took her hands between his own, kissing her fingertips.

'For us, more than enough. But my family is another matter. It's only a formality, I know, but the Dowager is quite adamant.'

Lia, hurt, snatched her hands away.

'A formality? Does she suspect there is bad blood in my family? Corsairs, maybe? *Lepers?*'

It was the first time since childhood that she had raised her voice to Berengar. A frown clouded his golden gaze.

'Your noble family is willing enough to receive the generous dowry my father settled on me.'

He opened his mouth to reply – then pursed his lips together and turned away.

She had forgotten how intractable he could be when crossed.

'I'm sorry. I didn't mean that, it was wrong of me.' She gently touched his sleeves, trying to be conciliatory. 'If only we could run away together, just the two of us, and forget all this . . .'

He did not answer.

Lia sat in the window seat in the empty house, tracing a pattern in the dust on the sill with her fingertip.

She and Berengar had never argued like this before. Nothing was going right. Suddenly it seemed they could not agree on anything.

Why was it so important? And why had the Belcastel notary waited till now to raise the matter – when her father was away?

There must be something left from those distant days, some over-looked document or letter . . .

Lia looked down at the pattern she had traced: the Belcastel shield.

Her mother was not at home; she had gone on one of her rare vists to her sister-in-law, Lia's aunt Béatrisse, on the other side of the city. She would not be back until dusk.

Even a brooch, a ring with a family name engraved on it . . .

Lia crept to the door and listened. Emmenza was snoring in the kitchen, indulging in an illicit siesta whilst her mistress was away. The house was still but for the buzz of a fly trapped in the shutters.

Lia crept out into the passageway and tiptoed towards the attic.

Why did it feel as if she was doing something terribly wrong? She had every right to know who she was.

Under the rafters, it was oppressively hot. The fine, powdery dust seemed tinged with a smell of burning; Lia could taste it, dry at the back of her throat.

Trunks filled with discarded clothes were stacked in a corner, alongside Lia's father's old sea chests full of curios and souvenirs brought back from his travels.

Lia knelt down and blew dusty cobwebs from the top of the nearest chest.

She opened the chest and a musty smell issued.

All kinds of imaginings began to fill her mind: suppose Zillaïs had a past to conceal? Suppose she had been a woman of loose virtue, a courtesan – and the seawreck story was a mere fabrication, concocted to veil a less than respectable truth?

Her mother a prostitute?

The thought was both outrageous and absurd.

Lia began to giggle – and sent a puff of dust into the sunbaked air. The dust began to tickle her nostrils as she delved into the contents of the chest. Dried artemisias leaves put in to keep the mothgrubs at bay crumbled to dust beneath her searching fingers.

When a tiny worn shoe with red ribbons dangling from it fell out, she picked it up and held it next to her foot; had her feet ever been that small?

Other baby clothes followed; delicate embroidered caps, tied with faded ribbons, a silver and ivory rattle marked with little teethbites, then a battered wooden dog with a broken leg.

'Ohh,' Lia said aloud, lifting up the dog, stroking its wooden flank. 'Toutou. Dear Toutou. I thought they'd thrown you away.'

A chest of memories . . . redolent not just with the scent of dried artemisias but forgotten babyhood . . .

She sneezed – and clapped her hands over her face to smother the sound, half-dreading to hear a voice cry out below, '*Who's up there in the attic?*'

It seemed somehow shameful to be searching in this secretive and underhand manner. There was nothing here to be found, only a mother's mementoes of her daughter's childhood . . .

Her fingers brushed against something sharp and hard. Another old toy?

Lia dug down and pulled . . . Whatever it was was well buried in the midst of all the baby clothes.

It was a shell.

A seashell, intricately whorled, about a handspan in length, pale pink and brown.

'I don't remember this.'

Lia weighed it in the palm of her hand. Had her father brought it back for her from one of his voyages? She could not recall; there was a mist, thick as seafog, veiling her memory.

The sea was rarely mentioned in the Maury household. The family never ate shellfish; Zillaïs insisted they were poison to her and would make her violently sick. She would not even permit Emmenza to eat them in the house. Besides, this shell was nothing like the common oysters, scallops and mussels regularly consumed by the people of Arcassanne.

Lia raised it to her ear to listen to the murmur of the distant sea . . . and as she lifted it she heard a rattle.

There was something inside the shell.

She examined it more closely . . . were those miniscule letters? If they were, they were in no script that she recognised; they seemed to have once been filled with a gold paint, maybe even gold leaf . . .

She sat back on her heels.

No ordinary shell, then . . . maybe a memento of some argosy of her father's, maybe a betrothal gift from a far country, Djihan-Djihar or the Isles of Ta Ni Gohoa, where bridal customs were so different from their own. Or a birth-gift from one of her father's sea captains, a rattle which had been put away because its sharp edges might cut a baby's soft skin? Perhaps the gilded letters were a birth charm in a foreign tongue, wishing long life and good health to the newborn; her father Auger was always bringing home fascinating trifles and treasures: feather fans made from the wings of talking birds; phials of powdered mummy; mermaid's combs . . .

But the most curious thing about this treasure was that she had no recollection of ever having seen it before.

CHAPTER 6

The courtyard of the Tour de la Justice was crowded with petitioners; people spilled out into the street beyond. Jaufré stood watching from the top of the wide steps that led to the hall. Feelings were running high in the city; there had been disturbances, little demonstrations of anger directed against the Tsiyonim. Yet he felt nothing as he surveyed the petitioners, oddly distanced from the hatred he had awakened. Since that night he had felt nothing at all. It was as if the power he had summoned had armed him for this encounter, burning away all human emotions, making him invulnerable.

He had placed his men around the courtyard – but they were outnumbered. If there was trouble, they would never be able to contain it.

A scuffle suddenly broke out and a wave rippled through the heaving sea of people as a dishevelled woman pushed her way through, collapsing to her knees at the bottom of the steps.

'Call yourselves men of the Watch!' She was almost incoherent with anger. 'Three days! Three days have gone by since my boy was found! And what have you done? Nothing!'

Jaufré looked down at her and saw a face distorted with grief, unwashed cheeks streaked with runnels of tears, wild hair a faded shade of a brighter angel-gold, escaping from under a stained veil.

So this was the mother. He could not concentrate on what she was saying; he could only wonder how such a drab creature could have given birth to a child of angelic beauty.

'Well?' she cried, shaking her fist at Jaufré. 'What are you going to do about it? I want justice for my boy!'

Two more women fought their way to the front of the crowd and raised the woman to her feet, half-supporting, half-restraining her.

'Justice! Justice!' The crowd took up her words, repeating them in a rising chant so loud that Jaufré did not hear the great doors dragged open behind him. The chanting died and, turning, Jaufré saw that Comte Aymon had appeared at the top of the steps.

'What is this noise?' Aymon demanded testily. 'Can't your men keep these people under control, Orbiel?'

'With respect, Comte,' Jaufré said, 'my men are outnumbered twenty to one.'

'Give me justice, Comte!' cried the woman. 'Justice for my boy!'

'Who is that loud-mouthed woman?' Aymon murmured in Jaufré's ear.

'The mother of the murdered boy.'

'Admit her and her companions to the court. The rest of you – disperse. Go back to your work. I have the matter in hand.'

The woman tried to climb the steps but sank down, as though her strength was exhausted. Her two companions put their arms around her and helped her up the steps. Jaufré signalled to his men to take their places on the steps, guarding the doors to the court. Before he followed the Comte into the building, he turned, gazing back over the courtyard. A few of the petitioners had obeyed the Comte's orders but many lingered on, arms crossed, stubbornly determined to wait.

A shadow seemed to darken the courtyard as he gazed down at the crowd, and instinctively he glanced up to see if a cloud had moved across the sun.

The sky was blue, hot-summer blue – and cloudless.

Jaufré shook his head, trying to clear his vision.

By the time he reached the hall, the woman was already making her deposition before the Comte. Behind Aymon's chair he noticed the lean figure of Prieur Maugis of the Order of the Sacred Lady, Arcassanne's spiritual leader. The Prieur watched in silence, fingers pressed together. What influence had he exerted in the matter? Jaufré wondered. The priests of the Lady rarely interfered in judicial affairs. But this had become much more than a simple matter of justice.

'My name is Guillemette. I live by the river. I'm a laundress, I support my family doing washing. My boy's name?' Her voice faltered. 'Jacou. Eight years old this summer.'

Jaufré felt something twist deep within him. *Jacou.* And he had not even known the boy's name till now . . .

'Your only child?' the clerk asked. Comte Aymon looked on from his chair on the dais, fingers slowly tapping the arms of the chair.

'No; I have four other little ones.'

Four! So what does one fewer matter? They breed like rabbits, these common women, she's probably ready to drop another at any moment . . .

'I can't rest, I can't sleep.' Guillemette's voice penetrated Jaufré's thoughts, harsh as the persistent whine of a winter's wind. 'I just keep seeing his face . . .'

'Captain Orbiel.' Aymon beckoned Jaufré to the dais. 'What have you done so far to bring the murderer to justice?'

'No one in the Tsiyonim community saw or heard anything that night, Comte.'

'And you believe them?' cried Guillemette. 'They're shielding someone! They're lying!'

'Who knows what they get up to in there?' said one of her friends, jabbing her finger at Jaufré. 'Remember what happened in Galicys. Twelve years ago. They were murdering children and drinking their blood –'

'Allegations. It was never proved,' Aymon said drily.

'I told him to stop running errands for that tailor. But we needed the money,' whispered Guillemette, sinking back, exhausted. 'Five mouths to feed, he was only trying to help me . . .'

'And that old man,' persisted her companion. 'The Tsiyonim priest. Where was *he* that night?'

Prieur Maugis leaned forwards and whispered in Aymon's ear. Aymon nodded – but his expression did not alter.

'Perhaps you'd better bring in some of the Elders of the community to be questioned, Orbiel,' Aymon said.

Question the Elders. Jaufré forgot about Guillemette as a wild surge of excitement thrilled through him. What better opportunity to twist the truth from the Tsiyonim?

'Do I have your authority?' he asked, carefully masking his exhilaration.

'You have,' Aymon said wearily.

Prieur Maugis cleared his throat; a rough, rasping sound like the grating of a key in a rusty lock.

'Comte,' he said, 'is this not a matter for my inquisitors? Are we not straying into matters of the spirit?'

Jaufré glanced at the Comte. Interference from the priests? That would ruin everything.

'Prieur Maugis,' Aymon said, 'my father granted the Tsiyonim his protection. I must – and I will – endorse that treaty.'

Although the Comte's expression remained bland, Jaufré saw that he had begun to twist the great onyx seal ring on his fourth finger as he spoke. 'Arcassanne is a state that thrives on a healthy trade with other countries. If we offend other faiths, other beliefs, we risk losing our trade – and our livelihood –'

'Torch the Quarter,' Guillemette cried. 'Smoke them out!'

'My good woman, you must not take the law into your own hands. We will find the murderer and we will bring him to justice.' Aymon rose to his feet. 'But if any one of you attempts to stand outside the law – then I shall make an example of him. This hearing is at an end.'

Jaufré sat hunched over his desk. Candles burned in every corner of the turret room; the air was rich with their golden radiance.

So why – when all was bright with candlelight – did he have the distinct impression that there was a shadow within the room, a patch of darkness that slid into the furthest edge of his vision – yet, as he glanced up, slid away again?

Every time he took up his pen, dipped it into the ink, he became aware of it; every time he set the pen down and turned around, he saw to his irritation that there was nothing there.

As a consequence he had written nothing.

What had he expected? That one brief glimpse into the numinous would rekindle the dying fire of his poetic gifts? His mind could conjure no delicate poetic conceits, no fanciful rhymes or *jeux de mots* . . . the only image that appeared was the waxen face of a dead child. Jacou.

He shut his eyes, pressing his fingertips against his closed lids. Jagged traceries of flame embroidered the darkness.

There must be something wrong with his sight. He had not seen aright since that chaotic moment of apocalyptic turbulence in the cellar. Some lingering damage must be causing this irritating visual distortion.

He heard feet on the stair – and moments later, the curt rap of a mailed fist on the door.

'Identify yourselves!' Jaufré said curtly.

'Men of the Watch, Captain.'

Jaufré rose to his feet. This was no time to reveal any sign of fatigue or weakness.

'Enter.'

The door swung open and two men appeared, half-dragging a third between them.

'We've apprehended the suspect you ordered us to bring in for questioning.'

Jaufré saw Rebh Jehiel, dusty, dishevelled, gazing in bewilderment around him.

'You've done well. Now leave us. Wait below.'

The men released Jehiel and tramped out.

The old scholar stood blinking in the candlelight, a nocturnal animal dragged from the darkness of its burrow.

Jaufré watched him, arms folded, saying nothing.

Jehiel's eyes narrowed. His breathing quickened. Suddenly he raised his hands, making the sign to avert evil, muttering under his breath words Jaufré could not catch.

Jaufré took a step towards him.

'What have you done?' Jehiel said, backing away. 'In the name of God, Captain, what have you done?'

Jaufré stopped, frowning. What could the old man sense? Could he detect his guilt, could he read it in his eyes? Or was there . . . something else?

'I warned you. Why did you not heed my warning?' The colour had faded from Jehiel's face; his skin looked pallid, almost grey. One hand crept to the collar of his coat, loosening it with shaking fingers.

'What are you babbling about?' Jaufré spoke harshly, fearing Jehiel might be about to have a seizure.

'Might I – might I sit down? Your men insisted that the matter was urgent. My legs aren't used to that kind of urgency.'

Jaufré gestured to a wooden chair; Rebh Jehiel eased himself into it.

'So? What do you want of me?'

'What did you see?' Jaufré's voice dropped to a whisper. 'Just now, when you came in?'

'Is that the question you had me dragged through the streets to answer?' The rebuke was mildly worded yet the scholar's eyes regarded Jaufré coldly.

'There's no one else in Arcassanne who can give me an answer.'

'But what of the murdered child? Aren't you going to interrogate me? You were so sure it was one of the Tsiyonim who killed him. But then it was you who planted the seed in the minds of the people of Arcassanne. Those few emotive words. *Ritual . . . sacrifice . . . Tsiyonim.*'

'Answer my question, Jehiel.'

'To answer your question could take a *yeshiva* of learned doctors a lifetime of study and debate.'

'Just answer my question,' Jaufré repeated, an edge to his voice. He was in no mood to play word-games.

'Once there was a man in Tsiyon, a scholar you understand, who desired above all worldly treasures to attain a state of enlightenment. But he made one singular mistake in his interpretation of the ancient texts. He assumed that in summoning up one of the elemental spirits, it would obey him – for good or for evil. Such a fundamental error to make –'

'Get to the point,' Jaufré said through gritted teeth.

'The point,' said Jehiel, fixing his eyes on Jaufré, 'is that you have made the same crucial error. Daemon kindred, spirits, Winged Guardians, angelloi, whatever you call them, do not obey the will of men. Summon them – and they will cleave to whatsoever is strongest in the summoner's soul. Do you begin to understand, messire?'

'No,' Jaufré said curtly.

'Only the man who can honestly profess to have led a pure, a holy life, a life without sin or blemish, may dare to open himself to such powerful influences. In the days before the Temple was destroyed and the Tribes scattered, the young scholars and warriors strove to perfect themselves so that they might be chosen when – and if – the need arose –'

'Spare me this lesson in ancient history!' Jaufré could not concentrate on what Jehiel was saying. 'It is of no interest to me. Tell me the truth.'

Jehiel sighed. 'Already it is at work.'

'You accuse me of conjuring daemons. Evil spirits. Devils.' Jaufré's fingers mockingly mimed horns. 'There are no such things. Tales to frighten children and simpletons.'

'But I sense a darkness in here,' Jehiel said, 'a darkness that clings to you, Captain Orbiel. A darkness that feeds on the despair in your soul – feeds and grows strong.'

Jaufré turned away abruptly so that Jehiel should not see the working anger in his face.

'This . . . darkness you claim to sense,' he said, mechanically leafing through the papers on the desk. 'Can it be exorcised?'

Jehiel remained silent.

'Well?' Jaufré whirled around. 'Can it? Or is this just some fantastical story you've invented to put me off the trail? To shield the murderer?'

65

' "*Blood of the pure, blood of the innocent*",' Jehiel said.

Jaufré tried to conceal the involuntary shudder that the scholar's words provoked. Had Jehiel noticed the effect upon him? Had he guessed? The muscles in his jaw ached with the effort of keeping his face expressionless.

'A literal translation from the pen of one not truly initiated. The fragment of text comes from the ancient *Sefer Razhiel*, the Book of the Unseen. It speaks metaphorically. Long ago in Tsiyon, the Guardian Warders of the Temple, they who were entrusted with the amulets of power, were enlightened scholars, chosen for their spiritual beauty. Their purity of soul.'

'Amulets of power?' Jaufré whispered the words. 'So you acknowledge they exist?'

'The amulets were destroyed when the Temple was razed to the ground,' Jehiel said with a sad, wry smile. 'And –'

'And that is why your Tribe wanders the world, your people proscribed, outcasts, yes, yes.' Jaufré rounded on the old scholar. 'How many times have I heard that from you, Jehiel? It's what you all say. And I say to you – it's a convenient lie.'

'A lie? How else could we have lost Tsiyon?' Jehiel said, slowly, regretfully shaking his grey head. 'The amulets were God-given. It was only through human foolishness that they were misused, and for that my people have paid the heaviest price of all – eternal exile. Have you any idea, Captain, what that is like? Never to call any place home. Always on the move, hounded from country to country, vilified, persecuted –'

Jaufré was wearying of the old man's constant harping on the past. Since Jehiel had spoken the words *amulets of power*, he had felt a gnawing deep within him, a terrible unassuageable hunger.

A sudden shudder of breeze made the candleflames flicker; Jaufré blinked as the golden radiance seemed to dim. It was as though a veil of dark gauze had been drawn across the chamber . . .

He put his hands to his temples, shaking his head to clear his vision.

Amulets of power . . .

He looked up, narrowing his lids. He no longer saw the benign elderly scholar whose lined face revealed a wisdom born of long years of prayer and study. Instead, as the smoke-veil dispersed, he saw a hunched, decrepit figure, with rheumy eyes that looked on him with suspicion.

'I'll strike a bargain with you,' Jaufré said. His voice sounded heavy, slurred in his own ears, as though drugged. 'Find me one of the Guardian Amulets – and not another word will be spoken about the child's death.'

There was a silence. 'A bargain?' Jehiel said eventually, as if he had not heard aright.

'One amulet – and I will ensure that the Tsiyonim community is publicly exonerated.'

Jehiel shook his head, as if in disbelief.

'Have you not heard a word I said? The Guardian Amulets were broken up, destroyed, scattered like the people of my Tribe. And even if we had one, we would not give it to you. They are not to be given away, bartered like merchandise on a market day. They are a sacred trust, a covenant not to be broken.'

'Is that your answer?'

'I thought you to be an honourable man, Captain. I believed you were searching for justice, for truth. Now I see you are driven by greed.'

Greed! Now Jehiel was openly insulting him. Jaufré struck the desk with his fist – and to his satisfaction saw Jehiel flinch.

'Maybe a day or two in the cells will make you change your mind.'

Jehiel said nothing.

His silence only confirmed to Jaufré what he had suspected; and the confirmation excited him deeply, though he took pains not to show it. Jehiel must know of the existence of an amulet within the community, maybe more than one . . .

He went to the door, opened it and called down the stairs for his men.

'He won't talk. Take him down to the cells and lock him up. Then get reinforcements and arrest the remaining Elders.'

'Interrogate me,' Jehiel cried, 'but let the others be. They are not scholars, they know nothing.'

Jaufré almost permitted himself a smile; it was working. 'If they are innocent,' he said pleasantly, 'then they have nothing to fear . . .'

He had taken a risk in revealing so much of his own desires to the old scholar.

Jehiel must never be released back into his own community alive.

CHAPTER 7

One of the idle pleasures of Lia's childhood summers had been to filch ripe raspberries from the canes in the kitchen garden.

Now Lia and Alissende sat together in the arbour, as if they were still ten years old, sharing their stolen provender, laughing at each other's juice-smeared mouths.

'Mmm. They never taste better than this,' Lia said, wiping the red juice from her lips. 'Raspberries should always be eaten immediately they've been picked. They should never be stewed in pies.'

'Or preserved in eau-de-vie.' Alissende made a face.

'I wish we could have fresh raspberries at our wedding feast. With thick cream,' Lia said greedily.

'As long as there's plenty of wine, no one will care much. And music for dancing.'

'And cake.' Lia sighed. 'Papa promised to bring back spices . . . and that delicious preserved ginger from Serindha.'

'What a pity you have no brother, Lia,' Alissende said with a little sigh. Curious how similar she looked to Berengar when she furrowed her brows – and yet in every other respect they were dissimilar, Alissende fair and freckled with hair of white-gold, Berengar darker, hair gilded bronze. 'Then there could have been a double wedding.'

'We shall wait till you find a man you want to marry,' Lia said, squeezing her friend's hand.

'Then be prepared to wait a long time.' Alissende flashed her a defiant glance. 'I find all Berengar's friends horribly dull.'

'Except Jaufré d'Orbiel?'

Alissende turned her head away but not before Lia had seen the flush of red darkening her fair skin.

'So I'm right! You *do* like him!'

'He's the lover of Grazide del Azénor. How can I compete with the White Lily of Arcassanne?'

'Grazide?' Lia made a dismissive moue. 'She must be as old as

my mother. The famed Lily is fading, withering on the stem . . .
whereas you, *ma belle* –'

'Me?' Alissende tossed back her hair so that the sunlight
caught its sheen of gold. 'Queen of the Tourney. D'you remember?'

Now Lia felt her cheeks burning.

'You promised we'd forget the whole incident.'

'It'll make a wonderful story for the wedding banquet!'
Alissende' eyes sparkled maliciously. 'How old were we? Ten?
Eleven? The boys were playing at paladins and you – as you
always did, you tomboy – how you begged Berengar to let you
be a paladin too. And he said –'

'I didn't beg! I was as good with a bow as any of them,' Lia
said indignantly.

'And he said,' continued Alissende, refusing to be distracted
from her re-telling, '"You can't be Queen of the Tourney
because she's got to have golden hair, so I suppose you'd better
be her lady-in-waiting."'

'I didn't want to be Queen. I didn't want to sit there – just
watching. I wanted to join in. You still don't understand that,
do you?'

'Always running around with your skirts hitched up like a
boy's tunic,' Alissende said, collapsing in giggles. 'Always
tangling your embroidery threads because you were testing
them as bow strings. And that time you had the quartan fever
and they cut your hair and you spoke up feebly from your
sickbed, saying, "Good, it only got in the way at target
practice –"'

'Dem'selle Lia!'

'It's Emmenza. What can she want now!'

'Ignore her,' said Alissende. 'Maybe she'll go away.'

'Dem'selle!'

Emmenza came puffing down the path towards the arbour.

'Too late,' whispered Alissende.

'What is so important that you must needs disturb us –' Lia
stopped, seeing Emmenza was not alone. Behind her stood the
young Tsiyonim tailor, Rahab.

'This man says he comes from the Sieur Belcastel. He says he
is a tailor . . .' Emmenza seemed flustered, turning from Rahab
to Lia and back again.

'The Sieur de Belcastel had arranged a fitting for this afternoon,' the tailor said. Lia noticed for the first time that his voice

was spiced with a slight foreign inflection. 'But when I went to the Great House, they told me he was not at home. They suggested I call here.'

'Berengar must have forgotten,' Alissende said.

'I'm sorry you've had a wasted journey –' Lia began.

'No matter.' Rahab gave a little bow and turned to leave.

'Wait!' Lia could not contain her curiosity. 'You said a fitting. Have you any of *my* clothes ready?'

'Dem'selle,' Emmenza said warningly, 'your mother is ill with a megrim. It would not be seemly –'

'You can be my chaperon, Emmenza.' Lia put her arm around Emmenza's plump shoulders, giving her her most winning smile. 'Don't you want to see my wedding gown?'

'*I* want to see it,' Alissende said.

'I don't suppose there'd be any great harm then . . .' Emmenza said, relenting. 'But no stripping down to your shift! Whatever you try on goes on over your daygown.'

'Bless you, Emmenza!' Lia gave her old nurse a hug.

In the cool of the solar, the tailor opened up his worn carrybag and carefully unrolled lengths of plain cloth; within, protected from dirt and sun by the cloth, lay the folds of ivory brocade, woven with threads of gold into an intricate formal pattern of lilies and acanthus leaves.

'Ohh . . .' Lia knelt down to gaze at the glittering brocade, stroking it with reverent fingers. 'Look, Emmenza, isn't it fine . . .'

'It pleases you?' Rahab said.

'Oh, yes. It pleases me very much.'

'This is going to be the grandest occasion in Arcassanne since the Comte married Elvire del Irhuna,' Alissende said, clapping her hands together.

Lia undid the fastenings on her bean-blue surcoat and shrugged it off as Rahab shook out the creases in the brocade overgown and eased it on over her light berry-sprigged dress.

'I must warn you, demoiselle, that the gown may look complete – but it's only held together with tacks, so tread carefully.'

It was heavy, the train falling in rich folds from subtly disguised tucks at the shoulders, yet when Lia turned, the gown flowed in a most pleasing way. She straightened her shoulders and essayed a few paces; the gown's weight forced her to move slowly, gracefully, as if taking part in a courtly dance.

'What d'you think?' she asked.

Emmenza had clasped her hands together.

'You look like a princess,' she said, her eyes glistening with tears. For the moment it seemed that she had forgotten her apprehension about letting a stranger into the house.

'Isn't the train a little uneven at the back?' said Alissende.

'If the demoiselle could just stand still a moment . . .' Rahab said through a mouthful of pins. He knelt down and swiftly pinned up the hem. Then sitting back on his heels, he watched critically as Lia walked up and down again.

'Better,' he said, nodding.

'And my gown?' Alissende demanded.

'The silver brocade?' The tailor was transferring pins back into the little velvet pin cushion he wore on his wrist. 'Maitre Schimeon has finished the cutting. Today he is sewing.' He stepped forwards to help Lia remove the heavy brocade, then began to wrap it carefully in its protective cloth. Lia watched wistfully, wondering if Berengar might be present when the gown was ready for its next fitting. 'Perhaps I might ask you, demoiselles, to tell the Sieur de Belcastel that I called . . . and will await his further instructions.'

'Isn't it ill fortune for the bridegroom to see his bride in her gown before the wedding day?' Alissende said.

'Not amongst my people,' said Rahab. Lia thought she caught the glint of a smile in his dark eyes as he fastened the straps of the bundle and hoisted it on to his shoulder.

'I will give my brother your message,' Alissende said, a little petulantly. 'And tell your Maitre Schimeon to make sure that *my* gown is ready for the next fitting.'

Emmenza insisted on calling Peire in from the stable to escort the tailor off the property and into the lane.

'He's quite good-looking . . . for a tradesman,' Alissende commented, watching Peire unbolting the garden door to let Rahab out.

'Is he? I didn't notice,' Lia said, affecting disinterest. 'Though obviously, you did, my lady Alissende.'

Then, before Alissende's mock-blow could hit her, she ran laughing into the garden, her friend in pursuit.

'Dem'selles, please!' Emmenza cried, trying in vain to shush them. 'Remember madame is not well, remember her head-ache.'

'Then we'll take our drinks outside so as not to disturb her,'

Lia said. 'Bring us a jug of borage watar, Emmenza. We'll be in the arbour.'

As soon as Rahab entered the Quarter, he sensed something was wrong. No one was about; the streets were deserted at the very time in late afternoon when the shadows had begun to lengthen and the Tsiyonim came out to take the air after the intense heat of midday.

Then he caught sight of Jaufré d'Orbiel's Hawks at the end of the street. He shrank into a doorway. There were three of them, coming swaggering down the street, coming towards him –

Mandel the Shoemaker appeared, hurrying along, head down, clutching a pair of boots.

As Rahab watched, helpless, the Hawks moved in, barring Mandel's way, pinning him up against a wall.

'Who found the body?'

'His name. Tell us his name and you shall go free.'

No weapons were unsheathed, there was no overt threat of violence – just their loud, arrogant voices and their rough handling.

Who found the body?

He should have gone to Mandel's aid. He should have cried out, 'Let him go, it's me you're looking for!' But instead he scuttled on, despising himself for his cowardice . . . yet knowing that to come forward would mean beating, imprisonment – death. His sense of self-preservation was too well honed by the years on the run.

They don't care about finding the murderer. They want a scapegoat. And Rahab the little tailor is just the man they're looking for.

He turned the corner of the narrow street and saw –

Beneath the tailor's sign of shears and thread, Schimeon's door had been wrenched off its hinges.

'Dear God, no.'

He ventured nearer, pausing on the threshold, his fingers moving out automatically to touch the prayer-case –

Sharp splinters grazed his fingertips. The prayer-case shell was gone. Ripped off.

He entered cautiously, a step at a time. Everything was turned upside down, chests had been forced open, their contents thrown out on to the floor. He stepped over spilled spices, yards of unspooled thread . . .

72

'Anyone at home?' he called softly. His voice shook. Had they taken them all? And why Schimeon – when the one they wanted was Rahab?

He stopped, listening. His ears had caught a faint sound, soft, like the mewling of a kitten.

In the kitchen he noticed what he took at first to be a heap of clothes in the corner by the fire. As he came nearer, he saw the heap of clothes move, heard the faint sound again, the sound of smothered weeping.

'Chadassah?' he said tentatively. 'Chadassah – it's me. Rahab.'

'Go away.'

Two little faces peeped out from the fireplace: Iudith and Thirzah, their eyes wide with fear.

'Mama. It *is* Rahab.'

Kneeling down, Rahab put one hand on Chadassah's heaving shoulders.

'What has happened here? Was it Orbiel?'

She raised her head from beneath her veils. Her hand clutched at his.

'They came – they tore the place apart – they arrested them, Rahab. My husband, m-my beautiful daughter.'

'Michal? But – why?'

'They wouldn't say. They just took them.' She reared up, eyes suddenly blazing. 'But if one of Orbiel's men so much as touches a hair on her head –' She turned away and spat.

The little girls ventured out cautiously from their hiding place, Iudith sucking her thumb.

'You can't stay here,' Rahab said. 'They may be back.' Thirzah silently curled her hand in his; her fingers felt hot and sticky.

Chadassah shook her head.

'For the sake of the little ones, Chadassah –'

'Where would we go? Nowhere is safe.'

'Please . . .' Rahab begged again. 'We must leave this house. We must go somewhere safe.'

Chadassah had stopped weeping. But now she sat like a statue amidst the ruins of her ransacked home, immobile, staring into nothing.

'It's what Schimeon would want.'

Chadassah's lips moved. The words came out in a halting whisper.

'I'm not going without Michal. Or my husband.'

73

'But it's not safe here. Come to Baruch's house. He has cellars big enough to hide the whole community. Schimeon will know to find you there.'

She looked up at him then, her eyes red with weeping.

'For the little ones' sake, then . . .'

Rahab let out a silent sigh of relief. 'Come on, girls.' He held out his hands to Iudith and Thirzah. 'We're going for a little walk.'

Thirzah shook her head.

'Nasty men,' she said vehemently.' Don't like the nasty men.'

'They've gone,' Rahab said. 'They won't come back.' He prayed he was right.

Iudith hung back.

'Not going without the rabbits.'

'The ra –' Rahab, aghast, stared at her. Had Jaufré's men searched upstairs too? 'Wait. I'll go fetch them.' He ran up the stairs, two at a time, flinging open the attic door.

'Don't let it fall into Gentile hands . . .'

His mattress lay on the floor, gashed and slashed, spilling its horsehair stuffing. His thread-bag had been turned inside out; costly spools of bright-coloured silks were tangled and coiled together. Even his clothes had been shaken and thrown down higgledy-piggledy.

And then he spotted a lone red ear poking up; he grabbed it and pulled out one felt rabbit – and then its twin. A quick pressure of the fingers reassured him that the shell was still intact, sewn inside its incongruous hiding place. The Hawks had found the toys – and discarded them.

Fools. He could feel a slow smile spreading over his face, exultant in the knowledge that he had tricked them.

'Fools!' he shouted aloud defiantly.

'I win – again.'

Lia and Alissende were playing each other at chequers for sugared comfits.

'Lia!' Alissende cried. 'You're cheating!'

'Don't be such a poor loser,' Lia said, grinning as she drew the pink and white comfits towards her and popped one into her mouth.

'I saw you move that counter. You thought I wasn't looking.'

'So what if I did?' Lia said with her sweetest smile. 'Raise the stakes this time?'

'I'm not playing if you're going to cheat,' Alissende said, sulking.

'Good evening, Peire. Is my sister Alissende here?'

Lia sprang up, recognising Berengar's voice.

'Berengar!' she cried. 'Where have you been?'

Peire, cap in hand, ushered Berengar into the solar.

'You forgot the fitting this afternoon,' Lia said, shaking her finger at her fiancé.

'Yes, you forgot,' echoed Alissende. 'We had to send the poor little tailor away.'

'And he'd struggled all the way here in the heat, carrying the clothes.'

'So you'd better have a good excuse.'

'There was trouble outside the Palais de Justice,' Berengar said when the girls had finished their chiding. 'I had to wait until the crowd had dispersed.'

'Trouble? What kind of trouble?' Lia said.

'The mother of the dead boy and her supporters. Aymon ordered arrests to placate the crowd. I'm damned if I understand what's going on,' Berengar said, shaking his head.

'Why? What is there to understand?' said Alissende, helping herself to Lia's comfits.

'Why the Tsiyonim don't do more to help themselves. You ask them a question, they answer with another. They turn everything around. If they have nothing to hide,' he said, frowning, 'why are they so obtuse?'

'So Jaufré still suspects it was one of them who –' Lia faltered. *Killed the boy.* She could not bring herself to say it out loud.

'And those shells.' He had not heard her question. 'Outside every front door, a shell. A seashell.'

'Shells,' Lia echoed.

'Whenever they visit each other, first they kiss the shell and mutter some kind of charm.'

'But what does it mean?' Lia asked in a whisper.

'Jaufré says the shells have some secret ritual significance.'

'Shells?' Lia said again. She felt a small, sick twisting in the pit of her stomach. Could the shell she had found hidden in the attic be Tsiyonim? Why would her father have brought home a souvenir of secret ritual significance?

'Ouf.' Berengar stifled a yawn behind his fist. 'I'm tired. Come, Alissende, we mustn't keep Gran'mère waiting.'

Alissende placed one hand on his shoulder.

75

'Why not leave the Hawks, Berengar?' she said. 'The Sieur de Belcastel has better things to do, more fitting to his status.'

'You could spend more time at the farm, the vineyard,' suggested Lia.

'Na. Farm talk bores me, sweeting.' He bent to kiss her farewell, brushing her cheek with his lips. 'Give my greetings to your mother.'

Lia nodded. She watched Alissende and Berengar walk through the garden to the gate. Usually she was sad to see them go, sad at the end to the merriment and laughter.

But tonight she felt confused.

Afflicted by a belated pang of guilt, Lia took her mother a tisane of feverfew.

The shutters in Zillaïs's bedchamber had been closed all day. Lia could only just make out her mother's face, pale in the gloom. Zillaïs had been plagued by these sick headaches for years; Lia had learned long ago to tiptoe about until the attack had passed.

'Do you need anything else, Mother?'

'No,' Zillaïs murmured. 'Thank you . . .'

Outside every front door a shell.

Lia went to her own room and shut the door, standing with her back against it, listening for Emmenza and Peire to bolt the outer doors and dampen down the kitchen fire for the night.

A seashell.

At last all was quiet. Holding her lantern, Lia crept out on to the landing and, hitching up her skirts, went up the open stair into the attic.

Kneeling down in front of the dusty chest, she opened the catch and delved down into the tightly packed layers to find the shell.

She felt the sharp edge graze her searching fingers as she drew it carefully from its place of concealment and held it to the lantern flame.

A gift. It must be a birth-gift. Her father met all kinds of people on his travels. Some Tsiyon merchant must have pressed the shell upon him eighteen years ago to celebrate the birth of a daughter.

Secret ritual significance.

She knelt in the lanternlight, staring at the shell, turning it round and round in her fingers, remembering . . .

Tentatively, she raised it to her ear.

76

The distant murmur of voices, many voices, rising like a distant stormwind . . .

'What are you doing?'

The shell dropped from her fingers. Looking up, she saw her mother's face, white in the moonlight, staring at her.

'I – I –' Lia could not speak; the expression on her mother's face was too terrible.

'What have you done, child? What have you done!'

Zillaïs crossed the attic floor and snatched the shell from her hands.

'I've done nothing!' Now that the shock of discovery had subsided, Lia was angry. What right had Zillaïs to shout at her? All she had done was unpack an old chest, full of mementoes . . .

'Nothing. Nothing!' Zillaïs clutched the shell to her; with her grey hair unplaited, falling loose about her shoulders, she seemed like some wild, demented fury. 'Do you know what this means? The end of your hopes, your dreams. The end of your betrothal to Berengar –'

'How can that be?' Lia cried.

'We should never have tried to ally ourselves to such a powerful house as the Belcastels.' Zillaïs sank down on to one of the chests, still clutching the shell. 'Your father only ever wanted the best for you – but he could not see the pitfalls. Because he is a good man, a compassionate man, he does not always understand that others are not like him –'

'Mother!' Lia's voice shook. 'What are you saying?'

'Berengar won't marry anyone tainted with Tsiyonim blood. That's what I'm saying.'

'Tsiyonim!' Lia went over to her mother. Questions buzzed in her head like angry bees. 'How can I have Tsiyonim blood? How can –'

'It is passed down through the mother, not the father.'

'*You?*'

'Yes. My name was Zillah bet Ithamar. Your father thought it was best I should change it.'

'But – but why?' Lia said, stunned. 'Why did you never tell me? Why keep it a secret?'

'Why? You have kept company with the Belcastels all these years and you ask me *why*?'

'I need to know!'

'Because I thought it best. Because I wanted your childhood to

77

be free of prejudice, free of fear. I wanted you to have the childhood I never had.'

'But I've been living a lie. I'm – I'm not who I thought I was.' Lia stared at the shell clasped in her mother's fingers. 'I'm someone else.'

'You are who you have been brought up to be,' Zillaïs said coldly. 'A demoiselle of Arcassanne.'

Lia could not understand why Zillaïs was so angry – wasn't she the one who had been deceived?

'No, I'm not. Not inside. Not any more.'

'You don't know what you're talking about,' Zillaïs said with a terrible, chilling disdain. Lia stared at her mother, open-mouthed. 'You have no idea of what it is to be Tsiyonim.'

'And now I'm – I'm nothing. Now I belong nowhere. Now you say my marriage can never take place –' Suddenly sobs rose in Lia's throat, stifling her voice. Weeping, she ran from the attic to her room, slamming the door shut.

If only Papa were home . . . he would make everything all right again.

But Papa would not be home for two long months.

Zillaïs stood with her back against her chamber door, as though to keep out the shadows of her past.

Why? Why now? After all these years?

She could hear Lia's sobbing, the uncomprehending, bitter sobbing of a child who does not understand why she has been rebuked. Poor, wilful, impetuous Lia, always rushing in where caution should prevail. Her heart pained her to hear her daughter weeping so bitterly – yet she could not bring herself to go to comfort her. Not yet.

She had tried to protect Lia by keeping the truth from her. Whenever Lia had asked about her grandparents, tears had filled Zillaïs's eyes. And Auger had always stepped in, protecting her, saying, 'It's still painful for your mother to talk about her family. Another time . . .'

Slowly, with dragging feet, she moved towards the round bronze mirror that gleamed dully on the wall. A bridal gift from Auger, brought from the far east. She gazed unwillingly into it. The reflection that gazed back shocked her: the colour had faded from her lips, fine worry-lines had appeared around mouth and brow, and her dark eyes looked warily back, beneath brows more silver than black.

The face of a ghost.

The ghost of her mother Liah.

Zillaïs steeled herself to look again at the bronze reflection. The woman who might have been her mother stared back.

'Mamma. Help me. What should I do, what should I do?'

A voice in the back of her mind whispered, *'You're a grown woman now, Zillaïs. You know what you should do.'*

Zillaïs sat down on the bed, the bed she had shared with Auger these past twenty years.

If only he were here, beside her, to advise her –

'It's your responsibility, Zillaïs, yours and no one else's,' came her mother's whispervoice again. *'Auger's a good man, a kind man, but he's not one of us, he wouldn't understand.'*

'All these years I have lived in this city as Dame Maury, the merchant's wife. No one has forced me to wear a saffron badge, no one has spat at me, called me names. I wanted that freedom for Lia. Was that so wrong?'

'Freedom? What kind of freedom forces a woman to live a lie? To abandon her faith? To creep to her room on the holy nights to light the candles in secret, to whisper the words of the evening prayers so that no one suspects, no one hears?'

'But she found the shell, Mamma, the shell. How can I begin to tell her about Tolonada –'

'Don't you think she deserves to be told what it means to be born into the House of Ithamar?'

'No,' Zillaïs whispered, her hands rising to press her temples as she felt a sudden throb of blinding pain. What was she doing, talking to a ghost? Arguing with a woman dead these twenty years? 'I wanted to spare her. It's my burden, not hers.'

' "Blood of the pure, blood of the innocent . . ." It's calling to her, Zillaïs, just as it once called to you.'

CHAPTER 8

'Sieur Berengar, Demoiselle Alissende. You are back at last!' Berengar's manservant Pons unfastened Berengar's cloak and baldric as he greeted them. 'The notary is here to see you. Your grandmother has been waiting dinner for you. And –'

'The notary?' For a moment Berengar had no idea why the notary should have come to see him. The mention of dinner quite distracted him. 'Can't it wait till morning?'

'A word with you in private, Sieur Berengar.' The notary must have heard his voice and come out to greet him; his drab robes were dusty and travel-stained.

'I'll go to Gran'mère,' Alissende said, hurrying away towards the old lady's chamber. 'But don't be long, Bera, you know how she hates to be kept waiting. She'll take it out on me.'

'There is someone else to see you,' Pons tried to interrupt. 'Cap –'

'Dinner, Pons!' Berengar said impatiently. 'Go!'

Pons opened his mouth to try again – then retreated.

'This will not take long, sieur,' said the notary.

'It had better not.' Berengar's attention was wandering; he could smell roast fowl – he hoped it was duck, with salt rubbed into the skin to make it crisp . . .

'It – is a delicate matter.' The notary's fingers wound themselves into a knot. 'Concerning the parentage of your betrothed. Or to be more precise – your betrothed's mother.'

Berengar stifled a yawn behind his fist.

'I have been to Tolonada and made the most exhaustive enquiries. No one knows anything of a woman called Zillaïs. But there is a record of a Zillah bet Ithamar – who is said to have perished with all of her family when the boat in which they were travelling was wrecked off the coast of Galicys.'

'Perished?' Berengar was finding it hard to concentrate. 'So this can't be Dame Zillaïs.' He began to walk down the panelled corridor, following the savoury scent of the salt-roast duck.

'But the lady in question maintains she was rescued from a shipwreck, does she not?' The notary pursued him. 'And as she was escaping from the massacre at Tolonada –'

Berengar stopped suddenly, swinging round.

'Escaping from the massacre? What massacre?'

'Perhaps I did not make myself quite clear,' the notary said carefully. 'The Zillah bet Ithamar said to have been drowned at sea was Tsiyonim. A few of the Tsiyonim inhabitants escaped – but most were slain. I came upon the records of the Ithamar family in the city archives because he was a physician, a respected physician by all accounts, in favour with the royal family of Tolonada, until –'

'Tsiyonim?' Berengar said the word under his breath, afraid lest someone – particularly the Dowager – should hear. 'But that would make Lia –'

'It would make the young lady Tsiyonim as well, through her mother's bloodline, yes.' The notary bowed his head low, as though deference might blunt the impact of his news.

'Lia?' Berengar stopped abruptly, turning on the notary. 'But surely if her mother is this same Zillaïs – Zillah – she would have had to convert to marry Auger?'

'Surely so.' The notary nodded his head. 'It would not, however, eradicate the indubitable fact that she was born Tsiyonim.'

'Well, well, well,' came a dry, mocking voice from the shadows. 'How are you going to explain this to Gran'mère Belcastel?' Jaufré d'Orbiel slid out from behind a tapestried door-curtain. His face was twisted into a wry smile. 'A Tsiyonim daughter-in-law!'

'Wh-what are you doing here?' Berengar stammered.

'Pons tried twice to tell you, but you dismissed him. An obedient servant, your Pons. He does what you tell him to do.'

Lia's face swam palely before Berengar's eyes, lost, confused, betrayed . . .

'And of course, one is forced to ask, has the Maury family deliberately concealed the truth from you?'

'Say nothing. For our friendship's sake, Jaufré, if nothing else, say nothing. All this is circumstantial evidence, there's no proof –'

'I have brought back copies of the documents in question, sieur,' said the notary in indignant tones.

Berengar glared at him.

'Mmm. That duck smells good,' Jaufré said, sniffing the air. 'Did you know the Dowager has invited me to stay for dinner?'

'Lia has been raised as one of us. She is no more Tsiyonim than I,' persisted Berengar.

Jaufré gave a little shrug of the shoulders.

'Berengar?' called a woman's voice, at once querulous and imperious. 'Where have you been? Why are you so late?'

It was his grandmother, the Dowager; Berengar could hear the tap of her stick coming closer along the passageway. She would never understand. Maybe she need never understand . . .

'Here's my purse,' he said, pulling it from his belt, pressing it into the notary's hand. 'You'll find ten gold courons in it. Now give me those copies. There'll be ten more if you produce documentary evidence of a different nature, understand me?'

After a moment's initial hesitation the notary nodded and discreetly made his retreat.

'Twenty courons.' Jaufré looked at Berengar, one eyebrow lifting. 'Is she worth it? Is any woman worth it? Oh – I quite forgot. She brings a considerable dowry to swell the Belcastel coffers, doesn't she?'

'Berengar!' The Dowager appeared, leaning on her ebony cane, Alissende hovering behind. 'Have you quite forgotten your manners? We have a guest. Whatever your business is, it must wait till after dinner. Captain Orbiel – give me your arm. You shall escort me into dinner.'

'My pleasure.' Jaufré bowed and offered his arm to the Dowager.

Berengar watched helplessly as Jaufré and the Dowager walked on ahead into the hall. That last jibe of Jaufré's still stung. It was true, Lia would bring him an impressive dowry. Merchant money – but who were the Belcastels to be proud when their coffers were nearly empty? Many Arcassanne marriages were built on such arrangements of financial convenience. But this marriage was to be based on more than money; he genuinely liked Lia, had always liked her. He did not want to see her hurt.

Alissende tweaked at his sleeve, hissing, 'Come *on!*'

Why was he worrying? Jaufré was his friend, had been his friend since childhood. Surely he would never betray a confidence, especially one as sensitive as this?

But as he followed his sister into the hall, the appetising smell of roast duck seemed to have lost its savour.

Snow falls from a leaden sky.

A wailing cry rings out over the empty landscape.

Jaufré shades his eyes against the chill brightness, scanning the snowfields. So faint, so inhuman the cry, it must have been a bird or a wild beast.

He looks down and sees footprints in the snow, small footprints trailing away into the distance. A child's footprints.

Who would send a child out alone in this wilderness of snow?

The cry rings out again, plaintive yet distant.

Jaufré begins to wade through the snow, following the trail of prints.

And then he hears the flap of wingbeats overhead.

He glances up, expecting to see a bird, a buzzard or an eagle, swooping down from the mountains – but the snow-speckled skies are empty too.

The blizzard-wind falters, dies a moment, and Jaufré catches sight of his quarry. The child. Lost. Alone. Struggling forward blindly through the snow.

A shadow falls over Jaufré, the shadow of great, slow-beating wings.

The child stumbles, falls full-length in the snow.

The sky darkens. Glancing up, Jaufré sees a giant winged figure swooping down out of the sky, arms outraised to scoop up the child. White feathers drop from its soft wings, swirl and eddy, falling cold and wet on to Jaufré's upturned face.

'Shalgiel,' Jaufré whispers into the sighing snow-wind, his tongue numbed by the winter's chill, 'Bringer of Snow . . .'

The snow where the child fell is stained darker than shadow. Jaufré drops to his knees, traces the icy outline of the imprint left by the boy's frail form . . .

His hands come away damp, sticky . . .

He looks down and sees they are wet with blood.

Jaufré sat upright, shivering. He fumbled in the darkness for his tinder to light the lamp. He looked down, checking his palms, his fingers by its wavering flame.

They were sticky with sweat. Not blood.

Why had he dreamed of snow? The night was stiflingly hot. His whole body was wet, his hair stuck to his forehead.

Did the juice of Mynezhil poppies bring dreams of the snowfields where they grew? There had been a time when a single phial would have ensured a night's oblivion. Now he was awake again after an hour or so's uneasy dozing, awake and on edge. He suspected the apothecary of diluting the drops to keep his customers coming back for more, still more . . .

Sleep . . . he badly needed sleep . . .

But no dreams. No more dreams.

Jaufré picked up his pen, dipped it in the ink – then paused.

What was he doing?

He used to while away the boredom of hot summer nights playing with words. Nights were a fertile time for conjuring images from the darkness, for poetry.

What was the point in even trying?

And then the pen was moving across the page, feverishly writing, as if driven by a will other than his own.

Jaufré stared down at what he had written. The ink – in the lamplight – glowed red as fresh-spilt blood.

> . . . the naked child shivers in the snow . . .
> comes a knight, his armour silvered hoarfrost,
> the child weeps but no one hears his cries
> 'Cold knight of winter, why have you used me so cruelly?
> For pity's sake –'

With a cry of anger, Jaufré ripped the page in two and held the pieces to the lampflame. He watched the flame devour the words until they crumbled to ashes.

Memories of a freezing, bare chamber, a locked door, a child beating his fists against the wood until they bled, crying until his throat burned . . .

He clenched his hands tightly, willing away the memory.

'Let me out, please let me out –'

'You will learn to take your punishment like a man.'

'But it's dark in here. So dark. Let me have a light. J-just one little light?'

The child Jaufré tries to still his own juddering sobs, listening in vain for an answer. But all he can hear is the sound of retreating footsteps. The harsh Lord of Orbiel believes that children must be schooled into submission by rigorous chastisement.

He huddles back into the farthest corner of the unlit chamber. His mind has already begun to conjure shadow-daemons out of the chill

84

darkness, daemons that come swarming to suck out his soul; he can almost smell the charnel foulness of their breath, see the voracious gleam in their luminous eyes, he can scarcely breathe for the choking terror. If he should die here, alone, forgotten –

Pray. Pray for help. He struggles to his knees, hands clasped together.

'Lady, help me, I'll be good, I'll bring offerings to your shrine,' he prays to the Lady of Arcassanne, pressing his hands tight together, trying to will her image to lighten the darkness, her pale, smiling face, her long tresses of golden hair, so like his mother, his dead mother . . .

Childhood was a time of defencelessness, vulnerability. He was strong now; he had armed himself against the world. Weakness was to be scorned. He had become the knight in cold armour.

So why, why did the child he had been still cry out, mourning its lost innocence?

This was not the verse he was renowned for, the villanelles, the rondeaux, barbed with acerbic wit, the love poetry, courteous and clever. This was some raw emanation from behind the door he had locked on his past.

Once poetry had been a consolation, a pleasing diversion in which he could mock the vagaries of life. Now, after months of drought, another child, cruelly abused, haunted his words, crying out for vengeance.

The lanternflame wavered. A thin, fine smoke guttered from its failing brightness. Jaufré stared at it, mesmerised. There was no stir of breeze in the sultry night and yet still the shadowsmoke unravelled from the wavering flame . . .

Suddenly he could not bear to be alone any longer. Snatching up his jacket and sword, he extinguished the flame and went clattering down the stairs, out into the sultry Arcassanne night.

'I can wait all night, tailor. But you will answer me.'

Schimeon had been brought from the cells to a room in the Tour de la Justice. He stood, hands manacled, before Jaufré and the clerk of the court, who sat ready with pen and ink to record the tailor's interrogation.

Jaufré's fingers strayed towards the carved shell he had torn from Schimeon's doorpost which he had placed on the table in front of him.

'On whose authority do you hold me here without charge?'

'Comte Aymon. Do you want to see the documents? He has given me power to interrogate anyone I suspect of involvement in the murder of the child. And you, Schimeon, are highly suspect. It was on your doorstep the body was found.'

'I don't deny it! But I had nothing to do with the murder.'

'How do you explain this?' Jaufré held up the shell and shook it. It rattled. To his satisfaction, he saw Schimeon blink; for a moment the master tailor's reserve faltered.

'Explain it? We put shells on our houses to remind us of the sea we have been forced to cross in our flight from Tsiyon – and that we hope to cross again one day when we return home. It is a custom of our people.'

'Does the tailor speak the truth, I wonder?' Jaufré took his dagger and slid the blade-point into a crack in the shell – then levered.

'No!' Schimeon cried out.

With a crack, the ivory shell shattered. Jaufré, trying to control his growing excitement, searched amongst the fragments. In the lanternlight he saw a piece of curled parchment. Opening it up, he could make out signs inscribed on it in an unfamiliar and ancient script.

'What's this?' He thrust it under Schimeon's nose. 'How do you explain this?'

'Part of a prayer. It's a good-luck charm.'

'It must have some ritual significance.'

'I told you. A good-luck charm, nothing more.'

'Very well.' Jaufré replaced the fragment of parchment on the table beside his dagger. His heart was beating fast with the thrill of his discovery. 'Let's return to the matter of the boy. Who found the body? Who was the first?'

Schimeon turned his face away.

Jaufré shrugged, keeping up his pretence of disinterest. But all the while his heart kept thudding, his fingers itched to touch, to caress the ancient piece of parchment again. 'Berengar!' he called.

Berengar came into the chamber.

'Go and bring me more of the Tsiyonim shells. Strip the Quarter of them. I want them brought here by dawn.'

He saw Berengar's eyes flicker towards Schimeon in his manacles.

'Why have you arrested my tailor?'

'The boy's body was found on his doorstep.'

86

'Are you determined to ruin my wedding, Jaufré?' Berengar asked, pleasantly enough. 'How can my wedding clothes be finished in time if you keep my tailor locked up?'

'If your tailor can prove his innocence, then he'll be released.'

Jaufré saw Berengar open his mouth to object – and then close it again. He was beginning to doubt Berengar's suitability as a Hawk; when they had been boys together, Berengar had always been his faithful lieutenant, a little slow to comprehend the task in hand but always eager to please. The lords of Belcastel were not renowned for their quickness of wit, though their loyalty and bravery in battle had never been in doubt. Yet recently Berengar had begun to question Jaufré's actions . . . was it Lia Maury's influence? Better he were absent from the interrogation.

As the door closed behind Berengar, Jaufré leaned close to the clerk and said – just loud enough for Schimeon to hear – 'Is the girl ready to be questioned?'

'In the next room, Captain.'

'Girl?' Schimeon raised his head. 'What girl?'

'Have her brought in,' Jaufré said, purposely ignoring Schimeon.

The Tsiyonim girl was young, maybe two or three years younger than Alissende de Belcastel, Jaufré reckoned, but with none of Alissende's pale insipidity. Her dark eyes might be red-rimmed with crying – but they flashed defiantly at him as she reared her head.

'You say your name is Michal. You are Schimeon's daughter. Where were you when the boy's body was found?'

'Asleep.' Her voice was sullen.

'You slept through the whole disturbance?'

'I'm a heavy sleeper.'

Jaufré rose from his chair and walked around the table to stand close to her, so close he could sense the apprehension she tried to hide beneath the defiant mask.

'How unfortunate.' He paused, savouring her discomfort. 'If you had been able to identify the member of your community who found the body, I could have let you go free. Now I shall be forced to keep you here until one of you recovers his memory.'

He could see the throb of the pulse at the base of her throat where her torn chemise revealed skin of a darker bloom than any pale Arcassanne demoiselle's. He had a sudden desire to reach out, to touch, to see her flinch away –

87

'I'll tell you what you what you want to know, Orbiel,' Schimeon said heavily.

'No, Father!' Michal whirled around, bound hands upraised. 'Don't –'

'It was Rahab.'

Michal let out a cry.

'Who is this Rahab?'

'My apprentice, sieur. Now let my daughter go, as you promised. She's only a child.'

'Bertran. Did you hear what the tailor said?' Jaufré beckoned over the man standing guard near the door. 'Go arrest the apprentice. He's called Rahab.'

'Father!' cried Michal, her eyes dark with anguish.

'Now let her go,' Schimeon said heavily.

'Oh, I'm not releasing anyone yet,' Jaufré said, studying his fingernails. The tailor was beginning to sweat; well, let him sweat a little longer. 'Not until this Rahab is arrested. Then we'll see if his story accords with yours.'

CHAPTER 9

'Down here, Chadassah my dear. Take care, the steps are narrow.' Baruch led the way into the cellar, holding high a lantern to illuminate the way.

Rahab picked up Iudith, balancing her on one arm, gripping the rail with the other. Thirzah took hold of a fold of her mother's gown, venturing tentatively down one step at a time.

In the lanternlight, Rahab saw faces, upturned to stare at them, fellow refugees from Jaufré d'Orbiel's interrogations.

'This madness will pass,' Baruch said. 'Aymon will put a stop to it.'

'The children must be hungry,' said Keziah, his wife. 'Would you like some honeybread, girls? Come with Auntie Keziah and we'll get you a nice big slice each.'

'Baruch! Baruch!' Tobiah appeared at the cellar door, waving his hands agitatedly.

'What now?' Baruch said wearily.

Tobiah kept waving and beckoning. Baruch slowly wheezed his way back up the steps; Rahab watched, listening intently.

'They're doing *what*!' thundered Baruch.

'Ssh, don't alarm the children.' Tobiah tried to pull Baruch away from the cellar door.

Rahab hurried after them.

'The shells,' Tobiah said. 'They're taking all the shells.'

'They took Schimeon's,' said Rahab. He saw Baruch and Tobiah exchange a glance.

'Someone must go warn them at Tifereth,' Baruch said.

'What's the matter?' Chadassah had followed Rahab up the steps, her face pale as whey. 'I heard Schimeon's name – is there any news?'

'No news. Only more desecration. They're taking the shells.'

'The shells?' Chadassah's hand flew to her mouth.

'Someone must get a message to Tifereth,' Baruch said again, this time staring Rahab directly in the eyes.

'Me?' Rahab took a step backwards.

'You're young, you're strong,' Baruch said. 'You're the obvious choice.'

Tifereth. Rahab swallowed. 'How can I go and leave Chadassah? And the little girls? I owe it to Schimeon to make sure they're safe.'

But Chadassah was not paying attention; she had turned away, wringing her hands.

'We should have listened to Schimeon. He was right. None of us wanted to hear what he was saying. Now it's too late.'

'It's not too late!' insisted Rahab.

'The truth is that we belong nowhere, we have no home, not even Tsiyon. We will always be outcasts. We –' She stopped, listening. Rahab glanced around.

He could hear the sound of running feet coming down the street. Rough voices, shouting, banging on the shutters.

'Rahab! Rahab the Tailor!'

Chadassah clutched at Rahab's hand.

'They've come for you.'

Baruch pointed down the passageway. 'Quick, boy – go through the backyard.'

'Chadassah –' Rahab still held her hand between his, looking pleadingly into her eyes.

The door shuddered under repeated blows.

'*Run!*'

He let go of her hand and made for the kitchen, scrambling out of the window, landing with a thud in the yard below. The impact jarred his ankles, sending pain shooting up his legs; he staggered and set off before he had fully regained his balance, lurching across Keziah's kitchen garden towards the high wall that rimmed the back lane, clambering up to the top, scraping the skin from his knuckles as he went.

'There he goes!'

They had seen him. He sped across the open and dived into the passageway that ran behind Efraim the Butcher's shop.

'Don't let him get away!'

'Split up. Two this way, two the other.'

He leaned against a wall, trying to catch his breath, ribs aching from running. He was damned if he was going to let Jaufré's Hawks catch him on his own territory; he knew the blind alleys and cul-de-sacs of the Quarter better than they. Dropping to a crouch, he edged along, wondering where to go, where to hide.

90

He could not ask any of the community to shelter him; Jaufré would only punish them as he had punished Schimeon.

And then the thought came to him. A thought so mischievous that it seemed daemon-sent.

The Gentile girl. Sieur Berengar's betrothed. Who would find him if he hid in the bedchamber of the Lord of Belcastel's bride-to-be?

He began to laugh – but his aching ribs pained him and the laugh caught in his throat, harsh as a sob.

Half the night, it seemed, Lia heard the footsteps overhead as her mother paced relentlessly to and fro whilst she sat, frozen, on her bed, staring into nothing, her brain frenetically shuttling thoughts to and fro.

Tsiyonim. How can I be Tsiyonim? And why did they never tell me?

Zillaïs had said it had been done to protect her, to shield her from the taunts and persecution she herself had endured as a child.

For the very best of reasons.

At this moment, Lia did not care about her mother's reasons, no matter how well intentioned.

The bleak fact was that once the truth was out, the Belcastels would break off the engagement. It would not matter to them that she had been raised as a Gentile. Their prime concern would be to keep their ancient bloodline pure, free from taint. They would find some clever legal way to withdraw from their contractual obligations, their honour and bloodline un-smirched. Even now their notary and his clerks were ferreting around the archives, sniffing out the truth –

Maybe clerks could be bribed, documents forged . . .

Lia started up, beginning to reckon on her fingers how much money she could raise to pay for false documents.

But it would not stop there. Once she had revealed her secret to another, there would be needs be further payments, pay-ments to secure silence – and the constant threat of revelation would be held like a knife at her throat. Her life could become an unending nightmare of concealment and blackmail . . .

What else have they withheld from me? What other lies have I been told?

She heard her mother's restless pacing start up again. Zillaïs had not slept all night. But frozen in her anger, Lia could feel no sympathy with her mother's anguish. A vast gulf had opened

91

between them, a gulf she would not, could not breach. Zillaïs had betrayed her; had ruined her life. She was no one now, not Tsiyonim, for she had not been raised to the faith, nor Gentile. Alissende would turn from her, cut her dead.

She stared at the mottled dawn sky as the sun warmed the pale clouds to gold. Her face felt stiff with dried tears.

She was an outcast, a nobody.

Rahab skirted the garden wall of the town house of Auger the Merchant, seeking for a place to climb over unobserved. In the prosperous Merchants' Quarter, the houses were large, each with its own walled garden, not huddled together in narrow lanes.

The sun was rising and the city of Arcassanne was waking to the new day. If he was to infiltrate the Maury household, he'd better be quick before someone spotted him and gave the alarm.

Red valerians covered the crumbling wall; it looked easy enough to climb.

He found a foothold and pulled himself up. A stone gave way – and he scrabbled to keep his hold.

A thick thatch of glossy ivy covered the garden side of the wall; Rahab gripped the wiry stems – but the ivy could not take his weight and tore away from the wall, taking him with it.

He dropped to the ground, scraping the skin from his knuckles as he fell.

The sting of the grazes centred him. He shaded his eyes against the sun, gazing up at the house, searching for a way in.

The shutters were barred – all except on one first-floor window. More climbing, he thought ruefully, sucking his knuckles.

Getting on to the sill of the ground-floor window presented no problem. But hauling himself up to the first floor nearly resulted in disaster – and instead of slipping with agility into the room as he had planned, he lost his grip and ended tumbling clumsily on to the floor – almost straight into the lap of the Sieur Berengar's betrothed.

Lia screamed.

The intruder rolled over and reared up on his knees, hands clasped.

'Demoiselle –'

'Keep away from me.' She edged away from him, one step at a time, making towards the door. Her whole body was trembling. 'I'll call Peire.'

'I mean you no harm. You've got to help me. *Please.*'

Now she recognised him. The tailor, Rahab. But so dirty, so dishevelled that he looked like a lazar.

'Wh-what do you want?' She had never screamed before – not in her whole life. Now she was disgusted with herself for having reacted so timorously.

He was silent, listening intently. There were footsteps in the passageway, shuffling footsteps.

'Don't give me away.'

'Lia?' It was Emmenza. 'What's wrong?'

She could see desperation in the tailor's eyes. Was it the desperation of madness – or fear?

'Nothing's wrong.' She kept her gaze fixed on his.

'But I heard a scream –'

'Oh – that!' She forced a little laugh. 'I picked up my shoe and there was a huge spider inside. So silly of me –'

'And you're sure nothing's wrong, my pet? I know how you hate spiders.'

'I put it out the window. It's gone.'

'All right, then. Do you want me to help you braid your hair?'

'No. I can manage.'

The footsteps shuffled slowly away. When she was certain Emmenza had gone, Lia turned on Rahab.

'Now you must go.'

'Shelter me. Until nightfall. Then I'll go, I promise.'

'Why? Why should I shelter you? Why are you on the run? Have you committed a crime?'

His eyes darkened. 'My only crime was to be born Tsiyonim.'

She flinched. *Tsiyonim.* But of course, he knew her to be Gentile, he could have no idea –

'Do you know what they did? They took my master's daughter, Michal – she's no older than you – they took her to be – to be questioned.'

'So you came here to take me hostage?' she said coldly. 'To exchange me for your Michal?'

All his anger seemed to die down, as if she had thrown water on the flames.

93

'No,' he said dejectedly. 'I fear it's too late for that.'

In the silence Lia heard a hollow, rumbling sound coming from the tailor. She glanced at Rahab. He looked away, embarrassed.

'I haven't eaten since . . . I don't exactly remember . . .'

He huddled in the corner of her room, unwashed, unkempt, unfed. Was this what it meant to be Tsiyonim?

She had made her decision before she realised it.

'Bar the door behind me. Don't open it to anyone but me.'

'Where are you going?' He jerked his head up, eyes wild, distrustful again.

'I thought you said you were hungry,' she said tartly. When she opened the door, he made no move to hold her back.

In the corridor she checked herself. What was she doing, getting food for an intruder, a wanted man? What was there to stop her from sending Emmenza to fetch the Watch?

The sound of pacing overhead had ceased. Perhaps Zillaïs had worn herself out and was sleeping at last? Lia hurried downstairs and slipped into the kitchen.

She caught sight of Emmenza trudging across the courtyard to the well to draw water. There was just time to grab a round loaf of this morning's fresh-baked bread, a pot of curd cheese and another of honey. Emmenza had cut a plateful of slices from a side of smoked, spiced beef for Peire's breakfast; she wouldn't miss two or three . . .

A sudden commotion in the garden made Lia jump, spilling apples on to the floor; as she knelt to pick them up, the door opened and Emmenza came in, flustered and out of breath.

Lia got up, holding the plate at her side, hoping Emmenza would not notice.

'What's that noise?' she asked.

'Dear, dear me.' Emmenza flopped into a chair, fanning herself with one plump hand. 'Barbe next door swears – that child-killer – came this way. This way!'

'Child-killer?' Lia began to edge towards the door.

'Dark as a devil, they say he is. Staring eyes. We could all be murdered in our beds. Make sure you bar your shutters, Lia. I'll get Peire to go check the outhouses. If you see anyone – just shout. Loud.'

In her room, Lia spread a clean napkin on the floor and laid the food on it. Rahab nodded his head in thanks and slowly leaned forward to take a piece of the loaf. Then all restraint vanished and he began to tear at the crisp-baked crust with his teeth, bolting the food down.

Lia watched.

'So, where are they?' he said, his mouth still full of food.

'Where are who?'

'Lord Berengar's men. You had ample opportunity to call them.'

'Perhaps I have called them. Perhaps even now they're on their way.'

He stopped chewing, regarding her with his head on one side, as though assessing what she had said.

Lia looked down at her hands; her fingers were repetitively knitting and unknitting themselves.

'*Why?*' he said. There was an intensity to his voice that disturbed her. 'When your betrothed finds out you fed and sheltered a Tsiyonim –'

'Why don't you tie my hands and feet before you go? That would make it look more convincing . . .' She could not keep an ironic smile from her voice. 'As for my betrothed –' Bitterness swelled in her throat, choking the words.

'Fools,' she heard him say. He moved to the window, wiping traces of crumbs from his beard as he gazed out. 'They seem to have given up the chase. They're probably too busy looting our shops and homes to bother . . .'

'Keep away from the window. If anyone sees you –'

He did not budge. 'Now's as good a time as any to make a break for it.'

'And where will you go?'

He shrugged.

'There is a place, some distance from here. In the mountains.'

'A place of safety?'

He smiled, shaking his head.

'And why should I tell you? So that Captain Orbiel can bring his troops to ransack it?'

'You don't trust me, do you?' Lia said.

'Why should I trust you? It'll make a good tale for the Great Hall at Belcastel, won't it? How the Tsiyonim tailor who should have been making your wedding clothes forced you to bring him food and ale –'

There was a mocking quirk in his words that Lia found infuriating.

95

'You'd better go, then.'

'Farewell.' He leaned out over the sill, gazing into the courtyard, and then swung his legs over the ledge. 'I'm afraid you'll have to find another tailor for your wedding gown –'

'Wedding!' Lia cried suddenly. 'There won't be a wedding!'

'Oh?' Rahab paused. 'And why so?'

'Because I'm like you. One of you. Tsiyonim.' It all came out in a gabble.

'You? Oh, don't try to stall me with that ploy. I'm off.'

She caught hold of him by the arm and pulled.

'You've got to believe me. Berengar doesn't know. No one knows.'

He swayed on the window ledge, grabbing at the sill to steady himself.

'"Hold him here by any means till I come." Were those Lord Berengar's instructions?'

'Listen to me, Rahab! We've got one of those – those shells. Do I have to fetch it to make you believe me?'

He froze.

'A shell? A prayer-case?'

'It's my mother's.'

'Your mother?' he echoed, his eyes suddenly misted, opaque.

'Must you repeat everything I say?'

'There came the sound of distant voices in the lane. They fell silent, staring at each other.

'Come back in, for mercy's sake,' Lia begged.

Poised on the ledge, Rahab was straining to see where the voices were coming from.

'There's a litter at your gate; the colours are blue and white –'

'Alissende!' Lia's hand flew to her mouth. She had completely forgotten she was to go with Alissende to the perfumier's this morning. At the door, she paused to look back over her shoulder. He was still sitting perched on the ledge, straining to see what was happening below. Lia flapped her hands at him, as if shooing a naughty child.

'Hide! Get out of sight!'

She was halfway across the kitchen, making towards the courtyard, when she stopped.

This might be the last time she saw Alissende.

The thought pierced her, sharp as a thorn.

She glimpsed Alissende alighting from her litter, heard her eagerly calling her name.

She hesitated, one hand on the door handle, frowning into the sunshine. When Alissende knew, would she greet her so eagerly? What would prove the stronger: lifelong friendship – or Belcastel blood?

A crowd had gathered outside Jaufré d'Orbiel's tower; even though it was bright daylight, Berengar noticed as he approached that many carried torches, the torchflames flaring palely.

'What are you doing here?' Berengar demanded.

'Waiting.' A woman turned to stare at him; he recognised the drawn features of Guillemette, the dead boy's mother. 'Waiting for justice.'

They parted to let Berengar through but he sensed as he entered the tower their growing impatience, a silent seething.

Berengar climbed the tower stair wearily, stumbling on the spiral tread. He had been up all night on this fool's quest for shells. He wanted a bath – and his bed. But first he had to report to his Captain on the night's activities.

But on the threshold, he stopped, gazing about him in bewilderment; scattered fragments of broken shells lay everywhere, crunched underfoot. It was as if the room had been transformed into a beach; he half expected to hear the wailing mew of gulls overhead.

'Well?' came Jaufré's voice, taut, tense. 'D'you have any more?'

Berengar picked his way towards him through the shells.

'No more,' he said, opening his hands to show they were empty.

'Damnation!' Jaufré turned away. 'Are you certain?'

'Unless the Tsiyonim removed them and hid them before we reached their houses, yes,' said Berengar, stung that Jaufré should doubt his word. 'Why do you need them? They were only good-luck charms.' His gaze strayed past Jaufré, trying to see what the poet had been doing at his desk when he came in.

'Good-luck charms? That's what they would have us believe,' Jaufré said darkly, his mouth still twisted.

'So what do you think they are?'

Jaufré went back to the desk and scooped up a handful of little scraps of parchment, leeting them sift through his fingers. 'I don't read the ancient script of the Tsiyonim.'

Berengar picked one up and peered at the faded text; the unfamiliar scrawlings meant nothing to him.

'Perhaps they told us the truth. Perhaps they *are* good-luck charms.'

Jaufré let out a harsh bark of laughter.

'Whatever they are, they've done the Tsiyonim no good.' Berengar let the fragment of parchment drop. 'Poor devils.'

'Poor? Don't forget they are shielding a child-murderer, protecting him from justice.' Jaufré said, rounding on him. 'They don't deserve your pity.'

'But just because my tailor found the body doesn't necessarily mean –'

'And did anyone see what happened before your little tailor called for help?' Jaufré's eyes burned in sockets darkly hollow with lack of sleep. 'They're keeping something from us. A vital clue.' He turned away and began to leaf through the sheets of written evidence that littered the table.

Berengar went over to Jaufré and laid a hand on his arm.

'When did you last sleep?'

'God knows.' Jaufré shook the hand off and continued to search.

'Well, I'm off home. I could sleep for a week.'

Jaufré seemed not to hear him.

Berengar turned on his heel and went down the stairs. At the doorway, Guillemette confronted him.

'Well? Have you found my boy's killer?' Her eyes terrified him; lit with a torpid yet intense gleam.

'Not yet.' Berengar drew himself up, hand moving instinctively to the hilt of his sword. 'Our investigations are still in progress.'

'You hear that?' she said to the others waiting. 'Nothing. Still nothing.'

'Then let's smoke them out.'

Berengar turned around, trying to identify who had cried out. But others took up the cry.

'Yes, smoke them out!'

'Burn! Burn!' Torch flames swirled close to his face as they turned and began to move towards the Tsiyonim Quarter, sweeping Guillemette along with them.

'Wait!' Berengar cried above the chanting. 'You could set the whole city alight –'

They took no notice. One lone voice would not dissuade

them. Berengar hesitated a moment, then went flying back into the tower.

'Jaufré! They're going to set fire to the Tsiyonim Quarter!'

Jaufré looked up from his desk. His face had a strange, blank expression.

'So?'

'One stray spark in this heat and the whole city could go up like a bonfire!'

'Then take the Hawks and go and stop them.'

'B-but you –' Berengar stammered. Jaufré was Captain; quelling civil unrest on this scale was surely his responsibility.

'I'm busy,' Jaufré said dismissively. 'What are you waiting for, Lieutenant?'

Berengar went to the window and looked out. There was a haze on the blue sky, a grey haze too dark to be cloud.

'Smoke,' he muttered. A faint acrid smell of burning wafted in on the breeze.

Any fire in Arcassanne in summer was dangerous. Once roof-thatch was alight, the hot, dry wind from the mountains would fan the flames –

He went hurtling down the spiral stair, calling to the Hawks who stood on duty at the entrance to the Tour.

'Hawks! *A moi*! To me!' It was the Hawks' rallying cry – and he had not used it since they were in Djihan-Djihar.

CHAPTER 10

'Lia!' Alissende seized Lia's hands in hers. 'Gran'mère's in the most terrible temper. I just had to get away. You know how horrid she can be when she's vexed. No one dare go near her.'

Lia beckoned Alissende to the arbour seat.

'Can't I come inside?' Alissende asked brightly.

'Ssh.' Lia laid a finger to her lips. 'Mother's ill. Another megrim. She can't bear any noise.'

'Ahh.' Alissende nodded.

'Why . . . why do you think the Dowager is so upset?'

'It must be something to do with Berengar. I distinctly heard her mention his name. Several times.'

'Berengar? You're sure?' A horrible suspicion began to form in Lia's mind.

'A clerk or someone delivered some documents this morning. She went to her chamber to read them. Then Pons heard her cry out and thinking she wanted help, in he goes. And guess what? Gran'mère was so angry she threw a cushion at him and chased him out, brandishing her stick!'

'Poor Pons,' Lia said, forcing a smile. Documents. Did the documents concern her? Had Berengar's notary discovered the truth? Did Berengar know yet? All her dreams for the future were fast vanishing, evanescent as river mist. She steeled herself to ask the question she had been dreading. 'And where's Berengar?'

'We haven't seen him since yesterday. Busy with his men, I suppose, searching for the suspect.' Alissende began to dart little glances around the garden. 'Lia . . . doesn't it make you nervous to be out here alone with a murderer on the loose?'

'I'm not alone – you're here. And how do they know they've flushed out the murderer? Is there proof?'

'What more proof do you need?' Alissende said, her blue eyes wide. 'If he's innocent, why has he run away?'

*

Rahab brushed the last breadcrumbs from his beard and leaned back against the wall of Lia Maury's chamber. He felt less light-headed now that he had eaten but he had lingered longer than he should at the Maury house . . . If only he was not so weary. His whole body ached; his limbs were more accustomed to sitting cross-legged than hurtling down alleys or clambering over high walls.

As for Lia Maury . . . she puzzled him. She seemed almost to be enjoying herself, relishing the adventure. Well, *her* life was not in danger.

But in the last half-hour or so she had become pensive; several times she had seemed on the point of speaking, of blurting something out – and then had checked herself. Then she had suddenly babbled this nonsense about being Tsiyonim. It made him uneasy. Now she had disappeared to greet her friend, Lady Alissende. Was she sending word to Lord Berengar? Was her plan to stall Rahab, to keep him distracted until the Watch arrived?

It was time to move on. He forced himself to his feet, casting a wistful look at the soft feather mattress on Lia's bed, wishing he could lie down for a few minutes, just a few . . .

No time for sleep now.

In the courtyard below he saw the servants lift the white and blue litter and carry it away into the lane. He hoisted himself on to the window ledge and was just waiting to clamber out when Lia reappeared in the doorway.

'Rahab. Wait.'

'Why?' he said wearily.

'I want you to tell me what this is.'

She held out an object wrapped in a length of faded wool. The wrappings fell away, revealing a shell.

A shell prayer-case.

Rahab got down from the ledge and, carefully taking it from Lia, examined it.

'Well?' she said.

It was old, much older than the one that had been torn from Schimeon's doorpost. The only other prayer-case he had seen like this was the one he had sewn into the felt puppet and stuffed inside his robe. Suppose . . .

Tentatively, he shook the shell . . . and heard a faint metallic rattle inside.

'How did you come by this?' he asked. His voice sounded odd in his own ears, stifled by growing excitement.

A strange sensation thrilled through his fingers, a vibration . . .

'I told you. It's my mother's.'

'Your mother?'

'Don't look at me like that.'

'Your mother really was Tsiyonim?'

'*Is*,' Lia corrected sharply.

He shook his head. 'She married a Gentile. She has lived as a Gentile.'

'Does that matter?'

'Yes.'

He saw Lia swallow hard.

'And – and me. What does that make me?'

'Tsiyonim by birth.' He could not stop staring at her. 'Gentile by upbringing.' A smile began to twitch at one corner of his mouth.

'What's so funny?'

'Lord Berengar. Marry a Tsiyonim.' Suddenly the situation seemed absurdly ludicrous, and in spite of himself he began to chuckle. 'I suppose he doesn't know, does he? Now the joke's on him!'

'Forget Berengar!' Lia hissed. 'Tell me about the shell!'

'Of course.' He placed the shell carefully down on its covering, serious again. 'A prayer-case.' He could not keep his fingers from touching it. 'It's like . . . so very like . . . and the lettering . . . Where did you say your mother's family came from?'

'From Tolonada. That's all I know.'

'*Lia!*'

A woman was standing in the doorway, staring at them. They had been so engrossed in their conversation they had not heard the door open.

'Who is this man?' the woman said, her voice low, hoarse.

This, Rahab realised from Lia's consternation, must be Zillaïs Maury, the merchant's wife. The owner of the prayer-case.

There was no point in dissemblng.

'My name is Rahab ben Chazhael,' Rahab said, bowing his head.

'What are you doing in my house?' Zillaïs demanded, coming forward. Her eyes were stony, suspicious.

'Hiding. The Hawks are arresting all the Tsiyonim.'

Rahab saw Zillaïs flinch – then make an effort to compose herself.

'And that gives you the right to hide in my daughter's chamber? To ruin her reputation, to –'

'Mother!' cried Lia.

'And you, Lia! How dare you bring this stranger into our house? If Orbiel's men have followed him, they'll ransack the place –'

'No one of Tsiyonim blood is safe in Arcassanne any longer,' Rahab said.

Zillaïs turned on her daughter, her face white with fury. 'You *told* him?'

'Yes, I told him,' Lia countered, defiant. 'We can't continue to pretend any longer.'

'We? You are your father's daughter. This doesn't concern you.'

'I'm also *your* daughter. Of course it concerns me.'

Zillaïs let out a little exclamation of exasperation. 'Don't you see, Lia, that this is why we kept it from you? To protect you. Go to Alissende. There's still time. They won't dare to touch you if you're with the Belcastels.'

'It's too late to seek help from the Belcastels.'

Rahab listened in growing discomfort, knowing himself to be the cause of their bitter disagreement.

'I know a place where you will both be safe,' he ventured.

Zillaïs turned her forbidding gaze on him. 'This place of safety,' she said coldly. 'What is it – and where is it?'

'In the mountains. Several days' journey from Arcassanne.'

'I would not be welcome there,' Zillaïs said in brittle tones.

'Anyone of Tsiyonim blood is welcome in Tifereth.'

'Tifereth,' Zillaïs echoed. 'So it still exists.' Her voice had softened.

A smell of burning, acrid and foul, drifted into Lia's room.

Rahab wrinkled his nose, frowning. That smell, that choking smell of fire and destruction woke terrible memories. Zillaïs glanced round, sniffing the air.

'Fire,' she said.

He saw in her eyes the reflected memory of past horrors. He went to the open window, leaning far out.

Dark smoke was rising from the Quarter, gusting on the breeze to smirch the clear blue of the sky.

Fire.

'The Quarter.' Suddenly the sun was too bright; it was making his eyes water. He knuckled his eyes like a child, wiping away the wetness. 'They've set fire to the Quarter.'

'With all the people still in their houses?' Lia said in disbelief.

'Chadassah,' Rahab whispered, staring at the rising smoke plume. 'Iudith. Little Thirzah.'

He tore himself away from the window and made for the door.

'Where are you going?' demanded Zillaïs.

'To give myself up.'

'And that will put out the fires? That will save them?' Zillaïs's voice was tart with scorn. 'By the time you reach the Quarter they'll all be dead.'

'Mother!' Lia said, shocked.

'I can't just stand here and let them burn.' Rahab's mind had filled with milling images; he smelt the choking, suffocating smoke, heard the faint cries of terrified children.

'No,' Zillaïs said shortly. 'Of course not. It must be stopped.' She went hurrying from the room and they heard her calling, 'Peire! Peire!' as she went downstairs. 'Go fetch the fire buckets. Rouse the neighbours. The city's on fire!'

Fire buckets. Rahab struck his fist against the window frame in frustration. What use were fire buckets against fire in a city tinder-dry in high summer? The Quarter would burn like a torch – and he would be forced to watch, powerless to save his people, his adopted family –

'I don't know what to do,' he cried aloud, sick with disgust at his own helplessness. 'Tell me what to do!'

A faint tremor emanated again from the Tolonada prayer-shell. And he felt an answering tremor from within the breast of his jacket, where he had concealed Jehiel's amulet.

Like calling to like? Was there still some way to access the power of Jehiel's broken amulet, to call on the Guardians to help them? If only he'd paid more attention to his studies with Rebh Jehiel, if only he'd read more, he'd know what to do, what ritual words to say –

'What's in this shell? Can you open it?' he demanded.

'Open it?' She stared at him, not understanding. She began to turn it round in her hands, feeling, searching with her fingers.

Another drift of smoke gusted across the blue sky, dark as a stormcloud.

'Please, Lia. It may be their only chance.'

'They? Those names? Your children, your wife?'

104

'Does it matter?' he said brusquely. 'They'll all die if we don't do something.' All the time they were dithering here, the fires were gaining hold. He kept seeing flashes of Chadassah, huddled in Baruch's cellar, clasping Thirzah and Iudith to her –

'How can you open a shell?' Lia asked, perplexed.

'Like this.' In desperation he drew out Jehiel's shell from the breast of his jacket. 'Forgive me,' he muttered as he took the shell in both hands and brought it smashing down on the stone sill.

'What are you doing!' Lia cried as fragments of shattered shell flew everywhere. A shiver rippled through the room.

Rahab bent to retrieve the object which lay amidst the shell fragments and showed it to her. The precious stones gave off a cold, clear light, like the rippling of cloud-covered water.

'What – what is it?' Lia asked. Her voice was hushed.

'Part of a Tsiyonim Guardian Amulet,' Rahab said. Now they were both whispering, caught up in the tension of the moment. 'And I suspect the other part is hidden in your mother's shell.'

'But how will it help them?'

'Trust me, Lia.'

She took up the shell and copied him, dashing it against the sill. Slivers of broken shell showered on to the floor. He watched, biting back his breath as she knelt down, eagerly sifting through the fragments.

'Ohhh,' she said softly, raising her hands to him.

The rich sheen of enamelled metals glimmered between her fingers, bronze and gold, set with slivers of burning ruby and topaz, red as fire.

Rahab stared. It was as exquisite a piece of craftsmanship as the one he held, inscribed with sacred symbols, centuries old . . . and dangerous as the hour it was forged, symbol of the ancient God-given covenant.

All his life he had prayed for a chance to put matters right, to go back to that night in Galicys, to keep hold of Shaoni's hand, to bring him safely through the chaos. Now that chance had come. It might not be Shaoni – but it was the closest he had to family. Now he knew what he must do.

'Lia – bar the door,' he said.

With trembling fingers, he slowly brought the two fragments together – and felt an irresistible force draw them close, meld them into one whole. The sacred symbols glinted like sparks; he slowly spelled them out, trying to make sense of the ancient letters.

'*Help us*,' he cried aloud in Tsiyonim. '*Guardian – help us.*'

'What are you saying? Why is it glowing like that?' Lia began.

The amulet glowed, hot as a flame, in Rahab's cupped hands; he could not take his dazzled eyes from its burnished lustre.

'Lia?' A woman's voice called from the corridor. 'Lia?'

'Don't answer.'

The door handle rattled.

'What's happening? Why have you locked your door?'

So hot now it was burning the palms of his hands, sizzling, scorching –

With a yelp he dropped it; it fell to the floor at his feet – and began to spin.

'Lia!'

The thrumming sound grew louder until the boards on which they stood began to vibrate.

'What are you doing in there? Let me in!'

Lia had turned as white as the folded sheets on the bed.

'Go, Lia. You don't have to be a part of this. Go now.'

'No.' Lia seemed to make an effort to control herself; Rahab saw her swallow hard, as though choking back her fear. 'I want to help.' He was as terrified as she. He had no idea what would become of him – but he must finish what he had started.

The room was darkening fast, as though a stormcloud had covered the sun. The boards trembled beneath Rahab's feet. The air began to buzz.

'It's coming,' he said in a small, triumphant voice.

He felt a sick, griping sensation in the pit of his stomach, as he always did when a thunderstorm was about to break. The room grew ever darker and a strange, dry wind began to rustle the creepers at the window. Yes, he was terrified – but also exhilarated now, charged with this vibrant, buzzing power that pulsed through his body like the crackle of an electric storm. This was an ancient, elemental force, drawn from the depths of his past. He had called on the powers of his ancestors – and they had responded to his call.

'Go, Lia!' cried Rahab above the roar of the rising wind. 'Get out!' The shutters banged on their hinges. The sky had turned a dun, leaden grey. In the distance they heard the first rumbling of thunder.

The amulet spun faster, a dizzying whirl of sky and cloud.

106

Rahab could not keep his eyes off it; he leaned closer and closer, hypnotised by its storm-dark vortex.

A shaft of white light suddenly shot from the amulet and pierced his forehead, sharp as a honed spear.

Flung to his knees, Rahab jerked forwards. Blinded, he felt himself fall, go on falling into turbulent darkness –

His cry, his terrified cry, as he plunged into chaos went on shrieking in his consciousness, merging with the wail of the stormwind.

Extinction – oblivion –

And then something – someone – was rising up out of the stormcloud to meet him. Outstretched arms were raised to catch him, enfold him. With the last of his strength Rahab held out his own arms, frantically clutching at the rising cloudfigure –

He was caught, held, borne upwards again.

For a moment he sank, naked, exhausted, into the comforting, sustaining arms . . . until he was merging, becoming one with the storm-veiled entity . . .

He was no longer Rahab the menial, Rahab the poor tailor.

He was cloud. He was storm. He was lightning.

Power crackled along his veins from his light-riven heart. Rain streamed from his wild hair, fell in torrents from his cloud-clothed shoulders, from the pinions of his beating wings.

He rose high into the air, gazing down upon the land beneath. Trees swayed, bowed, snapped beneath the turbulence of his beating wings. Streams swelled to rivers, burst their banks, overflowing, flooding . . .

He turned his gaze on the city far below.

Burning buildings were guttering, gusts of smoke rising, the thick black smoke of dampened fires. People ran about in the rain, small as ants; he could not hear their cries. He was the Bringer of Lightning.

He had brought the rain.

Jaufré d'Orbiel ran to the window to gaze out at the storm.

Where had it come from? It seemed to have blown up out of nowhere. One moment the summer sky was clear, not a cloud in sight. And now blue fire crackled from weather vanes. Silhouettes of buildings loomed up, black against the sudden flare.

The power of the storm was tangible. He could reach out and touch the lightning, be one with the storm.

Brief blaze of brilliance – then eternal darkness.

Consumed by divine fire – a fit end for a poet.

Jaufré flung back his head and laughed aloud. The thunder drowned the sound of his laughter.

He felt the power of the lightning fizzing in his bloodstream, a potent, erotic charge.

Lightning lit the room and he gasped, feeling again the electric charge of arousal sizzle through him.

This was no ordinary storm.

Blinded, he saw a gigantic shadowform silhouetted across his lids.

Outstretched wings clove the air.

Talons rent the sky, clawing a dazzling tracery of whitefire against the dark clouds.

He glimpsed a face, terrible yet beautiful, gazing down at him. Eyes seared with elemental fire sought him out, where he stood, transfixed. A taloned finger pointed to the *Sefer Rhaziel* which lay open on the desk.

One name was illuminated in the stormlight, one name stood out, silverwhite.

'Barakiel,' Jaufré whispered, 'Bringer of Lightning.'

The rain glittered in the lightning like star-shards. The air smelt of burning.

The stones of the Maury house trembled with a cacophony of thunder. Lia slowly, dazedly, got to her knees and crawled across the floor to unbar the door. She was shivering uncontrollably; her clothes were soaked with rainwater. The golden afternoon sky now loured as grim and dark as night. Lightning flickered and crackled across the blackness. The broken shutters dangled uselessly from their hinges; rain poured into her room through the open window.

Zillaïs caught her as she fell, holding her up.

'Are you all right? Lia – are you all right?'

'It took him,' Lia babbled. 'Lightning – struck him. And then – this – this whirlwind – sucked him – right up –'

Zillaïs was staring at the floor. Lia stared too. The floorboards were seared, scorched, as if the lightning had made a direct strike – yet in the midst of the charred circle of wood, the joined amulet lay gleaming, undamaged by the lightning's fire.

'Two amulets, joined . . .'

'Mother?' Lia said in a small voice. 'Wh-what happened to Rahab? Where is he? One moment he was here – and then – that flash –'

'Why did you give him my amulet? It was not yours to give. Have you any idea how powerful –'

'How could I have known?' Lia rounded on her mother. 'You never told me about it. You never told me anything –'

Another crack of thunder overhead made the roof timbers shudder. Lia gave a shriek.

'It's out of control. Do something, Mother. Make it stop.'

'There's no stopping it now,' Zillaïs said bleakly. 'The storm will rage until the boy's strength is exhausted. The Guardian works through him . . .'

'What Guardian?' Lia's teeth were chattering with shock and the sudden chill of the storm. 'What are you talking about?'

'Part of your Tsiyonim heritage.'

'Which you kept from me.'

'If I hadn't kept it from you, where would you be now? Trapped in a burning building with the other poor wretches –'

'And your precious amulet? Shouldn't we hide it in a safe place?' Lia bent to pick up the enamelled disc.

'No!' Zillaïs cried. 'We must leave it here – if Rahab is ever to be returned to us.'

'There's no need to shout at me.'

Lia saw that her mother's face had turned deathly pale. Another megrim; she recognised the signs only too well, the blank stare from eyes dull in dark-blotched sockets.

'It acts as a beacon, it calls him back.'

'He will come back then?' Lia said uncertainly.

Zillaïs turned to gaze out over the city. Behind her the rain poured down from a sky as dark as lead, streaked with fissures of lighting.

'Mother?'

She heard Zillaïs sigh.

'I don't know. I don't know. All we can do is watch . . . and wait.'

CHAPTER 11

A sudden gust of wind flapped the shutters wildly on their twisted hinges. A turbulence of mist gusted into the chamber, a whirl of rain-wet air and spinning thundercloud.

Zillaïs threw her arms around Lia, pulling her out of the way.

The whole house shuddered convulsively – then fell still.

Slowly the pall of cloud began to dissolve, revealing the figure of a man slumped face-down on the floor. Half-naked, soaked, his sodden clothes shredded to tatters, his hair plastered in wet strands to his head, he lay as if dead.

The Guardian had brought Rahab back to them.

'Is he – is he –' Lia stammered.

Zillaïs went to kneel beside him, reaching to feel for the pulse in his throat.

'Alive? Yes.' Only just alive, she might have added, but she did not wish to alarm Lia further. There were practical considerations, too. Rahab was still a wanted man; hadn't Emmenza told them he had been sighted in the Merchants' Quarter? It might be many hours before he returned to himself, and even when he did, it would be a day, maybe two, before he had regained enough strength to walk. And now that the storm was abating the Hawks would be on his trail again.

She looked up from the prone body and saw Lia watching her warily.

'You'll have to help me,' she said. 'I can't lift him on my own.'

'Lift him?' Lia's brows rose.

'Then pull your mattress on to the floor. We'll roll him on to it.'

'*My* mattress? But he's soaking wet!'

Zillaïs took a deep breath; it was understandable, she told herself, that Lia should react in this way. But there was no time for explanations now; she must tend to Rahab first.

'You can sleep in my bed. We'll tell Emmenza that your room was flooded by the storm and it will need a day or two to dry out.'

Lia paused a moment, mouth open as if to protest – and then she turned to the bed and, gripping the mattress with both hands, dragged it on to the floor.

Then between them they took hold of Rahab by shoulder and hip and half-pushed, half-rolled his limp body on to the mattress.

Zillaïs took out her kerchief and gently wiped his cold face, stroking the wet locks from his forehead.

'So young . . .' she whispered. He could hardly be a year or more older than Lia; he could have been her son.

'Why did you never tell me?' Lia said in a small, peeved voice.

'I told you all you needed to know.' Zillaïs kept her eyes on Rahab's still face. 'All that you were told was true. My father, Ithamar, was herbalist and physician to the court of Tolonada. He taught me all I know.'

'But the amulets,' Lia persisted. She was pointing at the metal discs, as if unwilling to touch them or get too near.

Zillaïs sighed.

'How shall we protect them now the shells are broken?' She went over to where the amulets lay, still dully gleaming amidst the water and shell debris.

'That's not what I meant, Mother,' Lia said.

'Later,' Zillaïs said, glancing around for something in which to place the precious talismans. 'What's this?' She picked up a piece of crumpled red material. 'It looks like some kind of child's toy . . .'

Drenched to the skin, Berengar forded the narrow street which still ran with rainwater.

The air was filled with choking smoke – but the fires were dampening down in the still-falling rain. The taste of the billowing smoke fouled his mouth, his throat.

Torches lay quenched in the streaming gutters where Guillemette's followers had dropped them as they ran to seek cover from the violence of the storm.

But where were the Tsiyonim?

The first row of houses was a charred shell, the roof timbers fallen in. He satisfied himself there was no one trapped in there alive – before coming to the last house in the lane, a fine stone building whose sign of beaten metal proclaimed its owner to be a moneylender.

The crowd had tried to batter down the doors, hoping, no doubt, to loot the moneylender's coffers. When Berengar and his men arrived, the mob had torched the roof. But though the roof still smouldered, the sturdy stone construction had survived.

Berengar hammered on the nailed door with his fist.

'Anyone inside?'

There was no answer.

Suppose they had been saved from the fire – only to be suffocated by the choking smoke?

'It's safe to come out. You won't be harmed. I give you my word. My word of honour as lord of Belcastel.'

And then, to his infinite relief, he heard the sound of chains being undone, latches lifted . . . and the door creaked slowly open.

Coughing, blinking in the cloudy daylight, they ventured out into the rain, clutching hold of each other, bedraggled, their faces smeared with smuts, men carrying little children, women supporting the elderly.

As they glanced uncertainly around them, Berengar heard their hushed murmurs of disbelief.

'So much burned down, so quickly . . .'

'All my goods, my livelihood gone . . .'

'Where shall we go now?'

'Do you have any news of my husband, Lord Berengar?' asked a soft, anxious voice. 'Or my daughter?'

Berengar turned to see a wan-faced woman with two little girls clinging to her skirts. He thought he recognised her but couldn't quite place . . .

'I'm Chadassah, Schimeon's wife,' she said. One of the girls started to whine and she stroked her dark head mechanically. 'Captain Orbiel arrested them both.' Her voice faltered. 'I – I have no idea why.'

'I'll see what I can find out for you,' Berengar said, aware how lame his offer sounded.

An old man approached.

'If we're to stay here, we need protection,' he said, thrusting his face into Berengar's, white eyebrows bristling. 'Guards to stop the looting of our damaged shops and houses.'

'I'll have to go to the Comte,' Berengar said, taking a step back. 'Until then I can leave four of my men here.'

'Four!' the old man said testily. 'What use are four against a mob?'

112

A man came running up, calling out, 'We can shelter in the *shul*, Baruch. It's undamaged.'

'An armed guard,' Baruch said to Berengar.

Berengar signed to the Hawks to stand by as the Tsiyonim shouldered bundles of possessions and set off down the lane. The Hawks followed at a distance, Berengar at the rear of the ragged procession.

'Witchcraft!' A woman's voice, raw with emotion, screeched out suddenly. 'I smell witchcraft!'

Guillemette had appeared at the end of the lane, with a few of her supporters. All were drenched to the skin, shivering with the wet and cold.

'That was no ordinary storm.' She went to Berengar. 'Didn't you hear? Didn't you see the daemon at the heart of the storm, the daemon *they* summoned?'

Berengar, fearing more trouble, beckoned his sergeant Arnault over.

'Get her away from here,' he said under his breath. 'Quickly.'

'You think you're safe under Aymon's protection?' Guillemette's rain-streaked face was contorted with hatred as she jabbed her finger at the bewildered Tsiyonim. 'You think you've escaped this time? I tell you – no witchcraft will save you next time, no hellspawn daemon will protect you –'

'Come, madam,' Arnault said, taking her firmly by the arm, 'time to go home.'

'You'll pay! You'll pay!' Guillemette screamed as Arnault dragged her away. 'We'll be back for you – and your children!'

Rain still beat against Jaufré d'Orbiel's high tower, still poured from the louring clouds on to the city of Arcassanne. But the thunder had ceased to roll over the river plain, the wind had dropped and a faint, thin line of light gleamed beneath the clouds towards the west.

Jaufré, still charged with excitement, went running through the wet streets to the Tour de la Justice, hurrying down the stairs to the interrogation room where he had left Jehiel manacled to the wall.

'You lied, Rebh Jehiel. You lied to me.'

The old scholar did not reply.

'You told me the Guardian Amulets were all lost. And now I have seen with my own eyes, all Arcassanne has seen, the destructive power of a Winged Guardian.'

Jehiel slowly, wearily raised his head.

'A Guardian? No, no . . . it's not possible.' His voice was a cracked whisper, issuing from parched lips.

'I saw it! With these very eyes!' Jaufré pushed his face close to Jehiel's. '*Barakiel.*' Why was the old man so intransigent? 'There's no point trying to deceive me.'

'Deceive you?' Jehiel's voice was so faint, Jaufré had to lean closer to catch his words. 'There were only two amulets left . . . and one of those . . . was lost . . . at sea . . .' As Jehiel's voice faded to silence, Jaufré realised to his annoyance that the scholar had fainted.

'Wine!' he shouted. One of the Hawks on duty brought over a cup. 'Give the prisoner a drink.'

Between them, the two Hawks tilted Jehiel's head back and held the cup to his lips. As the wine trickled down his throat, Jehiel began to cough and splutter.

'He's very weak, Captain. Shouldn't we take him down? He's not likely to escape in his condition.'

Jaufré swore.

'Sit him in the chair. But keep his wrists and ankles tied.'

The Hawks unlocked the manacles and propped Jehiel in Jaufré's high-backed chair. Jehiel's face was grey as cobweb-threads. A drop of wine dribbled from one side of his mouth.

'Now talk,' Jaufré ordered. He was in no mood for Jehiel's scholastic perorations. 'These amulets. Tell me more.'

'Nothing to tell . . .' Jehiel's lids fluttered; he seemed to waver between waking and unconsciousness. 'Belonged to . . . the Tribe of Ithamar . . . Ithamar of Tolonada was the last of his line . . . drowned at sea . . . twenty years back off the coast of Galicys . . .' His eyes opened suddenly and stared at Jaufré. 'I told you, Captain, those amulets are dangerous.'

'Ithamar,' Jaufré whispered. 'Ithamar of Tolonada.' So Berengar's notary had discovered a truth hidden even from the Tsiyonim community: that Ithamar's daughter was alive and living incognito in Arcassanne . . .

'A good man, a scholar and a healer . . . But even he was destroyed by the power of the Guardian. Do you understand me?'

Jaufré was not listening any longer. He took up his sword and slipped it into its sheath, seizing his cloak.

'Bertran – stay and watch the old man. Martin, round up six of the Hawks and meet me in a quarter of an hour.'

114

'Where?' Martin asked.

'The Merchants' Quarter. We're going to pay a visit to a lady. A very special lady. Madame Zillaïs Maury.'

Water dripped slowly from the roof gutter above Lia's bed-chamber window.

Lia went to close the broken shutter and stepped straight in a puddle of rainwater that had pooled on the floor.

'Ugh.' she drew back, shaking the cold drops from her foot in disgust.

The sky was white, a sheen of pale, high cloud washed clean by the storm. But the street had become a churned stream, running with mud. Roof tiles lay smashed into red shards on the paving below.

The gillyflowers in the courtyard garden, her mother's del-ight, had all but been destroyed; the herbs had been flattened, roses uprooted, leaves torn off by the force of the wind.

'All the young figs are down before they're ripe . . .'

In the midst of the devastation she saw her mother standing, just looking at the ruin of her garden.

'All the striped roses,' Lia mourned, gazing at the wildly strewn petals, once pink and white, now bruised and rain-sodden. 'There'll be none left to preserve this year.'

A distant flicker of movement beyond the garden wall caught her eye.

The Watch.

They moved swiftly, purposefully through the churned mud and storm debris.

Lia went running downstairs and out into the garden. The evening air felt wetly cold, chilled by the torrential storm rain.

'Mother! The Watch! Coming this way!'

Zillaïs merely said, 'Why didn't you put on a shawl? You'll catch cold.'

'Rahab . . .'

Someone was calling a name, calling in the far distance. He paid scant attention. He was not Rahab. He was Barakiel; he rode the wings of the storm.

'Rahab.'

Thunder still rolled and throbbed in his head. Within his skull, distant lightning flickered, flashes of electric blue that seared his senses.

115

'RAHAB!'

Rahab forced his eyes open. The light was too bright. He shut his eyes again. 'Leave me alone,' he mumbled, turning his head away.

'Wake up, Rahab. You must wake up.'

Blinking, he obeyed. Faces swam above him, faces in lamp-light, human faces, flesh and blood. He tried to make his lips and voice work together. All that he managed was a long, aching groan.

'Orbiel's men are in the street.' A woman's voice spoke in his ear, softly, insistently. 'You must go.'

Each word pierced his tender brain like a white-hot needle. He shrank from the pain.

'You have to take the amulets.'

'Wh-where?' he said muzzily.

'Don't you remember? To Tifereth. You told me so yourself.'

'Look at him, Mother, he's in no fit state to go anywhere!' A girl's voice this time, light yet tart. An apple-blossom voice. He remembered that voice . . . but from where? 'We'll have to hide him.'

'And they'll pull the place apart searching –'

'They'll never find him in papa's cellar. No one knows about that.'

Hands were touching him, pulling him into an upright position, supporting him. He sagged at the knees.

'We can't carry him . . .' the light voice complained.

Someone forced a flask between hs lips, leaking liquid into his mouth. The liquid seemed to catch alight, searing his throat. He coughed and gagged.

'Hurry!' someone urged.

Then they were dragging him downstairs; his limbs felt as if they were stuffed with sawdust. He lurched drunkenly from side to side, crashing into the wall.

A black hole yawned up to swallow him – he was falling into musty darkness –

Auger Maury had taken the precaution of adding another cellar below the wine cellar. Merchants liked to have a second, secret place to keep their more exclusive merchandise, hidden from any unexpected visits from the Comte's taxmen.

Lia and Zillaïs half-dragged, half-pulled Rahab down into the wine cellar. The second cellar lay beyond, the door hidden behind the ale cask. It smelt musty, the underground dankness mingled with the perfume of the rare liqueurs Auger stored there: aromatic alquer, mature brandies, bitter absinthe.

Rahab tottered inside and sank to his knees. Zillaïs pressed a little package into his hands, closing his fingers around it.

'Keep them with you. Don't come out till we tell you it's safe.'

She shooed Lia out and shut the door; together they heaved the ale cask back into its usual place and climbed the stairs.

'Hold still. You're covered in cobwebs.' Zillaïs brushed the dusty threads out of Lia's hair.

There came a pounding on the front door.

'The Watch! Open up!'

'The Hawks –' Lia whispered. 'They're here.'

'Lia.' Zillaïs caught her daughter by the shoulders. 'Run to the Belcastels'. Fetch Berengar. We may need his help.'

'But I can't leave you here alone to face them –'

'I've faced far worse than Orbiel's Hawks.' Zillaïs turned Lia around, propelling her towards the garden door. 'Now go. Hurry!'

The garden path was slippery with wet leaves and mud; Lia tried to run but kept losing her footing. At last she reached the ivy-grown side-gate that led out into the lane and dared to glance back behind her.

There were figures in the house; she could see them passing to and fro, at the open window of her room. In *her* room! Indignity rose, quelling her fear for herself, fear for her mother. Those men pawing her clothes, rifling through her belongings –

How *dare* they!

She would see what Berengar had to say about this!

Zillaïs stared coldly at the intruders.

'Was it really necessary to break down my front door? If you had given me time to reach the hall, I would have opened it to you. I trust, Captain, that your men will repair the damaged timbers before they leave.'

'Madame Maury,' Jaufré d'Orbiel said curtly, 'we have no time for repairs. We are on the trail of a murderer. We have reason to believe he may be hiding in your house.'

'In my house!' Zillaïs allowed herself a small, incredulous smile. 'I do not make a practice of sheltering criminals.'

'A man was seen climbing your garden wall. I would not like to think we had gone away and left you and your household unprotected.' Jaufré's voice was courteous; yet she thought she detected a strange shadowing in his gaze whenever he looked at her.

'Search, then, if you must,' she said. 'But be sure you put back anything you displace. And do not molest my servants.'

The Hawks dispersed; Zillaïs tried not to wince as she felt the floorboards shudder under their heavy tread. But Jaufré d'Orbiel did not go with his men; he stayed, still looking at her.

'Can I offer you any refreshment, Captain?' she said in level tones. She was surprised how easy it was to pretend politeness, in spite of his silent, intense scrutiny.

He shook his head.

'Now that my men are otherwise occupied, you can speak freely, Madame Maury. Or should I call you by the name of your Tribe? Ithamar?'

For a moment the room went dark. Zillaïs gripped the table to support herself. How had he found out? Who had betrayed her secret?

The door was flung open; Emmenza came hurrying in, her face flushed.

'Madame, madame, they're tearing the place apart, they're ripping open the mattresses, turning out the chests –' She caught sight of Jaufré d'Orbiel and advanced on him, wagging her finger. 'I don't know what you think you're going to find, but there's no need to wreck my mistress's house. You'll have the master to answer to when he –'

'*When* he returns,' Jaufré finished. 'How long will that be? Another month or two?'

Emmenza stared at him, open-mouthed, and suddenly burst into tears, loud sobs that shook her large frame.

Zillaïs, grateful that Emmenza had unwittingly caused such an effective distraction, went to her and put her arms around her shaking shoulders.

'I won't have you upsetting the members of my household, Captain.'

'Members? I see only your cook. Where is your daughter Lia?'

'She has gone to the Belcastels'.'

'The Belcastels'! I doubt she'll be welcome there.'

She looked at him and saw that the seemingly casual remark was deliberately intended to wound.

'Captain!' called a voice from upstairs. 'Come look at this!'

'Madame Maury.' Jaufré d'Orbiel gestured to her, extending his hand as if he were about to lead her on to the dance floor. 'Please accompany me.'

Zillaïs swept past him, ignoring the outstretched hand. She was still mistress within this house – and he was an uninvited intruder. What could they have found? She had taken the precaution of burying the shell-shards deep in the compost heap, but as she climbed the stair, her heart thudded so violently in her breast she was afraid Jaufré d'Orbiel would hear it.

'So? What have you found?' Jaufré demanded. The veneer of courtesy he had assumed downstairs was peeling away, revealing something more ugly, more dangerous beneath.

They stood on the threshold of Lia's room. Within, two of the Watch were puzzling over the scorch marks on the floor, the blasted shutters.

Jaufré went in and knelt down, tracing the scorched circle on the floorboards with one hand.

'A lightning strike,' Zillaïs said. 'You saw the force of the storm, Captain.'

'Oh yes, I saw the force of the storm,' he said. 'But this lightning strike seems to have originated *within* your house.'

'What you are suggesting,' Zillaïs said, holding the darkly shadowed gaze, 'is completely absurd.'

'I'm afraid, Madame Maury, that I am obliged to exercise the authority vested in me by Comte Aymon and place you under arrest.'

'Without proof, you cannot hold me against my will.'

'Oh, you misunderstand me, Madame Maury. I'm arresting you because you are Tsiyonim –'

Zillaïs heard Emmenza's stifled cry of shock. Years of trust betayed in one offhand remark.

'– just as I have been obliged to arrest the others of your community. Your presence in Arcassanne constitutes a threat to public order. We are forced to hold you in the Tour de la Justice for your own safety until Comte Aymon decides what is to be done with you.'

'Mistress –' Emmenza stretched out both hands to her imploringly. 'It's not true, is it?'

Zillaïs took Emmenza's hands in her own, pressing them.

'That I am Tsiyonim? Yes, it's true. Does it alter the good years we have spent together, Emmenza?'

119

Emmenza shook her head; tears began to roll down her broad cheeks.

'Wh-what shall I do now? With the master away –'

'Stay here for Lia. Just do that. Look after her – until I am released.'

She managed a smile to reassure Emmenza, but as the Hawks led her away, a voice whispered in her head, *If I am released.*

She had escaped with her life once before . . . this time she was not sure she would be so fortunate.

CHAPTER 12

Lia tugged at the iron bell-pull of the Belcastel mansion and stood tapping her foot impatiently as she waited for someone to answer.

Pons opened the door to her.

'Oh. Demoiselle Maury. You were not expected.'

There was something awkward, almost unwelcoming in his manner, but she pushed past him, running into the hall, calling out as she went, 'Where's Berengar? I must speak with him.'

Pons followed after her.

'Dem'selle.' His voice was hushed as though he didn't want to be overheard. 'Dem'selle, there's something you ought to –'

A figure appeared in the doorway. Lia started forward, words of relief and greeting on her lips, only to see it was neither Beranger nor Alissende but the forbidding figure of the Dowager; stooped, stiff, clutching her ebony walking stick in one gnarled hand, a letter in the other.

'Lia Maury. Well, well, child. I'm surprised you have the impudence to show your face here.'

Lia hesitated. The Dowager's eyes did not look on her kindly; they glittered, hard and cold as hailstones.

'How well you deceived us! And how well we were taken in! To think the wedding might have gone ahead –'

'Wedding?' Lia echoed, falteringly.

'All here. In this document. Tsiyonim!' hissed the Dowager, shaking the paper in Lia's face. 'Read it. Deny it to my face if you dare.'

'H-how did you come by this?' Lia took the document, hastily scanning the neatly penned lines. *Ithamar* . . . that name again. The name she had only heard for the first time yesterday, at the head of a family tree filled with the names of strangers, all unfamiliar save for one. The last, at the bottom of the tree: 'Zillah, daughter of Ithamar and Liah of Tolonada.'

'Deny that is your mother's name.' The Dowager snatched

the document back before Lia could read any more. 'Well? Well?' Her lips set in a smile of grim satisfaction. 'As I thought! Your silence confirms it.'

'I didn't know –' Lia burst out.

'You may consider the contract null and void. All gifts exchanged between the two of you will be returned. And you may tell your mother to expect a visit from my lawyer.'

One mottled hand reached out and grabbed the Belcastel emerald, tugging hard; Lia felt the thin chain snap.

'And Berengar? He has no say in the matter?' she managed, almost speechless with fury.

'My grandson will do what I wish him to do. He will do what is in the family's best interests.' The Dowager clutched the emerald to her breast possessively, the broken ends of the chain trailing from her claw-like fingers. 'And you, dem'selle, will leave my house this instant. I have instructed the servants that you are not to be re-admitted. Not under any circumstances.'

Lia felt tears in her eyes, burning tears of rage and humiliation that threatened to spill out. But she would not cry in front of the hateful old woman. She would leave with what little dignity and courage she could muster. She would turn her back, walk out whilst the Dowager was still spitting insults at her.

Somehow, through the haze of tears, she found her way to the door and fumbled for the heavy latch.

'Lia,' she heard someone whisper, so faintly she thought she had imagined it. 'Lia!'

Blindly, she turned around and saw Alissende frantically beckoning her from a doorway.

'I'm sorry,' Alissende said. She had been crying too; her milky skin was red and blotched. 'I'm so, so sorry, Lia –'

'Pons? Pons?' came the Dowager's voice, sharply imperious. 'See that Lia Maury is escorted off the premises. She is not to have any further communication with my granddaughter. See to it now!'

'Stand up to her!' Lia said through her tears. 'Alissende – you don't have to do as she says. Stand up for yourself.'

She saw Alissende hesitate.

'Alissende,' Lia implored. 'Do all our years as friends count as nothing?'

'Don't answer her!' cried the Dowager.

Alissende opened her mouth to reply – and then closed it again, her lips twisting in an anguish of indecision.

'Remove that young woman, Pons!'

Pons came down the hall towards Lia.

'Lissi,' Lia said, slipping back into childhood names, 'oh Lissi, I hoped you – you'd stand by me –'

Alissende turned away, shaking her head.

'Pons!' screeched the Dowager. 'Get her out!'

Pons opened the door. His gaze met Lia's for one moment, then slid apologetically away.

'I was just going,' Lia said with as much hauteur as she could manage. She stepped down into the rain-washed street and walked away without a backward glance.

Only when she had turned the corner did she stop, choked by tears of rage and humiliation.

Berengar would defend her. Berengar was the sole inheritor of his father's estates – he was Lord of Belcastel.

She dried her eyes on a corner of her hem and straightened her dress.

Who was the Dowager anyway? Just a sour, ill-tempered beldame. Lia Maury would not let a crabbed old woman get the better of her. She would send Peire into the city to find Berengar – and then they would see who held the most influence in the Belcastel household! She hesitated, tempted to go herself – but glancing up at the sky she saw that the cloudy twilight was fast fading to night. She shivered, remembering her mother's advice: 'No woman of good repute ventures abroad after dark in Arcassanne without an escort.'

She began to hasten her pace, still glancing uneasily around, fearing that there were prowlers lurking in every alleyway, waiting to molest her.

Just as she was almost in sight of home, she felt a sharp stab in the sole of her right foot. Stopping to shake out her shoe to see if she had picked up a stone, she heard the tread of marching feet approaching.

Her first impulse was to rush out to see if it was Berengar with the Watch – but some instinct made her hold back. She slipped into a doorway and waited.

A small detachment of the Watch passed by: eight men walking briskly, arms swinging. And in their midst – Lia pressed her hand to her mouth to stop herself from crying out aloud – was Zillaïs.

Jaufré d'Orbiel had arrested her mother!

*

123

The back door was open. Warily Lia put her head around the door, listening.

From inside the unlit house came the faint, muffled sound of weeping.

'Emmenza?' Lia crept inside.

Emmenza sat on the stairs, her apron over her face, rocking to and fro, speechless with grief.

'Emmenza?' Lia ventured closer, one hand extended to pat her on the shoulder.

Emmenza lowered her apron just enough to peep at Lia.

'Lia?' She burst into even louder sobs. 'Oh Lia, Lia . . . they took your poor mother . . .'

'Why did they take her?'

'Because she was – is –' Emmenza could hardly say the word through her sobs. 'One of *them*.'

'Tsiyonim?' Lia dared to say the word aloud, not knowing how Emmenza would react.

'As if it mattered!' Emmenza gave an outraged snort. 'She's been a good mistress to me all these years. I said I'd stand by her. And stand by her I will, no matter what people say.' She blew her nose loudly. 'But why aren't you with the Belcastels, my pet? Your mother was sure you'd be safe there.'

'I was turned away,' Lia said. 'The Dowager won't have anything more to do with me.'

'That evil, spiteful old woman!' cried Emmenza. 'The Belcastels are snobs. Nothing but puffed-up, self-regarding snobs.' She started to cry again.

Lia sank down on the stair below Emmenza and let her head rest against the old woman's knee. Suddenly all the fight had drained out of her. She felt weak with emotional exhaustion.

'What shall we do, 'Menza?' she whispered. 'What shall we do?'

She felt Emmenza's hand on her head, stroking the straying hairs from her forehead as if she were still a little girl.

'Don't fret now. We'll think of something.'

There came a distant tremor of movement deep below the stairs. Emmenza started.

'Lady love us, what was that?'

Rahab. Lia had forgotten all about him until now. He was still in the under-cellar – and it sounded as if he was trying to get out.

'What was what?' she said vaguely.

124

The sound came again; a faint, grinding rumble as if someone were moving the liqueur casks.

'There!' Emmenza stood up. 'You must have heard it this time. In the cellar. Someone's in the cellar.'

'Rats?' Lia said.

'I'm going for Peire. I'll get him to bring his pitchfork.'

'Emmenza – wait –'

'You come with me, Lia. That could be a thief, though Lady knows how he broke in –'

'I've a better idea,' Lia said, desperately trying to think of a way to distract Emmenza. 'You go get the pitchfork. Send Peire to find Lord Berengar.'

'I'm not leaving you alone here.'

'I'll barricade the cellar door with the kitchen bench. I'll be safe.'

'And if he has accomplices –'

'Take a lantern.' Lia shooed Emmenza down the stairs towards the darkened kitchen. Striking a tinder, she lit two lanterns, one for herself, one for Emmenza, and propelled the cook towards the unlit garden.

The turbulence in Rahab's mind slowly ebbed away, storm-clouds drifting apart, breaking up to let through the last light of the sun. But in their place, in the unearthly calm that followed the storm, all Rahab felt was emptiness. The calm was a void.

He came back to himself to find he was lying in musty blackness.

Dear God. They must have thought he was dead – and buried him.

He flailed around in a panic until his scrabbling hands hit against something large, wooden . . . barrel-shaped?

He sniffed the air. There was a faint hint of . . . spirits. The rich, mature smell of old grape liqueur, the burned-wood savour of oak casks . . .

Strange tomb . . . He had heard of pickling bodies in spirits to preserve them – but there was not a drop of spirits on him . . .

Not buried – but imprisoned, then. Orbiel's Hawks must have caught him and flung him into this horrible lightless oubliette.

'Help!' he shouted, struggling to his knees, crashing against a cask, hearing the liquid inside sloshing around. 'Help! Let me out!'

125

'Rahab?'

He froze, listening, certain he had heard a faint answering call.

Someone was outside; he could see a thin trace of light outlining the shape of a door.

'Here!' he called. 'In here!'

The door creaked open and lanternlight spilled into his musty prison.

'Quick!' someone hissed. 'You've got to get out!'

In the dazzle of lanternlight, Rahab could just make out the pale face of – of Lia Maury. He could also see the wine casks and barrels of spirits lining the walls.

What was he doing in her cellar?

Confused, he stumbled towards the light, crawling out on hands and knees.

'Hurry!'

He wanted to hurry but his legs would not cooperate. He felt sick and light-headed, as if he had been ill in bed for days with fever.

'You've got to get away from here. They've just arrested my mother.'

In the lanternlight he saw that her face was dirty with streaks of dried tears, her hair in disarray. Sudden flashes of memory illuminated the void in his mind.

'Your mother,' he said slowly.

'You've got to go to Tifereth. Remember? To get help?'

'How?' he said forlornly. 'I don't even know where Tifereth is.'

He heard her stifled exclamation of exasperation.

'At least get *those things* out of my house. Out of the city. They've brought us nothing but ill luck.'

What things? She was pointing at his hands. He looked down and saw he was holding a piece of crumpled red felt. Inside he caught a gleam of enamelled metal, colours darkly rich as gemstones.

The Guardian Amulets.

He looked up again and saw that she was watching him with a curious expression; half-pitying, half-scornful.

'Oh, all right then. I'll see you to the Aude Gate. Come on.'

Berengar yawned hugely as he waited for Pons to open the door.

Supper – and then bed. No . . . bed. He was exhausted.

The door opened.

'Bring bread and boiled ham to my chamber, Pons,' Berengar said – and then stopped, seeing the Dowager sitting bolt upright in her chair in the hall, one jewelled hand on her stick, watching the door.

'At last you deign to return home, Berengar. Where have you been? No, don't tell me, I don't want to know. Look at the state of you – your face is dirty, your clothes ruined –'

'I've been putting out a fire, Gran'mère.'

'Well, you've no time to change. You're needed on the estate. There's storm damage to be assessed.'

Berengar yawned again; he was not in the least interested in riding out to Belcastel.

'Can't Thibaud do it? Isn't that what stewards are meant to do?'

'These are your lands, your tenants, your inheritance. Thibaud is a paid servant – you're the master.' The Dowager bristled with indignation.

'At least let it wait until I've had some breakfast.'

'You've no time for breakfast. Saddle up Arbutus and ride out to the farm.'

'But Gran'mère, I –'

'Your father would not have said but. Your father would not have needed the prompting. He would have put his estates first.'

'Damn it all!' Berengar knew there would be no peace from her nagging until he acceded. 'Pons! Don't take the bread and ham to my chamber. Wrap it and put it in my saddle bags.'

Lia grabbed her father's old jacket from the back of the cellar door and draped it around Rahab's shoulders. It was the patched, mildewed garment Auger kept for working in the cellar or the garden – and was several sizes too big for the tailor. No matter. It would have to serve as a disguise.

When she looked back at him, he was shambling aimlessly around the kitchen. What had become of the brave, bitter man who had risked his life to save his family? Had the Guardian taken his wits as well as his strength?

And then she checked herself. What *was* she doing? Why had she taken pity on him?

She was just ridding herself of incriminating evidence, that was all. It wouldn't help her mother's case if the Watch were to find the wanted man sheltering in their cellar.

Her mother's straw gardening hat lay on the table; as Lia bustled Rahab into the hall, she snatched it, jamming it on her head. She patted her belt to check her little purse was still attached and felt a reassuring bulge of coins.

'Lia? Where are you, pet?'

She heard Emmenza puffing and wheezing as she came back into the kitchen.

'I couldn't find the fork but I've brought a hoe –'

Lia opened the front door and pushed Rahab out into the unlit street.

Rahab stumbled, almost missing his footing. She gripped hold of him by the arm.

'Can't you go any faster?'

'S-sorry . . .' He slurred his words as if he was drunk. That might work to their advantage; two staggering figures propping each other up was not an uncommon sight in the city after dark. But drunkards were also easy prey for thieves – and the wick in her lantern was already guttering. Heavens – suppose it should go out before they reached the Gate?

'For heaven's sakes, at least *try*.'

In the distance she could still make out Emmenza's voice plaintively calling her name into the night.

It was downhill from the top of the lane to the river; a winding, cobbled path that was too steep for carts. Weeds had sprung up through the cobbles, thick-spined thistles and coarse-leaved clumps of yellow ragwort. And since the storm, the cobbles were slimy with channels of mud washed down from the steep hillside above, making the descent treacherous and difficult to negotiate.

A breeze shivered through the knotted willow branches overhead, peppering them with raindrops. Far away, a dog bayed – and another answered. Lia glanced around uneasily. Had they brought dogs to track Rahab down? She could just make out the glint of water far below where a looping bend in the river Aude encircled the wooded western flank of Arcassanne. The Aude Gate lay beneath them; she could just make out the watchfires burning on the ramparts.

Unsupported, Rahab sank slowly down on to the muddy path, legs awkwardly folding under him like a newborn foal.

Lia gazed at him scornfully. He did not look much of a hero

now. Yet what he had dared was, she supposed, heroic. Or, at least, heroic for a tailor.

And now he sat slumped amongst the weeds, unable to put one foot in front of the other. How was he ever to make his way alone across country into the mountains?

She shrugged the question aside. She would buy him passage on a riverboat going upstream. And there her involvement would end. She would have done her best to ensure her mother's amulet did not fall into the wrong hands.

The lanternflame trembled in a sudden damp shiver of breeze. Lia lifted up the lantern and examined the wick; it had curled round on itself, with maybe no more than a few minutes' burning time left.

'Come on,' she said, prodding Rahab. 'Before this lantern goes out and we're left blundering around in the dark.'

'And where d'you think you're going?'

A voice rang out, challenging them as they approached the looming shadow of the Gate.

Rahab seemed not to hear and kept shuffling mechanically forwards.

'Hola, there!' bellowed the guard. 'Are you deaf? *Stop!*'

Lia tugged on Rahab's arm until he came to a halt. She kept hold of him, hoping he would not fall over, as the guard at the Gate came strolling out of the guardroom.

'It's after sunset. The Gate's shut till dawn. On your way.'

'But you'll let us through, won't you?' Lia smiled coquettishly at the guard.

'I said the Gate's shut. Wait till dawn like everyone else.' The guard turned on his heel and started back towards the guard-room.

'But we've got to get out of the city.' Lia cast around for a credible excuse. She ran up to the guard, leaving Rahab swaying on his feet. 'We're eloping.'

'Oh yes?'

'I'm to be married tomorrow to – to a man I hate!' Lia said, improvising wildly. 'An old man. Rich. A widower.' She lowered her voice. 'Incapable in a . . . a certain capacity. Ra –' she remembered in time to alter his name, 'Rahere and I, we love each other. But he's poor. If we don't get out of Arcassanne tonight, our lives will be ruined. Forever.' She paused to snatch a breath, trying to make out the guard's expression in the

129

lanternlight. Had her breathless plea moved him? Or was he still unconvinced?

The guard cleared his throat. She saw that his hand was outstretched, empty palm upwards.

Ah. She understood. A bribe.

She felt for her little purse, untying the ribbon strings, shaking out the coins into her palm. Thirty-seven oboles. She would need money to pay for Rahab's passage upriver; could she risk offering the man a whole ten oboles to let them through?

Smiling sweetly, she counted out ten coins into the man's outstretched hand. Without another word, he walked over to the side door and unlocked it.

She grabbed Rahab by the arm and hustled him forward, tugging him through the door.

It was not until she heard the door clang shut behind her – and the scrape of the key in the lock – that she realised she was on the wrong side. She was locked out of the city until daybreak.

A sharp pain pierced her foot. She swore under her breath. Another stone in her shoe? Had the stitching come undone between sole and uppers? This was not the time to discover she needed to visit the cobbler's. How far could she walk in shoes that needed mending?

'Wait.' She sat down on a mounting outside the Gate and tugged off the shoe, probing it with her fingers to find the hole. Rahab slumped down on to the damp gravel beside her, leaning his head back against the stone. The fast-moving clouds scudded aside to reveal a sliver of moon, casting a pale, wavering light on the river-path.

It was as she was holding the shoe up to the moonlight, squinting to try to make out the damage, that she heard the voices from behind the Gate. Loud voices, self-important, not caring whose sleep they disturbed.

'A girl's gone missing. Merchant's daughter. Abducted.'

Lia held her breath, straining to hear the guard's reply – but it was inaudible.

'Captain Orbiel wants her found. Yes, there's a reward.'

Orbiel. Lia felt a chill, sick feeling in the pit of her stomach. Not Lord Belcastel, her betrothed – but Jaufré d'Orbiel. The man who had arrested her mother.

'And a new edict from Comte Aymon. No Tsiyonim to be

allowed to leave the city. They're to be turned back. Any trouble
– and you have full authority to arrest them.'

She had planned on returning to plead her mother's case
before Comte Aymon. But now she began to realise that Aymon
might not listen to her.

'Not allowed to leave?' Rahab raised his head. 'Not even the
women and children?'

'Or my mother?' Lia pulled her shoe back on and started to
lace it.

'We put our trust in Aymon,' Rahab muttered. 'We believed
he would uphold the treaty his father signed with us. We
believed he would protect us.'

'Now what do I do?' Lia said. 'Do I go back – or do I go on?'

'For a few years, they tolerate us. Then something goes
wrong – and we get the blame.' Rahab appeared not to have
heard her. 'I told you – we're scapegoats. How could we be
anything else? We're the ones who lost our homeland – we're
obviously the bringers of ill-luck.'

'But what do *I* do now?' Lia snapped. The tension was
beginning to gnaw away at her self-composure. 'They think
you've abducted me. They'll come after us.'

Moonlight shimmered on to the path . . . and faded away
again as the clouds skimmed across the dark sky.

'Go back, then,' Rahab said. His voice was slurred with
weariness. 'I'm not asking you to come with me. Just don't
count on your Gentile friends to protect you.'

'And what precisely do you mean by that?' Lia's voice rose
sharply; she clapped her hand to her mouth, glancing fearfully
up at the moonlit walls.

The side door scraped open and voices drifted down to where
they sat.

'A girl and a young man. Can't have gone far.'

'Rahab!' Lia whispered. 'Do you hear?'

'It might not be the same girl. Abducted. You said abducted.
These two were courting.'

'Just think of the reward –'

'Courting couples are always coming out of a night in
summertime.'

'On a fine night, yes! But it's too wet to be cuddling on the
riverbank. Go on – how much did they give you?'

'I never accept bribes.'

'Tell that to Captain d'Orbiel.'

'Oh, all right, I'll split it with you. Half each. But what's the point in searching tonight? In this dark, we'd need the dogs . . .' The voices faded into the night.

'Quick!' Lia plucked at Rahab's sleeve. 'Off the path! There must be somewhere we can hide . . .'

Brambles tore their clothes; they slithered and slipped, grasping frantically at roots and tree branches to stop themselves from falling. Lia, gripping on to a knotted tree root with both hands, feared they might plummet off the steep hillside straight into the river far beneath.

'Lia –' came Rahab's voice close by in the darkness.

'Ssh!' Lia whispered, straining to hear if there were any sounds of pursuit. In the dank darkness, all she could hear was the monotonous whirr of crickets and the bizarre bubbling trills of little frogs.

'I think there may be – a cave – in the bank up here –'

Lia pulled herself back up the bank, clutching at the coils of ivy for support. Rahab had crawled into the gap between two ivy-hung boulders; it was barely wide enough for one, let alone two.

'That's not a cave!' Her palms stung from the wiry friction of the ivy coils; she rubbed them on her skirts to try to cool them. 'That's a hole.' She wrinkled her nose in disgust. 'A horrible smelly hole.'

Rahab did not contradict her. He seemed to have fallen asleep.

'Damn it,' she said softly. She sat down outside, propping herself against the rough stone. The air here was clammy with the river's chill; her arms were soon prickly with gooseflesh. She hugged them around herself, trying to stop her teeth from chattering.

'Rahab?' she said.

When he did not reply, she pinched her nose to keep out the fetid odour of the hole and quietly crept in beside him.

At first light, Lia and Rahab left their hiding-place. Stiff and cramped, they made their way slowly down the stony path towards the landing-stage.

Lia stopped once and gazed back at the city. From the pepperpot towers of the Belcastel mansion, pennants fluttered, blue and white against the dawn sky. She felt a sudden pang of homesickness. There was still time to change her mind . . .

The river Aude gleamed, a green sheen of silk through the rising gauze of the morning mist.

The path wound down through drooping willows and alders to the river-bank. Thick clouds of black flies buzzed in the sunlit grass-patches beneath the branches. Lia shuddered, holding her skirts close to her legs.

The riverboat crew were making ready to cast off. They had been cooking hot oats and honey and the clover-sweet scent of the honey only reminded Lia how desperately hungry she was. She untied her purse and shook out the remaining coins into her palm.

'Good morning to you, dem'selle.' One of the oarsmen looked up from the rope he was coiling as she approached. 'Better weather today.'

'Good morning to you.' She forced a smile, aware that after a sleepless night wandering the riverbank, she must look a fright. 'I want passage upstream for myself and my servant. How much?'

'Depends how far you want to go.'

'How far do you go?'

'We're going as far as the Gorge. No further. The river's swollen with rainwater. The Gorge is treacherous after a storm.'

'The Gorge it is, then.'

'That'll be twenty oboles for the two of you.'

Lia counted out twenty oboles into the man's hand. That left only seven; little enough to pay for food or lodgings. If there were lodgings to be had in mountain country . . .

Her empty stomach griped again; she narrowed her eyes against the brightness of the morning sun, feeling dizzy with hunger. The porridge smelt so good and she had not eaten since . . . since . . .

'How much for two bowls of porridge?' she heard herself asking.

'Passengers usually bring their own victuals,' the oarsman said, surprised.

'We had to leave early. My stupid servant forgot to pack the supplies.' Lia glanced at Rahab but to her relief he appeared not to have heard.

'I'd let him go hungry, then!' said the oarsman, laughing. 'Teach him a lesson he won't forget!'

'One bowl, then,' Lia said, unable to take her eyes from the steaming pot.

'One obole.'

'One obole? With extra honey for one obole!'

She was so ravenous that she burned her tongue as she spooned down the thick, creamy oats – and didn't care. But as she looked up over the rim of the bowl and saw Rahab sitting, propped against the end of the landing-stage, she felt a little ashamed of her greediness. She went over to him and silently offered what was left – a thin scraping at the bottom of the bowl.

The boat slipped through the cloudy waters, rocking gently as the oarsmen began to pull against the current.

Lia raised her head, shading her eyes against the glinting sun. The city was already behind them, rising from the misty river plain like a mirage. The Belcastel pennants had become insubstantial, distant gossamer shadows.

'Adieu, sweet Alissende, dearest Berengar,' Lia whispered. 'If only . . .' Her words trailed to silence.

The oarsmen pulled against the gentle flow of the river-current, onwards, upwards towards the distant mountains, still hidden from view by heat and cloudhaze.

Somewhere far beyond in that vague cloudhaze, Rahab had told her, lay Tifereth, their only hope of shelter in a world suddenly turned upside-down.

CHAPTER 13

The river mists slowly evaporated in the burning heat of the morning sun, to reveal the damage caused by the storm. On either bank Rahab could see the flattened fields of wheat and barley, young vines uprooted, the neat lines of the vineyards destroyed, the willows and alders ripped from the banks and tossed into the river.

'The harvest,' he said, stunned.

'All but ruined, they say.' The oarsman tugged on his oar. 'Never seen a storm like it. Great waves coming down the Aude. Almost capsized the boat. Almost drowned us all.'

Rahab felt chill and cold, as if a cloud had passed across the sun.

I did this. This is my doing. I may have saved them from death by fire . . . but what if the harvest fails? A long-drawn-out death, slow starvation because there is no bread . . .

He sat huddled, hugging his arms to his body, glad that Lia had charge of the amulets – in the face of such destruction, he might have been tempted to take them and hurl them into the green depths of the river.

He felt someone touch his shoulder, and looking up from the pit of his misery, he saw Lia looking at him, her sharp gaze as bright and curious as a blackbird's.

'What's wrong?'

How could he begin to explain his guilt to her? She could never understand. She had lived a Gentile's life in Arcassanne, protected from persecution, from fear.

'Tired,' he lied. 'Need to sleep.'

'Hm.' She gave a sniff. It sounded to him like a sniff of contempt.

He leaned his head against his arm, feeling the grate of the oars in the rowlocks as he closed his eyes.

What had he done, agreeing to let her come with him? Granted, he would not have left Arcassanne if she had not paid

135

his passage. But how could he admit to her that he had no more idea where Tifereth was than she?

Berengar steered Arbutus past pot-holes filled with rain-water on the road to the Belcastel estates. Everywhere the debris of the freak storm lay littered across the roads: shattered tiles, green leaves torn from the trees.

Great branches lay strewn across the mud-churned track; at the fork in the road, a massive oak, lightning-seared, blocked the way to the next village.

As Berengar turned Arbutus into the alley of chestnuts that led to the castel, he glimpsed a group of his peasants at work in the churned, rutted mud-patch that had once been a vineyard. One of them, looking up, spotted him and came hurrying over. Berengar recognised the weathered face of Thibaud, his steward.

'Welcome back, Lord Berengar.' Thibaud pulled off his hat, revealing his sunburned head, shinily bald. 'We're glad to see you came safely through the storm. I trust the Lady Esclarmonde is in good health?'

'My grandmother is in excellent health,' Berengar said through gritted teeth. And if it were not for her nagging, he'd be asleep in his own bed in Arcassanne. 'How has the estate fared? Can we make good the storm damage?'

Thibaud swallowed. 'See for yourself, seigneur. We've done what we can, but . . .'

Berengar turned around in the saddle, staring out across his storm-devastated fields. The corn stalks lay broken, flattened by the force of the rain and the wind.

'It was so sudden,' Thibaud said. Berengar saw tears glistening in the old man's eyes. 'The storm seemed to blow up out of nowhere. First the wind – then the rain. The hailstones were large as my fist. The stream burst its banks – water came through here in a torrent. Young Foulke was swept clean away. They're still searching for the body.'

'And the other vineyards?' Berengar asked, although he could already guess the answer.

The steward shook his head. 'I've never seen a storm like this, not in all my years. It was like the end of the world.'

Berengar opened his mouth – and then shut it again. What could he say? The prospect of a lean winter, a hungry winter loomed. Their grain stocks were low, depleted after last summer's poor harvest.

His people would go hungry . . . his people would starve.

'Come up to the castel,' Thibaud said, taking the reins to lead Arbutus up the alley of chestnuts. 'You must be hungry and thirsty after so early a start from the city.'

Berengar nodded. As he rode between the damaged trees his great-grandfather had planted, he felt chastened. These people spent their days working the land – *his* land – whilst he frittered his time away in idle pastimes at the court of Comte Aymon. He knew nothing of their lives, the drudgery of the farming calendar, yet he lived off the proceeds of their toil.

'*Farm talk bores me . . .*' The words, casually tossed aside to Lia, shamed him now. And yet she had been right; though he was reluctant to admit it, he had spent too much of his time acting as Jaufrés lieutenant –

Lia! Not until now had he thought of her – he had not even called at her house to check that she and her mother had come unscathed through the storm. A pang of guilt tweaked his heart. He would see to the farm business and ride straight back to the city.

'Who's this, who's this?' Esperte, Thibaud's wife, came out to welcome him, wiping her hands on her apron. She seemed to have dwindled since he had last seen her, but with her wizened red cheeks, she was still as ripe and sweet-natured as an autumn windfall. Esperte had had care of Berengar and Alissende when they were babies – and seeing her there on the step, beaming, arms wide open to greet him, he felt a pang of homesickness. Esperte and Thibaud were more like grandparents than Gran'mère Belcastel.

'I've just taken the bread out the oven. Walnut bread – that was always your favourite when you were little . . .' Esperte's voice brought back memories, childhood memories of the warm kitchen hearth, fresh-baked bread spread with bramble and apple jam, old songs hummed under her breath as she worked.

He hugged Esperte and followed her into the kitchen, where a fire crackled in the wide fireplace, the smoke sweet with the scent of burning applewood.

Sarrasin, the old wolfhound, got up from his place beside the fire, tail thumping enthusiastically.

'He, old boy, you remember me!' Berengar went down on one knee to stroke the shaggy grey head.

'You must be hungry,' Esperte said, starting to clear the table

137

and set out plates. 'There's a fresh-baked game pie just out of the oven . . .'

When they had eaten, Thibaud opened up the ledgers and insisted on showing him the estate accounts.

Berengar sat listening to the steward's voice droning pleasantly on about pecks and bushels, trying hard to keep his eyes open. Drowsed by the food in his belly and Esperte's home-brewed ale, he found it hard to keep his heavy lids from dropping shut.

The meticulously penned columns of figures blurred before his eyes.

'The lad's worn out.' He heard Esperte's voice, gently chiding. 'Put those books away, Thibaud. He needs his sleep.'

Berengar opened one eye. Something nagged him, something he had forgotten, someone he should have told . . .

'Why don't you put your feet up?' Esperte slipped a cushion behind his head, a footstool under his feet. 'You rest now. The estate business can wait.'

Lia . . . He had planned to return to the city before nightfall to make sure she was all right. He yawned hugely, stretching.

'Maybe just a few minutes, then . . .'

In the shallows beneath the trailing willows, the air became steamy as the sun's heat grew more intense. Lia saw damselflies, blue as slivers of turquoise, flitting in and out of the willow leaves.

The oarsmen pulled into the pebbled shore beneath the stone bridge at Yrioux to offload bales of cloth. New passengers came on board: a garrulous old man who kept telling anyone who would listen that he had been cheated at the market in Yrioux, and two farmer's wives, going back upriver after selling eggs. The oarsmen put up a canvas awning to protect their heads from the midday sun.

The further they travelled from Arcassanne, the more unfamiliar the country became. Lia had never been further upstream than Yrioux, and as the wide fields and nut orchards of the Arcassanne plain gave way to more rugged ground, she felt a slow, suppressed sense of panic begin to build below her ribs. This was wild country, harsh country, quite unlike the cultivated land, the farms and vineyards, surrounding Arcassanne. The foothills of the mountains loomed up out of the heat haze, and high in the pale clouds overhead, a bird of prey wheeled, its jagged wingspan too wide to be a lowlands kestrel or buzzard.

'An eagle,' she whispered under her breath, awed.

They had left the plains behind, and now the Aude grew narrower, ran faster, deeper. Lia looked over the side and saw that the waters were no longer limpidly green but churned dark against jagged rocks. The oarsmen were having to work hard now, fighting against the pull of the current. The banks rose higher on either side, sheer walls of rough lichened stone.

The gentle plash of the oars was drowned in the growing roar of the churning waters. Lia gripped the side of the boat as it rocked, buffeted by the strong current, setting little white-crested waves eddying into the stony shallows.

Under an overhanging ledge of rock, covered with stunted trees and gorse, Lia spotted a little bay where – to her astonishment for so wild a place – people stood waiting, women with baskets filled with cheeses, a man with a sheepdog which kept barking excitedly, the sound echoing off the walls of the gorge.

'Rahab,' she whispered, tapping his shoulder. 'We're here.'

One of the oarsmen gave the passengers a hand to climb down on to the little stony beach.

It was only as she was stepping on to the rough pebbles that the sense of panic Lia had managed to keep suppressed suddenly erupted. All the time she had been on the boat she had been in a state of limbo, drifting. Now here she was – alone in the wild, rugged country with a hole in her shoe and only six oboles to her name.

Her first instinct was to turn around and get back in the boat.

Rahab caught her by the arm.

'What are you doing?'

'What does it look like?' She twisted free. 'Going home.' She went marching up to the oarsman. 'How much back to Arcassanne?'

'Ten oboles.'

'Ten!' she cried, fighting back the tears. 'Can't you take me for less?'

'I'll take you for free, darling.' The oarsman caught the eye of his fellow crewmen; a snigger of lewd laughter passed between them.

'Lia.' Rahab came to stand beside her. 'Come on.'

'No, you come with me, darling!' called the oarsman, blowing kisses.

Lia stamped her foot on the pebbles and went marching away up the beach, trying to ignore the laughter from the river. Once she was out of sight of the shore, she sat down on a lichened rock, put her face in her hands and howled.

Rahab sat helplessly, watching Lia weep. At one moment he tentatively put out a hand to comfort her – and then thought better of it. He hadn't asked her to come with him. But she had come, whether he liked it or not. And she had paid for his passage. He owed her for that. Strange, though, he had a feeling she would never let him forget. Once a merchant's daughter . . .

He gazed around at the barren crags rising high above them. Such inhospitable country! Where would they find food and shelter for the night? And where, in this wilderness, was Tifereth?

The sun had passed overhead and the shadows were already beginning to lengthen in the gorge. Rahab was hungry. The meagre scraping of porridge this morning seemed all too long ago. The women from the boat had gone on ahead; there must be a village close to the little beach – or at least a farm where they could buy bread.

'Come on, Lia.' He tried to sound encouraging. 'We can't stay here till nightfall.'

'No,' she said, sniffling.

'We can ask for directions at the village. Someone's sure to know.'

'You've no idea which way to go, have you?' she said witheringly. 'We might as well take a twig, spin it and see which way it points.'

CHAPTER 14

'Nothing matters as long as Lia is safe.'

All the while the Watch had been escorting her through the streets of the city to the Tour de la Justice, Zillaïs had silently kept repeating the words to herself for reassurance. She had ignored the intrusive stares of the people they passed, closed her ears to the jeering cries and catcalls.

Nothing matters . . .

But when she was obliged to climb the bare spiral staircase of the Tour, past cell after cell, when they locked her into a narrow room, she felt her self-control begin to desert her.

She was a prisoner.

She sat down on the wooden bed and made an effort to compose herself.

Jaufré d'Orbiel had no legal right to confine her, of that she was certain. He had not officially charged her with any offence. No one had lodged a complaint against her.

The only reason he had cited for arresting her was the fact that she was one of the Tsiyonim.

So . . . what was driving him to act in this way? What did he really want from her?

A pigeon alighted outside the high slit window, and preened its mottled feathers, crooning softly to itself.

Fly away . . . if only she were free to fly where she wished, like the pigeons of Arcassanne . . .

She knew Jaufré d'Orbiel by reputation; she had read his verses – what woman in Arcassanne hadn't? She remembered them as accomplished, clever confections, charmingly witty. She remembered the love songs too, darkly obsessive, imbued with an unnatural passion for the woman who had inspired them . . . They had made her shiver when she read them.

'Madame Maury?'

The door opened and Jaufré d'Orbiel appeared.

141

'They tell me, madame, that you have some reputation in the city as a healer.'

She looked up at him, her gaze unwavering.

'You know so much about me already, Captain d'Orbiel, I'm surprised that fact escaped you.'

He carried on, ignoring her little barb. 'Rebh Jehiel needs attention. He refuses to see my own physician; he insists on a Tsiyonim healer.'

'I am the wife of a Gentile, he may refuse me too.'

'But you'll take a look at him?'

She hesitated. Then she said resignedly, 'I'll do what I can.'

But as she followed Jaufré d'Orbiel along the dank passageway, she found herself wondering what she was doing. She had kept herself apart from the Tsiyonim community in Arcassanne. She had spun herself practical reasons for doing so – but underlying her reluctance was one stark truth: she feared the pain of their rejection.

An elderly man lay on a pallet, his head raised on a little linen pillow. For one moment, noticing his white beard, his long sidelocks, his prayer-shawl wrapped about him, she saw again her own grandfather . . . and the sight stopped her on the threshold. So long since she had been amongst her own kind, so long . . .

'Go in,' said Jaufré behind her.

She nodded and approached the pallet. From the pallor of Jehiel's skin, the blue taint of his lips, the weak, ragged rise and fall of his chest, she recognised the telltale signs of a failing heart. Her simples would do little but relieve his condition; she could not work miracles.

She went down on one knee beside him.

'Rebh Jehiel,' she said. Would he reject her, turn his face away?

The wrinkled lids slowly opened and the old scholar stared up at her.

'Who – are you?'

'My name is Zillaïs Maury. Try not to exhaust yourself speaking. I'm just going to check your pulse.' She counted the irregular pulse beats, forcing herself to concentrate, trying to push all the crowding thoughts away. 'Just answer me with a nod. Is this the first time you've experienced this?'

A little shake of the head.

'And do you take any pills for your condition?'

Another little shake of the head.

'Rebh Jehiel, you should have consulted a physician,' she said, gently chiding. 'As it is, I can do little but alleviate your symptoms . . . it's beyond my skills to cure you.'

'Well?' demanded Jaufré, who had been standing, arms folded, watching.

'Everything I need is at my house,' she said.

'Give me a detailed list and my men will fetch whatever you need.'

'Very well,' Zillaïs said briskly, standing up. 'Though my recommendation is that the Rebh should not be kept confined in a prison cell. He should be taken somewhere where he can be properly nursed, properly cared for.'

'That's impossible,' Jaufré said. 'After the disturbances yesterday, we have been forced to bring all the Tsiyonim to the Tour de la Justice. For their own safety, you understand. The situation in the city is still volatile.'

'All of them?' Zillaïs said, astounded. 'For their own safety?'

'Just so. Now – that list, Dame Maury.'

'If you're bringing me pen and paper, I would like to send word to my husband.'

'Your husband is at sea.'

'There are ways of establishing contact, Captain d'Orbiel.' She saw with some satisfaction that she had unsettled him a little. He had not reckoned that she might be able to call on anyone for help. 'My husband has many friends outside Arcassanne, many contacts.'

There was a moment's pause.

'Very well,' he said. 'You may send word.' He turned on his heel and left the cell. She heard the key turn in the lock.

'It seems we are to be confined together . . .' she said to Rebh Jehiel.

'Why . . . has he arrested you? You are . . . Gentile.'

She saw the Rebh's eyes were fixed on her. Should she tell him the truth? Agitation almost overcame her. She turned away from the Rebh's bedside.

'Your letter . . . You know it will . . . never reach your husband . . .'

The grille in the door was opened and pen, inkwell and paper were pushed inside.

'The Captain says put the letters under the door when you've finished.'

Zillaïs looked around the little cell; there was nowhere to write but on the cold stone floor. She knelt down and swiftly penned her list. The letter to Auger was much harder to write. Eventually she settled on one stark plea:

'Please come home; we are in desperate trouble.'

She shook the papers to dry them, folded and addressed them – the list to Emmenza, the letter to messire Auger Maury, care of Maitre Guilbert at the Sign of the Red Lily – and pushed them under the door. She heard the guard take up the letters and walk away down the passageway. She waited for the footsteps to return, to take her back to her cell. No one came.

She began to pace.

'What is his purpose?' she asked aloud. 'What does Orbiel want from us?'

'What did you say your name was?' came a feeble voice from the pallet.

'I gave you my married name, Rebh,' she said, stopping her pacing. 'But now that Orbiel has uncovered my past, I should tell you that I was once known as Zillah bet Ithamar.'

She saw his eyes widen.

'Ithamar of Tolonada? But . . . we thought you all were dead.'

'Dead to my own people, yes.'

'You married a Gentile?' There was no censure in his voice, only surprise.

'I married the man who rescued me from the wreck of our ship.'

'So . . . everything was lost in the wreck?' he said weakly.

'Everything?' Zillaïs tensed. Was this some subtle form of interrogation, devised by Orbiel to inveigle the truth from her about the amulet?

'*All* your father's possessions?'

'His possessions? Has Orbiel set you up to this?' she cried – and then, seeing his face, was instantly ashamed of her outburst. 'You must forgive me, Rebh Jehiel. The past few hours have – have been most unsettling. I don't know what I'm saying –'

'For all I know, Orbiel has placed *you* here to entrap *me*.' There was a shrewdness in his gaze that she had not noticed when Jaufré d'Orbiel was in the cell. 'How can I be sure you are who you say you are?'

'Test me,' Zillaïs said, 'and I'll answer you as honestly as I can.'

'The first words of the evening blessing. The blessing said over the lighting of the candles.'

The blessing, whispered for years in secret to an empty room, came readily to her lips ... though it was disconcerting to speak the words aloud.

Jehiel listened without comment.

'The words spoken by the youngest child on the night we remember the fall of Tsiyon.'

Zillaïs swallowed. Once she had been the youngest child, the cherished youngest daughter. Once, long ago, she had spoken these words aloud at the candlelit supper-table, surrounded by her family, her father Ithamar smiling his encouragement. Haltingly, she began to repeat them – for the first time in years without number. And then the room blurred and she could no longer see Rebh Jehiel's face for unshed tears which stung her eyes.

'Zillah, Zillah,' he said gently. 'I had to be sure, sure I could trust you. We are all in such danger here.'

Zillaïs nodded, blinking away her tears. Such foolishness, to cry at the memory. What was past was past. Tears would not bring back the dead. But the living ...

Jehiel lifted one hand, beckoning. 'Come closer ... where I can see you.'

She drew nearer.

'If I die ...'

'Please, Rebh Jehiel, don't talk of dying yet!'

'It's important, Zillah. You don't mind if I call you Zillah? It was my mother's name, a beautiful name, it gives me pleasure to say it.'

'It's a pleasure to hear it spoken again.' She smiled at him tentatively. She had expected censure. She had expected him to turn his face away from her, to ignore her.

'Listen, Zillah. There is something ... wrong with Jaufré d'Orbiel. I fear he has come into contact with some evil influence. I fear he may be ... possessed.'

Possessed. Zillaïs felt a sudden chill at the word, the chill that comes with the confirmation of a long-held suspicion. That disconcerting shadowy stare ...

'He has ransacked the Quarter searching for ...' and Jehiel's voice sank even softer, 'an amulet. A Guardian Amulet.'

'To what purpose?' Zillaïs asked, feeling colder still.

145

'Ah, if we could only find out . . .' Jehiel let out a halting sigh. 'I can only pray that young Rahab got out of the city before the Quarter went up in flames.'

'Rahab?' Zillaïs said sharply. 'Rahab ben Chazhael?'

'The tailor's apprentice. Why – do you know the boy?'

'I know him. And he may have –' Zillaïs broke off, hearing footsteps coming closer in the passageway outside. She placed her finger over her lips. 'Not now. Later.'

'There may be no later . . .' Jehiel sank back, closing his eyes as the cell door was unlocked and Jaufré d'Orbiel came in.

'Here are the simples you requested. Your servant-woman assembled them for us.'

'And . . .' Zillaïs tried to make the question sound inconsequential as she examined the herbs Emmenza had sent, 'was my daughter Lia at home?'

'Bertran?' Jaufré called out into the passageway. 'Who did you see at the Maury house?'

Bertran came ambling back; a large man, with a face as craggy as the rough stones of the *causse*, he loomed into Jehiel's cell, towering over Jaufré d'Orbiel.

'Only the servant-woman. And she was half beside herself, shrieking and wailing.'

'Why?' said Zillaïs sharply.

'She said –' Bertran hesitated, glancing at Jaufré as if requesting permission to speak. 'She said your daughter had been abducted.'

'Nonsense!' Zillaïs heard herself saying. 'Emmenza doesn't know what she's talking about! Lia is at the Belcastels'.'

'Of course. At the Belcastels',' Jaufré repeated. He signed to Bertran to leave.

'What did he mean?' Zillaïs rounded on Jaufré d'Orbiel. 'What are you concealing from me? I want to see Berengar de Belcastel; I want assurance that my daughter is safe.'

'Captain,' Bertran called from outside. 'You're needed in the yard. We've brought the Tsiyonim in as you ordered. But they insist on talking with you.'

'Very well, very well . . .' Jaufré spun around on his heel and followed Bertran out into the passageway. He seemed relieved, Zillaïs thought, not to have to answer her question.

'Brought them in?' Jehiel said, trying to raise himself up on one elbow. A spasm gripped him and he clutched at his collar, gasping. 'Arrested – them –'

146

'Here. Put this under your tongue.' Zillaïs gave him one of the little pills Emmenza had sent. 'Try to lie still, try not to exert yourself.'

There were herbs to be crushed and infused, medicines to be mixed. She could not cure Jehiel – but she wanted to do what she could to alleviate his suffering.

This was not time to worry uselessly about Lia; the elderly scholar needed her. Maybe in caring for him she could atone in some way for the years she had spent in hiding.

Jaufré stood at the window, watching his men herd the last of the straggling line of Tsiyonim fugitives into the yard of the Tour de la Justice. Many had not had time to clean themselves from the ravages of the fire; their faces were stained black with smuts, their clothes dirty with cinder-smears. They shuffled along, glancing warily about them, herding small children, clutching the few possessions they had been able to salvage from their homes. They looked bewildered . . . and exhausted.

As the last of the ragged line entered the courtyard, he saw his men pull the heavy doors to, shutting them in. It was time to go down to address his new charges.

As he reached the stair, a jagged pain suddenly flared in his chest. He stopped, grabbing at the rail to steady himself. What could have caused it? Indigestion? He couldn't remember the last time he had eaten. Maybe it was hunger . . . though he had little appetite these days.

The instant the Tsiyonim caught sight of him, they surged forward, calling out a babble of questions.

Jaufré raised his hand for silence. Around the perimeter of the yard, the Hawks stood, armed with bows and swords in case of trouble.

'Have you no spokesman?' Jaufré shouted above the din of angry voices.

An old man came out of the crowd, leaning heavily on a stick.

'I am Baruch the Moneylender,' he said. 'I speak for my neighbours. And we want to know why we've been arrested. Have you some new charge to bring against us?'

'We have only confined you in the Tour for your own safety,' Jaufré said, forcing his lips into the semblance of a smile. 'The Comte has given his word that when the situation within the city has improved, you will all be freed.'

147

'Wasn't that the excuse given in Ebora twenty years ago?' Baruch said.

'Yes, and there they herded them all into the castel – and set it alight,' cried a woman's voice from the crowd.

'Your quarters may prove a little cramped.' Jaufré continued, ignoring her, 'but it should only be a temporary measure.' A reverberation of the pain nagged, dully, about his heart.

'So why not let us go free?' called the woman.

'Save the Comte the expense of feeding so many extra mouths!' shouted another. The child in her arms started to grizzle. The whining sound grated on Jaufré's ears.

'Until the case of the boy's murder is resolved . . .' he said, shrugging.

'So we *are* prisoners!' growled Baruch, shaking his stick at Jaufré.

The ache persisted; dull as the throb of an old battle-wound in damp weather. His hand slid to find the place . . . and encountered the metal disc of the amulet, concealed beneath his shirt.

'I request an audience with Comte Aymon,' Baruch said testily. 'No – not request – demand. It's my right as a citizen of Arcassanne. I demand my rights as a citizen. Haven't we all paid our taxes? Haven't we the right to be heard?'

Many nodded their heads in assent.

'I will see what I can do,' Jaufré said, forcing himself to continue to smile despite his growing irritation, 'but the Comte is a busy man . . .'

'Pah! His father was never too busy,' muttered Baruch.

'He has been good enough to accommodate you all here at his own expense whilst the damage to your homes is assessed.'

'Damage which would never have occurred if you and your damned Hawks had been doing your job properly!'

Jaufré signalled to Bertran to open the doors to the Tour. He was not going to stand arguing with the old moneylender all night; he had better things to do with his time. He went on ahead, leaving the Hawks to usher the Tsiyonim into the Tour. But as he climbed back up the spiral stair, he heard a little voice, piping high above the others, asking, 'Mamma, where's Rahab gone?'

Rahab. Schimeon's apprentice, the young man who had found the boy's body. Rahab, who had disappeared, in spite of an intensive search of the whole city.

Jaufré stopped, gazing down the stairwell, listening intently for the reply.

'Hush, Thirzi . . . Rahab's gone to Tifereth. He'll be back soon.'

Tifereth? Where was Tifereth? Jaufré leaned over the rail.

The child began to snivel, a dismal, irritating sound.

'I don't like it here. I want to go home.'

'But what about Papa? And Michal? You want to see Papa, don't you Thirzi?'

'I just want to go home . . .'

A child was crying, a thin, wailing sound that penetrated Jaufré's sleep.

It must be one of those whining Tsiyonim children . . . Why couldn't their mothers control them? Why must they let them disturb others' rest? He pulled his pillow over his head, trying to block out the sound.

The crying went on . . . and on . . . It nagged, keen as the ache of a worm-eaten tooth. It wailed like the Tramontan wind in late summer.

Jaufré lay sleepless in the dark until he could bear it no longer. He forced himself out of bed and flung open the chamber door.

The crying stopped as suddenly as if it were a snuffed-out candleflame.

He stood in the doorway, listening tensely to the darkness until his ears tingled with the absence of sound.

CHAPTER 15

'Tifereth? Never heard of any place called Tifereth round here.'

Whenever Rahab asked his question, he was greeted with suspicious glances or blank looks.

They had spent the last of Lia's money on bread, fruit and ale. They had sheltered the night in an empty shepherd's hut. At sunrise they had finished the bread and fruit and set off up into the mountains.

At first they kept to the shadows. But as the sun climbed higher in the cloudless sky, the shadows dwindled, offering scant shelter from the heat. The track wound on upwards through sun-baked pastures. Rahab walked doggedly on, although he could feel the perspiration trickling down the back of his neck. But Lia had begun to lag behind, and after a while he looked back only to realise that he was toiling on alone. Lia had disappeared.

He retraced his steps to find that she had wandered from the road and flopped down in the shade of a clump of walnut trees.

'Maybe you're asking the wrong question,' she said. She was tracing a pattern with the toe of her shoe in the dust. The air was noisy with the chatter of cicadas.

'Wrong?' Rahab, hot and cross, wiped his face with the corner of his shirt. 'What d'you mean, wrong?'

'Maybe you call it Tifereth in Arcassanne. But maybe they call it something else up here.'

'So I just ask if there's "something else up here"?' he said. The heat was fraying his temper.

'It's a college, isn't it?' She picked a grass stem and split it, holding it between her thumbs, trying to blow a note out of it. 'Ask if there's a college. A foundation. A place where people study.' She blew again on the grass and produced a piercing squeak.

To his irritation he realised that she was right. And he did not want to have to admit that he might have been in the wrong.

'We'd better find this place soon,' she said. 'I don't want another night under the stars. And I want something decent to eat.'

'Oh, I forgot,' he said, unable to stop himself, knowing it would provoke her. 'Demoiselle Maury is not accustomed to hardship or hunger. She has led such a sheltered life.'

'You haven't forgiven me yet, have you?' She glanced up and he saw her eyes had narrowed.

'For what?'

'For eating the last of the bread.'

'You could have split it between the two of us.'

'It was *my* money. It was my bread. I was starving.'

'Oh, and I wasn't?'

'Ssh!' She knelt up, shading her eyes into the sun. 'Someone's coming!'

Rahab listened; he could hear the gentle tonkle of bells in the distance. Gazing up the hillside, he saw a herd of mountain sheep grazing their way down the steep pasture.

'Only sheep,' he said dejectedly.

The air sizzled with the midday heat. His parched throat burned. He was desperate for a drink. He had hoped there might be a farm along this track where he could ask for a cup of water. Or a mountain stream, running cold and clear from the high peaks . . .

He tried to put the thought from his mind. The very idea of water was a torture. In his mind the memory of fast-falling rain was still fresh, the shimmer of grey haze streaked by lightning, the hail of raindrops that had guttered from Barakiel's cloud-feathered wings . . .

Some of the sheep meandered on to the track, their cloven hoofs kicking up a dustcloud.

A voice, high and shrill as a bird's, called out and the sheep bleated in reply.

'There!' Lia said smugly. 'Look.'

Rahab looked. Was it the sun beating on his head – or was it the swirling dust, gilded by the sun? A figure was emerging from the dustcloud, coming along the track with the sheep trotting beside him. For an instant Rahab thought he saw a glimmer of angei-light about the figure –

He shook his head to try to clear his blurred sight. The heat must be frying his wits! This was only a boy, a shepherd boy, he guessed, spotting the rough wooden crook he carried.

151

Rahab walked back out into the glare of the sun.

'Good-day to you,' he called, his voice hoarse from thirst.

Dust hazed the air. Rahab put up one hand to cover his eyes as the boy drew near.

'Good-day,' the boy replied, smiling. Sheep spread out around him, busily cropping the mountain herbs.

'Can you help us?' Rahab noticed the water flask slung on a strap over the boy's shoulder. 'We're lost. We're looking for a – a college. A place of learning. Have you ever heard of such a place round here?'

The boy grinned at him, a dazzling grin, white teeth in a sunburned face. There was something oddly familiar about his face, with its rough-cut fringe of sun-bleached hair – although Rahab could not identify what it was.

'The scholars? You've come the long way round. You should have gone up the valley and kept in the shade.'

'But there *is* a college?' Rahab was so excited he almost choked on his words. 'And we're on the right road?'

'Keep on up the track until you come to a fork. Take the right down towards the forest. A way further along, you'll come to a stream. Follow the stream up the mountain. Look out for the watchtower of the ruined castel.'

'Stream?' Rahab hardly heard the boy's last directions in his desperation to find water. 'There's a stream?'

'You look parched,' the boy said, holding out his water flask. 'Here. Drink.'

Rahab hesitated.

'I know where to find more,' the boy said, grinning again.

Rahab took the flask and tore out the stopper, pouring the water into his mouth. It was so cold, so clean, so sweet . . .

'Rahab!' Lia, seeing the flask, came hobbling over, trying to avoid the sheep.

Rahab lowered the flask, wiping the wet from his mouth with the back of his hand.

'Don't leave any for me, will you!'

He handed her the flask. She attempted to drink in refined little sips – then, overcome by thirst, tipped her head back and let the water gush down her throat.

'Thank you,' she said stiltedly, handing the empty flask back to the boy.

'Don't forget – right where the path forks.' The boy whistled up his sheep. 'Follow the stream.' He set off down the winding track, followed by his sheep, and as the dust eddied up about him, he was soon lost to view.

'Thank you!' Rahab echoed Lia. His eyes were still fixed on the shimmer of dust where the boy had been. How had he come to disappear from sight so swiftly?

That eerie thrill of recognition he had sensed when he looked into the boy's face. He had been thinking of Barakiel. And then the boy had appeared, almost as if he had called him. Could he have been –

'What is it?' Lia asked sharply.

No. It couldn't be. Rahab shook his head. 'Nothing. Nothing . . . of consequence . . .'

By the time they reached the stream, the light was beginning to fade and the mountains beyond were coloured an intense rose-gold. There was a stillness in the air, broken only by the rush of the stream waters. Blue shadows darkened the sheer forested slopes of a little hidden valley.

Lia shivered, rubbing her upper arms with her hands.

'It had better not be far,' she said. 'I'm not sleeping out again. There could be – wild things up here. Bears.'

Rahab hardly heard her. As he stood, gazing down at the hidden valley, the only shiver he felt was one of excitement. Tifereth. Were they really so close at last?

'Come on.' He forced himself to start walking again. 'If you want to find somewhere to sleep tonight – somewhere safe from bears.'

She let out a little whimper of fatigue and wearily began to tramp upwards after him.

He supposed he should ignore her complaining; after all, it wasn't her fault she had led such a sheltered life. She had probably never walked further than the market in Arcassanne; she had probably been carried everywhere else by litter. He did not like to think what state her feet were in by now. He was sure she would tell him.

Over and over again.

The sun was dipping between the high peaks when Rahab caught sight of a jagged tower silhouetted against the gold of the sunset. Perched precariously on the edge of the cliff, it commanded an almost impregnable position above the narrow valley.

'That's it?' Lia said in a wail. 'But that's a *ruin.*'

153

Twilight shadows darkened the slopes.

'The boy said it was here – so it must be here.' Rahab turned and began to trudge on up the steep track. The walking had rubbed raw blisters on both heels, and his toes were still throbbing from having stubbed them on a hidden stone on the path.

'How can a college be up here, so far from civilised life?' Lia grumbled as she trailed after him. 'Where do they get their food?'

'They grow their own.'

'But they're scholars. They're supposed to study, not grow vegetables.'

'I'm sure they find the time to do both,' Rahab said patiently, feeling as if he was humouring a fractious child.

The path was taking them closer to the side of the valley; looking down into the shadows, he saw that the cliff sheered away to a distant silver sliver of water far beneath.

'Keep away from the edge,' he cautioned Lia.

'Yes, yes . . .'

'It's a sheer drop.'

When she didn't reply, something made him glance back. She was drifting blindly towards the edge.

Sleep-walking.

He lunged out and grabbed her, dragging her against him away from the ravine. Dislodged stones rattled over the side, cascading down into the brambles far beneath.

'Get – your hands – off me!'

Dizzy with fatigue, Rahab lost his balance and they both fell down on to the path, Lia beating at him with her fists.

Awake now, she stumbled away from him, breast heaving, glaring.

'You're – an animal!'

Rahab lay back on the stony grass and closed his eyes. What did she imagine he had been trying to do?

'Next time I'll let you fall.'

She sat down a way off from him, rubbing her ankle.

'And you hurt my ankle. How can I walk with a twisted ankle?'

Rahab did not bother to reply. Getting to his feet, he went back to the edge of the cliff and forced himself to look down. It was rapidly growing darker and a chill breeze blew from the ravine beneath, wafting a faint, resinous breath of pine-sap.

'No sign of buildings below.' He drew back from the edge and started to trudge on up the path. 'So it must be further up.'

Lia made no comment.

He looked back to see her still sitting where he had left her, a pale blur against the gathering darkness. 'Surely you're not going to give up now, Lia? Within sight of the castel?'

'Within sight of a broken-down ruin.'

'At least it'll be somewhere to shelter for the night.'

'Huh.' She stood up and began to hobble up the path towards him. 'Some shelter.' He was sure she was exaggerating her injury. He would not give her the satisfaction of noticing she was limping.

She can't help herself. She's a spoilt little rich girl, Papa's treasure. Maybe this journey has opened her eyes to the realities of life outside the Merchants' Quarter . . . even if it's almost driven me to insanity . . .

He stopped again to gaze up at the jagged black outline of the watchtower.

Was that smoke, curling up in a thin, gauzy ribbon against the gold sheen of the twilit sky? He forced himself on, wanting to make certain it was not just a wisp of cloud he had seen.

'Lia! Lia!' he shouted. 'Smoke!'

'So?' came the sulky reply. 'Who cares?'

He pressed on up the path, ignoring the fiery blisters, the stubbed toes – and stopped as the ground levelled out into a grassy ridge. He could just see that in the fading light – set at a distance from the watchtower – stood an ancient, dilapidated castel, its crumbling stones mottled with lichens.

He set out eagerly across the soft, springy turf, hastening his pace, until he stood in the shadow of the walls.

The only sound of human habitation was the distant cackling of chickens; the only sign, the curling smoke.

No one had challenged him.

Surely there must be someone about? Rahab went – more cautiously – towards the gatehouse.

'It could be a brigand stronghold,' Lia said, catching up with him. 'The shepherd boy could be their lookout, sending unwary travellers up here to be robbed and murdered.'

Rahab, one hand upraised to knock at the door, paused. He too had heard stories of ruined mountain castels haunted by brigands . . .

'So why has no one stopped us?'

'They're waiting for us to go inside. Then they'll pounce. I'll bet you the door isn't barred.'

Rahab knocked. The sound rolled around the twilit ridge, hollow as a drumbeat.

From behind the ancient door, its faded paint cracked and flaking, a man's voice asked, 'Who is it?'

'Travellers. From Arcassanne.'

'At this hour?'

'We lost our way.'

'Do you know where you are? Do you know the name of this place?'

Rahab suddenly sensed he was being tested.

'Tifereth,' he said, risking all.

'And what is Tifereth?' came back the reply.

Rahab thought back to his studies with Rebh Jehiel.

'Tifereth is Beauty,' he said breathlessly. 'Tifereth is the Sixth Sefirah, Tifereth is at the heart of the Tree of Life.'

'Come in.' The heavy door swung slowly open. 'Come in – and be welcome.'

Cautiously, Rahab crossed the threshold, followed by Lia, who now walked so close to him, she had almost shrunk into his shadow.

A man stood in the courtyard, his arms open wide in greeting.

'Welcome to the Realm of the Soul,' he said, smiling. 'My name is Malakhi.'

Lia stood close to Rahab as curious scholars appeared in the torchlit courtyard, summoned by the man calling himself Malakhi.

Suddenly she found herself surrounded by the Tsiyonim; men, old and bespectacled – and young, with wisps of dark beard. All were wearing fringed shawls. Were there no women here? She edged closer to Rahab, feeling suddenly as if she had wandered into an alien country, clinging to the only familiar person.

The scholars peppered them with questions.

'Have you come far?'

'How long have you been on the road?'

'Was it hard to find your way?'

'Where have you come from?'

Malakhi raised his hand for silence.

'There'll be time to talk later. Can't you see our visitors are tired and hungry after their long climb? Rahab, Lia, would you like to share our supper?'

Supper. Lia nodded her head vigorously.

'Thank you,' she heard Rahab say. His voice sounded odd, as if he were overcome with emotion. As Malakhi led them across the grassy courtyard, she saw in the torchlight that the tailor's cheeks were wet with tears.

A few days ago, Lia would not have dreamed of appearing before strangers in a tattered, smelly, travel-stained dress, her skin sunburned, her hair unkempt. Now her hunger was so acute that she did not care who saw her looking such a mess. After a perfunctory splash of water to rub the dirt and perspiration from her sticky face and hands, she was ready and ravenous for supper.

The dining hall was a plain, lime-washed chamber with trestle tables and benches. All the furniture was rough-hewn and had a home-carpentered look. Only the many-branched bronze candlesticks were finely, ornately crafted, a legacy, she guessed, from earlier, more prosperous days.

There were women in the hall, busy laying plates, knives and spoons on the trestles. They nodded to her as she came in. Lia nodded back, suddenly overcome with shyness. She couldn't help but notice that most were wearing headscarves, twisted in the fashion her mother often favoured around the house. And to her surprise she saw that there were children present: a little girl and a boy of about ten years, carrying in dishes of salad and bread. Children in a college? Astonishment made her completely forget her hunger for a moment. She had assumed that the scholars were celibate. And then Malakhi was ushering everyone to the table. She sat between Rahab and Malakhi, hungrily scanning the laden dishes, reaching out to seize a piece of bread and begin.

'Baruch atah adonai elohenu . . .'

Lia felt her face reddening; looking around the table she saw that everyone had bent their heads as Malakhi pronounced words of blessing in a tongue she did not recognise, and the others murmured a response. Rahab had told them nothing but her name; naturally, they would assume she was one of them, that she knew their ways and customs. For a fleeting moment she had felt as if she were amongst friends – and now she knew

157

herself a stranger again. Even the dishes of food on the table looked unfamiliar. Was there some unspoken protocol here as well? She hesitated – remembering tales Papa had told of eating with foreign merchants and their families, remembering how she had laughed as he described his blunders. Now those stories did not seem so funny.

Malakhi turned to her, offering to serve her from the dish in front of him.

'Vine leaves? Stuffed with rice? They're very good. We grow all our own fruit and vegetables up here.'

Lia risked a questioning glance at Rahab. Was there any other custom she was unaware of? The smell arising from the dish was delicious, and she felt her stomach ache with emptiness. Then, seeing the scholars enthusiastically helping themselves, she nodded, holding out her plate.

'Please, please start,' Malakhi said, passing her the bread.

She needed no further encouragement. The stuffed vine leaves were delicious, and so were the stuffed peppers. After that came fruit: juicy plums, late greengages, sweet and ripe, and peaches.

'All from our own trees,' Malakhi said proudly.

'Listen to him!' exploded an older man sitting opposite. His hair and fiercely bristling brows were speckled with silver. 'You'd think he'd grown them himself!'

'Let me introduce Elon to you,' Malakhi said. 'Our authority on orchards. Apples, pears, plums, he knows all there is to know.'

'If only I did! The blight's back in the late-fruiting apricot,' Elon said to Rahab. 'Any tips?'

'I'm sorry,' Rahab said, smiling an apology, 'but I'm a tailor. I know nothing about gardening.'

'My mother –' Lia blurted out, and then stopped as everyone looked at her. 'My mother might be able to help,' she finished in a small voice, 'if she were not in Arcassanne.'

'So what's the news from Arcassanne?' asked a woman, an older woman about Zillaïs's age.

Lia looked at Rahab. The buzz of conversation at the table died and she realised they were all looking expectantly at them.

'Arcassanne . . .' Rahab repeated. There was something in his voice that made Lia glance sharply up at him. She saw a muscle twitch in his face as if he were making an effort to hold

158

back tears. And when he spoke again, his voice was choked with emotion. 'It's . . . a long story.'

'We've got all night to listen,' Malakhi said. He refilled Rahab's wine-cup and passed the jug along the table. 'Speak, Rahab. Tell us what brought you both here.'

Once Rahab began to tell the scholars what had been happening in Arcassanne, he could not stop; memories and details came pouring out in an impassioned, barely coherent flow. It was only when he came to Jaufré's tearing down of the prayer-shells that he became aware of a rustle of heightened attention around the table. He checked himself, catching Lia's eye. Thus far he had not once mentioned the amulets, nor had he said anything of Lia's involvement.

'So our kinsmen were forced out of their houses into hiding? By this – what did you say his name was?'

'Jaufré d'Orbiel,' Rahab said. 'He has much influence with Comte Aymon. Or so my master Schimeon says.'

'And he arrested your master?'

'My master, his eldest daughter and our teacher, Rebh Jehiel. It was Jehiel who said I should come here to ask for your help.'

'Jehiel!' Malakhi said, his voice softening. 'So he's still alive. I owe him and his wife Miriam a debt of gratitude. They showed me much kindness many years ago . . .'

'Miriam died three summers back,' Rahab said. 'And I fear for Jehiel's health. Prison is too harsh a place for a man of his years.'

'So this Orbiel has our people trapped in the Quarter?' put in a quavering voice from the end of the table. 'You say he won't even let them leave the city? This sounds like Tolonada all over again.'

'Tolonada?' Rahab heard Lia repeat under her breath.

'And what was the excuse there?' continued the wizened old scholar. 'Some nonsense about poison in the wells. But the true reason,' and he wagged his finger at Rahab, 'was that the First Minister was a practitioner of the Dark Arts. He wanted to learn our secrets.'

'That was only a rumour, Lamech,' said Malakhi as a buzz of discussion began at the old man's suggestion. 'It was never proven.'

'It was never proven because everyone was massacred,' Lamech insisted over the voices of his fellow scholars. 'And the talisman that he was so keen to seize for himself disappeared.'

159

Talisman. Rahab glanced at Lia and saw that she was staring at Lamech, her mouth half-open, as if she had been about to say something – and had thought better of it.

'But how are we to resolve this situation?' Malakhi asked, calling the arguing scholars to order. 'Our kinsfolk need our help. We have no army to ride down the mountain and relieve the siege. What was the situation when you left, Rahab?'

Rahab cleared his throat, which had suddenly become tense and tight. This was the part he had been dreading.

'They – they set fire to the Quarter,' he said.

'I told you! Just like Tolonada!' cried old Lamech over the murmurs of dismay.

'So – how did you both escape with your lives?' Malakhi asked, his face stern. 'How did you know where to find us?'

'We – we didn't know where you were. We lost our way. If it had not been for the shepherd boy, we would never have reached you tonight.'

'Shepherd boy?' Malakhi said, frowning.

'Way back, the other side of the hill. He said he knew you.'

Rahab saw the scholars look at each other blankly, exchanging shrugs.

'We've gone to such trouble to conceal our true identity. Yes, we are scholars, this is a college. But to our neighbours, to the landowner from whom we rent this castel, we are merely immigrant farmers from across the mountains in Galicys. The word Tsiyonim has never been mentioned.'

'You never told us how you escaped,' said a fresh voice from the far side of the table. Rahab looked and saw a young man sitting beside Lamech, watching him with clear, penetrating eyes. He suddenly felt uncomfortable under the scrutiny of the clear gaze; almost as if the young scholar had looked into his mind and learned that he was holding something back, something of vital importance.

'Yes, Bar Talmai,' Malakhi said, turning back to Rahab. 'Our guest has not told us how he escaped Orbiel's soldiers.'

Rahab looked again at Lia and saw her nod – almost imperceptibly – her permission. He took up the wine-cup and drained it, hoping the wine would give him confidence to relate the unrelatable.

'Rebh Jehiel asked me to bring this to you.' He reached into the breast of his jacket, brought out the folded scrap of cloth in which he had wrapped the amulets and laid it on the table.

160

There was just the faintest shock of sensation in his fingertips as he touched them . . . but nothing more. Slowly, he pulled back the protective folds of cloth until the two sections of amulet were revealed, their metallic enamel sheen gleaming in the candlelight, like the carapaces of two exotic beetles glinting in the sun.

The room fell silent. All the scholars stared at the amulet fragments. It was so still that Rahab could hear the hoot of an owl swooping across the courtyard.

'*Two* Guardian Amulets?' Malakhi said, his voice hushed. His long, slender fingers rested on the table-top but Rahab could sense that he longed to reach out, to touch them.

'Barakiel,' read out Elon, 'and Rashiel.'

Barakiel. The pronouncing aloud of the name of his Guardian sent an involuntary shiver down Rahab's spine.

'You *used* the amulets?' The clear voice of Bar Talmai broke the silence. How could the young scholar know what he had done? Had he read his mind? Or was his guilt all too easy to read in his eyes?

They were all staring at Rahab now. He could not find his voice to reply.

'Well?' Malakhi said. 'Did you?'

Rahab cast his eyes down, ashamed. He felt as if he had committed a terrible sacrilege. Now he was to be punished for daring to transgress their Holy Laws.

'It was the only way to save them,' he heard his voice saying. 'The storm put out the fires in the Quarter. But it . . . it ruined the harvest. I did not realise how powerful . . .' His voice trailed away.

He felt a hand on his shoulder. Looking up, he found himself gazing into Malakhi's frank, sun-burned face.

'But the Guardian chose you.'

Rahab nodded.

'"Blood of the pure, blood of the innocent",' quoted Lamech. Rahab started; he had heard those words before, in a very different context.

'But we have two amulets here. If one was Jehiel's – where did the other come from?'

'From my mother,' Lia said. Until this moment, she had kept – unusually, Rahab thought – her silence. But now all the scholars turned their attentions to her.

'And who is your mother?' asked the woman, Selima.

161

'Zillaïs, daughter of Ithamar of Tolonada,' Lia said, faltering.

'Ithamar's grandchild!' Lamech cried out gleefully. 'But Ithamar and his children drowned. In the tidal wave that followed the earthquake.'

'My – my mother was rescued.'

Rahab saw Lia staring at the old man.

'You said this amulet was . . . was Rashiel.'

'Bringer of Earthquakes, yes.'

'You mean – my grandfather used the amulet? To save them? And . . . the earthquake led to a tidal wave – and they were all drowned? All – all the ones he meant to save?' Lia clapped her hand to her mouth as though trying to stifle the words.

'Not quite all. I got away,' Lamech said, 'or I wouldn't be here to tell the tale. Until today, we believed the Rashiel amulet to be lost. Deep under the ocean.'

'Oh,' said Lia, very softly. 'Ohh.'

'Suppose this Orbiel is a practitioner of the Dark Arts?' Lamech insisted. 'Suppose he's trying to find these amulets?'

'What do you know of the man?' Malakhi asked.

'Of Jaufré d'Orbiel?' Lia said, frowning. 'He's a poet, a soldier, he's travelled . . . he was in Djihan-Djihar with my betro –' She broke off.

'Djihan-Djihar?' Malakhi exchanged glances with the other scholars. 'Do you think it's possible he might have –'

'Anything's possible,' said Selima grimly.

'And you're sure no one's come after you? No one's followed you?' Malakhi asked Rahab.

'Or, more to the point, no one's noticed you've gone,' said Lamech.

Lia nudged Rahab hard in the ribs. 'Remember?' she whispered. 'What I overheard at the Aude Gate. About my being "abducted"?'

Rahab tried to remember. But the events of that night remained veiled in a cloudy blur of exhaustion; he could not even recall how they had reached the riverboat.

'You think Jaufré d'Orbiel may . . . may be after the amulets?' he asked uncomfortably.

Malakhi rose to his feet.

'We need to give this matter very careful consideration,' he said. 'Let's not act hastily. We'll review the situation in the morning. You must be tired after your journey. Let us show

162

you to your rooms. Lia, will you go with Selima? Rahab – Bar Talmai will take charge of you.'

'And the amulets?' Rahab's hand hovered.

'I will place them in the Sanctuary for safe-keeping.'

A feeling of deep unease settled over Rahab. He had carried the amulets next to his heart since they left the Gorge. To be separated from them now seemed like . . . like losing a part of himself. He became aware that Bar Talmai was standing, waiting for him. But still he lingered, unwilling to relinquish the amulets.

'Don't worry.' Malakhi said. 'They will be safe in the Sanctuary. Much safer than they ever were in Arcassanne.'

Rahab nodded. He knew he must trust Malakhi. But as he watched the scholar wrap the amulets in silk with reverent fingers he felt a sense of rising disquiet, of disorientation . . .

He reached out towards Malakhi, wanting, needing to keep hold of the Barakiel amulet – no, *his* amulet, it was a part of him now; without it he felt incomplete.

'Come,' said a light, clear voice behind him.

Rahab turned and saw Bar Talmai patiently standing waiting in the soft light. Behind him Selima was snuffling out the candles, one by one, murmuring the words of the evening prayer.

Seeing the pattern of light and shadow on Bar Talmai's face, hearing the familiar murmured words, Rahab blinked, cast back years without number to his house in Galicys, remembering his mother extinguishing the evening candles whilst his father patiently watched her with the same scholarly stillness and intensity he saw now in Bar Talmai. If Shaoni had grown to manhood, he would be about the same age as this young scholar. Could Talmai be . . .? For one moment Rahab found himself wondering, wishing . . . and then put the thought firmly from his mind. What was the point in wishing? He would never find Shaoni now. Shaoni was dead.

'Your room is next to mine. East-facing. The sun will wake you early.'

Rahab yawned, stretching.

'Don't worry – nothing will wake me!'

CHAPTER 16

The moon was climbing high in the black sky as Berengar rode Arbutus slowly back through the vineyards towards the walls of Arcassanne. Towers and turrets glimmered, white shadows against the darkness of the night. Arcassanne looked as insubstantial as a city in a *conte des fées*, confected from phantasms and spidersilk shadows.

He had stayed longer at Belcastel than he had intended. After an uninterrupted night's sleep – his first in days – he had put aside his fine Arcassanne wool jacket and gone out to help salvage the few vine plants that had survived the storm. It had been hard work, muddy work, but it had purged the unpleasant miasma that still lingered in his mind after the firing of the Tsiyonim Quarter.

The city was quiet. Maybe the long-simmering atmosphere of suspicion and hatred had been washed away by the storm rain . . . or maybe it was just a lull as Guillemette and her supporters planned the next stage of their campaign.

Berengar turned Arbutus's head towards the Merchants' Quarter.

He had some explaining to do. He hoped Lia would not be too harsh with him for not sending any word. He hoped she would understand that he had been obliged to fulfil his duty to his estates. He smiled wryly, anticipating that he would not be let off lightly; Lia could be quite as forthright as the Dowager when she saw fit.

Lia.

He could have chosen one of a dozen or so eligible girls from good families in Arcassanne . . . but he had picked Lia because she seemed like . . . like one of his friends. He felt at ease in her company, much as he felt at ease amongst the Hawks. Around Lia he did not have to pretend. But there was also the matter of her dowry. The Belcastel estates desperately needed the Maurys' money. Gran'mère might insist on preserving the purity of the bloodline ... but she had not looked at the ledgers in years. Thibaud had confirmed his worst suspicions. The family fortunes were badly depleted. Berengar would have to sell the estates to keep the mansion in Arcassanne – or sell the Arcassanne mansion. Years of poor harvests had emptied the family coffers. He had not mentioned it to Gran'mère because he knew only too well what her response would be: 'Increase the tithes! Make the tenant farmers pay! Why should they receive charity from us? We're not a charitable institution!'

As Arbutus plodded wearily up the lane, Berengar noticed that there were no lights burning outside the Auger mansion. Unusual. It was not over-late to be calling. As he drew closer, it became evident that there were no lights lit inside either, no patterned glow of lamplight and shadow spilling out on to the cobbles.

Dismounting, he went to knock at the door – and hesitated, seeing in the moonlight the signs of forced entry, splintered timbers hastily patched up.

Had there been a robbery? He lifted the metal door-knocker and rapped hard.

There was no reply. He tried again.

This time he thought he could glimpse a snail-trail of light inside, trembling tentatively closer. Emmenza's voice, muffled by the door, asked, 'Who – who's there?'

'It's Berengar,' he said.

'H-how can I be sure you're who you say you are?' came back Emmenza's quavering reply.

The household must have been attacked by robbers. What else would have caused Emmenza to be so suspicious? Berengar took off his signet ring and held it up to the keyhole so that she could see the Belcastel crest.

'Oh, Lord Berengar, it *is* you!'

He heard her pulling back bolts and turning keys, and moments later she opened the door a crack. Even in the moonlight he could see that her face was wan and puffy with weeping.

'How's your mistress, Emmenza?' he asked, alarmed. 'What's happened here?'

'Sieur, sieur ...' Emmenza started to weep. 'You'd better come in.'

'Tell me what's happened.'

165

It took several minutes of patient questioning and reassurance to coax the facts out of the old woman. And even when he began to make sense of what had happened, none of it seemed to add up.

'So Captain Orbiel arrested my p-poor mistress and I haven't seen her since –'

'But had Dame Maury ever told the Captain that she was Tsiyonim?' Berengar said, frowning.

'No, not that I recall . . .' Emmenza shook her head. 'No one knew.'

No one but the notary and Jaufré d'Orbiel. And as the notary had little reason to betray his client's confidence, everything pointed to Jaufré. Anger gripped Berengar. Jaufré was his closest, his oldest friend; he had promised. How could he break his word?

'And Lia? Where is she? With my sister?'

The mere mention of Lia's name set Emmenza sobbing again. Between heaving sobs, he saw she was shaking her head.

'She's not with my sister!' What had possessed him to stay so long at the estate without sending to check what was happening in Arcassanne? 'Where, then? Did Jaufré arrest her too?'

Emmenza, incoherent with grief, shook her head more violently.

'Ab-abducted –'

'What do you mean, abducted?' Berengar asked, bewildered.

'She went to your grandmother's – and your grandmother turned her away. Wouldn't have anything to do with her. Then we heard someone – in our cellar. A – a robber. I went out to get Peire. When I came back – my lamb was gone!' Emmenza said, stuffing her apron into her mouth to try to stifle her anguish.

'Gone!'

'The – Watch sent to your grandmother's. Searched everywhere. The only – clue – a man and a girl – took a riverboat up into the mountains early yesterday –'

'A man? What manner of man?' Berengar demanded. A host of possibilities jostled in his mind, all of them hideous. Lia could have been kidnapped – raped – murdered by now . . .

'Dark. Bearded.'

'Half the men in Arcassanne answer that description,' Berengar said, tugging his fingers through his hair, trying to think. 'And there's been no ransom demand?'

'N-nothing,' wailed Emmenza.

166

Emmenza's weeping was getting on Berengar's nerves. He needed to take action, not to stand helplessly by.

'I'm off to my grandmother's,' he said. 'Send word to me there if you hear any news!'

But outside in the lane, he struck his fist against the wall in frustration.

He did not know what had hurt him the most, Jaufré's betrayal or Lia's disappearance. He knew only that Jaufré had shattered years of trust and friendship in one single ill-judged act.

Arbutus let out a soft whinny of recognition, nuzzling up against his shoulder. Berengar patted the soft nose absently as he reached to untie the reins.

'Home, Arbutus.'

A whole day had passed – and the only person Zillaïs had seen was the gaoler who brought her food and drink. The bread, though stale, proved just about edible when dipped in the watery vegetable soup; there was also some weak-brewed ale in a mug. Zillaïs politely but firmly rejected the ale, asking the gaoler to fetch her some hot boiled water in which to steep some of the herbs Emmenza had sent.

There was nothing to do but pace and fret. No book to read, nothing with which to occupy her hands or her mind. She hoped that camomile and spearmint tea would calm her nerves.

She lay down on the bed and began in her mind to weed and prune her garden, one bed at a time, forcing herself to visualise each plant in turn in vivid detail: feathery fennel leaves, turning from fresh green to brown, verdigris to copper, as the seeds ripened, giving off their strong scent of aniseed in the midday heat, the tiny white stars of the thyme flowers beneath, carpeting the herb bed . . .

When she heard the footsteps outside her cell door, it was a shock to open her eyes and see that the light was fading from the sky.

Keys grated in the lock – and Jaufré d'Orbiel came in, lantern in hand.

'How is Rebh Jehiel?' she asked.

'A little better.' His face looked darkly sallow in the lantern-light; his eyes sunken into shadow-sockets. Was he suffering from some wasting disease? Or was his ravaged appearance the result of his dissolute way of life?

'I should like to check his progress,' she said.

'I'll take you to him.' Yet still he lingered, making no move to leave the cell. Zillaïs felt a flutter of unease. What did he want of her?

'And I wish to see my daughter's betrothed, Berengar de Belcastel.'

'But he may not wish to see you, Dame Maury.'

'Whyever not?'

'Your future son-in-law was far too thorough in his investigations.'

'Berengar?' Zillaïs said, stunned. 'Berengar has found out?'

'His notary traced you to Tolonada. You and your family were said to be dead. Drowned. But we know otherwise.'

She saw again his eyes darken oddly as if a scrim of shadow had been drawn across his face. *We* know. He spoke oddly too, now that they were alone; his voice had a whispering timbre to it that made her senses crawl.

'I and the notary are the only other living souls party to this knowledge. So you need have no worries, Dame Maury. Our silence is assured . . . on one condition.'

'What condition?' Zillaïs said.

'That you give me your Guardian Amulet.'

The words came at her with the force of a blow; she staggered, trying to keep herself upright. Her secret. How could he possibly know?

'Think, Zillaïs . . .' His voice began to penetrate the chaotic tumult of her thoughts, persuasively soft now, sweet as incense smoke. 'The happiness of your daughter, her place at the head of the Belcastel household assured. Would you destroy Lia's future just for the sake of an ancient relic?'

She dug her nails into the palms of her hands.

'I don't know what you're talking about,' she said.

'Oh, come now!' He laughed lazily, fixing her with his dark, drowsy eyes. 'Rebh Jehiel told me the amulet was kept by your family. A sacred trust. A covenant.'

Zillaïs shook her head, forcing a smile.

'Rebh Jehiel is obviously mistaken. He is old, ill, confused –'

'Which amulet was it? Barakiel? Rashiel? Shalgiel?'

She heard herself gasp – and then wished she had not given herself away. But she had never heard a Gentile pronounce the sacred names of the Guardians before. It seemed somehow . . . profane.

168

'Captain Orbiel,' she said, taking control of herself. 'You know the truth of the matter. My family was drowned in the wreck of the ship that was taking us from Tolonada. We lost everything in that wreck. All our possessions. Does that answer your question?'

'Everything,' he repeated flatly. Did he believe her?

'Now, would you be so good as to conduct me to check on the progress of Rebh Jehiel? That was the purpose of your visit, wasn't it?'

Shadowflicker across the hooded eyes watching her ... and then Jaufré bowed and said with cold courtesy, 'Please ... come with me.'

Zillaïs managed to disguise her growing anxiety beneath a front of professional calm as she tended to Rebh Jehiel.

She made great play of examining each little bottle and sachet she had brought, distractedly shaking her head as she replaced it.

'What's taking you so long?' demanded Jaufré d'Orbiel impatiently.

'My tincture of *cenelle*,' she said, feigning confusion. 'Hawthorn berries.'

Knowing she would have need of a distraction, she had contrived to leave it behind in her cell.

'Is it essential?'

'It is most effective for a weak heart.'

He hesitated a moment – and then went outside to tell the guard to go back for the tincture. Whilst he was explaining, Zillaïs leaned close to Rebh Jehiel, whispering, 'You told him about my father's amulet. How *could* you? Now you have put my daughter's life in danger.'

'Your daughter?' The old scholar's eyes flickered open, fixing upon her face. 'You never told me your daughter was involved.'

'How could I tell you, with that man spying on us, watching us all the time?' Zillaïs's fingers knotted themselves in a fold of her gown. 'Even now we can't be sure he isn't spying on us.'

'Then let us carry on our conversation in the old tongue,' he said.

'I – I'm a little rusty in Tsiyonim. It's been so many years.'

'These things you never forget. It'll come back to you.'

She nodded. Outside she could hear Jaufré d'Orbiel remonstrating with the guard.

'You must understand,' Jehiel said in Tsiyonim, speaking slowly, 'that I had no idea you were alive when I told Orbiel about the Guardian Amulets.'

'Orbiel has – no right – to know,' she said haltingly.

'And your daughter's part in this?'

'I – I believe she may have gone to Tifereth. With Rahab ben Chazhael.'

'Ahh,' Jehiel said.

'Remember what you said about Orbiel?'

'Possessed?'

'Could it be a *dybbuk*?'

'Ah. So you sensed it too –'

Jaufré d'Orbiel threw open the door. He was carrying the little bottle of medicinal tincture in his gloved hand; he thrust it impatiently at Zillaïs.

'Idiot of a guard neglected to tell me that he can't read.'

'Thank you, Captain,' Zillaïs said, icily polite.

'I have retired to bed!' came the Dowager's voice from behind the tapestry bed curtains, stiff with affront. 'I will see no one till the morning. Go away!'

Berengar drew in a breath to steady his temper. This was not going to be easy. But he would not let himself be intimidated by the formidable old lady. He was master of the house now.

'I want an explanation, Gran'mère,' he said to the drawn curtains. 'And I won't leave your bedchamber until I have one.'

There came a spluttering sound from within the great curtained bed.

'I do not explain myself to anyone.'

'Do you know what has become of Lia Maury?'

'I neither know,' came back the reply, 'nor care.'

'So you don't deny that you sent her away when she came to you for help?'

'She had no business coming here! She's Tsiyonim.'

'Gran'mère, she's missing. Because you sent her away, she had nowhere to go. Now no one knows where she is. She's disappeared.'

'Good.'

'Good!' He reached for the bed curtains and tugged them open. Within, he saw her sitting glowering at him, a little brocade nightcap covering her sparse white hair. 'She's my betrothed, Gran'mère!'

'H-how dare you!' She clutched her nightgown to her. 'How dare you invade an old woman's privacy!'

'So when did Jaufré d'Orbiel tell you?'

'Orbiel? What are you talking about?

He had no time now for her prevarications.

'How did you find out, Gran'mère? About Lia Maury's family history?'

'It came in a letter, if you must know,' she snapped back.

'And where is the letter?'

She pursed her lips together.

'Who is Lord of Belcastel, Gran'mère?' He had not intended to threaten her – but if she was going to play stubborn, he would have to stand up to her. 'There's a little cottage on the estate. Two rooms. Just the right size for you.'

'You wouldn't dare!' Her bead-black eyes challenged him – but he noticed that her lower lip had begun to tremble. 'You wouldn't send your old grandmother to the country . . . the damp, the cold, the . . . the loneliness.' Tears appeared in her eyes. She had played on his feelings too many times before. Now he knew she was manipulating him. Folding his arms, he turned away from her.

'Bera,' she said in a small, pathetic voice, using his childhood pet-name. 'Dear Bera, you've always been my favourite, you know that . . .'

'I want that letter,' he said, still with his back to her.

He heard her give a fretful little sigh.

'Here. Here you are.' She was fumbling in the front of her nightgown; out from between her shrivelled breasts came the folded paper.

He took it and opened it. He did not recognise the writing; it was not the notary's neat, formal script, so who else could have penned it?

He crushed the paper in his hand.

'She's gone, Bera,' the Dowager said softly. 'Forget her.'

'I made Lia a promise,' Berengar said, rounding on her. 'And a Belcastel does not break his word. Wasn't that what you taught me? Belcastel honour – before all else.' He turned on his heel and went out of her bedchamber, hearing her screeching behind him, 'You're a besotted, lovesick fool, Berengar! You'll regret it!'

'Berengar.' A soft voice from the gallery made him gaze upwards. Alissende stood at the rail, watching him. Her hair was unbound, her face dirty, streaked with tears.

171

'Why didn't you stand by Lia? She was your friend!' he cried.

'I – I wanted to –' Her voice was half-stifled with crying. 'But Gran'mère – she forbade me –'

'So you just stood there, weeping, and let Lia go?'

'And where were you when she needed you?' she cried back. 'Why weren't you here for Lia?'

The accusation stung all the more because it was just.

'Pons! *Pons!*' Berengar turned his back on Alissende, calling for his servant.

Pons appeared in his shirt sleeves.

'Arbutus is spent; give him a good rub-down, will you? And saddle up Tramontan for me.'

'What? Off again, sieur? You've only just got back . . .'

Berengar was not easily provoked to anger; he was known in the Hawks for his affable, easy-going nature.

But now he was charged, vibrant with fury.

Lia was *his* choice, *his* bride-to-be. It was of little importance to him that her mother was Tsiyonim; he was not marrying Zillaïs! Yet to hear Gran'mère rant, anyone would think he had decided to convert to the Tsiyonim faith himself.

He gazed back at the storm-shredded Belcastel pennants, still fluttering bravely in the night breeze.

Azure and argent: the colours of purity and honour. He swung away, sick at heart. What honour was there in a family that turned its back on a plea for help?

'I'll find you, Lia,' he whispered.

The stained-glass windows in Jaufré d'Orbiel's turret room were open to the stars.

Berengar had come running up the stairs – but now he stopped in the doorway, staring.

On the tiled floor, Jaufré had drawn a star; a black candle was placed at each of its five points. Jaufré, dressed in a long, loose robe, stood, his back to the door, at the centre of the pentagram, holding an open book . . .

As Berengar drew nearer he heard Jaufré reading aloud from the book.

'*Barakiel . . .*'

Incense fumes issued from a silver burner in serpentine wisps; the dusty, acrid spice irritated the back of Berengar's throat.

'Rashiel . . .'

Were they names? Pronounced in Jaufré's deep, hoarse voice they sounded to Berengar like some maleficent invocation.

'Shalgiel . . .'

Berengar began to cough.

'In God's name, Jaufré, what are you playing at?'

The glowing incense grains sputtered in the silver burner.

'This is magic, Berengar. Tsiyonim magic.'

Berengar's rehearsed speech of accusation vanished from his mind.

'B-but if you use a Tsiyonim occult book, that makes you as culpable as they –'

'Culpable?' Jaufré wheeled around, the hem of his robe setting the candle flames wildly guttering. 'This is proof that one of the Tsiyonim conjured up that storm.'

'Proof?' Berengar repeated automatically, shocked by Jaufré's haggard appearance. What was happening to his friend? Maybe it was the guttering incense smoke – but Jaufré's face looked drawn and gaunt and his sunken eyes were hazed with shadows.

'Did you know the Tsiyonim were once protected by Guardian Spirits, Winged Guardians whom they could unleash to subdue their enemies? Did you know that?' Jaufré hooked one arm around Berengar's neck, pulling his face close to his own. Warm, poppy-fumed breath made Berengar blink; what had Jaufré been drinking?

'But that's just an old legend. No one believes it.'

'Unimaginable elemental powers. Earthquake. Blizzard. *Lightning.*'

Berengar began to laugh; forced laughter, hoping to humour Jaufré out of this bizarre mood.

'If they can call on such terrifying elemental powers, why haven't they used them before?'

'Because they lost the sacred amulets that linked them to the Winged Guardians. Divided them up for safe-keeping.'

'And you're saying if these pieces were put back together, the Tsiyonim could destroy us with one of these . . . Winged Guardians?'

'With these amulets a man could control the world,' Jaufré said, gazing past Berengar to the starlit sky beyond.

'But – magic?'

'"*Blood of the pure, blood of the innocent* . . ."' Jaufré read aloud from the book. 'The ritual won't work without blood sacrifice. You saw the ritual cuts slashed into that child's body.'

Yes; Berengar remembered the gaping wounds marring the white skin, silent mouths crying for vengeance. He still felt a ripple of nausea deep in his belly at the memory. Yet . . . something did not make sense here. He knew he was not quick at reasoning . . . but even he could see the flaw in Jaufré's argument.

'If,' he said slowly, 'if the child was killed to summon the storm . . . why did the storm happen days after the murder?'

Jaufré looked up at him from the open book. Berengar met his eyes; for a moment he was plunged back into the desert night of Djihan-Djihar, trudging over endless dunes of black sand beneath a starless sky . . . Blinking, he shook his head to clear the clinging darkness from his mind.

'Jaufré!' he whispered. He gripped hold of Jaufré by the shoulders. 'What's happening to you?'

Jaufré suddenly sagged, as though drained of strength.

'Very . . . tired, Bera . . .' he said. 'Not sleeping well . . .'

'Easy, there, easy.' Berengar helped him into his chair and took the book from his hands. It felt distinctly unpleasant to the touch: warm, almost greasy, like ill-washed human skin . . . Berengar hastily dropped it. Once it was out of his hands, he turned on the incense burners, the black candles, and kicked them over, extinguishing them. He stamped on the five-pointed star, rubbing out the marks with his foot.

'It's no good, you know . . .' Jaufré said faintly in the starlit darkness. 'Nothing you do can alter it now. What's done . . . is done . . .'

Berengar had found the tinder box and was trying to kindle a spark to light the lamps. At last he succeeded, and the gentler glow of the oil-lamp illuminated the turret room. He brought it close to Jaufré – who turned his face away from the light as if it hurt his eyes.

'Why?' Berengar demanded. 'Why did you do it, Jaufré? Why did you tell Gran'mère about Lia?'

'For your own good, Bera . . .' Jaufré's voice seemed to come from a long distance away.

'And what gave you the right to be arbiter?'

'To save you heartache . . .'

'What do you think I'm feeling right now? Now that she's disappeared?'

Jaufré opened one eye.

'Disappeared?'

'Thanks to your interference, Gran'mère turned Lia out. She was last seen going upriver – with a man.'

A shadow of laughter flickered across Jaufré's face.

'So she's jilted you.'

'And if she's been abducted?' Berengar said, choked by anger.

'You're going upriver after her?'

'I have to know what's become of her. I don't know how long it will take . . . days, weeks maybe . . . so I want you to release me from the Hawks, Jaufré.'

'Release you?' Jaufré said, straightening up, alert again. 'A simple leave of absence would cover your time away. You surely don't mean to resign your commission? Not after all the years we've served together?'

Berengar studied the tiled floor. It was difficult to ignore Jaufré's plea, especially when it was spoken so simply, so movingly. They had been friends, companions-in-arms, for so long . . . 'I'm needed on the estate. I've shirked my responsibilities long enough. It's time I earned my title, Jaufré.'

There was a silence.

'Lia Maury,' Jaufré said, so softly Berengar hardly caught the words. 'Ithamar's granddaughter . . .' He looked up. 'Abducted, you say?' His eyes glittered in the darkness, bright as painted enamel. 'What d'you say to taking a small detachment of the Hawks upriver to catch this abductor?'

'B-but what about the unrest here?' Berengar could scarcely believe what he was hearing.

'I can spare a few Hawks to help an old friend. Go after her, Bera.'

'Th-thank you.' Berengar swallowed back his anger. Maybe he had been too hasty in threatening his resignation.

'Take Arnault and the men from the west quarter; things are quiet there. But be careful.' Jaufré put his hands on Berengar's shoulders. 'We may not be dealing with the Djihari here – but there've been rumours of brigands attacking travellers beyond the Gorge.'

'Brigands?' Berengar said, dismayed. 'You don't think that Lia –'

'You go rouse Arnault,' Jaufré said, releasing him. 'I'll go to the Comte. You'll need a signed authorisation.'

175

Berengar turned to go – and then swung back, gripping Jaufré's hand warmly in his own. He had been wrong to doubt Jaufré's sincerity, and he was ashamed of it.

'Thanks, Jaufré,' he said.

'Take care,' Jaufré said.

Jaufré stood watching from the window until Berengar had untied Tramontan and disappeared from sight.

Then he went to his desk and scribbled a few lines to 'Arnault Bazanet at the House of the Golden Bee':

Accompany Lieutenant de Belcastel into the mountains. But keep me informed of your whereabouts at all times.

Orbiel

CHAPTER 17

Bright sunlight woke Lia.

'Mm . . . not yet, Emmenza,' she murmured, turning over. The bed seemed so much harder, narrower than usual. And why did every bone in her body ache so?

She opened her eyes. For one moment, she lay unmoving in the column of mote-speckled sunlight, staring at the unfamiliar rough-stone walls. And then, hearing the clucking of the chickens outside the window, the bleating of goats, she remembered.

She was in Tifereth.

She struggled out of the narrow wooden bed and went over to the little window, wincing with each step. Even the slightest movement was an agony; she was stiff all over.

The window was set deep in the thick stone wall and she had to stand on tiptoe, leaning on the stone ledge, to see out.

Brown hens pecked and chattered in the gravel below her window. A little girl, barefoot, was trying to guide white ducks towards a pond with a stick. Goats were nibbling the sparse grass. The yard was more like a farmyard than the inner courtyard of a college. How could the scholars study with all this clamour?

She limped back across the bare boards and sat down to examine her feet. Blisters had rubbed and broken, leaving raw red weals on her heels and toes. She sucked in her breath as she tried to touch the tender places. If only she could remember the herbs her mother used to make a soothing foot-bath . . .

Mother.

She would not allow herself to admit how much she missed Zillaïs.

She would ask Selima if she had any salves for blistered feet.

But first she would have to find Selima.

She picked up her worn shoes, wondering how she could squeeze her sore, swollen feet into them. Gingerly, she tried to ease the right one on.

No. She would rather go barefoot than rub the little remaining skin from the blisters. She picked up the shoes and slowly, painfully set out to locate Selima.

Rahab had – out of habit – been up since sunrise. He had washed, eaten delicious fresh-baked bread and fruit from Elon's orchard . . . and now he did not know what to do with himself. Picking up the irresistible scent of frying onions, he sniffed his way down the winding passageways and found the kitchen, where Selima was busy chopping vegetables. A little girl of five or six years sat at her feet, happily engrossed in making patterns with the peelings.

'Where's Malakhi?' he asked Selima.

'In council.' She stopped to rub her cheek with her knuckle. 'With the Elders.'

'I see.' Rahab nodded, absently picking up a chunk of carrot and nibbling it. 'In council' meant that he and the amulets were the subject under discussion. The very thought of it made him uneasy.

Selima darted to and fro between the chopping board and stirring the vegetables in the soup pot. Watching her work reminded him suddenly, vividly, of Chadassah in the kitchen in Arcassanne, the little girls kneeling up at the table beside her, playing at being bakers with lumps of dough.

The memory brought tears to his eyes . . . though it could have been the pungent juice of the onions . . .

'Do you need any help?' he asked, wanting something to do.

Selima smiled up at him, expertly chopping the carrots into thin slivers.

'You could go fetch me some herbs. I need thyme, marjoram and basil for the soup. Oh – and some parsley.'

'Where's the herb garden?'

'Outside, beyond Elon's orchard. You'll find Talmai there. If you lose the way, one of the children will show you. Ask my boy Laban.'

Rahab set out to find Elon's orchard. Beyond the crumbling walls on the western side of the castel he spotted a cluster of trees, their branches laden with fruit: russet apples, purple plums and late peaches. As he came nearer he saw a man busy with a hoe at the far end of the orchard.

'Is this the herb garden?' he called.

The man turned and Rahab saw that it was the young scholar Bar Talmai.

'Selima's sent me to fetch some herbs.'

Talmai beckoned him closer.

'Be careful where you tread. The wasps are busy amongst the windfalls.'

Rahab made his way through the rough grass between the rows of trees; the air was noisy with buzzing wasps and flies, gorging themselves on the rotting fruit.

Talmai stood, leaning on his hoe, watching Rahab.

'So what does Selima want today?' he asked.

Rahab counted the list off on his fingers.

'Help yourself,' said Talmai, returning to his hoeing.

Rahab hesitated.

'I know quite a bit about tailoring,' he said, feeling foolish, 'but when it comes to herbs . . .'

Talmai laid down the hoe, and without comment went to pick the herbs for him. 'Here,' he said, holding out a bunch of aromatic green leaves, still wet with dew. As he handed them over, his clear gaze locked with Rahab's.

'How do you like Tifereth?'

Rahab gave a small, noncommittal shrug of the shoulders.

'It's . . . different from what I expected.'

'Oh?' Talmai said, still regarding him intently. 'In what way different?'

'It's – it's too quiet up here, for a start.' Rahab said. Talmai's scrutiny was making him feel awkward. 'Except for the whine of the wind. Doesn't that get on your nerves after a while? There's nothing here between you and the sky. I'm city-born. I like the noise of the city, the clatter of carts, the street cries, the bustle. The feel of cobbles under the feet. It centres you.'

Talmai was quiet for a few moments, and Rahab wondered if the conversation was at an end. But then Talmai suddenly turned to him and said, 'Barakiel is still with you.'

Rahab felt his eyes narrow, frowning. Till that moment all he had been aware of was the green, earthy fragrance of the herbs, the brilliance of the morning sun, burning off the heavy dew. Now a seed of disquiet stirred, deep inside him.

'I can sense His presence.'

'What do you mean?' Rahab found his voice.

'How do you feel?'

'Me?' Rahab was caught off-guard by the directness of the

179

question. 'A little shaky still . . . like when I'd had the quinsy. I was nine, maybe ten. When the fever dropped and I tried to get out of bed, my legs were so weak I fell over. Even seven days later I was staggering round in a daze. That's how I feel now,' he ended lamely.

Talmai looked shocked.

'You have been touched by the power of the Covenant,' he said sternly, 'and that's the only way you can describe it? The aftermath of a childhood illness?'

'It's an honest answer,' Rahab said, stung by the young scholar's sanctimonious attitude. What did Talmai know, sheltered up here from the dangers of life in Arcassanne? 'What did you want me to say?'

'But what was it like? When the Guardian took you?'

Rahab opened his mouth and then found he did not know how to give an honest answer. How did you put such an experience into everyday speech?

'It was like – like nothing else that has ever happened to me. Terrifying. Yet exhilarating.'

Talmai said nothing. When Rahab glanced up at him, he saw that the scholar was staring out across the valley.

'How old are you?' Rahab asked, seized with a sudden, strange apprehension.

Talmai glanced up.

'How old? Is my age relevant?'

'I . . . I just wondered how you came to be here. At Tifereth.'

Talmai looked away, as though unwilling to elaborate.

'I don't know how old I am. Malakhi . . . found me. I was six, maybe seven years. Wandering. Starving. Abandoned. I have no memory of what was before.'

'Wandering?' Rahab said, his throat tightening. 'Wandering where?'

'On the road from Galicys.'

Galicys. The sky seemed to spin. Could . . . could Talmai be . . .?

'And you remember nothing? Not even your name?'

Talmai shook his head.

'Malakhi has been a father to me. He gave me my life back. He gave me my name. Before him . . . nothing. I remember nothing.'

Now Rahab could not stop staring at Talmai, trying to match the tall, ascetic young man who stood before him with his hazy memories of a hot, stickly little hand clutched in his own, a tangle of tousled golden curls . . .

'So now you must be, say, eighteen, nineteen years?'

'Why does my age matter?'

'I lost a brother in Galicys.' The constriction in Rahab's throat was so great he could hardly whisper the words. 'He would have been about your age.'

The clear eyes clouded.

'There were many children orphaned in Galicys.' Talmai's voice sounded distinctly hostile.

'Our father's name was Chazhael; he was a scholar. Our mother's name was Ariel.'

Talmai stared blankly at him.

'We lived next to the *shul* in the Street of Blue Fishes. There was a mosaic on the wall; chips of blue and green pottery set in white plaster. Shaoni used to like to count the fishes. Whenever we went past we had to wait whilst he counted; there were nine but sometimes he insisted there were ten . . .' Rahab's voice died away. It was as if he was talking to himself; Talmai was not paying attention, his eyes had fixed on a buzzard wheeling high above the ravine.

Rahab felt bruised, angry. Why had he revealed so much of himself to this austere young stranger? Even now, years later, just saying his parents' names aloud was difficult. Maybe it was too much of a coincidence that after all this time he should find his lost brother, waiting for him here in Tifereth . . .

The fresh smell of the herbs reminded him of the reason for his coming; without realising, he had been crushing them in his hands. 'Selima will be needing these,' he said. He wanted to put some distance between himself and Talmai. 'I'd best take them to her.'

Talmai gave a little shrug and picked up his hoe.

As Rahab strode away, he heard the chip of the metal biting into the stony earth.

'You walked all the way from the Gorge in *these*?' Selima held up Lia's battered, blood-stained satin shoes in horror. 'These are shoes for dancing – not for walking!'

'There wasn't time to go back and change,' said Lia wryly.

Selima shook her head as she examined the torn soles.

'You won't be walking far today with those blisters . . . or tomorrow. But feet heal quickly – if you bathe them regularly.

You can help yourself to hot water and salt from the crock in the corner.'

Lia nodded her thanks.

'No matter as it's *shabbath* tomorrow evening; no one will be going anywhere,' Selima said, wiping her hands. 'Still, you could polish the *besamim* box; I was going to get one of the girls to do it, but it's a fiddly job.'

'The *besa* – excuse me?' Lia had no idea what Selima was talking about. And when the older woman brought out a little tower of intricately crafted silver and placed it before her with a cloth, she sat staring at it, baffled.

Selima had said polish it – so she began to rub the cloth over its tiny pinnacles, and a wonderful gingery-cinnamon smell spiced the air. She stopped to sniff. It reminded her of going on board her father's barque just after it had returned from overseas: dustily, richly aromatic, redolent of the strangeness of distant countries.

'What's inside?'

'Spices.' Selima was busy chopping vegetables again.

'A spice-shaker? Like a salt-shaker?'

Selima stopped chopping.

'You mean – your mother never taught you?'

There was such incredulity in her voice that Lia felt rebuked. Defensively, she snapped back, 'It was difficult for us in Arcassanne. You have no idea how difficult.'

'Difficult? It's always been difficult for us.' Selima turned back to her preparations. 'But what kind of a mother doesn't teach her daughter about *shabbath*?'

Lia put down the cloth. She wanted to shout out, 'It wasn't her fault. She's a good mother. She did what she could.' What was she doing defending her mother? It was Zillaïs's desire for secrecy, for concealment, that had caused all this mess. It was Zillaïs who had kept the truth of her heritage from her. Now nobody wanted her, neither the Gentiles, with whom she had grown up – nor the Tsiyonim, her blood-kin.

CHAPTER 18

All day the Elders of Tifereth had sat in council behind closed doors. Rahab waited to be summoned . . . but no summons came. He wandered around the grassy college courtyard, not knowing how best to occupy his time. He even offered to help with the livestock – but the girls busy milking the goats laughed and shooed him away.

'She was looking for you,' they said, with meaningful glances.

'Who was?'

'Your *shiksa*. Lia,' they said, giggling.

'You're not to call her *shiksa*.' Rahab glared at them. 'She's Tsiyonim.'

'But she doesn't know anything.'

'And that's your business?' he said.

The tallest of the girls gave a little sniff, wrinkling her freckled nose at him. Michal would have answered him back – but this girl was not family.

'We won't tell you where to find her, then.'

'As you wish.'

He walked on, hearing them whispering together – and another burst of giggling erupted as he reached the gate.

His. They had called Lia 'his' *shiksa*. He felt his face suddenly burning. Silly girls. What did they know? What would he want with Lia, anyway, wilful, indulged rich girl that she was? Or more to the point, what would she want with him?

He found Lia sitting on a boulder, chin resting on her hand, gazing out over the lilac-shadowed valley. The red fire of sunset had softened the rough stones of the castel to rose and gold. The air was sweet with the smell of woodsmoke and wild thyme.

'It's nearly time for supper.'

'I'm not hungry.'

'You! Not hungry?' he said, gently teasing.

183

'It's no use,' she said. 'I don't belong. I'll never belong. Not up here – nor down there.' She gestured out over the valley towards the distant river plain, hidden from sight by the blue haze of evening.

He sat down beside her on the cropped grass.

'Watch where you sit, the goats have been busy round here,' she said, offhandedly.

'Busy?' He leapt up again, hastily checking the grass beneath for goat-droppings, brushing off his clothes. 'You could belong here if you wanted. We would teach you.'

'Oh yes?' She looked at him, lips twisting in a wry, self-deprecating smile. 'That'd be a good joke, wouldn't it?'

'No one means to make fun of you.'

'But it's still funny, isn't it, the Gentile girl who dosen't know what to do?'

'You mustn't be so . . . sensitive.'

'That's easy for you to say!'

'Lia,' Rahab said, serious this time, 'if you're to acknowledge your Tsiyonim heritage, you can't afford to be sensitive. Down there in Arcassanne, we're the odd ones out, the butt of jokes and ridicule. It's no different anywhere else. We're the chosen people who lost their way, lost their country, lost their right to divine protection. We're losers. We're bad luck.'

'You were losers,' she said, turning to gaze at him, 'until you brought the amulet to my house.'

The audacity of her suggestion shocked him.

'We can't use the amulets every time someone insults us, puts us down!'

'You can use them as a threat. As a deterrent.'

Even though her face was half in shadow now, he could see that she was in deadly earnest.

'Use them as if they were weapons?' he said.

'Isn't that what they are?'

He was silent then, knowing that what she said was true.

They had lit the lamps in the council chamber. Rahab, drowsy with the mountain air and the after-effects of a good supper, was trying to keep his drooping lids from closing. Lia sat beside him, hands demurely folded in her lap.

He could hear Malakhi addressing the Elders, and the drone of his voice was pleasantly restful . . . until he caught his own name and jerked awake.

184

'But there are things of which you, Rahab, are not aware. Hidden things, known only to the scholars. You see,' and Malakhi hesitated, 'we had to be certain that you were telling us the truth.'

Telling the truth? 'Now wait a –'

'I'm not casting doubts on your integrity, Rahab.' Malakhi turned his brown eyes on him, warm as amber in the lamplight. 'But you could have been decoys. Unwitting decoys, marking out a trail for our enemies to follow.'

Rahab sensed that Lia had turned to look at him. He did not want to meet her eyes.

'We're not impregnable up here. We've enough food and water to survive a lengthy siege – but we have no fighting force, we are vulnerable to attack.'

'But who would attack you?' Rahab burst out.

'That's where we hoped you might enlighten us,' said Elon.

'Show them,' said old Lamech. 'Go on – show them.'

Malakhi placed a casket on the table in front of Rahab. It was of a dull, dark metal, unadorned except for one carved symbol on the lid: the letter *daleth*, which also means the number four.

'Open it, Rahab.'

Even before Rahab had touched the casket, he felt a filament of cold fire flicker through his mind.

Inside, cushioned on silk, lay the Barakiel amulet – and beside it he saw the fiery gleam of Zillaïs's Rashiel amulet. But what made his fingers start to tremble violently was the unmistakable enamelled glint of a third amulet, white and blue, brilliant as sun on fresh snow.

'Three?' he said hoarsely.

'Shalgiel,' said Malakhi.

'Then – only one is needed to make –'

'Only one more,' Malakhi said, closing the casket lid, 'and that one, God forbid we should find it, is Lailahel.'

'Don't say that name aloud!' hissed old Lamech, making the sign against evil.

'Will someone explain to me what all this means?' came Lia's clear voice in the silence.

'The Guardian Warders in ancient days were chosen for their purity of soul, their strength of character. The Guardians feed on the strengths – or the weaknesses – of their Warders.'

'But what did they guard?' Lia persisted. Rahab stole a glance at her and saw that her forehead was furrowed with the effort of trying to understand.

'Your mother did not teach you, then?' Malakhi said. There was no censure in his voice, only sadness.

Rahab saw the Elders glance questioningly from one to the other; he wondered if they would deign to answer an uninitiated girl. But after Malakhi had consulted the others with a look, he turned to Lia.

'They were created to guard the Books of Holy Law in the Temple in Tsiyon, one for each of the four Gates: North, South, East and West. They were tokens of the sacred covenant between the Lord our God, the God of Itshak and Ibrahil, and the Tsiyonim, proof that we were the chosen people. You have already witnessed the elemental power of Barakiel. You have heard the story of Rashiel and the destruction of Tolonada. But imagine the devastation that could be wrought if all four Guardians were summoned at once. Lightning, Blizzard, Earthquake – and Eternal Night.'

'So Lailahel is the Bringer of Eternal Night?' said Lia.

'Eternal Night,' Malakhi said softly, 'or the extinction of all life. The final darkness.'

'The end of the world,' said Lamech, shaking his white head.

'But – why was such a terrible thing ever forged? What was its purpose? Why has no one destroyed it?' Lia asked.

'You have never read the writings of Alevi the Prophet?'

Rahab hoped Lamech would not challenge him to quote from the Book of Alevi. His brief studies with Jehiel had been constantly interrupted by the demands of the workroom. And, he had to admit, he had not been the most dedicated of Jehiel's students. But Lamech raised one hand and began to recite in a hoarse, harsh voice, '"Let he who summons my servant Lailahel in vain, beware. Let he who has ward of the Western Gate be chosen for the purity of his spirit. For Lailahel feeds on the evil in men's souls and His darkness is the darkness of evil and despair. In the shadow of His wings, all but the pure in heart shall lose hope, all shall perish –"'

'Someone must have primed the amulets,' broke in Elon. 'Someone must have woken the Guardians. Rahab – was it you?'

Suddenly all ten Elders were looking at him. Mortified, Rahab could only stutter an incoherent reply.

'Primed? I – I don't understand –'

'What Elon means is that there are ritual words to be spoken to awaken the Guardians. Words known only to the initiate.'

'Words misused, mistranslated into the common tongue in that so-called *Sefer Rhaziel*,' spluttered Lamech. 'Words that should never be spoken by the uninitiate.'

'How can words – mere words – hold so much power?' Lia asked.

Rahab held his breath. This time she had ventured too far. He would never have dared to question the scholars. Yet at the same time he also felt a certain grudging admiration.

'Young woman,' Elon said sternly, 'how can you ask such a question? You admit you have had no instruction in our faith or our language. The word is sacred to us. The power of the word is supreme. Was not the first *golem* given life by the power of the mystic word?'

'But the girl is right . . . in a way,' said Lamech, pensively pulling at his thin wisps of bread. 'Whoever primed the amulets must have performed some kind of ritual.'

'But if it wasn't me or Lia's mother . . .' Rahab tried to cast his mind back to Arcassanne. But his memory was still shrouded in cloud; he still could not remember anything clearly.

'Maybe Rebh Jehiel,' Malakhi suggested.

'Then why didn't he tell me what he had done?'

Silence fell as the Elders looked from one to the other, each seemingly unwilling to speak first. Eventually Malakhi sighed.

'The Guardians are powerful spirits,' he said. 'Even if they are summoned by a wise man, a good man, they may yet overwhelm him.'

In the silence that fell again in the chamber, Rahab could hear the wind sighing outside, a soft, eerie whisper. An elemental music, raw and wild, untamed, unshaped by man. A whispered echo of the force of the swift-moving stormwind, the stormspirit that Talmai had told him was still a part of him. He wanted to ask, 'Overwhelm? What does that mean? Will that happen to me?' but he did not dare disturb the Elders' deliberations.

'We are all agreed on one point, at least,' Malakhi said at length. 'Our fellow Tsiyonim in Arcassanne have asked for our help. So we have written an open letter to Comte Aymon.'

'It was my idea.' Lamech took up the letter from the table and brandished it triumphantly. 'We inform the Comte that if he will set them free, we will shelter them here in Tifereth.'

'And if he won't let them free? What about this charge of child sacrifice?' Elon said, peppery brows drawn together.

'Surely he'll accept the Tsiyonim land and houses in exchange for safe passage?'

'That's not Elon's point,' said Malakhi. 'He's talking of justice.'

'Why should they take the blame for a crime they haven't committed?' Elon said sternly. 'Why should they perpetuate the myth of the blood sacrilege?'

'Surely it doesn't matter as long as they are safe?' Rahab heard himself saying. Pent-up words began to pour out of him in a torrent. 'We mustn't let it be another Galicys. I lost my parents, my brother, everyone I knew and loved in that massacre. I have never forgotten that terrible night. Never. And I won't let it happen to Schimeon and his family!' He stopped, shuddering – and realised that they were all staring at him again.

'Galicys,' Malakhi said quietly. He put out his hand and let it rest on Rahab's shoulder. Rahab sat, mute now, feeling the shudders of memory gradually die away. 'Later, when there is more time, you will tell me about Galicys.'

Rahab, choked with emotion, could only nod his head. The other Elders were murmuring together, their eyes flickering towards Rahab and away again. He felt his face burning under their scrutiny. And then – to his amazement – the solemn, learned faces beneath the curling white beards suddenly crinkled up and they began to chuckle with laughter.

'Why? What's so funny?' he asked, still smarting.

'Now we understand why Barakiel ch-chose you!' Lamech said, wiping his eyes. 'There's a tempest of a temper hiding behind your mild, meek manner, Rahab the Tailor. All these years you've been carrying that anger around with you. I'd love to have seen that storm over Arcassanne.'

'You're saying that I –' Rahab looked up, anguished, at Malakhi. 'But I – the storm – flattened the harvest. It was – out of control.' And Talmai had said Barakiel was still with him. What further damage was he capable of inflicting?

Malakhi kept his hand on Rahab's shoulder. The firm pressure centred him.

'So who will take the letter to Arcassanne?' asked Lia.

'I'm still not happy about this, Malakhi, not happy at all,' Elon said, shaking his grizzled head. 'We've gone to such trouble to keep this place secret. Now we're saying to Aymon, "Here we are, come and get us."'

'We've been over this ground again and again. There is no other solution. Other than to ignore our people's cry for help. You've heard from Rahab how dangerous Arcassanne has become.' Malakhi tightened his grip on Rahab's shoulder. 'If the crowd turn against our people again – how shall we live with our consciences? Knowing we had the chance to save them – and ignored it?'

'We're out of Aymon's territory,' argued Lamech. 'If he sends a force against us, he'll have to answer to Maureil of Foix.'

'Ha!' Elon said dismissively. 'And what makes you think Maureil is more likely to honour his agreement with us than any other Gentile? The mountain air has softened your wits, Lamech.'

'Let me deliver the letter,' Lia said over the bickering.

'You can't go back!' Rahab said. 'They'll arrest you.'

'I don't really belong here, Rahab, you know that.'

'You've only been here a day.' He could see the unhappiness in her eyes – and now he felt ashamed of his earlier feelings of exasperation. He wanted to make things better for her, but he had no idea how to begin. 'Give it time.'

'We'll send the letter by courier on the riverboat,' Malakhi said, intervening. 'Talmai will deliver it tomorrow when he takes the fruit and eggs to market.'

'So you're a tailor, young man?'

Rahab still sat at the table, lost in a mist of bitter thoughts; startled, he looked up to see Lamech watching him.

'I propose a trade of skills here. You want to know more about your Guardian . . . and I'm sorely in need of a little stitchery.'

'Show me,' said Rahab, grateful to be recalled to normal, mundane tasks.

'My eyesight isn't what it was . . . and besides, I'm no use with a needle. Selima's so busy in the kitchen, I don't like to bother her.' Lamech shuffled out of his coat and held it out for Rahab to inspect.

It was far more worn, more threadbare than Rebh Jehiel's beloved coat which he had repaired in Arcassanne. Shreds of faded silk lining clung to the seams. Moths had nibbled holes along the hem and cuffs.

'Well?' enquired Lamech hopefully.

189

He could take a strip off the hem and use it to patch. If only he had brought the tools of his trade with him . . .

'I'll do what I can. But I'll need needles, thread, shears that can cut.'

'Mind you make a good job of it; I've had that coat twenty years and I've never seen another I liked better.'

Scholars. Rahab raised his eyes to the ceiling. Twenty years! No wonder the coat was so threadbare. Yet he could not refuse; and though more decrepit, more eccentric, Lamech reminded him of Rebh Jehiel. In serving Lamech, he felt he could in some intangible way repay a little of his debt to his old teacher.

'Now to my part of the transaction.' Lamech raised one bony finger, twisted by rheumatism, and beckoned. Rahab gathered up the coat and followed.

The room to which he led Rahab was filled from floor to ceiling with books and scrolls. The scholars had put up linen blinds to keep the blinding summer sun from spoiling their precious texts, and the room was dim, lit only by a couple of suspended lamps. Rahab sniffed the air. He knew that dusty smell of ink and parchment; it tossed him back to Jehiel's study, and further back again, through the distant years, to childhood and his father Chazael's booklined room.

Suddenly he had shrunk in height; he was straining on tiptoe to look at the open book his father was working on, with its jewel-bright illuminated letters in gold and scarlet and blue, fingers itching to touch the gleaming gold leaf . . .

'Will you let me do the gold leaf?' the child Rahab asked his father. 'Please, please say yes –'

'All in good time,' his father said, laughing. 'First you must learn to read the letters. No running before you can walk!'

But Rahab had barely learned to read when Galicys erupted into madness and all his father's skills as scholar and scribe were lost forever –

'Now where did I put that Tolonadan *Sefer Bahir*, mm?'

The memory blurred in a sudden film of tears; Rahab hastily blinked the past away. Lamech was muttering to himself as he peered his way along a shelf of books. To Rahab's relief he had not even noticed his moment of weakness.

Books lay open on the tables; pages yellow with age. Annotations had been made on the black text, additions and alterations marked in red and blue ink.

'Here it is!' Lamech's cry of triumph ended in a catarrhal wheeze as he staggered under the weight of a great leather-bound volume. Rahab hurried to take the book from him and put it on the table.

'Thank you, young man.' Lamech groped for the eyeglass which lay nearby, and leaning over the book, began to thumb through the ragged vellum pages.

'What is this book?' Rahab asked.

'The *Sefer Bahir*, the Book of Brightness. I brought this out of the destruction of Tolonada, I rescued it from the flames of the College library.' Lamech paused, shaking his head. 'That's why the pages are a little singed, see?'

Rahab leaned over the old man's shoulder to look. The edges of the pages were brown and crumbling; he could see all too clearly how the fire's heat had singed the vellum.

'Lost my hair in the fire.' Lamech ran one hand over his sparsely covered scalp. 'Never grew back properly. Still . . . I'd do it again to save the wisdom in this book from destruction.'

'Someone should make a copy,' Rahab said.

'I've set young Talmai to the task.' Lamech licked one fingertip and continued to turn the crumbling pages. 'Maybe it's put too many abstruse ideas in his head . . . but he seems to spend more time day-dreaming than copying . . . Ah. Here we are. What d'you make of this?'

Rahab bent forward, trying to decipher the ornate script. If only he had been granted more time to study . . .

'"I looked and I saw a – a –"' He stumbled over the first words.

'"An Angel,"' Lamech prompted.

'"And the Angel spoke with – with –"'

'"With a voice of thunder,"' another voice said over his, a young voice, fresh and fervent, '"saying, 'O, ye foolish ones. Whilst ye did quarrel amongst yourselves, Tsiyon the Great fell. Set down these words, Alevi, and make them known unto the scattered children of Tsiyon. For not until these Four are One again shall Holy Tsiyon be built anew.'"'

Rahab saw Talmai standing in the doorway, reciting from memory, his eyes closed as if in prayer.

'A very reasonable interpretation,' Lamech said, nodding, 'although too literal for my tastes. I subscribe to the view that Alevi was writing rather more metaphorically. I would rather render it thus.' He cleared his throat with a series of little dry

191

coughs and recited, '"When the Four Guardians of the Covenant are reunited, then Holy Tsiyon –" which I have always taken to mean a divine state of grace, not a place, Talmai, "–will be restored to the children of Tsiyon." In other words, we will be granted divine forgiveness.'

'I – I've never heard of this *Sefer Bahir* before,' Rahab ventured.

'I have a theory,' Lamech said, 'that it should be called the Second Book of Alevi.' His rheumy eyes glittered with scholarly zeal. 'Not the *Sefer Bahir* – but the Lost Book of Alevi. It was obviously written just after the fall of Tsiyon.'

'Yes, yes,' said Talmai impatiently, 'but how can it be Alevi when he perished in the fall of Tsiyon?'

'How did Alevi die?' Rahab asked, sensing an argument was about to erupt.

'"Weep, daughters of Tsiyon,"' Talmai said, his words breathless, charged with excitement. 'Rather than be taken into captivity by the Djihari, Alevi and the last surviving Tsiyonim set fire to the Sanctuary themselves, perishing in the flames of the Temple.'

'Pah! Self-immolation? Where's the proof?' Lamech rapped on the table with one yellowed fingernail. 'I say show me your proof!'

'That's not what we were taught in *shul*,' Rahab said. He wished he had not asked the question now. 'You're saying that Alevi set fire to the Temple himself?'

'If they didn't die in the Temple, how do you explain the Lamentation?' Talmai said. 'It says quite clearly, "Shall the infidel defile Thy Holy Temple? No, rather Thy servants perish in the flames than –"'

'"In the flames". It doesn't state they did perish in the flames.'

'It doesn't say they didn't.'

'You heard what Rahab said, that's not what we teach our children,' Lamech said.

'And I would have been in ignorance, like Rahab, had I not come here and read the original texts for myself.'

Caught between the two scholars, Rahab felt himself a feather on a shuttlecock, batted to and fro between battling opponents. Raising one hand in silent farewell, he took up Lamech's coat and slipped out.

As he went down the passageway, he could still hear their

raised voices, arguing passionately about the authenticity of interpretation.

He wanted to laugh off the dispute, to dismiss it as another display of scholarly eccentricity. But what Talmai had said had disturbed him to the roots of his soul. All his life he had believed what he had been taught in *shul*: that the Tsiyonim had fled the burning ruins of their city. It had never occurred to him that the city might have been set alight by the priests and scholars in a last, vain gesture of defiance in the face of their enemies.

'An obole for your thoughts,' said a voice. He looked up to see Selima watching him from a doorway, arms folded, a half-smile hovering about her lips.

'Oh, nothing . . .' He returned her smile.

'You look as if you've taken the troubles of the world on your shoulders.'

'Mm.' He nodded. 'It feels a little like that.'

'Would you like something to drink? Some wine?'

Rahab glanced up, wondering why she was being so hospitable. Her eyes, dark in the lamplight that spilled from the room, were warm, welcoming . . . He began to wonder whether it was just a glass of wine that she was offering.

A fretful little voice called from the lamplit room, 'Mama . . . it's too hot, I can't get to sleep . . .'

Selima sighed. 'Jael,' she said. 'The summer heat makes her restless.'

'Maybe another time.' He was not sure whether he felt relieved – or disappointed.

'Goodnight then, Rahab.'

'Goodnight,' he said, and went on towards his room, tiptoeing so as not to disturb the sleeping children.

CHAPTER 19

Lightning flickered fitfully through Rahab's dreams. He tossed and turned on the narrow wooden bed.

'Rahab . . .'

He is standing on a long, white seastrand. Stormclouds lour over the tossing sea. In the distance, lightning flickers across the grey waves.

The pounding breakers toss a shell on to the white strand. He runs to pick it up.

Lightning sears the sky. Lightning strikes the shell from his hands, shattering it to fragments.

The shell is empty.

He woke, his chest tight for want of breath, as if he had been running hard, running for his life.

He felt under his mattress for the amulets . . . and remembered. Malakhi had taken them to the Sanctuary for safekeeping.

He lay back in the dark, heart still pounding. Something was wrong. Malakhi had assured him the amulets were safe. Why, then, had his dreams been riven with lightning? What had woken him?

Amulets . . .

He shut his eyes . . . but little streaks of lightning still flickered a warning across his closed lids. He was too jittery now, too tense to find sleep again.

Must go check the amulets are safe.

He found himself pulling on his coat and tiptoeing out along the moonlit passageway.

The carved wood door to the Sanctuary was closed – but not locked. The scholars were so trusting . . . too trusting for their own good. He pushed the door open, hearing the hinges creak.

Suspended in its dish overhead, the sacred flame glowed, a red glimmer of fire. For a moment he stood, blind in the darkness, not knowing which way to go. And then he sensed a faint charge, a flickering vibration, that drew him into the heart

194

of the Sanctuary. He moved towards it, hands reaching out . . . until they closed on the cold metal of the bronze casket.

'What are you doing here, Rahab?'

Rahab started, turning to see Malakhi standing in the open doorway.

What *was* he doing? He passed a hand over his forehead; his fingers came away wet with perspiration.

'I – I couldn't sleep.'

Malakhi looked from the bronze casket to Rahab questioningly.

'I – I had to check it was still here. That it was safe.'

'And why shouldn't it be safe?'

Rahab felt a chill shiver ripple through him.

'I don't know. I just . . . had a feeling . . .'

'You can see it's safe. There's nothing to concern yourself about.'

Rahab nodded slowly. But the feeling of unease had not been dispelled. 'Is it true?' he blurted out. 'Talmai said Barakiel was still with me. How can that be?'

'Talmai said that?' Malakhi came towards him. As the glow from the crimson flame overhead illuminated his face, Rahab saw that the expression in his eyes had become guarded, suspicious.

'What does it mean? That I shall always be tied to that – that –'

Rahab stabbed his finger at the casket. He couldn't bring himself to say the word 'Guardian'. It seemed such a small word to encompass a being so vast, so elemental as the power to which it had connected him.

Malakhi's hands moved to Rahab's face, fingers moulding themselves to his temples, his cheekbones. Rahab instinctively shied away – and found he could not move. Eyes dark as ancient prophecy probed his.

Don't make me remember. No –

He found himself hurled back into the black heart of the storm. Robed in thunderclouds, he felt the rush and roar of the wind as he hurtled through the rainwet air. Water drops glittered in his streaming hair, brighter than starlight. Stormrain streamed from his naked body – yet for all its wet chill, he felt nothing but the charged power of the Guardian and the righteous anger that had fused the two of them into one. The anger began to crackle in his mind, a terrible, destructive anger that burned away all self-control –

A tremor of blue fire suddenly streaked across his mind, and Malakhi snatched his hands away as though his fingers had been singed.

'I – I didn't mean –' Rahab stammered. His brain still crackled with lightning. 'I didn't know I could –'

'So Talmai was right,' Malakhi said wryly, nursing his hand. 'Barakiel *is* still with you.'

The spinning clouds slowly cleared from Rahab's mind. He put his hands to his pounding head. The charge had drained his strength; he felt dizzy and faint. Worse still was the realisation that – like it or not – he still retained the power to burn, to destroy. He had become dangerous; a danger to himself – and to others.

'But how long will it be before I – before I'm normal again?'

Malakhi shook his head. 'We know of no one who has survived a summoning before. Even those who witness the moment of possession are said to be marked for life . . .'

'There must be some way for me to learn control,' Rahab said, conscience-stricken. He had not meant anyone else to be harmed. He had acted to protect, to defend. Now it seemed he had caused nothing but damage. 'There must be something in the Books of Law. Malakhi – I need help with this.'

'Meet me in the library after the morning prayers have been said and I will show you what little written evidence we have collected. It may help to answer some of your questions –' Malakhi broke off, one finger raised to his lips.

There were footsteps outside, soft, stealthy footsteps coming steadily closer. Malakhi beckoned Rahab away from the casket, lifting the tapestry curtain of crimson and gold where the Books of the Holy Law were kept, gently pushing him inside.

Someone else had entered the Sanctuary.

'Stay in here,' Malakhi murmured in Rahab's ear. 'Let me deal with this.' As he let the curtain drop back, Rahab heard him say in a quiet, quirked voice, 'So what brings you to the Sanctuary? Isn't this a little too early for morning prayers?'

'Talk, all everyone does is talk! Use me, Malakhi.'

Rahab recognised Bar Talmai's voice.

'Isn't this what I've been training for all my life?'

'Sometimes talk is the best way,' came back Malakhi's level reply.

'When Tsiyonim lives are at stake? Do you truly believe Aymon is going to let our people go?'

196

There was a passionate urgency in Talmai's voice that made the hairs rise on the back of Rahab's neck.

'We must deliver our letter to Aymon. We must give him the chance to negotiate, to act honourably.'

'Honourably! Honour is the last thing on Aymon's mind. We must get them out of Arcassanne before it's too late. I'm ready, Malakhi. Ready to do what I have trained to do.'

'Didn't you hear a word Rahab said? Didn't you understand? The danger to our own people is as great as to our enemies.'

'Oh yes, I heard what *Rahab* said.' There was no mistaking the rank bitterness in the young man's voice. 'But don't you see? He was untrained, undisciplined. He hadn't undergone the proper initiation. He's just a tailor.'

Just a tailor. Even though it was true, the words stung. Rahab scowled at the curtain.

'I have spent all my years at Tifereth preparing myself,' Talmai said. 'I have learned the Holy Laws and the mystic texts by heart. I have undergone a strict training – both in mind and body. I have tried to purge myself of impure thoughts. I have dedicated my life to one path: the path of the Guardian Warder. I thought that if ever Tifereth needed defending, I would be ready. Ready to sacrifice myself for the community. Ready to become one with Shalgiel. And now it seems I need not have striven so hard. A mere tailor from Arcassanne has beaten me to it.' There was still bitterness in his voice . . . but also, Rahab heard, incredulity.

'Talmai, you must be patient,' came Malakhi's voice again. 'There is no immediate threat to Tifereth. If a troop of soldiers were to come riding up the mountain, then matters would be different. But as it is –'

'You may be prepared to live with the death of our people on your conscience, Malakhi,' Talmai burst out, 'but I am *not*.'

Silence followed. Rahab cautiously lifted a corner of the tapestry and scanned the Sanctuary; Talmai had gone and Malakhi was alone.

'I apologise for Bar Talmai,' Malakhi said. 'He is young, impulsive. He doesn't always think before he speaks.'

Rahab said nothing, eyes fixed on the dark doorway through which Talmai had gone storming out.

'He's still haunted by what happened to him in Galicys.'

Rahab slowly turned his head.

'I thought he couldn't remember what happened.'

'That's what he maintains. That he remembers nothing before I found him in the ruins of that burned-out house.'

'Do you believe him?'

'I've seen others like him, other casualties healed in body . . . but irreparably damaged by spirit. They block out the horrors of the past, insist it never happened. Even when confronted with the truth, they deny it.'

'So – what happened to Talmai?' Rahab asked. It was difficult to form the question, oh so difficult, because when he looked at Talmai, he still thought he saw . . . a likeness. An indefinable likeness. An echo of a memory. And there had been no amnesia to block out *his* past; he had had to live with his memories.

'Your guess is as good as mine. There were no clues. Just a malnourished, filthy, terrified child with a festering gash across his temple. The few feverish words he babbled made no sense. There were bodies everywhere, mutilated, fly-blown . . . We assumed his family was dead in the massacre. It wasn't a place to linger. But . . . I'm sure you remember all too well. How old were you? Ten? Eleven?'

Rahab nodded. Malakhi's words had re-awakened feelings he did not want to remember. Cobblestones slippery with blood. The charred smell of smoke on the wind that made eyes water, the foul taste of smoke in the mouth, at the back of the throat . . .

'We distil an excellent eau-de-vie from Elon's plums.' Malakhi took him by the arm. 'I think we could both do with a glass.'

An oil lamp was burning in Malakhi's room. Rahab took the little glass and took a sip of the eau-de-vie; at first its sharpness made his eyes water . . . until a golden glow burned down his throat, sweet with the juicy tang of ripe orchard fruit.

'I asked Talmai about Galicys,' he confessed, turning the little glass in his fingers, watching the pale gold of the liqueur eddy. 'He was . . . angry.' He gazed up at Malakhi. 'It was just that for one moment I believed he might be my brother Shaoni.'

'Shaoni,' Malakhi repeated, his face closed, unreadable. 'Shaoni ben Chazhael.'

'It was stupid of me,' Rahab said. He took another mouthful of eau-de-vie. The burn of the liqueur seemed to take the edge off his own anger.

'Do you think Talmai is your brother?'

The directness of Malakhi's question startled Rahab.

'You see ... Talmai has been like a son to me,' Malakhi said, before he could reply. His face was in shadow. 'I lost my wife and children in Tolonada. Finding Talmai all those years later seemed like a gift from God. I've tried to be a good father to him. But he is fragile – oh, not in body; as I said, his physical wounds healed years ago. His mind, his spirit, is vulnerable. I would not want to see him hurt again, Rahab.'

'So you think I shouldn't have spoken out.'

'I merely wanted to warn you.'

It stung that Malakhi had spoken to him so bluntly. Did he think he was completely lacking in sensitivity? He took another gulp of the eau-de-vie, but instead of soothing the hurt, the liqueur only seemed to inflame it.

'If Talmai's so vulnerable, why train him as Guardian Warder? What was that passage you referred to? "The Guardian cleaves to that which is strongest in the Warder's soul?" Wouldn't summoning one of the Guardians be too much for him? Wouldn't it destroy him?'

'Training as Warder has given Talmai a purpose. It has centred him, given him a goal to strive for. It has helped him gain strength. But we –'

'But you never imagined a time would come when he would be tempted to use the amulet.' Rahab finished Malakhi's sentence for him.

'And I intend to keep it so.' Malakhi's voice hardened.

'Suppose it's true?' Rahab set down the empty glass with a crack. 'Suppose – just suppose – he is Shaoni?'

'You're still not certain?'

'How can I be certain!' Rahab cried. 'Sometimes ... when the sunlight glints across his face, I think I see ... I see ...' His voice faded. It was so tenuous a clue. The shadow of a memory. The memory of his mother's face. How could anything so tenuous be claimed as evidence of kinship? A fragment of memory, fleeting as a dream?

'Of course you want him to be your lost brother.' Malakhi spoke less harshly now. 'I spent years trying to find my wife, Rivkah. Sometimes I caught sight of her in a crowd ... yet whenever I fought my way through, I would find myself staring at a stranger. I just couldn't accept the idea that she was dead.'

Rahab shrugged. He understood what Malakhi was saying well enough. Talmai was Malakhi's foster-son. Malakhi was warning him – quietly but firmly – not to interfere.

Morning mist was rising from the ravine deep below the castel. The chill air had a faint crispness to it, tart as unripe apples.

Rahab shadowed Bar Talmai as he set out down the winding path, bearing the letter to Comte Aymon in the basket of fresh eggs he was taking to market.

Rahab kept glancing up at the sky to see if clouds had moved to darken the sun's brightness – but the darkness was the darkness of presentiment, the presentiment that had woken him at dawn.

He was seized with a sudden irrational impulse to take charge of the letter himself and send Talmai back . . .

Or maybe he could keep Talmai company, they could talk of inconsequential things, get to know each other . . .

He saw Talmai stop, frowning, and look around. Had he sensed he was being followed? Rahab shrank behind a knotted pine trunk, hoping he had not been seen.

Why was he fooling himself? There was not the slightest chance of a meaningful conversation now. Talmai felt nothing but resentment towards him.

Talmai turned around and set off at a fast pace down the steep track. He walked purposefully, energetically.

Rahab stood watching him go, still gripped by the feeling of unease that had woken him.

Talmai was only going to market. He would have to be back by sundown to celebrate the start of *shabbath*. Surely the worst that could happen was a stumble on the stony path – and a few cracked eggs?

A fly had got trapped in the college library and was buzzing around one of the stained blinds.

Rahab sighed. He had been puzzling over the faded text of the Tolonada *Sefer Bahir* until the spidery characters had begun to crawl before his eyes. Like the fly, he wanted to escape.

He rose and tugged on the rope to raise the blind. Dazzling mountain light pierced the dusty gloom of the library as the fly zoomed out into the hot sunshine.

Rahab returned to the ancient text, mumbling under his breath as he traced the letters from right to left with the silver pointer.

' "When these Four are . . . are . . . One –" '

'Ssh!' hissed another scholar from behind a great leather-bound book.

Rahab sighed again. He feared it was too late to make a scholar of him now. He had painstakingly been spelling the words out, character by character. Malakhi had pointed out several significant differences between the script of old Tsiyon and that currently in use. But with no background knowledge to fall back on, Rahab found himself constantly defeated in his attempts to interpret the relevant passages.

Why could no one agree about the meaning? He sat, elbows on the table, chin resting on his cupped hands, trying to make sense of it. Every Tsiyonim child knew that Tsiyon fell because the Guardians were divided. Each Guardian, separated from His brethren, became an uncontrollable force of devastation, indiscriminately destroying both Tsiyonim and Gentiles alike. Surely that was never the original purpose of the God-given Covenant? There must be a clue somewhere in Alevi's writings, in these charred and blood-stained parchments, the only written record from the time of the Fall of Tsiyon.

'But where?' he said out loud, bringing down his fist on the table in frustration.

'Sssh!' came back the answering hiss of irritation from behind the leather-bound book.

Why was he wasting his time here? He was a tailor; tailors should leave scholarship to the scholars. Besides, there was work to be done; a *mitzvah* for Lamech. He quietly closed the precious manuscript, replaced it in its protective covering and tiptoed his way out of the library.

Tifereth was busy with preparations for *shabbath*. A great pan of chicken soup was simmering over the fire and Selima was directing operations in the kitchen.

Rahab sat down to unpick the seams of Lamech's coat. He wanted something to do to distract him from the ever-present sense of disquiet.

How long did it take to walk to the market and back? It had taken a whole day to reach the castel – but then they had lost their way. If it hadn't been for the shepherd boy who had put them on the right track, they might still be wandering, searching . . .

He put down the coat. To make a good job of it he needed

201

shears, chalk, needles and thread. He set off to ask Selima if she could lend him anything to help him complete the task.

But as he approached the kitchen, he heard a crash of breaking crockery – and then Selima's voice raised in tones of exasperation.

'How many times have I told you not to play ball in my kitchen, Laban!'

Rahab peered around the door and saw Selima down on her knees, mopping up a mess of spilt eggs. Her son Laban stood watching, head hanging, face red as one of Elon's plums.

'My best bowl, too. How could you – when I'm so busy!'

Maybe now wasn't the best of times to interrupt.

He wandered out of the courtyard, back towards the path that Talmai had taken earlier that day.

Just to check all is well . . .

The sun had burned away the last wisps of mist, and the high plateau shimmered in heavy midday heat. The birds were silent; only the chirring of the insects could be heard as he walked slowly down the track, feeling the sun hot on the back of his head.

'Damn.' The voice came from the long grass in the meadow beside the track. 'Damn, damn, damn!'

He knew that piqued tone. What was the matter with the girl now! He went down into the meadow and saw Lia sitting on a stone. Her face was twisted in an expression of tortured concentration as she tried to sew up the holes in her satin slippers.

'Here – let me.' Rahab took the slipper from her and shook his head over her botched attempt at mending. 'Why did you bring this to me?'

'You're a tailor, not a cobbler.'

'These stitches will all have to come out.'

'I was never interested in needlework,' she said defensively. 'But I'm good with a bow and arrow. D'you think –'

'No,' he said, squinting into the sun as he re-threaded the needle. 'Who gave you these?'

'Selima.'

'Maybe I could make myself useful mending clothes. I've one commission already, from Lamech . . .'

'Useful?' He heard a note of surprise in her voice, sharp and cold as the first drop of rain. 'But I thought this was where you wanted to be. Where you'd feel at ease, at home. With your own people.'

He shook his head. 'This slipper is so badly worn, there's little I can do. Maybe we could find some material to patch it.'

'Rahab,' she said.

He looked up.

'What's troubling you?'

'Me?' He forced a little laugh. 'Nothing.'

'You're a poor liar, you know. You've been going round with a wan face, sighing.'

'I can't help thinking about Chadassah and the children.' It wasn't entirely a lie, he supposed; he had been worrying about them too. 'That's all.'

'Is it?'

'Here. Try this on.' He handed her the darned slipper and took up the other one, noticing with a twinge of guilt the brown blotches of dried blood staining the once-pale satin. And he had made her keep walking!

'I saw you talking with Bar Talmai,' she said, wincing as she tried to ease her swollen foot into the slipper.

'Mmm?' He was not paying much attention to what she was saying; he was concentrating on the slipper.

'Has anyone else noticed how alike the two of you are?'

Taken by surprise, he pricked his finger. 'Ow!' he cried, dropping the slipper. A bright bubble of blood appeared. 'Alike? How do you mean, alike?' he asked, sucking his punctured fingertip.

'You're not related, are you?' When he did not reply, she leaned closer. 'Rahab?'

'I don't know. At first I thought – I hoped –' He broke off. How could he begin to tell her?

'You said your family was dead.'

'I had a brother, Shaoni. Younger than me.' It was still so difficult to put into words. 'In the massacre – in Galicys – we were separated. I never knew what happened to him.'

'Shaoni?' she said. 'But he's called Talmai.'

'He had lost his memory when Malakhi found him, so Malakhi gave him his name. Oh, and Malakhi doesn't want me distressing him by raking up painful memories from the past.'

'Whyever not?'

'Because I'm obviously such a disappointment as an older brother.'

'Obviously!' she said – but she was smiling as she spoke.

203

He had expected a more pungent retort. And yet the conversation had been flowing quite naturally between them, almost as if the soft air of Tifereth had melted away her earlier hostility. He found himself asking her, 'It's too much of a coincidence, isn't it? To have searched for him for so many years . . . and then to find he's been living only a few leagues from Arcassanne?'

'Living in Tifereth,' she said. 'What did you call it? Place of harmony? What better place to find a long-lost brother?'

'Tifereth.' Rahab felt a catch in his throat as he pronounced the name. 'For so long I dreamed of coming here. When I was working late into the night to finish a garment for Schimeon, I used to imagine what it might be like . . . I always thought it might be a little like Tsiyon. But Tsiyon here, Tsiyon now, not some unattainable fantasy far away in Djihan-Djihar.'

'Well, I'm no use to anyone here, and that's certain,' Lia announced. 'I don't know how to make chopped liver, my mother never taught me the right way to prepare meat and I don't know one end of a chicken giblet from the other.'

Rahab glanced up and caught the dry glint in her eyes; the line was throwaway, self-deprecating. Was she trying to cheer him up?

'Selima could do with an extra pair of hands in the kitchen. When I came past, her boy Laban was playing handball around the pots and pans.'

'Well, she'll just have to manage as best she can without the benefit of my help. I'm going to lie back here in the sun and forget everything.' She stretched out on the grassy slope and tipped the battered hat she had brought from Arcassanne over her face to protect it from the glare of the sun.

Rahab sat looking down at her a while. He found her helplessness at once endearing and frustrating. How was she ever to make a new life for herself in Tifereth, so far from the comforts of city life? How could she manage without her maid to wash and arrange her hair, to prepare the creams and perfumes that Arcassanne women liked to pamper themselves with? He picked up the slippers he had mended for her; the faded, stained satin had once been pale gold, a delicate shade known as 'Hay Flower' in Arcassanne. Maybe she had a gown to match? He would have dressed her for court in an undergown of bronze silk with an overgown of Hay Flower gauze, slashed sleeves caught in at the wrist and elbow with bronze ribbons, low-cut bodice subtly shaped with little darts to emphasise her slender waist . . .

He hastily put the slippers down beside Lia. What *was* he thinking of? He pocketed the precious needle and thread and set off back towards the castel. There was work to be done.

Lia opened one eye and squinted into the sun from under the brim of Mother's hat. The mended slippers lay beside her on the grass. Rahab was walking away towards the castel. She caught herself smiling.

What was there to smile about? Her life was in chaos. A few days ago she had been betrothed to the most eligible bachelor in Arcassanne . . . and now she was a nothing, a no one, cast out to fend for herself with only the dress she was wearing and a broken-down pair of slippers to her name. And Mother's hat . . .

Whenever she thought of the wedding, tears came to her eyes. The wedding feast, the eminent guests invited, the cream of Arcassanne's aristocracy, the clothes, the beautiful gowns Rahab had been making . . .

Rahab.

She had not planned on spending so much time in the company of Berengar's tailor. If she had once imagined when he was measuring her for her wedding gown –

His hands, deftly moving the measuring-cord about her body, his breath warm on the nape of her neck as he measured the distance from shoulder to waist . . .

Ouf! She was suddenly hot, her face burning. She fanned herself hastily with the hat. How could a mere memory conjure up such thoughts?

She could hear Alissende's voice whispering, 'But Lia, he's only an apprentice. A common apprentice.'

'He's not only common,' she said aloud, 'he's infuriatingly opinionated.' Yet as she lay back in the sun, closing her eyes, her hand stole out to touch the slippers he had mended.

White doves circle in the blue sky above the towers of Arcassanne. The musicians are playing.

Lia gazes down at herself, admiring her exquisitely embroidered wedding gown. Elegant folds of silk and brocade, ivory, gold and russet, rustle softly as she slowly ascends the steps to Comte Aymon's Palace, on her father Auger's arm. Her hair has been braided with pearls; chains of pearl and gold are looped around her throat. Crowds

205

have gathered to watch and cheer; little children dressed in white cast scented flower petals in front of her. The air is sweet with the heady scent of orange blossom and tuberose; garlands of roses, cream and pink, hang from every pillar. Court ladies watch, whispering enviously behind their hands as they admire the richness of her gown. And at the head of the stairs, Berengar stands waiting to greet her, to lead her into the Comte's presence so that the last formalities of the wedding can be completed . . .

But as she climbs the long stair, the costly gown of silk and brocade begins to disintegrate, to fall away to tatters.

'Papa?' She turns to Auger in her distress – but he has vanished; she is alone on the steps. The ladies of Aymon's court have begun to laugh at her, pointing maliciously, their laughter strident as the cries of magpies.

And now the children start to pelt her with mud, their little faces distorted, gargoyle-sharp, as they shriek, 'Tsiyonim, Tsiyonim!'

'Berengar, help me –' She runs to him, arms outstretched, imploring. She looks up and sees – a blank, a void where his face should be.

Mud-spattered, humiliated, she clutches the last shreds of her ruined gown to her nakedness –

'Ai!' She sat up, her arms still clutched tightly across her body. The mocking laughter echoed in her mind – even though she was alone in the grassy meadow and the only sound she could hear was the chitter and whirr of the insects.

She could still feel the slap of the cold, stinking gutter mud on her naked body . . . but more terrifying still was the memory of Berengar, face as blank as a defaced statue.

She was marrying a blank. She had contracted to share her life with a stranger. In spite of all the years she had known Berengar, she had never once experienced that sudden flush of heat she had felt thinking of Rahab – not even when they kissed. Berengar was more like a brother, an indulgent elder brother, than a husband, a . . . she could scarcely bring herself to articulate the word . . . a *lover*.

'This is all nonsense,' she told herself, briskly brushing the dry grass from her skirts. And then she stopped, hearing the sound of running footsteps.

Someone was hurrying up the track, someone whose stumbling, headlong gait sent loose stones rattling away down the side of the ravine.

She knelt up, fully awake by now, looking down the track to see who was in such a hurry.

It was Talmai. To move faster, he had hitched up his robes, belting them like an athlete's tunic. She thought for one idle moment how long and brown his legs were . . . and then she heard his gasping breaths, saw how the sweat had soaked his curls, plastering them to his dripping face. No one would run in this heat merely for pleasure or exercise.

'Talmai?' she called, jumping up. She wanted to run to meet him – but her blistered feet were too sore. 'What's wrong?'

'H-horsemen!' he cried over his shoulder as he passed her.

'Horsemen?' Lia said, hopping after him.

By the time she caught up with him he had reached the courtyard and collapsed on to the grass. The goats were regarding him with baleful eyes; a kid tried to butt him from the patch of grass it had been grazing.

One of the girls came hurrying over to Talmai with a cup of water; he cupped it in his shaking hands and drained it in one long draught.

'You should sip the water after such strenuous exercise.' Malakhi came out into the courtyard. 'Whatever possessed you to run back uphill in this heat?'

'There are – horsemen coming this way.' Talmai gestured wildly back over his shoulder. 'I – I passed them. I heard them ask for – the ruined castel.'

'Horsemen? What kind of horsemen?' Malakhi went hurrying over to Talmai's side, gripping the young man by the shoulders.

'Armed men. Soldiers.'

CHAPTER 20

'Jaufré . . .'

Through half-opened lids, Jaufré saw a figure in his room. The first time he had fallen asleep in days, and now they had roused him!

'Go away, Bertran,' he muttered. Then he remembered. It couldn't be Bertran. He had locked the door, double-locked it so as not to be disturbed.

'Why did you break your word to me, Jaufré . . .?'

'Who's there?' He fumbled for his sword – but clumsy with sleep, he dropped it and it fell with a clatter to the floor – out of his reach.

A breath of laughter, dry and chill as a desert wind, stirred the hair at the nape of his neck.

In the dim light before dawn it was difficult to see clearly . . . his sight seemed veiled in spidersilk; he wanted to claw away the obscuring veils –

A hand appeared above him, insubstantial, etched in sepia.

'Why do you still carry it close to your heart? Can't you feel it draining the life from you?

The fingers reached down, clawing towards his breast. A dry ache seared through him with every halting breath he attempted.

'Give it back, Jaufré . . .'

'N-no –' he gasped, struggling to sit up.

The air burned with the hot, dark wind of the sandstorm. His lungs were seared by its black heat.

'Have you forgotten so soon what it can do? Look at me, Jaufré. Look – and remember . . .'

Alois's eyes, blue as an Arcassanne sky, were gazing down into his.

'Alois?' he said – but even as he gazed on his dead friend's face, the blue pupils began to fade, to shrivel as though burned by intense heat. Until all that was left was the desiccated, shrivelled mummy-face he had seen that last night in Djihan-Djihar, grinning horribly down at him.

'*Is this what you truly desire?*'

'N-no –' Jaufré stared, transfixed.

'*Then give the amulet back. Give it to the scholar Jehiel.*'

Jaufré felt for the amulet. He tried to untie the thong from around his neck. He tried to tug the amulet free from his breast.

'I – I can't,' he whispered.

A distant murmur of voices broke on the dark shores of Jaufré's dreams like the incessant rise and fall of the tide. Slowly he drifted back to consciousness . . . and lay, listening, trying to puzzle out what the source of the noise could be.

The room was filled with light; he must have slept longer than he intended. His mouth was dry and foul, his head heavy with the afterthrob of the sleep draught. And his sleep had not been refreshing; there had been dreams, confusing, muddled dreams –

'Alois,' he whispered, remembering. His shirt was damp with sweat, sticking to his back as if he had been tossing in fever all night. The foul taste in his mouth was the taste of gravedust.

The voices droned on outside; a constant, ominous buzz.

He blundered his way to the window and looked out. Then he rubbed his bleared eyes and stared again.

The Tour de la Justice was surrounded.

People had filled the streets outside the courtyard; in whichever direction he looked, he could see crowds, in Horloge Street, the Carrefour, Peppermill Lane . . .

And standing facing them on the steps to the Tour stood a thin woman, drably dressed, clutching her patched shawl to her as though she could not feel the day's sticky heat.

Guillemette.

Jaufré could not hear what wild words she was shouting to the crowd, what arguments she was using to harangue them into a frenzy of hatred – but he could see her hunched shoulders, taut with grief and fury.

If she knew, if she only knew who the murderer really was –

For a moment he found himself gripped by an overwhelming desire to confess, to throw himself down at her feet and beg her forgiveness. Anything, anything to free him from this tyranny of concealment, this stifling shroud of lies he had woven for himself.

And then a soft, persistent voice began to whisper in his mind.

Why couldn't the foolish woman accept her son was dead?

If she was so hungry for vengeance, let her have it. Let her have one of the Tsiyonim, if needs be . . .

A child's life for her son's?

'Captain! Captain!' Bertran pounded at the door. 'Guillemette wants to talk with you!'

'Can't you deal with her, Bertran?'

'She wants you. The Captain. No one else will do.'

'Very well,' Jaufré said wearily.

Why must it be him? Why must he be forced to deal with the woman face to face, to see the shadow of the child's bright countenance in her worn features?

He took up his jacket, belted on his sword and went out into the street.

The murmur of voices slowly stilled as they turned to stare at him. He sensed blatant, sullen defiance. He also saw that many had brought makeshift weapons: axes, scythes, pitchforks, shears.

As he walked towards Guillemette, he felt the dull burn of the amulet pressing against his skin.

Why should he fear these rebels? He was protected. The Guardian he had summoned would watch over him.

'Dame Guillemette.'

Guillemette turned around.

'I must ask you and your supporters to disperse peacefully and go about your business.'

She narrowed her eyes as she looked at him, as though the daylight were too bright to see him clearly. The last traces of late summer bloom had faded from her face, leaving the wary, withered features of a woman old before her time.

'Another day has passed, Captain. You promised me justice. I'm still waiting.'

'Waiting? Is that what you call this?' Jaufré's curt gesture encompassed the crowds. 'With a besieging army?'

'Why do you protect *them*?' Guillemette said. She spoke slowly, strangely, as if she were talking in her sleep. 'They're harbouring a murderer.'

'You burned down their houses. The Comte was obliged to offer them shelter.'

'Shelter!' She spat. 'How much have they paid him? There has to be money involved. Whose interests does Aymon represent? Those of the Tsiyonim foreigners – or those of his own people?'

'That's treasonable talk. I could have you arrested,' Jaufré said.

'Arrest me?' she said, folding her arms across her thin breasts. Her eyes burned, dry as fever. 'On what charge?'

'Slandering the good name of the Comte in public.'

'No one heard what I said but you.' The burning gaze openly defied him.

'Your supporters set fire to the Tsiyonim Quarter.'

She let out a harsh, brittle burst of laughter.

'A spark from a torch caught in some thatch. That's an accident – not an offence.'

'The third charge is laying siege to the Comte's courts of justice.'

'I am holding a vigil,' she said, her voice suddenly soft, breaking, 'in memory of my murdered child. I and my friends will hold vigil until you bring his murderer to justice.'

Jaufré was fast losing patience.

'Vigil?' he said. 'Do you need weapons to hold a vigil? Go home – and hold your vigil there.'

'And until you find his murderer,' she continued, ignoring him, 'we will hold all the Tsiyonim accountable for his death.'

Jaufré's hand crept towards the collar of his shirt, feeling for the thong on which the amulet hung, tempted to call on its powers to silence her. He needed the Tsiyonim. If he were to let her have her way, he would lose the only bargaining ploy at his disposal.

'I am on my way to Comte Aymon now,' he said. 'I will put your case to him again.'

As he walked past her, he could feel her gaze still on him, searing like a burning arrow into his back.

'Justice,' she whispered.

Comte Aymon was at dinner in the Great Hall. Jaufré lingered beneath the pillared gallery, watching his patron. Aymon sat under the embroidered banners of the Seigneurs of Arcassanne who had sworn fealty to the Comte's house, prominent amongst them Orbiel's crimson and black, the blue and white of Belcastel . . . and the gold and green of the House of Azénor. Jaufré scanned the long table . . . and saw Grazide in a gown of willow green and white, inclining her long neck with a slow,

211

swanlike grace to hear what Aymon was saying. So Grazide del Azénor was back in favour with the Comte. Well, and what did it matter to him? He had tired of her long ago.

A savoury smell of grilled pork flavoured with rosemary drifted down the hall to where Jaufré stood. He felt a faint stirring of hunger. When had he last eaten? He could not remember.

One of the Comte's musicians was playing softly, plucking fashionable melodies on a Galicyan lute; on seeing Jaufré appear, he suddenly struck up the sombre strains of the poet's last song, 'Winter Lilies'.

The melody was greeted with a ripple of discreet applause from the courtiers at the Comte's table. Grazide was regarding him, an enigmatic smile curving her full lips. The song had been written for her, in a last, bitter outpouring of regret . . .

Jaufré forced himself to acknowledge the compliment with a bow, hiding the anger in his face. He felt exposed, betrayed. The next moment, one of Aymon's damoiselles would ask him when he would sing them his latest song, to whom it was to be dedicated . . .

Had they no idea how it tormented him to be reminded of his lost gift?

The Comte dipped his fingers in a fingerbowl and, shaking off the waterdrops, beckoned Jaufré forward.

'Orbiel . . . I want this Tsiyonim business wound up.' He wiped the pork grease from his lips with his napkin. 'Why is it taking so long to arrest the murderer? Don't you even have a suspect?'

Jaufré had been half-anticipating, half-dreading this question.

'I have the name of a suspect. Rahab. A tailor's apprentice.'

'So why haven't you arrested him?'

'It seems he may have . . . slipped through our fingers.'

'It's not good enough, Orbiel.' Aymon began to tap out a repetitive rhythm on the table with finger and thumb. 'Not good enough at all. Have you any idea how much it's costing the city to feed all these Tsiyonim? And now that woman Guillemette is back with her supporters, stirring up trouble again. I don't want a riot on my hands.'

Jaufré nodded.

'For God's sake find the murderer, let's have a trial and an execution and be done with it.'

One of Aymon's servants came pushing his way through the waiting courtiers and, approaching the Comte, whispered in his ear.

'Well, let's see this urgent letter,' Aymon said, holding out his hand.

The servant placed a sealed paper in his master's hand and withdrew, bowing. Jaufré watched Aymon break the seal and read; watched Aymon's expression change to a puzzled frown.

'What d'you make of this, Orbiel?'

Jaufré took the letter and read:

We, the scholars of the college at Tifereth, wish to inform Comte Aymon that we are willing to accommodate our Tsiyonim kinsfolk who have lost their houses and possessions in the recent fire in Arcassanne. We therefore ask the Comte to release our kinsfolk so that they may join us here.

'It seems like the answer to our problems. No more hungry Tsiyonim to feed at the city's expense.'

'How did they hear about the fire?' Jaufré said, looking up from the letter.

'Does it matter? Bad news travels fast.'

'And where is this Tifereth?' Jaufré persisted. 'Who brought the letter? How do we know it isn't a hoax? A trick?'

Aymon gestured the liveried servant who had brought the letter back to his chair.

'How was this letter delivered? Is anyone waiting for a reply?'

'It came by riverboat, seigneur. From the mountains. It appears that money was paid for one of the boatmen to make the delivery. He has already left the Palace.'

'The mountains?' Jaufré's gaze slid to the Belcastel standard. So Tifereth was in the mountains? Suddenly all the seemingly disconnected facts began to link together: Lia Maury's abduction, the sightings at the Aude Gate, the disappearance of the suspect Rahab . . .

'Didn't you just say your suspect had slipped through your fingers? Let's negotiate an exchange with the Tsiyonim. We'll let them go free to this Tifereth college, on condition they first return the suspect – Rahab, did you say his name is? – to stand trial in Arcassanne. That should placate the boy's mother, don't you think?'

'And if they don't hand Rahab over to us?'

213

'This woman's campaign is disrupting my city.' Aymon's expression was no longer so affable. 'It must be brought to an end.'

Jaufré looked at the Comte but saw only Guillemette's face staring at him, saw only the accusation burning in her red-rimmed eyes.

'Then let me arrest her,' he said.

'You know as well as I that arresting her will start a riot. She wants justice.' Aymon grasped Jaufré by the arm. 'And we must be seen to give her justice. Understand me?'

'I understand you,' Jaufré said, between gritted teeth. Aymon had left him little room to manoeuvre.

'I expect an arrest. And a full report.'

'You shall have it. Trust me.'

Aymon relaxed his grip. 'Jaufré, Jaufré ...' A slight sigh escaped his lips. 'You should not be writing official reports; you should be putting your pen to better use.'

'No.' Jaufré turned his face away. Aymon had touched the raw wound in his soul. 'There'll be no more poetry. It's finished.'

Zillaïs pressed her fingertips to her forehead, trying to will away the sudden, ominous throb that preceded one of her attacks.

She called them megrims, sick headaches, and her household had never questioned the explanation. No one had ever thought to link them to the weather. And no one knew, save she herself, the cause. They were a misery she must endure alone, every time the dry Tramontan wind, storm or snow threatened, legacy of an event so extraordinary that she could not even now bring herself to talk of it. Even thinking of it evoked a feeling of such stifling terror that she had never been able to tell anyone the truth of what had really happened in Tolonada; not even her husband, Auger.

But every time she saw the distant gloom of stormclouds or tasted the tingle of lightning in the air, she felt the telltale ache within her brain. Sometimes – if the storm was distant, rumbling far out over the river plain or high in the mountains – she could contain the attack with tisanes or herb-compresses of oil of lavender and bergamot.

The attacks would never be cured. She knew that now. She had been touched once – just once – by an elemental force. She would have to endure the consequences until the day she died.

214

The throbbing pulse began again.

The last time had been when Rahab had summoned Barakiel. Surely he would not hazard another summoning so soon after the last? Had he no idea of the risks? Did he not know that the Guardian Powers depleted the strength of their human Warders, leaving them debilitated, drained?

Zillaïs gazed up at the sky outside the high barred window. It was the intense hot blue of a late summer afternoon, without even a wisp of white cloud.

Not a single hint of a stormcloud.

'Tifereth,' Jaufré said, watching Rebh Jehiel's face for any sign of a reaction.

The scholar gazed impassively back at him.

'Well? What is it?'

'Tifereth,' said Jehiel, 'is beauty. Harmony. It is a state of mind that we strive to achieve.'

'Then how,' Jaufré said, trying to contain his impatience, 'can someone be said to have gone to Tifereth?'

Jehiel blinked.

'We know it exists.' Jaufré waved the letter in Jehiel's face. 'The scholars at Tifereth have written to us, offering you and your people refuge.'

'Let me see.' Jehiel took the paper and held it close to his eyes to read it. 'Ah,' he said, nodding, when he had finished reading.

'So where is this place, this college?'

Jehiel handed the letter back.

'Does it matter where it is?' he said. 'Surely it is of no importance to you, Captain.' There was an air of contentment about him, a serenity in his manner which irritated Jaufré.

It didn't take a scholar to piece together the facts. Someone must have gone to Tifereth from Arcassanne soon after the storm – and Jaufré had a strong suspicion that it was Rahab, his only 'suspect' in the child sacrifice case.

He had been lenient with the old scholar in the last few days. But now his patience had been exhausted; it was time to force the information out of him.

'Come with me,' he said abruptly.

'Where are we going?' Jehiel pulled his fringed shawl closer about his shoulders, as though the worn material were a defence against Jaufré's inquisition.

Jaufré did not reply.

Outside the Tour, late afternoon had settled in a haze of stifling heat over the city. But inside, the thickness of the ancient stone walls kept the atmosphere mustily cool and damp.

Jaufré led Rebh Jehiel down the torchlit spiral stair, trying to contain his impatience as the old scholar moved slowly, uncertainly from one narrow step to another. Jaufré stopped at a barred observation window cut into the inner wall of the tower. From here they could stand at the rail and gaze down into the dungeon of the Tour de la Justice.

The air was faintly fetid, tainted with the smell of unwashed bodies confined too close together too long.

The Tsiyonim lay wrapped in their cloaks and blankets. A baby started to cry fitfully; the mother tried to hush it, rocking it in her arms. An elderly woman coughed in her sleep; a mucusy, wheezing cough.

Jehiel shook his head, murmuring under his breath.

'What's that, Rebh Jehiel?' Jaufré said.

'Herded in here like beasts in a barn!'

'It's for their own safety,' Jaufré said softly.

'Safety! You can smell the damp in here, even though it's summer. What will you do when they all fall sick? Keep me in Arcassanne to answer the charges if you must, but let them go, let them leave the city.'

A child woke up below, whimpering. 'Mamma . . . I don't like it here, I'm frightened . . .'

'Then tell me what I need to know,' Jaufré said, 'and I will negotiate their release with Comte Aymon.'

'Their release? Do you give me your word, Captain? Your word of honour?'

'My word of honour,' Jaufré said.

Jehiel looked at him, and Jaufré saw the bleak resignation in the old scholar's eyes.

Jaufré pushed past his servant Jehan and went flying up the staircase of the Tour d'Orbiel. He had come running all the way back, his head buzzing with excitement. At last he had broken down the old man's resistance, at last he would get some answers to the questions which obsessed him.

'Captain,' called out Jehan. 'You've a visitor waiting to –'

'Tell him to come back later,' Jaufré called back impatiently, flinging open his chamber door. 'I've no time for visitors.'

216

And then he stopped on the threshold, staring, wondering for a moment if he had unwittingly conjured a vision of the Virgin Lady herself –

She was dressed in a gown the intense purple-blue of wild hyacinths, sunlight from the jewel-paned windows glinting in the rich, dark honey of her hair. But surely no manifestation of the Lady ever wore such a low-cut gown that displayed her white, azure-veined breasts so immodestly.

He frowned, recognising her.

'Grazide,' he said. 'What are you doing here?'

She slowly held out her hand towards him.

'You might at least have the courtesy to greet me properly, Captain Orbiel.'

Her eyes, blue as her gown, scanned his as he took her hand and brushed it briefly with his lips. A faint breath of her perfume, powdery-sweet as golden lily pollen, brought back a rush of memories he had put from his mind, sensuous, erotic memories he had schooled himself to forget.

He let go of her hand abruptly and turned away.

He was irritated that she had come here, irritated that she had sought him out. Didn't she understand? Their affair was over. He thought he had made that clear before he left Djihan-Djihar. He had returned her gifts, written an envoi to her gilded with his most elegant poetic conceits.

'So. You have nothing to say to me. And yet you used to call me your muse.' Her voice was sweet as her lily perfume. Grazide del Azénor could be so very persuasive when she wished.

'So I did.' He started to shuffle through the papers on his desk, hoping she would take the hint.

'You wrote me a very charming farewell,' she said. There was a breath of wormwood in her words now, bitter, cold. 'Never can a woman have been humiliated so poetically.'

He wished she would leave. What did she want? Did she think she could seduce him back to her bed? Had she no pride?

'So now you have another muse.'

'What?' He glanced up from the papers, not understanding.

'Who is she, Jaufré? Some dark-eyed dancing girl you brought back from Djihan-Djihar?'

'Grazide.' He steeled himself to take her hands in his own. 'I thought you understood. There is no one else. There is no other muse.'

217

'I thought you loved me.' Her full lower lip, carmined with rouge, began to tremble.

'Loved you? Yes, after my fashion. But I could never give you the love you want, the loyalty you deserve. I believe I am incapable of that kind of affection.'

'I could live with that, Jaufré –'

'No!' How could he explain to her? He could not risk the closeness, could not risk the pain of betrayal, loss.

'So it's true, then, what they're saying at court.' The green eyes brimmed with tears.

'What's true?' he said harshly. He hoped she was not about to cry.

'Alissende. You're pursuing Alissende Belcastel. That insipid little scrap of a thing.'

'Why should I be after Alissende!' he cried.

'You spend all your time with her brother these days. Ohh.' Her hand flew to her mouth. 'Is that it? You've tired of women?'

'He's my lieutenant. My oldest friend. We were squires together.' Exasperation was driving away all civil thoughts from his mind. What did she want of him? 'By the Lady, Grazide, you *know* that –'

'There was a child,' she said suddenly.

'What?' Jaufré's voice stifled in his throat, as if someone had caught him in a stranglehold.

'I received your letter on the morning you sailed for Djihan-Djihar. The morning after I discovered I was carrying a child. Your child.'

'My child.' For a brief moment, he was overwhelmed by an extraordinary surge of emotion, bright and painful as the first flares of passion.

'I was so happy. I was carrying our child. Child of our love. And then, in the space of a few hours, it became a nothing, an irrelevance, a burden – because you had rejected me.' She had begun to pick at a loose thread on the pointed cuff of her blue sleeve. 'So I got rid of it.'

He just stared at her.

'I thought you should know,' she said, her voice flat, expressionless.

'Why?' He saw her white body bloodied, writhing with cramps. The image revolted him. 'Why tell me this now?'

'You returned my gifts. It's my way of returning yours. Except the songs. Those will always be mine.'

218

'There will be no more songs,' he said quietly, still staring at her. The pale ivory of her face was calm again, unshadowed by emotion. Was this all they had left in common? A dead love affair . . . and the blood of innocents on their hands?

'So. There's no more to be said.' She went to open the door – and then paused, as though listening.

'What's that?' she said sharply.

'What?' He was still shaken, angry with her for having hurt him, having exposed his vulnerability.

'That child. Crying downstairs.'

He listened – and felt a sharp chill shiver through him. He could hear it too, a thin, desolate crying that went on and on, as though inconsolable. And it seemed to be coming from below. From the cellar –

'Not downstairs. Out in the street,' he said dismissively.

'Why doesn't someone go to it?' she said, and he saw her shiver too, clutching her arms to her body as though she was cold. 'Sweet Lady,' she said, her voice cracked and raw, 'why doesn't someone *make* it stop?' With a sudden convulsive movement she twisted around, and gathering up her blue gown, went hurrying from the chamber as though she could not bear to stay a moment longer.

CHAPTER 21

'Which way now, Lieutenant?' Arnault reined in his horse, shading his eyes against the merciless sun.

The Hawks sprawled in the long grass, taking out their water flasks, drinking till the water ran out of the sides of their mouths.

Berengar gazed around him at the steep wooded crags and the hazy mountain peaks beyond. He didn't want to admit it but he was utterly confounded; he didn't know which way to go. Lia's trail had gone cold the moment they left the Gorge.

Up here the air was keen, clear and hot. Insects droned and darted from bright sun to dappled shade . . . in the distance he could hear the lowing of mountain cattle in the pastures. But they had not passed anyone to ask directions since the last village. And there the villagers had been suspicious, grudging in offering food and water, even when he had paid them generously. Other soldiers, less scrupulous, would have just taken what they wanted.

'What d'you reckon, Lieutenant?' Arnault pulled off his broad-brimmed hat to wipe the sweat from his forehead. His tanned skin gleamed in the hot sun. 'There's been no sign of a ruined castel. Those villagers – surly bunch – could be in the pay of these brigands we're after. Suppose they've sent us up the wrong way – into a trap?'

'It's possible.' Berengar uncorked his flask and took a swig of water; it was warm and slightly bitter to the taste.

'They could've poisoned the water they gave us too.'

Poison. Berengar spat the water out on the dry path – and looked up to see Arnault grinning at him.

'Damn poor joke, Arnault,' Berengar said. 'Remember Alois?'

The grin faded from Arnault's sunburned face.

'I'll never forget,' he said.

'Jaufré said he drank bad water. Poisoned . . . or stagnant.'

'Those Djihari bastards,' Arnault said.

'You're right, though, Arnault. No point in relaxing our guard.'

'Which way, then?'

Berengar shook his head. The track forked, one way going on upwards, the other winding away out of sight. No one had mentioned a fork in the road.

'Upwards,' he said, guessing wildly.

'On your feet!' barked Arnault. 'Look lively, there!' The Hawks stumbled up, brushing the grass seeds and dust from their clothes.

Berengar cast a long, appraising look at them as they marched doggedly on up the track. How alert would they prove in an ambush?

Suddenly Tramontan stumbled. Berengar, jolted forwards in the saddle, swore – and dismounted. Tramontan jittered around nervously as he knelt beside him.

'Let's take a look then,' Berengar coaxed. He wished – not for the first time since they set out – that he had brought Arbutus instead, steady, reliable Arbutus. Tramontan was too nervy, too easily startled for this mission.

'What's the problem?' Arnault called back. 'Stone?'

'Mm. I'll have to prise it out.' Berengar took out his knife. 'Shouldn't take long – I'll catch you up.'

Tramontan's tail flicked as the flies began to gather, buzzing close to Berengar's head. He raised one hand to bat them away. Tramontan whickered, showing his teeth, and rolled his eyes threateningly.

'Steady there, steady,' Berengar murmured, patting the horse's flank.

'Need any help?'

The clear, high voice made him start. Looking round, he saw through the dazzle of sunlight a boy standing watching him.

'Where did you spring from?' Berengar asked, shaken that the boy had crept upon him so silently. If he had been one of the brigands . . .

The boy grinned a wide smile. The brilliant sunlight transformed his spiky fair hair to a translucent halo of silvered gold. Berengar tried to focus on his face . . . but his eyes watered with the strength of the sunlight and the boy's features became a blur.

'Lost, are you?'

Berengar nodded. 'There's said to be a castel up here.

221

Ruined.' Best not to give too much away; the boy might be a lookout for the brigands, sent to lead them into a trap.

'The old castel? You're going the wrong way.'

'Oh?' Sweat trickled into Berengar's eyes; he put his forearm up to wipe it away.

'You need the lower fork; you must have passed it a short way back.'

'What are you doing up here all alone?' Berengar asked, still suspicious.

'I'm on my way home,' the child said, completely unselfconsciously. 'Don't forget – the lower fork.'

'Thank you,' Berengar said. It seemed churlish now to suspect the child of any kind of deception; he was probably a shepherd's son, out searching for straggling members of his father's flock. Perhaps he should toss him a coin in thanks for his help . . .

He dug in his purse for a coin – but, looking up again, saw that the path was empty. Only dust swirled around, the motes sparkling with sunlight, where the boy had stood.

Berengar stood up to scan the barren, sun-scorched pasture but there was no sign of the boy.

Arnault and the others were waiting for him a little further around the bend; stretched out, lounging in the shade as he toiled upwards, leading Tramontan, to meet them.

'We're on the wrong route,' he called, feeling the dust rasp at the back of his dry throat.

'How d'you know it's wrong?' Arnault called back.

'Didn't you see the boy? Back there?'

'Saw no one,' Arnault said, shrugging.

'Because he's been asleep!' called out one of the Hawks. Arnault turned on him, beating him with his hat until the man howled for mercy. The others looked on, laughing.

Berengar, sweating and thirsty, shook his head. He was a seasoned enough campaigner to know that a little horseplay was good for dispersing tension on a long march. But every minute wasted was another minute in which Lia was in danger.

The seam of frayed cloth blurred. Rahab rubbed his eyes and bent closer over the work. What was the matter with his sight? He hoped he did not need spectacles; tailors' sight often deteriorated after years of intricate sewing in poor light, it was recognised as a risk of the trade . . .

222

A blue haze of pain, cold as ice, shimmered through his head. For a moment, his vision dimmed, his hearing faded.

Barakiel . . .

The pieces of unpicked coat dropped to the floor.

He staggered out into the passageway. His eyes. He couldn't see properly. Swirls of light, white as snow, went zig-zagging across his vision.

He could hear voices in the distance. He moved slowly towards them, feeling his way.

'I say we shouldn't make any assumptions. How are we to know this isn't Aymon's response? Armed men sent to massacre us all?'

The voices of the arguing scholars faded and swelled as if heard from far away. He wanted to shout, 'Something's wrong!' but his tongue was frozen in his mouth.

'There hasn't been time for Aymon to respond. Talmai only delivered the letter this morning.'

'T-Talmai –' Rahab stammered out. They turned to stare at him. 'Where is – Talmai?' And then his legs gave way from under him and he collapsed on the floor of the council chamber.

'The lad's ill.'

'Too hot in here. Open the shutters.'

'N-no.' Rahab tried to make himself understood. 'M-must – find Talmai.'

'Why?' Malakhi caught hold of him by the shoulders, fingers bruising into the bone. 'What's happened to him? What do you know?'

'When last I saw Talmai, he said he was going to water his herbs,' said Elon.

Rahab felt the weakness passing. He twisted free from Malakhi and went stumbling from the chamber towards the Sanctuary. He had to be sure – before the next fit overwhelmed him again. The others bustled along behind him – but he outran them easily, making for the bronze casket, lifting the lid –

'Gone!' he cried. 'They're gone!'

'What does he mean?' demanded Lamech from the rear as the other scholars crowded into the Sanctuary.

'Look for yourselves!' Rahab lifted the casket, thrusting it towards Malakhi. 'It was unlocked, Malakhi. Who had access to the key?'

223

Malakhi's hand crept to his neck, fishing for the chain. 'Here it is. I only took it off while I slept. No one could have . . . unless . . .' A slow frown crept across his face.

'The amulets have been stolen!' said Lamech, the last to push forwards to look in the casket.

'One of you go check the herb garden!' ordered Malakhi. 'Find Bar Talmai.'

Another icy tremor overwhelmed Rahab. He staggered, reaching out blindly to try to hold himself upright against its devastating blast.

Clouds scudded through his brain, grey with the promise of snow.

Through the turbulent clouds he felt someone grip hold of him, supporting him.

'What is it, Rahab?' Malakhi's voice whispered in his ear. 'Is it Talmai?'

'Must – get to him – Must – stop him –'

'You're too vulnerable. Tell me where he is.'

Rahab shook his head, trying to clear the chill clouds from his mind.

'C-can't tell.' There was nothing but a dull swirl of confusion. He could not sense anything more clear than the building clouds – and the intense cold. He began to shiver.

'You have a fever. Here. Sit down.'

He felt Malakhi ease him down into a chair, wrap a blanket about him. He clutched the blanket, hearing his teeth clicking together uncontrollably. Maybe Malakhi was right . . . and it was just fever chills.

'Stay here. Leave Talmai to us. We'll find him. We'll recover the amulets.'

The steep track skirted a forest of pines and spruce that resonated with a constant chitter of cicadas. The resin-scented shade was welcome after the fierce heat of the upland pastures. The path was soft underfoot with drifts of brown pine needles and Berengar found the dappled light filtering through the high branches a relief after the merciless glare of the sun. But the hushed shade of the forest made him wary.

'Be on your guard,' he cautioned the Hawks, turning in the saddle. 'They could be lying in wait for us anywhere.'

The trees began to thin and they found themselves toiling upwards again, the forest falling away beneath them into a sheer-sided valley. The sun still dazzled in a cloudless sky – but they were walking in the shade.

The longer the hot afternoon wore on, the more Berengar found his mind wandering to Lia. And the more he began to doubt the facts of Emmenza's account of her disappearance.

Nothing made sense. He had seen no evidence of a struggle at the Auger house. No ransom note had been delivered – in fact there had been no clues at all. All he had to go on was the report of the guards at the Aude Gate – though one of the riverboat men remembered transporting a girl to the Gorge.

He looked at his men toiling up the steep track ahead. There were no jokes now, not even grumbling, no sound but the tramp of their boots on the rocky track – and the grunt of their laboured breathing. A sudden appalling thought struck him. Had he dragged them all the way up here on a fool's errand?

'Lieutenant!' Arnault, who had been riding in the vanguard, waved to him, pointing on up the hill.

'Halt!' Berengar dismounted and, tossing Tramontan's reins to one of the Hawks, clambered on up to where Arnault had stopped.

'Up there,' Arnault said. 'The boy was right.'

As Berengar gazed to where Arnault was pointing, he saw the broken towers and jagged walls of a derelict mountain castel. To their right, on the edge of a dizzy promontory above the ravine, stood a single watchtower, its ancient walls swathed in thick garlands of dark ivy. The afternoon sun gilded the old stones with the ambered hue of thick honey.

'Looks deserted to me,' Arnault said.

Berengar shaded his eyes, squinting into the sun. A thin wisp of smoke was slowly drifting upwards from behind the walls.

'There,' he said. 'Woodsmoke.'

Arnault swore under his breath by way of reply.

Maybe there was some point to this hot, exhausting climb after all. Maybe they really had tracked down Lia's abductors. Or maybe all they would find would be a family of itinerant tinkers camping in the ruins. Berengar turned to the Hawks.

'Weapons at the ready. We're not taking any chances.'

The intense sunlight suddenly dimmed. He glanced up at the sky – and saw to his astonishment that a great grey cloud had come scudding up over the mountain.

'Looks like rain,' Arnault said wryly.

'Then let's get this over with before the heavens open!'
Berengar said. He climbed back into the saddle and drew his
sword from its sheath, raising it high over his head. 'Hawks –
forward!'

Rahab sat shivering in his blanket whilst all around him he
heard the scholars running, searching, calling Talmai's name.

'Rahab?'

He looked up to see Lia standing before him.

'What's wrong?'

'T-Talmai,' he said, against the chattering of his teeth.
'Amulets.'

'Talmai's taken the amulets? After everything Malakhi said?
About the – the end of everything?'

'G-got to stop him –'

'Rahab.' Lia had put her hand on his arm; she was gripping it
hard. 'Listen to me. Concentrate.'

'I'm – trying to –' The shivering was calming a little – but now
he could sense through the swirling clouds in his mind something else. A presence. A distant presence.

'Suppose they're Arcassanne soldiers. Hawks.'

The presence was slowly coming closer. Like a clear, cold
shaft of light penetrating the clouds in a wintry sky, it illuminated the foggy landscape in his head. He struggled to
focus on Lia's face, to hear what she was saying. He knew it was
important.

'Wh-why Hawks?' he said.

He heard her give a short, sharp exclamation of impatience
and the grip relaxed on his arm. Through the swirling snowclouds in his mind he saw her leaving the room. And knew he
must stop her.

'Lia!' he called, struggling to his feet. 'Wait!'

Every step he took was like wading through thick drifts of
snow. She had not heeded his warning; she was already far
ahead of him.

And she was running directly into danger.

He staggered into the courtyard, the blanket still draped
about him like a cloak. The golden light of late afternoon had
gone; blinking, he looked up into the cloud-sheened sky and
something cold, white, wet drifted down on to his lashes. A
thin, bitter wind whined about the broken battlements.

'Snow?' he said aloud.

The clouds were no longer within his mind; dark and heavy with snow, they filled the summer sky.

Now he could identify the presence. Not his volatile Guardian, Barakiel, but his colder brother Shalgiel. Shalgiel, merciless as the winter's blizzards, had recognised the cold emptiness in Talmai's soul, the chill logic that informed his actions.

The sky grew darker as Rahab set out across the courtyard, looking for Lia. All about him there was disorder; the scholars were running about in the falling snow, calling Talmai's name, the women and children were herding the goats into the barn.

And then he caught sight of a slight figure high on the jagged battlements above the gate, hair blown hither and thither like the tatters of a ragged war-banner.

Lia.

Was she trying to get herself killed? The ancient masonry on the battlements looked unsound even in clement weather.

Rahab clambered up the worn steps, already slippery with snow, to reach her.

'Go back, Rahab!' Lia cried against the whine of the wind.

He braced himself against a block of stone and gazed down. Snow swirled about the promontory, obscuring the ravine from sight. Vertigo made him feel dizzy and sick; he had never had a good head for heights.

'Go back,' she cried again. 'You're sick.'

'And so will you be if you stay out here without a cloak.'

'But there are men down there. Caught in the snow. I *saw* them.'

Rahab forced himself to look down. She was right. Far below in the swirling snow he could see figures struggling through the blizzard. Even from this height he could tell that they were disorientated, staggering blindly in different directions, some wandering close, too close to the edge of the promontory.

'Talmai's soldiers?' he said.

'Berengar!' Lia cried suddenly. 'It's Berengar!'

'How can you tell?' Rahab peered into the blizzard.

'Berengar! Look out!' shrieked Lia, leaning far out over the battlements. A loose stone, dislodged by her sudden movement, went hurtling down on to the ground far beneath.

Rahab grabbed hold of her, tugging her back.

'He can't see the edge of the cliff.' She seemed oblivious to the danger. 'He'll go over the edge!'

'Suppose they've been sent to kill us?'

'And suppose he's come to find me?' She began to shout his name again, voice straining against the howl of the wind. 'Berengar! *Berengar!*'

'He'll never hear us from up here!' Rahab said.

'Then we've got to do down –' Lia broke off suddenly.

A great turbulence came swirling, spinning through the cloudy sky, towards Tifereth.

'Shalgiel,' Rahab whispered. Looking upwards he saw a face at the heart of the blizzard. It was Talmai's face – but Talmai transformed, all human emotion seared away. Cold, clear light streamed from eyes as grey and chill as ice. Eddies of snowflakes came tumbling from frozen rivulets of snow-streaked hair, from the frost-grey feathers of great, slow-beating wings.

And as Shalgiel swooped low over Tifereth, the Hawks scattered in panic.

Berengar raised one arm to shield his face from the swirling blast of snow. Tramontan started to buck and shy, whickering in panic.

'Hawks, *à moi*, to me!' Berengar bellowed. He could see nothing but snow, could hear nothing but the banshee shriek of the wind. He hoped the old rallying cry would draw them back towards him.

'Lieutenant –' came a faint cry.

They were going the wrong way, stumbling towards the edge of the ravine.

He hugged hard on Tramontan's reins, wheeling the horse around, forcing the terrified animal after his men. He had to stop them. He had to stop –

'Halt! *Halt!*' he shouted. The freezing air made his throat and lungs ache. The ground was already slippery with snow. Where was Arnault, damn him?

And then the blizzard came sweeping down, unleashing its full fury upon him, blinding him with snow.

For one moment he looked up and saw – in astonishment – a face at the heart of the blizzard gazing down at him, a face of inhuman beauty, its sharp bones sculpted from translucent ice, its eyes chill and cruel.

In those cold winter eyes he read one word.

Death.

*

228

One Hawk alone, on horseback, was trying to rally his men, calling them back. But they, heedless of the danger, went running towards the ravine. He spurred his horse after them –

Rahab felt Lia stiffen in his arms as the horse slithered in the snow – and came crashing down, pinning the man beneath its thrashing body on the edge of the ravine.

'No!' she whispered. 'Oh no!'

Suddenly she twisted out of his grasp and went flying towards the stair.

'Enough!' Rahab cried, shaking his fists impotently at the fast-swirling cloud overhead. 'Talmai! Hear me! This must stop!'

Then he turned and went after Lia towards the worn steps, hurtling down, skidding on the slushy ice.

The courtyard below was white with thick snow. Lia's footprints were already filling again as he went after her to the door.

But as he came sliding across the yard, Malakhi barred the way.

'There's a man injured out there!' Lia's voice was shrill with anguish. 'We've got to help him.'

'No,' Malakhi said sternly. 'You must stay here until the blizzard subsides.'

'Rahab,' Lia said pleadingly. 'Tell him. Tell him why.'

'I must put the safety of my people first,' said Malakhi. 'If we open the gates and let these soldiers in –'

'He's hurt!' Lia cried. 'He won't harm anyone.'

'I'll go with her,' Rahab heard himself saying.

'You?' Malakhi said. His eyes reflected the chill cold of the grey sky above. 'How can we trust you both? This could all be part of some Arcassanne plot designed to bring Tifereth down. We open the doors – and in come the soldiers to massacre us all.'

'For God's sake, Malakhi,' Rahab cried in exasperation. 'Has Shalgiel frozen your wits? Can't you understand? Talmai made a mistake. A terrible mistake. These are friends, they meant us no harm.'

'Friends?' Malakhi's eyes were still cold. 'You told us these Hawks rounded up our people in Arcassanne. Arrested them.'

'Must we stand around arguing whilst Berengar is lying trapped out there?' Lia pushed past Malakhi and started to heave up the heavy bar holding the great outer door shut, grunting with the effort.

Without another word, Rahab went to help her. Malakhi made no attempt to hold him back.

They lifted the bar between them and dragged the massive door open. Snow gusted into their faces, hard, cold flakes of stinging snow.

Both stopped, staring.

An hour ago, the mountain had glowed warm in the hot golden sunlight of late summer. Now all that could be seen was a bleak, barren snowscape, filled with eddies and flurries of driven snow, thick as fog.

'Which way?' Lia whispered.

Rahab took the blanket from his shoulders and wrapped it about her. She seemed not to notice, head tilted a little to one side.

'Listen? Did you hear that?'

Against the chill keening of the snow-wind, a distant sound came echoing back.

'Over there!' She set out, trudging doggedly through the drifts, head down against the wind.

'Remember the ravine,' Rahab cautioned, following behind.

'Berengar!' Lia called into the wind. The falling snow muffled her voice.

'Berengar!' Rahab joined his voice to hers.

'Help . . . me . . .'

'There.' Lia clutched at Rahab's sleeve.

The faint voice seemed to come from the left. Rahab turned to look behind him, trying to get his bearings from the castel – but in the snow, even its solid outline had dwindled to a dull shadow in the dying light.

The intense cold was beginning to numb his feet and hands; his nose tingled with the bite of the snow. Yet Lia waded determinedly on, forging her way through the drifts, without a single complaint.

A thought pierced his heart, keen as a jagged thorn. *She must really love Berengar.*

There came a wild, nervous whinny from nearby.

As the snow mists swirled around them, he saw the shape of a horse materialise in the gathering darkness. Beside the horse a man lay sprawled in the snow.

Lia gave a cry and ran forward, flinging herself down beside him.

Rahab rubbed the snow from his lashes, peering to try to see more clearly.

'Bera,' Lia was repeating brokenly. 'Bera, Bera, it's me. Lia.' As Rahab approached, she looked up at him, her eyes brimming with anger. 'He's unconscious. I don't know what to do. Tell me what to do.'

Rahab dropped to his knees, wincing as he felt the cold snow soak into his leggings. Berengar lay twisted, his face whiter than the falling flakes. The tailor put out his hand and tentatively felt for a pulse. At his touch, a faint moan escaped and he saw a bubble of blood-soaked froth form and break on Berengar's blue-tinged lips.

'He's not dead,' he said tersely. 'But he soon will be if we don't get him out of the snow.'

'How can we move him?'

She had a point, Rahab thought wryly; Berengar was a tall man, broad-shouldered, muscularly built. Even between the two of them, they would not be able to drag him far.

'I'll go back for help,' he said.

He had only gone about ten paces when he saw shapes in the snow-mist, three figures struggling towards him.

'Who is it?' he called nervously, remembering the other soldiers they had seen from the battlements.

'Rahab?' It was Malakhi; relief sent a flush of heat through his frozen body.

'Here! Over here!' he cried.

Malakhi and two of the younger scholars appeared, swathed in thick cloaks. They were dragging a short ladder between them.

'Elon lent us one of his orchard ladders,' Malakhi said. Ice crystals were collecting on his thick brows and beard.

They laid the ladder down in the snow beside Berengar and lifted him on, securing him with straps of leather to the rungs.

Then the four men heaved Berengar up and began to make their slow, awkward way back towards the castel.

Lia caught Tramontan by the reins.

Berengar, unconscious, was a heavy, unwieldy weight to lug through the eddying snow; Rahab, not accustomed to carrying anything heavier than bales of cloth, felt as if his arm was slowly being tugged out of its socket.

'Why don't we – get the damn horse to drag this ladder?' he said through hard-gritted teeth.

'He's lame,' Lia said. 'Can't you see? He can hardly even hobble.' She stroked Tramontan's head, murmuring reassuringly to him. 'There, there, Tramontan, you're with friends . . .'

231

The castel walls loomed up out of the curtain of still-falling snow. With one last effort, they hefted the ladder into the courtyard.

'Rest,' puffed Malakhi.

On his count, they set the ladder down. Flashes of black and scarlet flickered across Rahab's vision as he nursed his aching arm. He could hear himself wheezing for breath, could feel the indrawn air, cold as frost, burning his throat, his lungs.

Other scholars appeared, lifting the ladder, carrying the unconscious Berengar away. Lia went hurrying behind them.

Rahab shot Malakhi a look of gratitude.

'You – said – they were – friends,' Malakhi gasped.

Rahab nodded. He raised his snow-soaked sleeve to wipe his hot face.

'No sign – of – the others?'

'No – sign,' croaked Rahab. He started slowly, exhaustedly out across the courtyard, following after Lia.

Malakhi put out a hand and stopped him.

'You were right about Talmai,' he said gruffly. 'I should have heeded your warning.'

Rahab nodded again, too tired to do more than acknowledge the apology.

'Let's go change out of these wet things.' Malakhi beckoned him across the courtyard. 'No sense in us all catching cold.'

'And – Talmai?' asked Rahab.

Malakhi glanced up at the sky. 'Snow's falling less fast,' he said. 'And the wind's dropped.'

As Rahab tugged off his wet clothes, leaving them in a pool of snow-water on the floor, he sensed that what Malakhi had left unsaid was true: the blizzard had blown away from the castel. He felt whole again now, weak but clear-headed.

But somewhere out there on the mountain Talmai lay, alone in the snow, abandoned by his Winged Guardian.

Lia and Zillaïs had tended Rahab when Barakiel left his body; they had clothed and warmed him. Without anyone to rescue him, Talmai would die of cold and exposure on the frozen mountainside.

Malakhi had brought him dry clothes. Rahab hurried into them, pulling on extra layers for warmth, lacing the worn leather boots tight to his ankles to keep out the snow. Then he went to find Lia.

The scholars had laid Berengar on a trestle table before the warmth of a swiftly kindled woodfire. They had cut away his snow-soaked clothes to try to assess the extent of his injuries. Jorah, the college scholar of medicine, was gently prodding and pressing with expert fingers.

Lia, hair plastered down with melting snow into dripping strands, stood watching close by, agitatedly twisting her fingers together.

When she saw Rahab, she hurried up to him, clutching hold of his hand.

'He's still unconscious. D'you think he's very badly injured?'

Rahab looked over at Berengar. The young lord's skin was still pale as whey – except where the livid stains of bruises marred the pallor.

'He is going to be all right, isn't he, Rahab?'

Rahab looked into Lia's face and saw the anguish in her eyes.

'He's going to be all right,' he said, pressing her hand. He hoped he made a convincing liar.

From the table he heard a faint groan. Lia let go of his hand and hurried back to Berengar's side. Rahab heard her softly, urgently calling his name. 'Bera. Bera, it's me, it's Lia . . .'

For a moment he stood watching her, his hand still warm from the pressure of her fingers. And then he heard Berengar whisper her name.

'Lia . . .'

Rahab's heart felt cold and heavy in his breast, a lump of ice.

'Try not to talk,' Jorah ordered. The scholars gathered closer round the trestle, busy attending to their patient. 'Where does it hurt? Here? Or – here?'

Rahab turned and walked swiftly, silently away.

In the courtyard he turned his face up to the grey sky. Only the odd flake of snow drifted down now. He closed his eyes, feeling the light, wet kiss of the last flakes on his lids, seeking, calling . . .

Lia might not need his help any more . . . but there was one who insisted he was not his brother who was in desperate need.

The bleak snowscape lay before him, altered beyond recognition, even the dark pines of the forests in the ravine below powdered with white.

'Barakiel,' he prayed, 'help me find him . . . before it's too late.'

CHAPTER 22

Zillaïs stood with her back against the cell door.

The walls wavered, distorting, dissolving before her dimming sight. Her temples throbbed a warning.

'No,' she whispered. It was happening again. First the warning. Then the sickness, the pounding, devastating headache.

Streaks of red flashed across her vision. She shut her eyes tight.

'No, no,' she whispered again, pressing her fingers to her closed lids.

Behind her the Tolonada Ghetto is red with fire, people are running towards the sea, the burning air is filled with their cries.

The Rashiel amulet glows hot in her hand, hot as a coal plucked from the brazier.

'Rashiel,' she whispers, 'save us, only you can save us now.'

The red-hot amulet sears her hands; she can hold it no longer and with a cry casts it to the ground.

Suddenly she feels the ground begin to shake. The shuddering shoots up through her body until her temples ache with the tremors.

'Papa,' she cries, as the trembling ground cracks beneath her feet, throwing her forward. 'Papa, help me –'

Her father comes running out into the courtyard. He stops, staring at the glowing amulet.

'Zillah, Zillah, what have you done?

Where her father had been standing, arms upraised, she sees the air become a swirling vortex. And in the midst of the vortex stands a winged figure of air and shadow whose eyes burn with the raw heat of molten lava, whose cloudy hair is spun from particles of swirling dust –

She strives to speak, to call his name – but she is dumbstruck, staring at the great winged creature.

'No-no, not me –'

And then Rashiel opens his arms to embrace her, to gather her up,

and she is drawn into the searing vortex of flame and dust. Her words of
protest are drowned in the roar of beating wings.

With every beat of Rashiel's wings, the earth beneath shudders – and
cracks go darting along the whitewashed walls of the houses, fissures
appear in the cobbled streets.

'Earthquake!' goes up the terrified cry.

Smoke and dust billow around her, blotting out the light of the sun.

Only the amulet still glows on the spot far below where she was
standing, fiery red as volcanic lava.

Zillaïs forced her scorched eyes open.

One of the Guardians was close; she could sense its presence
in the storm-charged air, winging closer . . .

She braced herself, waiting for the first tremors to start.

If this was a rescue attempt by the scholars in Tifereth, then
they were not as wise as she had believed. Did no one remember
what had happened in Tolonada? Didn't they realise that the
summoning of another Guardian could destroy everyone in
Arcassane, Tsiyonim and Gentiles alike?

The cell grew steadily darker; the air was no longer still or
sultry. It burned with the keen, clean tang of snow, a tang that
made the nostrils ache with cold.

'*Shalgiel?*' she said aloud, gazing up at the barred window.

'Tifereth . . . Tifereth . . .' Jaufré thumbed through the faded
pages of the *Sefer Rhaziel*, feverishly searching for a clue.

Now a shadow fell across the scrawled occult letters. The
room suddenly grew dark and Jaufré found himself shivering, a
sick, chill shivering that made his bones ache.

He hurried to the open window and looked up at the sky.

Grey clouds had come scudding across the sun, massing like
hostile forces, blotting out its golden glare.

His usual view from the tower room stretched far across the
red-tiled city rooftops to the green river plain beyond . . . and
even further, to where the distant mountains were veiled in a
shimmering summer-haze of heat.

But what he saw now made him grip the stone windowledge
to steady himself.

The clouds were hurtling towards the city from the mountains, fast-propelled as though blown by hurricane winds,
swirling and billowing like tattered grey robes. And the
winds that drove them bit him to the bone, blowing his hair back
from his face, stinging his skin with sleet-slivers of bitter ice.

Still shivering in the winds' blast, he remained stubbornly where he was, clinging on to the ledge. Below he saw people staggering to keep upright as the winds tore through the narrow city streets; he saw them clutch in vain at headscarves, hats, papers, all tossed up into the freezing air . . . as down came spiralling cascades of white snow.

Faint cries of dismay and astonishment reached Jaufré's ears through the whining howl of the winds as women swept children up into their arms and ran for cover and tradesmen struggled to pull carts out of the storm.

'Snow?' Jaufré whispered. 'In summer?'

Icy flakes swirled in at the open casement, stinging his cheeks. His fingers were turning blue with the sudden intense cold, yet still he stayed where he was, intently watching the sky.

This was no natural storm; this was Tsiyonim mischief. There had never been snow in summer in Arcassanne; the snows never came till Year's End.

'I know you!' he cried into the whirling snow. 'Shalgiel! I command you – reveal yourself to me!'

The blizzard swirled around the tower – and Jaufré, almost fainting with its intense cold, saw the ragged snowclouds trailing like tattered clothing as a winged figure came sweeping down out of the storm.

A face stared into his, the white face of a young man, a sculpture chiselled from snow, the blue eyes gleaming, cold with the chill of eternal winters.

With every beat of his great wings, snow feathers fell over the city.

'*Shalgiel!*' Jaufré cried again with all the force of his snow-burned lungs. And he felt a sudden answering throb within his breast, a dark pain which pierced him like a spear of ice.

The Guardian passed on by, swooping away from the tower towards the river plain, turning back towards the mountains.

Jaufré, hand extended as though to hold the fleeting angel back, fell to one knee. The amulet glowed at his breast, a pulsating star of dark ice. He strove to speak, to cry out for help, but each gasped breath was an agony.

Words formed in the blackness of his mind, etched like hoarfrost on a wintry sky.

He fell to the floor – and the spinning tower room was extinguished.

'It – has – started.'

He could hear voices speaking, voices like the rush of the wind, the glitter of the lightning; he could not identify the tongue in which they spoke but he knew, he knew what they were saying.

'Now – it – shall – be – accomplished.'

'Captain!'

The glittering voices merged together, sucked into the void.

'Captain! Can you hear me?'

Someone was lifting him up, calling his name. He opened his eyes to see Bertran's battle-scarred face close to his own.

'Wh-what happened?' he heard himself asking. He tried to sit up and felt Bertran's brawny arm supporting him.

'Looks like you were hit on the head by one of the shutters. All this snow's blown in.'

Jaufré scrambled to his feet and brushed the snow from his clothes.

'I've never seen anything like it.' Bertran leaned out of the window. 'Must be bad up in the mountains.'

'The mountains,' Jaufré repeated, remembering Berengar and his Hawks. Was this some form of retaliation from the Tsiyonim, a show of strength?

The thoughts in his mind tingled with the buzz of the icy air. He sat heavily down in his chair, staring at Bertran's bulk and the frame of white, wintry sky behind.

'The grapes'll all be spoilt. The *vendange* will be ruined,' Bertran said gloomily.

A flicker of cold, dark fire flared beneath Jaufré's ribs. He wanted Bertran to go; he wanted to be alone.

'But if you're here – who's on duty at the Tour?' he said, making an effort to conceal his pain.

'You – you were supposed to relieve me, Captain. An hour ago.'

'An hour!' He must have been unconscious all that time. 'Go back to the Tour, Bertran. I want you to check on that Tsiyonim priest. Make sure he has nothing concealed about his person. No . . . talismans, jewels, amulets . . .'

'Very good, Captain.'

Bertran was halfway out the door when he turned on his heel, his heavy features crinkled up in an expression of puzzlement.

'It went right out of my mind, Captain, but –'

'What!' barked Jaufré, one hand pressing on his ribcage.

237

'As I came in, I passed this boy. Pale, scrawny little fellow, lurking in the shadows. "What're you doing in here?" I asked him. And he says, "Waiting." That's all. Just "Waiting." "You'd best be on your way!" I said to him . "If the Captain catches you –" But when I looked again, he'd vanished. I'd get your servant to check if anything's gone missing –'

'Thank you, Bertran, you're dismissed,' Jaufré said, feigning disinterest.

The instant the door banged shut, Jaufré let out a long, thin breath.

What had Bertran been babbling about? A boy? Maybe a child had crept in to shelter from the blizzard –

A boy. *Waiting.*

Jaufré felt another shiver chill his body.

Waiting for whom?

He reached for the *Sefer Rhaziel*, opening it with trembling fingers. The obscure incantations tantalised him, the elaborate magical diagrams and pentagrams that promised initiation into the secret powers of the dark – and delivered so little.

Shalgiel. He brushed the luminous lightning-script with his fingertips, reading the text Barakiel had revealed to him:

'Barakiel, Wielder of Heavenly Fire, shall come from the East; from the North, cold Shalgiel with snow-feathered wings; the earth shakes at the tread of Rashiel. The last of these is Lailahel, Bringer of Eternal Night.'

He shut the book with a snap. The Tsiyonim had two of the four amulets in their possession: all Arcassanne had seen the proof. But was his amulet Rashiel – or Lailahel? Earthquake or Eternal Night?

Jaufré went to rise from his chair – but another dark flare of pain shot through him. The amulet burned like a brand against his breast. Shalgiel's manifestation seemed to have charged it, to have increased its power.

It was killing him.

He must be rid of it. He must give it to Rebh Jehiel.

Right now he was not even certain he could make it across the room and down the stairs. Trying not to breathe in too deeply, he lurched to the door and went down the spiral stair, leaning against the stone wall for support.

At the bottom of the stair, he struggled to open the door.

A cold, wet blast blew in and he found himself standing in a pile of half-melted slush. The street beyond was muddy with snow-melt; the louring sky above the yellowish grey of old vellum.

'*Waiting . . .*'

He glanced back over his shoulder, certain he had heard someone whisper the word. He had the brief impression that he caught sight of a small figure slipping into the shadows of the stairwell.

'Come out!' he rasped, remembering what Bertran had told him, clutching at the ache in his side. 'Come out, you little thief!'

He ducked under the stair, arms extended, ready to grab hold of the intruder. He found himself clutching dusty darkness.

There was no one there.

'Dame Maury!' whispered the gruff voice.

Zillaïs awoke, shivering. The cell was dim – and freezing cold. A large man loomed over her bed.

'Who's there? Who is it?' she asked, frightened. She could remember nothing but the blinding megrim that had struck her down at the height of the blizzard.

'Bertran, lady.'

Now she recognised him: Captain d'Orbiel's corporal, Bertran, a great lumbering bear of a man. She sat up slowly, wishing she felt less muzzy-headed.

'It's the old man, Jehiel. He doesn't look too good. Can you come and attend to him?'

Zillaïs gathered up her simples and followed Bertran's lumbering frame down the passageway.

Jehiel lay unmoving on his bed, wrapped in his prayer-shawl against the cold.

'Rebh Jehiel?' she said, setting down her bag of simples.

'Did you see the blizzard?' he whispered. 'That was no ordinary storm.' His pale eyes gleamed, bright with the memory of the snow.

'I saw,' Zillaïs said, pressing his hand, noting how cold, how clammy it felt.

'Listen, my dear.' He seemed excited, almost delirious. 'There has been a letter. From Tifereth.'

'From Tifereth?' She felt his forehead, checking for signs of fever, but he brushed her hand away.

'Orbiel showed me. Our kinsfolk have offered us safe haven. They have written to the Comte asking that we be allowed to go free.'

239

Could it be true? Or was it only another of Jaufré d'Orbiel's subtle snares?

'Don't you see what it means, my dear Zillah?' Jehiel said. 'Our messenger got through.'

'Rahab?' she whispered.

'Who else could have told them?'

If Rahab had reached Tifereth, it was possible, just possible, that Lia was with him. If only –

Zillaïs hastily swept the idea from her mind. She did not dare to begin to hope.

The walk from the Tour d'Orbiel to the Tour de la Justice usually took Jaufré no more than five minutes. But as he struggled against the icy gusts of the dying blizzard wind, it seemed to last an eternity. And with each step he took, the burning amulet scorched his labouring ribs.

It was almost as if the power that possessed him knew what he intended, was trying to slow his steps. It did not want to let him go.

At least the snow-covered square in which the Tour stood was empty. He stood, teetering on the edge of the square, looking around. Guillemette and her followers must have gone to seek shelter.

Now would be the time to open the gates of the Tour and let the Tsiyonim go free. Before Guillemette realised what was happening. What did it matter that it was freezing cold and that half of them would fall sick and die on their journey? He would be free of them at last.

He started out across the desolate square. Each step was an effort. The Tour seemed so close – and yet so far. The wet snow glittered in the darkness.

'Captain.'

He looked around to see Guillemette trudging across the snow towards him, clutching her wet rags to her. Damn the wretched woman to hell – was she never to be satisfied?

'Go home!' he said. 'Go take care of your children.'

'That's what you'd like, isn't it?' Her eyes gleamed with fever in the gloom. 'You want me to give in, to give up.'

'Yes,' he said wearily.

'But then he wasn't your son, was he? You don't have children, do you, Captain Orbiel?'

The pain in his chest intensified; a dark mist obscured his

sight. He was having difficulty breathing –

'I haven't time for this now!' he said, pushing past her.

'They'll pay,' she cried after him. 'The Tsiyonim will pay for his death!'

'You can go home now, Bertran!' Jaufré said. Bertran handed over the cell keys – but still lingered, shuffling awkwardly from foot to foot.

'Well?' Jaufré snapped. 'What are you waiting for?'

'I've had Madame Maury give the old man more physic,' Bertran said. 'But I don't like the look of him.'

'You're not usually this tender-hearted towards our prisoners.'

'Drunks, pickpockets,' Bertran shrugged, 'they deserve what they get. But he's just an old man.'

A night of black, bitter cold had settled over the city. Jaufré could smell the frost in the air as he staggered towards Jehiel's cell – and yet his whole body burned with the amulet's dark fire.

His hand shook as he unlocked the cell door. He went inside, leaning back against the door, gasping for breath.

Jehiel sat up, clutching his prayer-shawl to his shoulders.

'What do you want, Captain Orbiel?'

Give Jehiel the amulet. There's still time.

Jaufré's hand moved to unfasten his jacket, to pull out the burning amulet on its chain, to fulfil his promise to Alois at last . . .

A numbness spread through his fingers, moving up his wrist into his forearm, his elbow. His whole arm was paralysed, he could not move.

'I – I c-can't,' he whispered aloud. Jehiel was looking strangely at him.

'Something is here . . . in the room with us. I can sense it . . .'

Jaufré tried to wrest himself free – but it was as if he were held tight in the grip of an invisible adversary. He struggled – wrestling with shadows – but his shadow adversary only gripped him even harder.

'Help me, Jehiel.' Jaufré just managed to gasp out the words before he pitched forward on to the cold flagstones.

'God of Tsiyon!' Jehiel whispered, sinking to his knees beside him.

241

Paralysed, Jaufré saw Jehiel raise his hands over him as if in blessing. The old scholar's eyes closed and he began to murmur rapidly in Tsiyonim, repeatedly bowing his head.

The dark pain no longer smouldered; it burned, searing through Jaufré's ribs to his fast-thudding heart.

'B-beneath – my jacket –' Jaufré stuttered. 'T-take it – in God's name, take it away –'

Jehiel's eyes opened, startled. He reached forward, and with palsied fingers, undid the fastenings of Jaufré's jacket and shirt. As the shirt fell open, Jaufré saw the scholar recoil, his hands raised to shield his face.

'No,' he said hoarsely. 'No. It can't be.'

'*Please.*' Jaufré heard himself begging aloud.

'I cannot take this amulet.' Jehiel still held his hands before his eyes.

'Wh-why not?'

'I – I am no *tzaddik*. I am only a scholar, I have not the skills to control a Guardian – especially not this Guardian –'

'You know its name?'

'And yet if I do not attempt exorcism, what further wrongs may be perpetrated . . .' Jehiel did not hear him; he appeared to be deep in internal debate. He leaned forward and placed one hand on Jaufré's forehead, the other on his breast.

'In the name of Ibrahil the seer and of Itshak, I command you, come forth!' he said in the common tongue. 'In the secret name of the one, the true, the ineffable God, come forth, leave the body of this man.' And then he lapsed into Tsiyonim and Jaufré could no longer understand what he said; he could only feel the intensity and the power of the words.

The lanternflame wavered wildly as though a sudden gust of wind had blown through the cell. Guttering smoke swirled outwards, dark as shadow, dark as encroaching night.

Jehiel lifted up his head and cried aloud into the darkness.

'Lailahel! Lailahel! Lailahel!'

The flame went out, sucked into the gathering darkness. The black air writhed and shuddered. Jehiel gave a faint, choking cry and fell forward across Jaufré's body.

The turbulence in the cell suddenly stilled.

Jehiel's weight – a dead weight – held Jaufré pinned to the ground.

'Rebh Jehiel?' Jaufré said shakily into the darkness.

There came only the weakest of groans in reply. Jaufre tried to

242

move – and found he had the use of his limbs again. He inched himself out from underneath the old scholar's prone body and felt his way across the cold stone floor to the lantern. His hands shook as he tried to strike a light from the tinder to rekindle the flame.

In the lanternlight he saw that Jehiel's face was pallid, his eyes wide and fixed. Yet his fingers still feebly scrabbled at his shirt collar, and his lips, grey, bloodless, moved as if he was trying to speak.

Dropping to his knees, Jaufré lifted the old scholar's head, supporting him. He lowered his ear close to Jehiel's mouth, trying to catch the wisps of words.

'S-Sefer Bahir . . .' Jehiel's fingers plucked at Jaufré's sleeve. 'Keep . . . keep the night . . . at bay . . .' A rattling wheeze extinguished the last of his words.

'Bahir?' Jaufré tried to pull Jehiel's collar undone to ease the old man's breathing; buttons flew off as he tugged, clumsy in his haste. 'Who – or what – is Bahir? Tell me, Jehiel. *Tell me!*'

Jehiel's lips opened again. Jaufré leaned closer.

On the exhaled breath of a sigh Jaufré heard him whisper, 'Tif . . . er . . . eth . . .'

And then the old scholar's eyes slid upwards, his mouth went slack and the scrabbling fingers stilled . . .

'Jehiel!' Jaufré shook the old man, put his mouth to his, tried to blow breath back into his frail body. After a while he realised that all his frantic efforts were of no use.

Rebh Jehiel was dead.

CHAPTER 23

'Cold, so very cold . . .'

Ever since the blizzard blew away, the messages had come shivering through Rahab's brain. But they were growing fainter, less distinct now, as though the sender was gradually slipping into unconsciousness.

'Shalgiel . . . help me . . .'

Rahab looked out from his window. It must be near to sunset. The grey of the snowclouds was slowly darkening to a chill sheen of violet-blue, streaked with veins of liquid fire. The effect was both lurid and chilling, promising a night of bitter cold.

Better to wait till dawn.

So why, Rahab asked himself, was he wrapping himself in layers of clothes, why was he borrowing Lia's old hat to protect his head from the night's cold? Why was he making a bundle of clothes and blankets to carry with him?

He would need food and drink, a flask of eau-de-vie . . . and gloves. He delved deep into Selima's old clothes chest, rejecting one worn and patched garment after another. There was nothing that he could adapt into mittens; there was no time to cut and sew now, the light was fading fast.

And then he remembered. They would make unconventional gloves – but as he had brought them all the way from Arcassane, he might as well use them.

A little while later, he made his way to the kitchen, tiptoeing past the chamber where Berengar lay. Jorah had finished tending to his injuries and was tidying away the bottles of tinctures and lengths of linen bandage. A strong smell of witchhazel came from the open doorway, masking another, more insidious smell: drying blood.

'Rahab!' Lia rose from Berengar's side.

Rahab paused, wishing she had not spotted him, wondering if he could hurry on with a whispered promise to see her later.

'How – is he?' he asked stiltedly.

'Difficult to tell,' she said, equally stiltedly. She was holding a damp cloth; Rahab could see the bloodstains on the white linen. 'Where are you going?'

'Oh – just out to check on the animals.' He forced himself to mime a shiver, rubbing his arms. 'It's freezing outside.'

'What are *those*?' Lia demanded, pointing.

'These?' Rahab had forgotten he was wearing the rabbit-gloves. He looked down at them, feeling foolish. 'Rabbits.'

'Let me see. No, let me.'

She reached out and drew his hands close, examining the bright-coloured stitching.

'Glove-puppets?' she said. The corners of her mouth twitched – yet she did not let go of his hands.

'Just a little frivolity,' he said. 'I made them for Schimeon's children.'

'They look more like mice than rabbits.'

'Thirzah insists they're rabbits.'

'Then rabbits they are.' Still she held his hands, and he made no effort to withdraw them from hers.

'What will you do now?' he asked softly.

'Stay and watch till he regains consciousness,' she said.

Her eyes met his over Berengar's prone body and he knew that she had understood the unspoken subtext to his seemingly simple question.

'I am still betrothed to him, after all,' she said, letting go of his hands.

'Yes.' He turned away. 'You are betrothed.'

'He came after me. In spite of all the Dowager said. If he hadn't come to find me, he wouldn't be lying here so badly injured –' He heard the little catch in her voice.

'Don't. Don't blame yourself. Lia –'

'Yes?' She looked up at him, almost eagerly. For a moment he wondered if he had misinterpreted her protestation of fidelity to Berengar; for a moment he dared to hope –

A groan came wheezing from Berengar's lips. Lia started.

'Bera?' she said. She bent low over him, fingers stroking his forehead, his bruised cheek. 'Bera, can you hear me?'

What was he thinking of, was he crazy? She would never consider him her equal. She was a merchant's daughter; he was an apprentice without a sou to his name. Besides, she was a shrew, a selfish sharp-tongued little spitfire. She would be hell to live with . . .

245

'C-cold. Dark. Help me . . .'

The voice shivered through Rahab's mind again, chill as falling snow. He withdrew on tiptoe from Berengar's chamber. He had lingered here far longer than he should and night was drawing in.

The other scholars would be gathering in the Hall, preparing to continue their disturbed preparations for *shabbath*. The sun had nearly set. Would they miss him at their table as Selima lit the candles? Was there anything in the Books of Law that forbade one man to set out on *shabbath* to go rescue another?

The kitchen was empty – but the delicious smells of *halkes*, herb-seasoned meal balls, simmering in chicken soup made his stomach ache with hunger.

Damn fool Talmai, rushing off in an idiotic act of self-sacrifice, believing he was the hero, the saviour of his people – without once stopping to question what he was doing.

After all, I should know, Rahab told himself as he helped himself to a plaited *challah* and some fresh-baked pastry *pastales* stuffed with pine nuts. *I set the precedent.*

Hearing voices, he grabbed a lantern and hurried out into the courtyard.

The chill almost took his breath away. Beyond the castel, he stood on the snowy ground, gazing to the west as the last streaks of sunlight bled crimson on to the distant peaks.

The drowsy nighttime chorus of cicadas was silent. There was no sound but the icy rustle of green leaves frozen by the sudden cold. Tomorrow, Rahab suspected, they would begin to count the cost of the blizzard; tonight, all he could do was search for the perpetrator – and ensure that he did not summon Shalgiel again.

'What am I doing out here?' he muttered, remembering the soft light of the *shabbath* candles he had left behind, the golden crispness of the savoury *pastales*.

'Help me . . .'

The mindvoice was fainter now, fast fading away as if the caller's strength was failing.

He stood tensed, listening, in the freezing air whilst the shadows in the ravine slowly darkened from violet to indigo.

'Come back, Shalgiel, don't leave me here alone . . .'

There was a poignancy now in the faint cry. For a moment Rahab heard the voice of a little child, trusting, overwhelmed by disbelief that he could have been abandoned.

He let out a short, resigned sigh. 'No chicken soup for me tonight.'

The way was treacherous; the snow that had not melted had frozen, creating a thin, glassy crust over the softer slush beneath. He went forwards slowly, uncertainly, walking flat-footedly to try to stop himself from sliding. Listening to the voice in his mind, making it his lodestone, he saw that he was being drawn towards the edge of the ravine. And he hadn't even thought to bring a rope. All he had was the cord with which he had tied the bundle of clothes. If Talmai had fallen over the edge –

Cursing his lack of foresight, he went cautiously forward one tentative step at a time, testing the ground.

A faint draught of ice-chill air stirred the flame of the lantern beside Berengar's bed. Outside the castel, the mountain slept under its spell of snow. Inside, the faint drone of the scholars' voices, muttering prayers, issued from the Sanctuary.

Lia sat beside Berengar, unmoving, frozen into immobility. she had reached a state beyond tiredness; she was floating in a lucid dream-daze.

'Why has everything gone so wrong?' she whispered to Berengar. He could not hear her. He lay, pale and still as a painted funeral effigy in the Belcastel vault.

All her hopes rested on the letter Talmai had dispatched to Comte Aymon. But had it even reached Arcassanne before the blizzard struck?

What daemon had possessed Talmai to undermine their plans?

Snatches of dream-vision kept flashing across her sight. She saw her mother confined in a bare, narrow cell, sitting, waiting patiently for release. A release which might never now be negotiated . . .

'Mamma, I'm sorry, I'm sorry,' Lia whispered. Tears pricked her eyes but she was too exhausted to cry.

And then there was Berengar.

He had come all this way in pursuit of her. So like Berengar, she thought wryly, true to the chivalric code of his house, an ancient chivalry, long-since abandoned by the other self-seeking nobles of Arcassanne.

What drove you up here, Bera? she asked him silently. *Was it because you do love me? Or was it to avenge the slight on the honour of your house?*

Her hand crept out to smooth the lion-gold hair from his temples. It was like touching a statue; there was no response, not even the faintest alteration in his breathing, the slightest twitch of a muscle.

Perhaps she would never know the answer. Perhaps he would die without regaining consciousness.

Rahab had no idea how long ago he had left Tifereth. The intense cold had numbed his mind as stealthily as it had numbed his fingers and shuffling feet. He might have walked only a few hundred paces from the castel ... or a few thousand.

It took a while for his brain to register that the shadow ahead, dark against the purple-black of the sky, was the ruined watchtower, built on the sheer edge of the ravine, on the promontory's tip.

'Talmai?' Rahab shouted, his voice crisp and hard in the chill black air. 'Talmai!' And then clapped his hand over his mouth, remembering stories of avalanches in the mountains.

'*Here . . .*'

Raising high the lantern, Rahab gazed up at the ruin. The crumbling stones were almost completely covered in creepers; he ducked in beneath a low-hanging swath of ivy and brambles.

The tower was open to the sky; Rahab crunched over shards of broken tiles and clumps of weeds that had split the ancient flagstones apart. The leaning walls afforded a little shelter from the keen wind – but there was a dank taint to the air that reminded him of the odour exuding from the Arcassanne street gutters after heavy rain. He hoped that no wild creature had made the ruin its lair and was lurking inside, lying in wait for unwary visitors.

'Talmai?' he called again, more cautiously.

And then a sudden faint shock set his nerves quivering. The Barakiel amulet was close by, he could sense it. The lodestone drew him across the broken flagstones towards a dark archway, half-blocked by fallen masonry. Dropping to hands and knees, he pushed the lantern in and peered around.

A man lay huddled in a corner, clutching the tattered rags of his clothing to his shaking body.

'Talmai!' Rahab crawled in, pulling the bundle of clothes and food behind him. He was so glad, he could have hugged the young man.

248

'Go away,' Talmai said in a muffled voice.

Rahab had started to unwrap the bundle of clothes. He stopped.

'You called for help,' he said.

'I called Shalgiel.' Talmai spoke slowly, his voice slurred, as if he were barely conscious. 'Not you.'

Shalgiel. One blizzard had caused enough havoc; another so close to the first would be a disaster. Rahab abandoned the dry clothes and began to search the chamber for the amulets. Little shocks – which made his searching fingers tingle – drew him to the darkest corner, beyond where Talmai lay slumped.

Talmai stretched out one trembling hand as though trying to stop him. Rahab pushed the hand aside. Dully gleaming in the dirt lay the three amulets, still fused together; pulling off his gloves, he picked them up – and then with a yelp of pain dropped them, nursing his hand. They were deadly cold; the chill of the charged metal had seared his palm. Iceburn.

'Shalgiel resists you,' said Talmai faintly. 'I am His Warder, only I can touch His amulet.'

Rahab shot him an exasperated glance and pulled the gloves back on. Picking up the amulets, he hastily dropped them on to his handkerchief and wrapped them up, tucking them inside the breast of his jacket.

'You've done enough damage for today,' he said shortly. 'Let's get you back to Tifereth. Can you stand?'

Talmai shook his head. He began to shiver again.

Rahab sighed. He had no desire to spend the whole night in the ruin, without a fire to keep him warm.

'Let's get you into some dry clothes,' he said. He held out the woollen robe that he had brought. 'Wrap this round you.'

Talmai turned his head away.

'Very well, then.' Rahab shuffled across the little chamber on his knees and tried to wrap the robe about Talmai's hunched shoulders. Talmai did nothing to help him, staying rigid, like a little child in a tantrum, consumed by its own anger.

'Eau-de-vie?' Rahab offered the flask. Talmai shook his head. Rahab shrugged and took a mouthful himself. He did not feel like humouring Talmai. He had not expected thanks – but he had hoped for a little cooperation.

'I'm telling you now that I don't plan on spending the night out here. I need my hands for my work; I didn't come out to lose a few fingers to frostbite.'

'Go back, then,' Talmai said listlessly.

Rahab sat back on his heels, looking at him.

'I might just do that.'

Now that his eyes had adapted to the gloomy light, he noticed a dark trickle staining the side of Talmai's face.

'You're hurt.'

'Hit my head. The descent was . . . very swift . . .'

Serve you right! Rahab bit back the obvious retort which had sprung to mind. There would be time for recriminations later. Now he had to try to determine how serious Talmai's injury was. It might just be a flesh wound . . . or the gash could mask some more serious damage.

'Let me see.'

Rahab brought the lantern closer and reached out to part Talmai's curling hair. Some of the locks were matted with dried blood, and Talmai drew in a sharp breath.

'The bleeding's stopped.' Scalp wounds bled a lot, Rahab remembered . . . and suddenly found himself back in Arcassanne with Chadassah bending over him, dabbing at his gashed head with hot salt water and discovering –

Rahab drew back the hair from the side of Talmai's face squinting in the flickering lanternlight.

The mark could have been mistaken for a bruise. If Rahab had not seen a blue and red whorl-tattoo just like the one behind Talmai's ear before, he might have ignored it. But there it was, as unmistakable as his own; he traced the pattern with gentle fingertips. The mark of his House and Line, Jehiel had told him, the ancient Tribe of Chazael.

'What . . . is it?' Talmai moved his head away.

Rahab tried to speak and found he could not force out a single word. Even if Talmai were not his brother, he was of the same House; they were family.

'What?' Talmai asked again in a dull, irritated voice.

'Nothing,' Rahab said, sitting back against the wall. 'Nothing . . .'

CHAPTER 24

Jaufré sat staring at Rebh Jehiel's body.

Outside he could hear the steady drip of melting snow as the rising sun brought a slow thaw to the icebound city.

A paralysing lethargy of despair had overwhelmed him.

There was no hope for him now. Jehiel had tried to exorcise the Guardian spirit that possessed him. And the Guardian had crushed the life from the old man, as swiftly as a child crushes an ant. Now there was no one to save him.

Why do you ask to be saved? asked the subtle shadow-voice in his head. *Why fight what you know now to be inevitable? Give yourself to the darkness. Surrender . . .*

'I will not surrender!' Jaufré said aloud. He clapped his hands to his ears, trying to black out the insidious shadow-words.

He knew he should release the body to the Tsiyonim so that they could perform whatever burial rites were customary in their faith. But how was he to explain it to them? They would accuse him of torturing the old man, of deliberately causing his death. The body was an embarrassment, an impediment to the fulfilment of his plans.

Why not simply order the Hawks to throw the carcass in the paupers' lime pit?

He went to the door, hand resting on the handle, ready to call for assistance. The Hawks had followed him unquestioningly across the sands of Djihan-Djihar. They would do anything for him. Disposing of an inconvenient body would be no problem . . .

His hand dropped back to his side.

Had the corrosive darkness burned away every last shred of honour in his soul? He could not deny the old scholar the final rites of his faith.

Zillaïs had hardly slept all night for the cold. She sat watching the drips of melting snow run down the rusting bars of her window.

251

'My speckled lilies,' she murmured. 'My strawberry tree . . .'

There would have been no time for Peire to protect the tender plants in the garden. The intense cold must have shrivelled them by now. It had taken her years to nurture the rare specimens that Auger had collected for her on his travels.

'Wait till you see what I've got here . . .'

She saw Auger, eyes twinkling in his sun-burned face, carefully unwrapping something concealed in his silk handkerchief.

'What is it, what is it?' Lia cried eagerly, and then – as she saw the contents, small, brown and shrivelled – she let out a sigh of disappointment. 'Just a few boring bulbs.'

'Lily corms,' Auger said, placing them in Zillaïs's hands.

'Not –' She had suddenly been unable to say the words.

'Yes,' he said, closing his hands around hers. 'Speckled cinnamon lilies from Aten Maia.'

Lia pulled a face.

'For your wedding chaplet,' Zillaïs said to Lia. 'Have you any idea, my girl, how rare these corms are? These speckled lilies have the sweetest scent . . .'

Lia. The memory brought sudden, sharp tears to her eyes. Lost Lia. Even at her most contrary – and only a mother could know how contrary Lia could be – Lia was her daughter, her only daughter and precious beyond the price of lilies.

Zillaïs sighed, angrily wiping her eyes. What use were tears? It was easier to fret about rare lilies than to admit her worries about Lia's disappearance.

Where was Berengar de Belcastel, why had he not come to her aid? Had he, too, turned against her? Even if he wanted nothing more to do with her, surely he would not have rejected Lia, surely he would come to her rescue?

She had sat idle long enough; she needed to know where her child was, that she was safe –

The door opened and Jaufré d'Orbiel came in. She rose, ready to confront him.

'Captain Orbiel –' she began. And then she saw his face. 'Captain,' she began again, 'are you all right?'

'Come with me,' he said, his voice hoarse. His eyes burned, dark with dissipation, in a sallow, haggard face. Had he been up all night drinking? Or was Jehiel right? Was he possessed?

'Come where?' she asked, wary.

'Just come.'

There was something in the roughness of his voice that warned her not to argue.

Two Hawks stood guard outside the door to Jehiel's cell; they moved aside to let them enter.

Armed guards? So even Jaufré d'Orbiel is losing his nerve . . .

And then, as the door closed behind them, she saw the body on the floor.

'Ohh,' she said. For a moment, grief overwhelmed her, a cloud of darkness, blotting out all other thoughts. '*Jehiel.*'

She knelt down, reaching out to feel his face, his pulse, just to check, to make certain, hoping, wishing . . . But his skin was chill to her touch and there was no trace of a pulse in his thin wrist. And when she looked into his face, she saw only stillness, the utter absence of the animating spirit she had known. The remote, calm features blurred; she put one hand up to rub her eyes – and felt the wetness of tears on her fingers.

'I tried to revive him,' Jaufré was muttering – though whether to her or to himself, she could not be sure. 'But he was gone. A flame, snuffed out, extinguished by the darkness . . .'

'I – I'm sorry?' she said, looking up at him. His face was distorted, twisted as though with some internal struggle. Aware that she was looking at him, he seemed to make an effort to force himself to adopt a more amenable expression, like a carnival mummer swapping masks: jovial-handsome for malevolent-grotesque.

Darkness. Now that he had said the word, it seemed to her that she could still hear it distantly resonating, like the slow tolling of a deep funeral bell.

'What darkness?' she said, rising to her feet. 'How did he die?'

'A sudden seizure.' Jaufré had averted his eyes; he was staring down at an open book on his desk. 'You said yourself he could die at any time.'

'But what provoked this seizure?' Zillaïs went over to the desk. 'And why didn't you bring me to him?'

'There was nothing you could have done,' he said shortly.

'You have witnesses, I trust,' she said, leaning across the desk towards him.

He closed the open book and snatched it away, as if he did not want to let her see it. But she had already caught a glimpse of cabbalistic symbols etched in stained brown writing, dark as

253

dried blood. This was no ordinary book; it exuded the unwhole-some aura of an occult treatise.

'What should I do? With the body? What do you Tsiyonim *do* with your dead?' His questions came out roughly, crudely, as though the emotion of the moment had chipped away the veneer of civility.

'We are not savages, Captain,' she said coolly. 'But it is our custom to bury our dead soon after death. You must speak to Baruch and the other elders. They will perform the necessary rites. There are special prayers to be said.'

'Bury? Where?' he said. A muscle twitched at the side of his mouth.

'In the ground,' she said, 'in the cemetery.'

She could still hear the dull, dark tolling – but now it beat with the rhythmic throb of blood pounding. She glanced up, sensing against the evidence of her eyes that there was . . . someone else in the chamber.

'You mean the Tsiyonim cemetery.'

'Of course the Tsiyonim cemetery!' she answered back scorn-fully. 'Anywhere else would be sacrilege.'

'It's impossible.'

She rose up.

'Deny this good old man the burial rites of his faith?' She did not care if she antagonised him. 'Is there no spark of decency left in your soul, Jaufré d'Orbiel?'

'And who precisely is going to perform these rites?'

'The men. There must be ten men. That is our way.'

'How can I guarantee the safety of your men if I let them accompany the body to the cemetery?'

'That is your problem,' she said, each word clipped, curt, 'and your responsibility.'

The darkness shadowing his face intensified, and for a moment she feared she had pushed him too far. And then she heard the wail of a thin, high voice outside, faint and faraway.

'What is that?' she asked, listening intently.

'It's only the wind,' he said. But she saw from his eyes that he had heard the thin voice too, and it had shaken him.

The cry came again, and this time it was closer, more distinct. There seemed to be words too, barely coherent, barely articulated.

'That's not the wind,' she said. 'That sounds like . . . like a child crying.'

'Outside in the street,' he said.

254

He went to close the shutters, banging them shut as if trying to block out the sound. But the crying went on and on, the cry of an abandoned child, desolate and alone. Zillaïs could not bear to hear it.

'That child is in this building,' she said sternly. 'In the Tour.'

'Then it's one of the Tsiyonim children,' he said. He was unnerved now, she could see it from the way his hands twitched, rubbing against each other as if washing away some indelible stain. 'Maybe one has fallen sick . . .'

Dybbuk. Jehiel had feared Orbiel was possessed. Was she listening to the voice of the *dybbuk*?

'I must go and see,' she said, moving towards the door.

'No!' he cried, moving to block her way.

'If the child is sick, then let me tend to it.'

'There *is* no child –'

There came a thunderous knock at the door. She saw Jaufré jump, startled by the sudden sound, his hand move to his sword hilt.

'Message from the Comte, Captain.' Bertran put his head around the door. 'You're to go to the Palais straight away.'

Zillaïs saw Jaufré's tense, hunched shoulders relax a little. His hand fell away from the hilt of his sword.

The crying had ceased – as abruptly as it had begun.

'Bertran,' he said. 'Take Madame Maury to tend to the Tsiyonim children.'

'Ten men,' Zillaïs said. 'Ten men to bury Rebh Jehiel.'

'Very well.' Jaufré's shoulders sagged now, almost defeatedly, as he turned to Bertran. 'I want you to make arrangements for ten of the Tsiyonim Elders to be released to bury the old man. But watch them every step of the way, to the cemetery and back.'

Zillaïs knelt beside Jehiel's body one last time and bowed her head.

'Goodbye, my friend,' she whispered in halting Tsiyonim. 'When all this is over, I'll come and put pebbles on your grave. That's a promise.'

The Comte's Hall was thronging with people and Jaufré had to push his way through the crowd. Aymon was seated in his carved chair, listening patiently to the furious complaints of a petitioner. Jaufré guessed from the man's homespun clothes that he was a farmer or a *vigneron*.

'First the storm and now this – this blizzard. Snow just at the time the grapes are ripening on the vine. I'm ruined, seigneur. Ruined!'

Aymon glanced up and, catching sight of Jaufré, nodded to him to approach. Jaufré moved closer, positioning himself behind the Comte's chair. He had heard enough angry comments as he forced his way through the crowd to guess why Aymon had summoned him; he sensed both bewilderment and anger amongst the farmers. He scanned the Hall, searching out his Hawks. He wanted to be certain that he had enough men on guard in case of trouble.

'Look, seigneur.' The *vigneron* held out a bunch of blackened, withered grapes. 'See? The rot has already begun to blight them.'

Aymon took the grapes to look more closely, wiping a smear of greyish blight from the hardened fruit with his fingertips.

'And you know what they're saying? That this is the work of those damned Tsiyonim.'

'Really?' said Aymon drily. He handed the grapes to a waiting servant, fastidiously wiping his fingers on his silk kerchief.

'They're not like us. They practise dark arts, they can summon ancient forces to do their bidding.'

There was a murmur of assent from the waiting petitioners.

'All the more reason for not antagonising them, then,' Aymon said with a thin smile.

'I want compensation, seigneur. For me, for my workers. With no wine to sell, there'll be no food to fill our bellies this winter. We'll starve.'

'But surely you've made provison for the lean years, the poor harvests?' Aymon said.

The *vigneron* looked down at the tiled floor, suddenly silent and subdued.

Clever Aymon. Jaufré listened to the Comte in grudging admiration. Only Aymon had the diplomatic skill and charm to deflate such a potentially explosive situation.

'I will look into the matter of compensation,' Aymon continued. 'But I make no promises. Not until the extent of the damage has been properly assessed.'

'Thank you, seigneur –' began the *vigneron*, but broke off as a commotion of voices erupted at the back of the Hall. Frowning, Jaufré looked around, his right hand instinctively gripping the hilt of his sword.

'Let me through! I must see the Comte!'

A soldier, haggard and filthy, came staggering into the Hall, pushing aside the servants who tried to restrain him.

'Comte,' the soldier said, tugging his battered hat from his head, clutching it to his breast in salute.

'Who is this?' Aymon enquired. 'Is he drunk?'

But Jaufré had recognised the weathered features. He hurried forward just in time to catch hold of the soldier as he swayed on his feet.

'Arnault!' he cried, steadying him. 'What in God's name –'

'Dead,' Arnault muttered 'all – d-dead –'

'Bring this man some wine!' Aymon raised his hand to his servitors.

One of the servants came running up with a chair and Jaufré eased Arnault down into it. Another poured a cup of red wine, which Arnault seized in both hands and drank down in shuddering gulps.

'Who is dead?' demanded Jaufré.

'The Lieutenant. The Hawks.'

Berengar dead? Jaufré heard the hushed exclamations of disbelief from the other listeners – but he felt numb, numb as if gripped by winter's cold.

It could not be true.

'Killed in the blizzard. The storm came upon us out of – of nowhere.' Arnault held up the cup for more wine. 'We were on a ridge, within sight of the castel, Captain. Then – the sky went dark – and the air was filled with snow, wind-driven snow. No one could see where they were going. The – the men ran towards the edge. The Lieutenant spurred his horse after them, trying to stop them. His horse slipped – and crushed him.'

There was silence. The only sound that could be heard in the Hall was Arnault gulping down his second glass of wine.

'Lower the Belcastel colours,' Aymon said to his servants, 'as a sign of respect to his house.'

'Who will break the news to his family?' someone asked.

'I will go,' Jaufré said automatically.

'You were close, weren't you, Orbiel?' Aymon said. 'Friends since boyhood, mm? I liked young Belcastel. Good-natured, sunny fellow. A loss to the court, a tragic loss. But tell me, what in God's name was he doing up in the mountains with a patrol of my men?'

Berengar dead. Jaufré was still trying to digest Arnault's news. He forced his numbed mind to think.

'Don't you remember, Comte, the brigands, the abduction of Demoiselle Maury?'

'We had your authorisation, seigneur,' said Arnault, wiping the wine from his frost-cracked lips with the back of his hand.

'Your Hawks are employed to keep the streets of my city safe, Orbiel,' Aymon said, leaning closer. 'What's all this wild talk of brigands and abductions? Since the murder of that child, there's been nothing but unrest and lawlessness. I want you to put a stop to it.'

'Me?' Jaufré snapped alert again. Aymon, unknowingly, was offering him the opportunity he had been waiting for. 'Then let me take the Hawks up into the mountains. Arnault can be my guide.'

Aymon slowly stroked his chin, considering. 'And leave Arcassanne unprotected?'

'I'll leave a detachment under Corporal Bertran's command at the Tour.'

'And what of the Tsiyonim?'

'If my suspicions are correct,' Jaufré said, 'the murder suspect is hiding out in this castel. Once I have brought him back to Arcassanne to stand trial, you can let the other Tsiyonim go free.'

'No more extra mouths to feed. Hmm,' the Comte said pensively. 'That has distinct attractions in view of the disastrous weather and the ruined harvest. We're in for a lean winter . . .'

Jaufré closed his eyes a moment. Constructing this elaborate fabrication of half-truths and implications was as complex a task as composing a *rondel*, with its strict rhyme-scheme. The effort was becoming too much of a strain. He feared that he might forget himself – and blurt out the truth.

For one distorted moment out of time, he glimpsed himself falling at Aymon's feet, heard his own voice crying, 'I killed the child Jacou. I did not intend to harm him . . . yet still he died and since his death I have not had one moment's peace of mind.'

And then a dark smoke swirled across the vision and a voice darker than smoke whispered of torments too terrible to endure, of fire and disembowelling hooks, a long, lingeringly painful death . . .

'Do not confess your crime, Jaufré. You are my Warder and I will protect you.'

Within the swirling smoke in his mind, Jaufré sensed a powerful presence, intense as a candleflame, the words searing into his soul.

I will protect you.

'Are you all right, Orbiel?' Aymon was staring at him. 'Are you sure you're fit to undertake this journey?'

The smoke cleared from Jaufré's vision.

'Berengar's death,' he said stumblingly. He hoped Aymon would believe his preoccupation to be caused by grief. 'So unexpected.'

'Indeed.' Aymon rose to his feet. 'And as a mark of respect to the late Lord of Belcastel, I declare this session concluded,' he said, addressing the waiting crowd. 'My steward will collect all written petitions.'

'I've waited all morning!' came a voice from the crowd. 'I'm not leaving till my case has been heard!'

Others began to shout out, and a few at the front of the crush, jostled from behind, came lurching towards the Comte. Aymon stood his ground, unflinching.

'Way!' Jaufré cried. 'Make way for Comte Aymon!'

Arnault jammed his battered hat back on his head and stood shoulder to shoulder with Jaufré.

'Back!' he snarled, revealing a mouthful of yellowed teeth. 'Or I'll show you a sword-trick or two I learned in Djihan-Djihar.'

The petitioners moved slowly back, letting the Comte pass. Jaufré and Arnault followed close behind, hands on sword-hilts.

In the antechamber, the liveried servants closed the doors behind them.

'Farmers!' Arnault said, spitting contemptuously.

'Close,' the Comte said, dabbing at his glistening forehead. 'Too close. Jaufré, make sure you arrest this man Rahab. I must be seen to maintain law and order in Arcassanne. They're losing confidence in me. And once you've lost the confidence of the people, my father used to say, you've lost control of the city.' He put his hands on Jaufré's shoulders, looking him directly in the eyes. Jaufré felt his left eyelid begin to twitch uncontrollably under Aymon's steady gaze. 'I'm relying on you. Don't let Arcassanne down.'

'You can depend on me,' Jaufré replied.

'Comte,' came a voice from the gilded chair near the fireplace, 'as your spiritual adviser, I have kept silent long enough. I must speak with you.'

Jaufré saw Prieur Maugis rise from the chair and come forward to the Comte. Aymon's shoulders sagged.

'Not now, Maugis,' he said, shaking out his linen kerchief and tucking it into his sleeve.

'What better time than now?' said Prieur Maugis quietly. 'You will forgive me for pointing this out, Comte, but Arcassanne is a troubled city. We have tolerated the Tsiyonim here long enough – but their malign influence has been well documented in other cities. Their religious beliefs are barbarous. They do not acknowledge the Lady or Her ways. I say the time has come to confront them, to give them the chance to abjure their old faith – and convert to ours.'

Aymon let out a slow sigh. Jaufré suspected he had heard this argument many times before.

'And if they do not wish to be converted?' said Aymon.

'Why, then they must die,' the old man said, folding his hands together.

'I will not hear of it.'

The murmur of angry voices in the Hall beyond surged up again.

'The woman Guillemette has been to see me,' Maugis said, his voice still soft. 'She is greatly distressed.'

'Then I hope you were able to offer her consolation,' said Aymon smoothly. 'That is, after all, Prieur, your role in Arcassanne. To administer spiritual consolation and advice. Nothing more. Do I make myself clear?'

Maugis's eyes narrowed.

'Only too clear, Comte,' the Prieur said. But Jaufré saw that although the old man's lips smiled, his eyes were cold and hard.

Jaufré returned to his room to make certain that Rebh Jehiel's body had been removed. Bertran must have followed his orders; the room was empty . . . though Jaufré felt he could still sense a lingering aura of death. Or had the news about Berengar tainted everything he encountered?

Bera, he cried silently, mouth twisted in grief. *Bera. Why you? Now there's no one left. I am alone. Utterly alone.*

He poured water into a bowl to lave his hands and face. Leaning over the water, he caught a glimpse of his own

260

reflection. Fevered eyes stared hollowly back from a face so drawn and sallow he hardly recognised it as his own.

'What's happening to me?' he cried aloud, his voice catching in his throat like a sob. 'Am I sick? Is this some Djihari fever burning in my blood?'

And then he saw a flicker of shadow moving behind his reflection.

'You are not sick. Neither are you alone.'

He shuddered.

'But you are in torment, Jaufré . . . Let me soothe away your pain, let me salve your hurts . . .' The voice breathed on the skin at the back of his neck, stirred through his hair, hot as the desert wind.

'Who's there?' Jaufré whispered.

'Don't you recognise me? You awoke me, you summoned me. You know my true name. Call me by my true name.'

'No,' Jaufré said. Yet even as he said the word aloud he could feel his resolve beginning to waver.

'But I can give you so much of what you desire. Look. Look at what I can give you, Jaufré . . .'

The flicker of shadow wavered, spread, darkness pooling into the room, sucking him in, swallowing him before he could even cry out in protest.

Blinking, Jaufré found himself standing in a fast-darkening garden, watching the last glimmers of twilight fade from the sky.

'Do not fear the coming of the night, Jaufré. Come, walk with me.'

A figure had materialised beside him, tall, robed in darkly shimmering shades of night: cobalt, purple, ebony. Long locks of wild black hair streamed behind, like a living cloak. Yet when Jaufré tried to look into his companion's face, he had to turn away, dazzled by the reflected glitter of starlight from the sky overhead.

'Where are you taking me?' he asked, shaken.

'Here, you can forget your pain, Jaufré . . .' The voice enchanted his senses; it breathed with the sweetness of night-scented blossom, white and pure. *'Night is not to be feared, it is to be welcomed . . .'*

A trickle of clear, liquescent notes fluted across the dew-wet paths of the dark garden.

'A nightingale?' Bewitched, Jaufré stood unmoving, listening. He hardly noticed that his companion had drawn closer . . . until he felt again that hot, desert-perfumed breath on his skin. And this time he did not draw away.

'A nightingale. Without the coming of night, how could you hear

that heartbreaking song? How could you see the dazzling brilliance of the stars? Think of the night-scented flowers, the jasmine that only releases its poignant scent in my sweet hours of darkness . . .'

As Jaufré's eyes became accustomed to the dark, he saw that they were walking between drifts of night-flowering plants, petals ghost-pale beneath the dazzling star canopy.

'I can give you all this and more . . . but first we must agree on one matter, we must be of one mind. Your will, my will.'

The voice was so soft, so seductive that Jaufré almost found himself agreeing before he knew what he was doing –

And then a warning beacon flared in his mind. All the grimoires and alchemical texts he had studied had emphasised one point. The summoner must never relinquish his control of the daemon he had conjured.

'I hold the amulet,' he said.

'You know that I can lead you to the other amulets. Isn't that what you truly desire, Jaufré? And that is all I desire . . . to be reunited with my fellow Guardians.'

'If you're so powerful, why can't you bring me the other amulets?' Jaufré demanded, his suspicions aroused.

He felt a ripple of energy move through the darkness, an emanation of a potent emotion . . . no longer soothing but fiercely, darkly angry. Frustrated.

'I can do nothing without you.'

'Why?' Jaufré could not stop himself from demanding further proof of his mastery over the Guardian.

'Because you are my Warder. I need your strength, your will to fulfil my purpose.'

He was master of this dark daemon, this beautiful creature of the night that walked beside him, breathing perfumes on his skin . . . This feeling of mastery was more seductive in its potency than his love for Grazide, for dead Berengar, than any transient human emotion. It intoxicated him, it flowed through his veins like a rich, dark wine. If this Garden of Perfumed Night was just one of the marvels the Guardians could show their Warders, what other wonders could the Guardians create?

'Captain!'

Dazed, he looked up to see the exquisite garden shimmering, disintegrating before his eyes.

'What's happening?' he asked, bewildered, disoriented.

'Captain!' The voice was Arnault's. 'Are you ready? It's time to go to the Belcastels'.'

CHAPTER 25

Zillaïs stared around her in bewilderment. Forty, maybe fifty Tsiyonim women and children had been crammed into a dungeon built to accommodate no more than a dozen. The smell of stale urine and unwashed flesh made her eyes water – or were they tears of shame and anger? How could Aymon treat her people with such callousness?

'Where is the child who is sick?' she asked.

'Here! Over here!'

In the corner she saw a woman rise up, frantically waving and beckoning.

'Who are you?' the old woman beside her asked, her voice querulous with suspicion.

Zillaïs sighed. This was not going to be easy.

'She's the healer, Auntie,' the woman said, chiding.

The child was a girl, no more than five years old, Zillaïs suspected. She lay still, listless, her cheeks red with fever. Another little girl crouched beside her, clutching a scrap of dirty blanket.

'When did this start?' Zillaïs asked as she felt the sick child's forehead.

'Last night. After the snow came.'

'She was sick,' announced the other little girl. 'All down her dress, eugh, eugh.'

'Mamma,' the little girl said in a faint, fretful whine, 'want Rahab. Want rabbits.'

'Hush, Thirzah, hush.'

Thirzah? Zillaïs wondered if she had heard aright. Hadn't Rahab mentioned the name Thirzah? If these people were friends of Rahab, then perhaps they might have news . . .

She gently slid her hands from the girl's sticky forehead to check for swelling in the throat and behind the ears.

'Mmm,' complained Thirzah, trying to wriggle away from Zillaïs's probing fingers.

263

'What's wrong with her?' the mother asked anxiously. 'Can you cure her?'

'Thirzah,' Zillaïs asked, 'does it hurt when you swallow?'

Thirzah nodded.

'And here?' Zillaïs gently pressed the child's stomach and saw her wince.

'Hurts,' complained Thirzah. 'Want to go home.'

'Is it bad?' asked the mother.

'It's very damp in here,' Zillaïs said. 'It might be quinsy. Let's hope it's not the quartan ague. I'll give her some powdered willow for the fever and ginger to calm her stomach pains.'

'Sit up, Thirzi. The lady's brought some medicine to make you feel better,' coaxed the mother.

'Nasty medicine.' Thirzi shook her head. 'Don't want nasty medicine.'

So like Lia at the same age. 'Open wide, Thirzah,' Zillaïs said. 'Pinch your nose. Then you won't taste it at all.'

Thirzah began to wriggle from side to side, turning her face away.

'Like this.' Zillaïs mimed. She knew that the medicine would taste bitter – and she had no honey to disguise sourness or comfits to take away the aftertaste.

Thirzah, fascinated, stared. Zillaïs took advantage of the momentary distraction and popped the spoon into her mouth.

'Ugh. Horrid, horrid,' wailed Thirzah, trying to spit the medicine out.

'Is it really horrid?' asked the other little girl gloatingly.

'I don't know how to thank you,' the mother said.

'Don't thank me yet. She's still feverish. She must be kept cool.'

'What is your name?'

Zillaïs hesitated. How much was it wise to reveal of herself? She contented herself with saying, 'Zillaïs Maury.'

'Maury?' The woman looked up from her daughter, a look of puzzlement on her worn face. 'I know that name . . . wait. One of my husband Schimeon's customers. Lia Maury?'

'My daughter,' said Zillaïs, trying to conceal the rush of emotion she felt at hearing Lia's name. 'So you must be –'

'Chadassah.' The woman put out both hands in a gesture of greeting. Zillaïs hesitated again – and then reached out to press Chadassah's hands.

'Madame Maury –' began Chadassah.

'Please. Call me Zillaïs.'

'I – I cannot pay you. We lost everything in the fire.'

'I need no payment. I am a prisoner here, like you. We must all help each other.'

'*You?*' Chadassah pushed a straying lock of lank hair back under her headscarf. 'But why?'

'Because I am Tsiyonim too,' Zillaïs said softly. And then, before Chadassah could ask any more awkward questions, she said, 'Chadassah. I bring sad news. Rebh Jehiel is dead.'

'Oh!' Chadassah's hands flew to her mouth. 'Our dear Jehiel – dead?'

Heads turned, the low, desultory murmur of chatter stilled.

'Dead?' quavered the elderly woman Chadassah had called 'Auntie'. 'Or murdered?'

'His heart was weak,' Zillaïs said, and instantly despised herself for saying it. Why should she excuse Jaufré d'Orbiel?

'If that Orbiel hadn't arrested him, he'd be alive today. It's disgraceful! Keeping an old man locked up. Jehiel deserved better. I say it's as good as murder.'

'Who will say *kaddish* for him?' Chadassah asked. Her eyes were bright with tears.

Zillaïs quietly withdrew. She had no wish to intrude upon the grief of the community. She was a stranger, she had only known Rebh Jehiel a little while; her grief at his passing was insignificant compared with theirs.

She gathered up her simples and went to the locked iron door, tapping.

The little window in the top was opened and one of the Hawks peered in.

'Yes?' he said curtly.

'I'm ready to go back to my cell.'

'Ready?' He looked askance at her. 'I've no instructions about that.'

'Ask your Corporal. My name is Maury. Madame Maury.'

The guard shook his head.

'Corporal's busy. Can't be disturbed.'

'But I was distinctly told –'

'Then you were distinctly told wrong.' He slammed the metal cover shut.

Zillaïs looked around her. The fetid air was damp, oppressive. Jaufré d'Orbiel had tricked her. She was no longer of use to him. Now she was just another nameless prisoner.

265

She slid down, back against the wall, her eyes closed.

'Oh Lia, Lia, may you be spared this . . .' she whispered.

Someone tugged discreetly at her sleeve. She opened her eyes to see the large, dark eyes of Thirzah's sister solemnly staring at her.

'Mamma says will you come back? Thirzah's been sick again.'

Pons led Jaufré and Arnault to the solar. Berengar's manservant, discreet as always, did not ask what the news was that had compelled Captain Orbiel to come visit the young mistress so urgently. Yet there was something in his doleful manner that implied he guessed the gravity of the situation.

Alissende de Belcastel was sitting at her embroidery by the open window. Her long hair, pale gold, was bound back from her face with a band of twisted ribbons of blue and violet. Her underlip was caught under her white front teeth in an effort of great concentration as she tugged her needle through the linen.

'Visitors, demoiselle,' Pons said quietly.

'Thank you, Pons.' As she looked up, Jaufré saw – as he had never seen till now – how like Berengar she was. The likeness jarred.

'Captain Orbiel?' She smiled at him and he saw that the similarity was not so much in the features but in the way her mouth curved when she smiled, the way she tossed back her hair. 'What brings you here?'

Jaufré was silent a moment. Now that he stood here before her, in Berengar's house, he found that he, the poet, had no adequate words to tell her that her brother was dead.

'Where is your grandmother?' he said stiltedly.

'What's wrong?' The smile faded from her face; she rose up, bright skeins of embroidery silks falling from her lap to the floor like flower petals. 'Oh, Jaufré – it's Berengar, isn't it? He's – he's –'

'Dead,' Jaufré said softly.

Her hand flew to her mouth; her pale face flushed red – then all colour blenched from her skin and all he could see was her eyes, dark with tears, staring at him.

'Demoiselle,' Arnault said, clutching his hat to his chest, 'There was nothing I could do to save him.'

She had turned so white now that Jaufré feared she was about to faint. He crossed the solar and caught hold of her, easing her back into her chair.

'Dead?' she whispered. 'How – how dead?'

'We were caught in the blizzard,' Arnault said. 'His horse slipped. Fell on him.'

'Tramontan,' she said in a dull, distant voice. 'Pons always said Tramontan was unreliable. If only he had taken Arbutus, dear, dependable Arbutus . . .' She looked at Jaufré suddenly. 'How shall I tell Gran'mère? Berengar was . . . was all she had left.'

'Tell me what?'

Jaufré turned around to see the Dowager standing in the doorway.

'How dare you visit my granddaughter unchaperoned, Captain Orbiel!' The Dowager jabbed her stick at Jaufré. 'Have you no regard for her reputation?'

'I come on a formal matter,' Jaufré said coldly.

'Berengar's dead, Gran'mère,' said Alissende, her voice breaking.

'Speak up, girl, don't mumble!'

'Your grandson, Lord Belcastel, is dead,' Jaufré said bluntly. He was weary of the whole affair; he wanted to get out of the Belcastel mansion. Everything here reminded him of Berengar: the hunting trophies on the walls, the boar spears they had played at tournaments with, the wide fireplace in which they had smashed wine bottles in a drunken wager to see who could down the most of the best Belcastel vintage . . .

'Impossible!' said the old woman.

'It's true, Gran'mère,' Alissende said. Her lower lip trembled now but no tears came spilling from her eyes.

'Absolutely impossible!' the Dowager repeated stubbornly.

Jaufré nudged Arnault.

'I was there,' Arnault said. 'I saw it.'

The Dowager suddenly sagged. Alissende darted forward and caught hold of her. The old woman stared into her face, eyes narrowed.

'Why?' she said. 'Why my boy, my bright, beautiful boy? Why couldn't it have been *you*?'

Alissende flinched as if the Dowager had hit her.

'What use are you, you simpering little thing?'

Alissende backed away from the old woman's venomous tirade, one step at a time. Suddenly she turned on her heel and went running from the room. Jaufré could hear the sound of her stifled sobs as she fled towards her room.

'Berengar!' cried the old woman, her voice cracking. Tears began to run down her wizened face.

Jaufré bowed curtly to the Dowager and retreated, Arnault following hastily behind. He could not bear to stay in the mansion a moment longer. As they crossed the galleried hall, they saw Pons closing the shutters and drawing the blinds, shutting out the daylight. The old servant said nothing, but from his hunched shoulders and slow gait, Jaufré suspected that he was silently, respectfully mourning in his own fashion for his dead master.

'They're saying in the city that this was no natural snowstorm,' Jaufré said to Arnault as they walked away from the Belcastel mansion, down the steeply winding lane that led back into the city. 'What do you think?'

'How should I know?' Arnault shrugged the suggestion aside.

'They're saying that the Tsiyonim conjured up the storm. By magic.'

'I don't believe in magic,' Arnault said bluntly.

'Good,' said Jaufré. Arnault's hard-bitten cynicism was exactly what was required from his second-in-command on this mission; he would suspect nothing. 'Now, Lieutenant, I want the men ready to leave at dawn. Meet me at the Aude Gate. All Hawks fully armed, on horseback.'

'Lieutenant?' Arnault said, alert now. For the first time Jaufré saw a gleam of pride lighten Arnault's world-weary eyes.

'You're the obvious choice now that Lieutenant Belcastel is no longer with us.'

'The men'll be ready before dawn, Captain, rely on me!' Arnault saluted Jaufré with alacrity and set off; he no longer dragged his feet but moved swiftly, almost jauntily.

'The Aude Gate,' Jaufré called after him.

As soon as Arnault was out of sight, Jaufré felt a sudden weakness overcome him. He reeled, righting himself by clutching at the wall of a house, feeling the roughness of the plaster grazing his fingers.

He had managed to keep his feelings under control till now. Now a debilitating sense of loss and fatigue overwhelmed him utterly.

This was no time to give in to weakness. He had a journey to make, a long and arduous journey into the mountains.

'I'll be all right after a glass of wine . . .'

At the Tour Orbiel he rapped at the door and waited for his servant, Jehan, to let him in. No one answered. After a while, he took out his key, unlocked the door and went in. The lamps were unlit and the staircase was in darkness.

'Jehan!' he shouted into the darkness. His own voice echoed back to him. 'Margotte!' he shouted again. Where were his servants?

The sound of muffled sobbing echoed around the darkened stairwell.

'Who's there?' he called.

'F-frightened –' The voice was high, trembling, the voice of a child.

Suddenly Jaufré was seven years old again, locked terrified in the lightless darkness of the Tour Orbiel vaults. He was so cold his teeth chattered. His body ached from the bruises and weals of the violent beating he had been forced to endure. His stomach ached with hunger and his throat was parched.

He did not understand what he had done to incur his father's hatred. There seemed to be nothing he could do to please him.

'So – frightened –'

Was it his own voice he could hear, plaintively calling for help from the locked cellar of his childhood?

He stopped, frozen in his own memories, unable to move.

'Help me,' whispered the voice in the darkness.

'Who are you?' he whispered back.

'Open the door,' came back the faint voice. 'Let me out. Let me go free.'

Jaufré's hand hovered over the door handle. He did not want to see what lay beyond the door in the darkness of the cellar – and yet he wanted to be rid of it.

'No!' he cried, turning, stumbling up the stairs, making for his bedchamber, flinging the door shut, locking it.

'Help me. Help me!'

He fumbled in the little casket for the amulet. He could not endure the torment any longer. What had the daemon said? You are not alone. The enamelled metal burned his fingers; the metal glowed, dark as the last light of a dying sun, casting its light through his skin so that his flesh seemed on fire.

And a voice came shuddering through the chamber, a voice of beaten bronze, dull as the tolling of a night bell.

'Call me by my name. My true name.'

'Lailahel,' he gasped, 'Lailahel, help me.'

Lailahel.

Jehiel had revealed its true name, the name of the daemon spirit he had summoned. His Guardian. The name, darkly sinuous, wound about his brain like the glistening coils of a black snake, lithe and dangerous.

'Lailahel, Bringer of Darkness . . .' Jaufré whispered. 'Come to me. Tell me what I must do.'

The shadows in his chamber stirred, rustled by a hot, dry breeze. The air in the chamber burned, as if scorched by the desert sun, until only a deep copper glow remained.

'*I am here.*'

'Help me,' Jaufré said.

A figure, darker than the shadows, materialised in the burnished air. His arms were open, beckoning Jaufré towards him. Jaufré found himself moving forwards, helplessly drawn into the embrace of the dark.

'*Why do you still fear me? I bring you what you most desire. Forget your guilt, forget your fears. Your will is my will.*'

The darkness moved over his body like a slow flame, setting every nerve burning. It was the darkness of the desert night, hot as fever. And that spiced breath, perfumed with desert rose and spikenard, breathed over Jaufré's skin like balm. Suddenly Jaufré was shuddering with desire, aroused.

He raised his face – and felt the flicker of a tongue tipped with fire parting his lips.

The dark heat scorched through his body in a sudden cresting wave of fire.

'I am here,' he said, yielding to the Guardian of the Night.

CHAPTER 26

A drop of moisture splashed on to Rahab's face. He huddled down in his blanket. Another drop, icily cold, splashed down.

'Why doesn't Schimeon get the roof mended?' he mumbled sleepily. And then, opening his eyes wide, he looked up and saw the ivied roof-joists above, crisscrossed against a pale sheen of ice-blue sky.

He sat up, stifling a groan as his stiff limbs creaked. Why had he fallen asleep? He had meant to keep watch.

Talmai lay curled asleep beside him. Rahab looked down at him. Asleep, Talmai looked so young, so defenceless. It was difficult to believe that only hours ago he had brought devastation to the mountainside, had sent men hurtling to their deaths over the side of the ravine.

And now the snow was melting. The random drips were fast becoming a steady patter; it was time to go back to Tifereth before the thaw drenched them.

Rahab leaned forward to touch Talmai's shoulder to rouse him. And paused a moment, wanting to check again the birthmark he had discovered last night – yet not wanting to draw Talmai's attention to it.

He sat back on his heels, looking at Talmai's face, trying again to match the features to his faded memories of his mother, his father . . .

'What is it?' mumbled Talmai crossly.

'The thaw's set in. We'd better go back.'

'N-no . . . I'll stay here . . . You go.'

Rahab tried to remember his own exhaustion after Barakiel had abandoned him. His memory was blurred; all he knew was that he had slept for countless hours hidden in the Maurys' cellar.

He tapped Talmai's shoulder again, firmly this time.

'You may not want to break your fast but I'm starving. And if we stay here, we'll get soaked to the skin.'

'Who cares?' murmured Talmai.

'All right!' Rahab said with a sigh. 'If that's the way it is . . .' He pulled Talmai's arm around his shoulder. 'On the count of three, we stand up. Ready? One, two, three . . .'

Lia yawned again until her jaw cracked. The wick was smouldering in the lamp beside Berengar's bed. It wasn't worth trimming now, for the first, dull light of dawn had begun to penetrate the cracks in the shutters; she would let it burn itself out.

She had kept vigil beside Berengar's bed all night . . . but now exhaustion threatened to overcome her. Her head began to droop . . . She forced herself awake, sitting back, stiffly upright, in the hard-backed wooden chair. She must not fall asleep! Suppose Berengar should need her?

Or Rahab . . .?

There had been something about the way Rahab had looked at her when he bade her farewell that had made her stomach flutter as if invaded by a flock of butterflies.

What was she doing even thinking of Rahab when Berengar lay here so seriously injured? She must stay alert, ready to respond if he regained consciousness . . .

She tried to stifle another yawn.

Must stay awake.

Her head drooped lower, lower . . .

She is standing beside the sea on a long, empty stretch of sand, pale sand, white as crushed pearls.

Smoke billows across the shore, acrid, bitter smoke. She turns – and sees a city in flames behind her. Distant cries reach her through the smoke, faint as the keening cry of gulls far overhead.

The ground shakes beneath her feet, flinging her down on her face in the pale sand.

From out of the smoke-choked sky comes swirling a vast presence; dust and molten fire rain down on the city from its fast-beating wings. The earth trembles, the walls of the city crack and crumble. Terrified, Lia gazes up into the heart of the turbulence. And sees a figure materialising, falling to earth, tumbling on to the white shore.

From this distance she cannot be certain . . . but there is something familiar about the slender, wild-haired figure . . .

And now there comes a roar of churning waters. Looking behind her, Lia sees the grey sea boiling, gathering itself in one great foam-crested wave, higher than the highest spire in Arcassanne.

The beach is water, the sky is water, as the monstrous wave comes crashing down.

'Help me!' she cries, arms outstretched, imploring. 'I'm – I'm drowning –'

At last the figure slowly turns, and she sees with a shock of recognition that it is her mother.

'Lia.' Zillaïs holds out her cupped hands. 'This is for you.'

Muddy quicksand is sucking her down; water crashes over her head, a cold, winter drowning-tide.

'Help me –' she gasps.

'Take it. You must take it.'

Zillaïs places something in her hands. It is a shell, a prayer-shell, smooth as ivory –

'Mother?' Lia cried, and opened her eyes to find the scholar Jorah staring sternly down at her.

'You were asleep,' he said accusingly.

Lia blinked. She was still mired in the quicksand of her dream, disoriented, uncertain where she was. Her mouth was dry and foul with the taste of the choking mud.

'Have you been checking his progress as I asked you?'

She looked down at her empty hands. She could still feel the contours of the amulet-shell, worn smooth by the passing of time. What did it mean? Had Zillaïs been Rashiel's Warder? Was this the secret her mother had lived with all these years? That she, not Ithamar, had caused the destruction of Tolonada?

'Well?' demanded Jorah.

'No change,' she said. Her voice came out muzzy. This was not the time to puzzle over a dream.

'I need to change his dressings,' Jorah said. 'Selima's busy. You'll have to help me instead.'

Still half-asleep, Lia nodded. What she really wanted now was a mug of Emmenza's hot spiced tea: apple, cinnamon and ginger. And fresh bread.

'You're not squeamish, I hope,' Jorah said, pulling back the sheet, revealing Berengar's bruised, broken body beneath. 'You're not going to faint?'

'Do I look the sort of girl who faints?' Lia snapped back.

And you're not going to complain that your modesty is offended? For I'm going to have to cut away these nethergarments.'

In truth, the sight of the dried, oozed blood had begun to make her feel a little queasy. But stronger still was the sense of utter helplessness in the face of such terrible injuries; she had always believed Berengar to be indestructible. And she was damned if she'd let Jorah see her show the slightest sign of weakness.

'Give me the knife, Jorah,' she said, putting out her hand, palm upwards. 'I'll do the cutting for you.'

At the door of the watchtower, Rahab stopped to get his breath. Talmai slid slowly down towards the ground; Rahab, leaning against the wall, let him lie there.

Outside, the light of the rising sun sparkled on the wide expanse of melting snow, a dazzle of ice and water, bright as crushed diamonds. Above, the sky was a swathe of palest blue silk, the last fleeting ribbons of cloud tinged with gold.

Golden cloud, Rahab thought, remembering a distant day in Arcassanne. *Wasn't it a spool of Golden Cloud thread the child Jacou brought me that day from old Sorel the Silk Merchant?*

The child . . . whom he had found lying dead on the workshop doorstep, the golden-haired child who had reminded him so vividly of lost Shaoni.

His gaze slid from snowfields to the corner where Talmai slumped against the mossy wall.

'Shaoni?' he said softly. *'Shaoni?'*

Talmai mumbled something inaudible in reply.

It might just have been a response to the sound of his voice. An instinctive reaction. Now was not the time to go into family history.

'Come on, then, whoever you are,' he said, heaving Talmai to his feet again. 'Let's get going.'

'Stay here,' murmured Talmai. 'Too tired . . .'

They set out across the slush. Talmai leaned so heavily on his shoulder that Rahab wondered if he could support him all the way back to the castel. Far above, the high mountain crags glistened with snow. But the sparkling air was utterly still; there was no sound of dawn birdsong or buzzing insects.

Something crunched hard in the slush under Rahab's foot. He looked down – and let out a soft cry of dismay. The fast-melting snow had revealed the stiffened corpses of little birds and the shells of cicadas, frozen to death in the sudden chill of the blizzard.

'Shalgiel's harvest,' he whispered. 'Oh, Talmai, Talmai, what have you done?'

*

274

Rahab gazed up at the castel walls and almost lost his balance as Talmai sagged heavily against him. Malakhi was waving to him from the battlements, his white hair silvered by the sparkling sun.

'We'll come down and help you!'

'Good,' Rahab muttered. 'About time too.' He was sweating with the effort of supporting Talmai, a hot, soaking sweat, and his legs were trembling with fatigue.

The castel gate was tugged open and Malakhi and Elon came squelching out to meet them across the glistening slush.

'You're safe,' Malakhi cried, hugging the young man. 'Thank the Lord you're safe.'

'Well done,' Elon said gruffly to Rahab. 'We feared we'd never get him back.'

Rahab felt a sudden pang of envy; Talmai might have lost his blood-family but he had found in Malakhi a second father who loved him as dearly as if he had been his own son. And much though Rahab had come to care for Schimeon, he had always been his indentured apprentice; there had always been the distance of servant and master between them.

'What's this?' Malakhi touched the gash on Talmai's head. Talmai shied away. 'A head wound? We'd better have Jorah take a look at him.'

Melting icicles dripped from the eaves of the castel roofs as Rahab tramped across the muddy courtyard behind Malakhi and Talmai.

What he really wanted right now was a long soak in a steaming-hot tub. But everyone was so busy mopping up after the blizzard that he suspected no one would have time to heat the water for him. In Arcassanne, he would just have strolled down the street to the Bath House where the water was hot at all hours and the brown soap smelt of rosemary oil.

No bath, then. Even though he was dirty, aching, stinking of sweat. And all because of Talmai.

He trudged up the steps and entered the castel.

Talmai.

If only he could stop thinking about that faded whorl of tattoo-pricks stained red and blue he had discovered last night behind Talmai's ear. Had he dreamt it? Had he been so desperate to find lost Shaoni that he had begun to imagine connections where none existed?

He stopped outside Talmai's room, seeing Jorah bending over the bed, busy cleaning the gash on Talmai's head.

Had no one else in Tifereth ever discovered the birthmark? Had no one else ever asked what it signified? Jehiel had recognised it straight away. Was it known only to the sons of the Tribe of the Chazhaelim? Or had Malakhi seen it – and sought to hide the truth from Talmai, wanting to keep his adopted son from the pain of his past?

Maybe it was better to let the past be, to forget what he had seen. And yet, if it was true, how could he ignore it? How could he walk away from his own brother?

Jorah came out of Talmai's room, carrying his box of tinctures and bandages.

'How is he?' Rahab asked.

'Remarkably well,' Jorah said, 'considering the stresses his body has undergone.'

'Can I go in?'

'Just for a few minutes.' Jorah said punctiliously. 'He needs rest. I'm going to mix a draught to help him sleep.'

Talmai lay on the narrow bed, eyes closed. Rahab hesitated, wondering if he should creep away without disturbing him. He had reassured himself that he was all right; he could return later . . .

Talmai's eyes suddenly opened and stared at Rahab, then slewed away, as if deliberately ignoring him.

'I knew what the risks were,' Talmai said. He stared straight ahead. 'I had no wish to endanger others. I made my choice – I expected to deal with the consequences. You had no business coming after me.'

Rahab did not know what to say to this. It was not at all what he had expected.

'I'm a grown man, a scholar. I was capable of looking after myself.'

'I only thought you might be hurt. When I heard you calling –'

'Nobody asked you to play the hero. Nobody asked you to go risking your life to find me. So don't expect me to thank you, to be grateful.'

'But I didn't come here for thanks –' Rahab began stumblingly. 'I –'

Talmai's eyes fixed on his; they glittered with the grey sheen of winter ice.

'You know what I mean,' he said. 'Don't expect it to make any difference between us. Understand me?'

Jorah reappeared, carrying a phial filled with a dark liquid.

'I think you'd better go now,' Talmai said, each word hard as a chip of ice.

Rahab backed away.

Life as a Tsiyonim apprentice had accustomed him to slights and cuffs – but he had been completely unprepared for such an unprovoked assault.

He went hurrying out through the courtyard, not heeding the greetings of the scholars he passed, dashing wildly on until he could be sure he was well away from prying eyes.

At the back of the castel, the crumbling boundary wall ran almost to the edge of the ravine; the cliff-face dropped away into the deep wooded valley far beneath.

Rahab sank down, back against the wall. Talmai's rejection had hit him with the full force of a punch in the stomach: at first he was too dazed, too winded to notice the hurt. Now his whole being smarted.

What had he done wrong? What had he said to deserve such a rebuff? Why was Talmai so angry with him?

The revelation struck as violently as one of Barakiel's lightning shafts.

Talmai *did* recognise him. And maybe he didn't like what he saw, maybe he didn't want to be the brother of Rahab, the tailor's apprentice; he wanted to retain the glamour of his cloak of anonymity, his lack of identity. Maybe he had constructed a fantasy brother in his mind, an impossibly erudite, heroic and powerful brother who would come striding back to claim him. And the real Rahab ben Chazhael had proved a considerable disappointment.

And worse still, maybe Talmai hated him for abandoning him in Galicys. Maybe he thought he had done it on purpose, out of brotherly spite –

Little children were like that; he had seen Thirzah furious at some imagined slight, at first uncomprehending, then utterly inconsolable.

Galicys. The pine-covered crags, the misty blue of the clear sky dissolved, and Rahab found himself flung back into the burning streets of his home city.

Fires light the sky. Everywhere smoke, choking smoke, and the acrid smell of burning. People fighting, pushing, stampeding to escape.

277

'Stay with me!' Rahab cries, trying to hold on to his little brother's hand.

A floodtide of people breaks, the force pulling them, tugging them apart.

'Mama!' The little one twists and cries, panicked. 'Where are you, Mama?'

He jerks his hand free – and the crowd sweeps him away. Dazed, Rahab can only stand and gaze numbly at his empty hand.

Rahab blinked. He was still staring down at his hand, a man's hand now, hardened and callused by years of pushing a needle through cloth.

Shaoni had trusted him. How could a child that young understand what had happened that night? He would remember nothing but his fear. He would only remember that his brother had not held on to his hand, had abandoned him.

Could he undo the damage done by those lost years? Could Talmai ever come to forgive him?

Rahab covered his face with his hands. And something small and scrumpled fell out of his sleeve. He leaned forward to pick it up and saw that it was the stained felt of the rabbit puppets which he had absent-mindedly scrunched together into a ball after handing the retrieved amulets into Malakhi's care.

He began to straighten out the crumpled felt, trying to smooth back some semblance of their original shape. One frayed eye stared rakishly up at him. In his mind he heard the faint laughter of Iudith and Thirzah, saw them doubled up, giggling at the silly antics of the two 'mossieus'.

And suddenly his eyes misted over and the rabbit's stitched features blurred. He had not realised till then how much he missed his adoptive family. He might not have been able to be a brother to Shaoni – but he had tried to do his best for the little girls.

A hot breeze stirred the pine branches in the ravine far below, wafting up a resinous whisper . . . and another sound, the faint, plaintive sound of a child crying.

He listened, trying to determine where the crying was coming from. Perhaps one of the children had fallen and hurt themselves. And no one else was around this side of the castel to hear them.

He rose, still listening, and followed the sound of the crying. It was quiet crying, interrupted by sniffs and sad little sighs. What was it Chadassah used to say? 'I know they're all right if

278

they open their mouths and scream at the top of their voices. It's the silence that brings your heart to your mouth . . .'

The crying drew him to the very edge of the cliff, below the tumbledown wall. Huddled in a heap, was Jael, Selima's little daughter, her shoulders heaving with racking sobs.

'What's wrong?' Rahab asked.

'Go away!' she said fiercely.

'Are you hurt? Did you fall over?'

Slowly she raised her head until he could see that her puckered face was red and stained with crying. 'I hate him,' she said in a gasp. 'He won't let me play. He called me a – a *baby*.' The tears began again.

'That was very unkind of him,' Rahab said, wondering which of the children had so upset Jael.

'He never lets me join in. Just 'cause he's older than me. I hate him!'

'Your brother?'

Jael nodded, tears still spurting from her eyes. Rahab reached into his pocket, searching for his kerchief. His hand encountered the rabbits. He wondered . . . and then wriggled one hand into the red puppet, the other into the brown. The rabbits confronted each other, nose to nose.

'Guess what these are,' he said.

'Don't know. Rats,' she said disconsolately.

'Rats! We're rabbits, I'll have you know,' Rahab said in the voice of the red rabbit.

'You're never rabbits,' Jael said, turning her head away. 'Your ears are all wrong.'

'They're brothers,' Rahab said. 'They like each other really. But they can't get on. They fight over things.'

'What sort of things?' Curious now, she sat up, wiping her nose on her sleeve.

'Oh, the usual . . . carrots and suchlike.'

He saw a shadow of a smile in her eyes.

'What are their names?'

'Names?' Thirzah and Iudith had never named them; he thought for a moment and then said, '*You* choose.'

'This one,' she said, touching the brown puppet, 'is Smudge because he's got dirt on his nose. And the red – is Cross-Eyes.'

Rahab squinted down his nose at Cross-Eyes, making Cross-Eyes squint back.

'My sight is perfect!' objected Cross-Eyes. 'I don't know what those two little girls can possibly mean.'

'Two?' echoed Jael. The shy smile had broadened into a delighted grin.

'And I haven't got a dirty nose,' put in Smudge, 'I was just snuffling around looking for a carrot –'

'Carrot?' Cross-Eyes turned on Smudge, squashed ear flapping. 'So it was you who stole my carrot!'

Jael burst into a sudden peal of laughter. 'One carrot?' she said. 'Or two?'

Rahab made Cross-Eyes go searching around the wall.

'Thief!' he cried. 'Now they've all gone!'

'So this is where you've been hiding.'

Rahab, red-faced, glanced up and saw Selima watching him. Her lips were pressed together – but he thought he caught the glint of a smile in her eyes.

'Don't stop, don't stop!' cried Jael.

What must Selima think? Here he was, making a complete fool of himself. Now his credibility as a Guardian Warder was ruined forever.

'Mama's been looking everywhere for you, Jael.' Selima held out her hand to the little girl. 'I was worried. Why didn't you stay with Laban?'

Jael stuck out her tongue, pulling a face.

'Here, Jael,' Rahab said, taking off the glove-puppets and offering them to her. 'You can help them sort out their quarrel.'

Jael beamed at him and eased the puppets on.

'It's been hard, bringing these two up on my own,' Selima said, gazing out into the pure blue of the mountain sky. 'Jael never knew her father. Laban doesn't really remember. He was only three when Jaered died.'

'I – I'm sorry,' Rahab said. Her candour took him by surprise. 'How did he die?'

'Avalanche,' she said. 'My Jaered was a dreamer. Not very practical, not used to the mountain ways. Malakhi has been kind to us, allowing us to stay on . . .'

'Smudge is being naughty,' announced Jael. 'He hit Cross-Eyes.'

'Then he'll have to go without his dinner,' Rahab said in a voice of great severity.

'You hear that, Smudge?' Jael asked the puppet. 'No dinner for you!'

'You've got a way with children,' Selima said, smiling at Rahab. 'Do you have a family of your own back in Arcassanne?'

'Me? Oh no. No . . .' He was flustered now, recognising what lay behind the seemingly innocent question. She was asking him if he was single. Unattached. Available. 'I – um – I helped look after my master's children.'

'If you stay here in Tifereth, you can be your own master,' she said softly. Her eyes reflected the colour of the mountain sky, startlingly blue in her sun-browned face, yet her brows and lashes were brown and gold, as was the stray strand of hair she tucked back beneath her plaited headscarf.

'My own master? That has its attractions,' he said, smiling back at her. He had never been so openly propositioned before and he had to admit that he was rather flattered. His first impressions of Selima had been of a strong, self-sufficient woman, proud of her independence. Now he glimpsed someone much younger, two or three years older than him at most. Married at seventeen, widowed at twenty, twenty-one . . .

'Besides,' she said, 'I've never been much good with a needle. And though I've tried to train them to look after themselves, these scholars have their heads in the clouds. It'd be nice to have someone to take care of all that.' She placed her hand on his, gently pressing to emphasise her sentiments. It was a simle gesture, the touch of hands between friends, no more . . . although Rahab was aware that it had the potential to lead to something altogether less innocent.

'Selima –' Jorah came around the corner. He stopped, seeing the two sitting together, hands touching. A swift succession of emotions flashed across his face, like wind-driven clouds on a stormy day.

'What are you doing here?' he demanded.

'Talking,' Selima said coolly. 'Is there a Holy Law against two people talking together?'

'A man and woman talking here alone,' Jorah said, his voice strangely choked, 'that could be misinterpreted.'

'Obviously only by you,' Selima said. Her manner had become formal – and she did not remove her hand from Rahab's.

Rahab felt distinctly uncomfortable; the instant he saw Jorah's expression change, he suspected there must be some understanding between Jorah and Selima . . . and that the attachment was evidently stronger on Jorah's part. And from his brief acquaintance with the doctor, Rahab had observed that Jorah was a humourless, inflexible man, unlikely to tolerate a rival.

'I'd better be getting back,' he said, hastily getting to his feet.

'What about Cross-Eyes and Smudge?' Jael asked, lower lip beginning to droop again.

'Would you like to take care of them for me?' Rahab said. 'For tonight?

'Yes, yes!' Jael went dancing off, a puppet on each fist.

Jorah came striding after Rahab, planting himself in front of him, blocking his way.

'Don't sneak off, Ben Chazhael, I've something to say to you.'

Rahab shot him a weary glance. He supposed he'd have to hear the man out, if only for Lia's sake. There was no point in antagonising the only doctor in Tifereth capable of healing Berengar.

'Make it short, will you? I'm tired.'

'I think it would be better for Tifereth if you moved on. Don't you?'

'Better for Tifereth – or for you?' Rahab said. He was damned if he'd let Jorah bend the truth to suit his argument.

'This was a peaceful community until you arrived. Look at the havoc you've caused.'

'I've caused? Look, Jorah. Say what you really want to say.'

'All right. You want plain speaking?' Jorah drew himself up to his full height, looking down on Rahab. 'Then here it is. Stay away from Selima. Is that plain enough? Stay away.'

'Fine.' Rahab nodded. A few paces on, he turned and said over his shoulder, 'I'll stay away from her. But . . . what if she doesn't stay away from me?'

It was a foolish jibe – but he just couldn't resist it. Jorah came after him.

'No, Jorah!' Selima caught up with Jorah, taking hold of him by the arm. 'Will you stop interfering in my life? What I do, who I talk to, that's my business.'

Rahab did not wait to hear Jorah reply, but hastened on out of earshot. In Arcassanne Schimeon had often warned him that women would confide secrets to their tailors and dressmakers that they did not share with their husbands. And jealous husbands, Tsiyonim or Gentile, were bad for business.

If he had been in Arcassanne, he could have laughed the whole incident off, could have decorated it as a good tale to tell in the workroom: the pretty widow, the handsome young tailor and the jealous doctor. But this was Tifereth. Tifereth, named for the central sphere at the very heart of the Tree of Life. He had cherished secret hopes of finding a resolution to the troubles that beset him in Arcassanne. And all he had done was uncover problems, more problems.

Perhaps Jorah was right. Perhaps his presence had disturbed the equilibrium of Tifereth. Perhaps he should quietly pack his few possessions . . . and leave.

CHAPTER 27

'Bandage.' Jorah raised one hand to Lia as he dextrously swabbed the oozing cut on Berengar's forehead with the other.

Was he this rude to all the women? Lia wondered mutinously. Or was this boorishness reserved for Gentiles? He had called her Gentile. And he obviously resented wasting time tending to a Gentile's injuries.

A bitter steam wafted up from the bowl of steeping medicinal herbs she held, making her eyes sting.

'Another length of bandage,' said Jorah curtly.

Lia fumbled with the cut lengths of bandage draped over her arm.

'No, not the thin stuff,' the young doctor said in tones of exasperation. 'The same as I'm using now. Please make some effort to concentrate!'

'You didn't say,' Lia said, her voice deadly quiet. If he used that tone of voice to her once more, she would stuff his precious bandages down his throat. Why did Jorah have to be the only scholar in Tifereth with medical training? Berengar's recovery depended on his skills – so she supposed she must endure his scorn and his rudeness, if only for Berengar's sake.

A shadow fell across the bed, and glancing round, she saw Rahab in the doorway. Relief at the sight of a familiar face sent a flood of warmth through her; she had never imagined she would feel so glad to see him again.

'Not now,' Jorah said without looking up. 'Can't you see I'm busy with my patient?'

Rahab ignored him and came into the chamber.

'You found Talmai?' Lia asked.

'I brought him back.' His expression, usually so frank, so open, was guarded. She sensed that he did not feel inclined to say more in front of Jorah.

'Is he hurt?'

'Just a few cuts and bruises. He was lucky.' Rahab gazed

284

down at Berengar's prone body. She guessed what he was thinking but did not say: *unlike Berengar.*

Jorah drew the sheet back up to Berengar's chin and rinsed his hands, wiping them clean on a linen towel.

'Wait! Lia cried. 'Is that all? Isn't there anything else you can do for him?'

'The horse fell on him,' Jorah said brutally. 'I can't work miracles.'

'What do you mean? He is going to live, isn't he?'

'His leg is broken in two places,' Jorah said. 'I've made a splint. What with the crushed ribs and the head injury . . . if he survives the next two days, he may pull through. But it'll be a slow process. And he'll be lame for the rest of his life.'

'Lame?' Lia repeated dazedly.

'And now, if you'll excuse me, I must go attend to my other duties.'

'Lame,' Lia said again. 'Berengar lame?' Her hands began to shake. Till then she had thought only of life or death. The possibility that Berengar would survive, but as an invalid, permanently disabled, had not occurred to her. And it would all be her fault, her fault –

Rahab took the salve-bowl from her hands and set it down. His fingers brushed against hers. Startled, she looked up. That touch, so brief, so fleeting, sent a shiver of warmth through her.

And Berengar shifted his head on the pillow, letting out a faint, fretful groan.

'Bera?' She turned hastily away from Rahab, blushing as if she had been caught *in flagrante.* They had only touched hands, her thoughts had only strayed for a moment . . .

'I'll leave you two alone.' Rahab turned to go.

'Wait –' She started after him. She did not want to be left alone with Berengar. She did not want to have to break the news to him.

'Lia . . .' came the dull, drugged voice from the bed.

Berengar was calling for her. She turned back to see him open his eyes. She watched, biting her lip, as his gaze wandered past her . . . then slowly focused on her face.

'Lia?' he said again. 'You're safe?' and then, after a slight hesitation, 'You're . . . unharmed?'

He knew her.

'I'm well,' she said, pressing his hand. 'How do *you* feel?'

285

'Me?' He tried to shift his position. She saw him wince as the pain of the broken bones kicked in; the look of surprise on the face of a bare-knuckle fighter as he goes down in the market-place ring, defeated.

'Would you like a . . . a drink?' she asked, wishing she did not feel so helpless to alleviate his pain.

He nodded.

If only she had taken the trouble to learn from her mother about simples and medicines . . .

She leaned forward and tried to raise his head. But it lay heavy against her arm, and as she tipped the cup of water to his lips, most of it spilled down his chin.

'Sorry, sorry,' she whispered, dabbing the wetness away with a cloth. Even this small movement seemed to cause him pain; he lay back, closing his eyes again, exhausted. She turned away from him, busying herself with mopping up spilt water. Why was she so clumsy?

'My men . . . where are my men . . . ?'

This was the question she had been dreading. Should she lie, for fear the truth might prove too strong a shock to his system? Or would he come to hate her for lying?

'They didn't make it,' she said.

'I . . . don't understand.'

'You were the only surivor.'

'They're dead? Every single one? Even Arnault?' He seemed not to be able to comprehend what she was telling him.

She nodded.

'And Tramontan?' He tried to sit up, but the effort was too great and he slumped back, panting for breath.

She looked down at the floor. How to tell him that poor, jittery Tramontan was lame when she must break the news to him that he was lame too?

'They've taken good care of him. He's in the stable below . . .'

'So now I'm captured. Taken prisoner too.'

Prisoner? Lia placed one hand on his forehead. His skin felt cool; there was no sign of fever. But she had heard of men losing their wits after suffering injury to the head. She began to fear . . .

'Berengar,' she said gently, 'you are not a prisoner here.'

She saw a frown pass across his face, a frown of puzzled incomprehension.

'But the brigands –'

'There are no brigands. These people are scholars.'

'B-but you –' He was exhausting his strength with the effort of speaking. 'Emmenza – said – abducted. Jaufré –'

'Jaufré?' Now it was her turn to frown. 'What did Jaufré say?'

'G-good friend, Jaufré.' Berengar's eyes closed. 'Good friend, Arnault.' Suddenly he reached out and gripped her wrist hard.

'Must know. Must be sure. Arnault. Could be . . . lying out there . . . wounded . . .'

'It's all right, Bera.' His fingers burned into her skin, rough-callused as rope. 'I'll go and find out.'

'Have to know, Lia . . . difficult . . . breaking it . . . to their families . . .'

His grip gradually relaxed. She looked down and saw the marks of his fingers impressed, angrily red, on the soft skin of her wrist.

'Berengar?' she said. He did not answer. Seized by a sudden irrational fear, she leant forward, her ear close to his mouth. A faint halting breath warmed her cheek. He was still alive.

A bizarre funeral procession wound its way from the Tour de la Justice through the muddy streets. Tsiyonim men, wrapped in their shawls, shuffled slowly along, carrying a bier on their shoulders. Two of Jaufré d'Orbiel's Hawks went ahead of them, driving away any curious onlookers, clearing the streets so that they could pass unmolested.

The Elders stood by Jehiel's grave and watched as Schimeon reverently placed a handful of pebbles on top of the freshly dug earth. They had buried the old scholar beside his wife Miriam in the quietest corner of the walled cemetery.

'Rest in peace, old friend,' Schimeon whispered.

'Hurry!' called one of the Hawks from the gateway.

'Take no notice!' said Baruch loudly.

'I said hurry!' said the Hawk. There was an edge to his voice.

'Show some respect for the dead, young man,' said Baruch.

'Listen.' Schimeon straightened up. 'Can you hear something?'

'Hear what?' Baruch shook his head. 'I can't hear anything.'

'You're deaf as a post, that's why.' Tobiah cupped his hand to one ear, listening intently. 'Sounds like voices. Coming this way.'

Schimeon brushed the clinging earth from his robe and went through the gravestones towards the gateway. As he reached the gate the murmur of voices suddenly became a roar as a crowd of people came running into the street. The Hawks began to back inside the cemetery, hands on sword-hilts.

'There they are!' shrieked a woman.

Schimeon flung the iron gates together with a clang. They would not keep the mob out for long.

'Kill!' came the chant from outside the gates. 'Kill them!'

'We're trapped,' said Tobiah. 'Where can we go from here?'

'This way. Over the back wall.' Schimeon hurried the Elders along the winding path.

'How can you expect a man of my years to climb over that!' protested Baruch.

'Here.' Tobiah, straddling the wall, leaned down to pull the old man up; Schimeon, the last, pushed from below.

A hail of stones came hurtling into the cemetery, cracking against the tombstones.

'Hurry, Schimeon!' Tobiah urged, ducking as a cobblestone flew past his ear.

The Hawks still lingered below.

'Well, go on, go,' Schimeon said from the top of the wall to the Hawks. 'Their quarrel is with us, not with you.'

The Hawks hesitated, looking uneasily from one to the other.

'Our orders were to take you back to the Tour,' one said.

The gates flew open and the crowd came bursting into the cemetery, trampling over the graves, knocking down headstones and monuments.

The Hawks took one look and shinned up and over the wall, after the Elders.

'Where now?' Schimeon cried.

'The *shul*. Into the *shul*.'

The little *shul* stood beside the burned ruins of Jehiel's house; the fires had not touched it.

'Divine protection?' Schimeon said wryly, pushing the Hawks inside and slamming the door shut behind him. 'We've never needed it more than now.'

They bolted the door and barricaded it with benches. Untended for days, the sacred flame in the Sanctuary had burned out, and only a dim, dusty light lit the *shul*, drifting in from the high windows of patterned stained glass, green and gold and red.

'That won't hold them for long,' said one of the Hawks. 'Is there another way out?'

'How dare they defile the cemetery!' cried Baruch, almost beside himself with rage. 'Give me your sword and I'll show them –'

Someone began to hammer on the door; a stone broke the star-shaped window above the door, sending fragments of glass showering down on their heads.

'Down here.' Tobiah guided Baruch away from the entrance, towards the inner door to the Sanctuary.

Their pursuers battered on the front door of the *shul* with fists and staves until the bolt gave way and the door swung open.

'Into the Sanctuary.' Tobiah pushed Baruch into the gloom beyond.

There was a moment's pause – and then there came a sudden ear-grating screech, as something exploded, hissing and spitting into the darkness. The Elders had a brief impression of wild yellow eyes, bristling fur and vicious claws hurtling past.

'Daemons!' one of their assailants shouted in terror, turning to flee. 'The place is haunted –'

The intruders, thrown into confusion, blundered around in the dark, trampling over each other in their haste. And counterpoint to their cries, a low growling could be heard, menacing and inhuman.

The Hawks slammed the broken door shut again.

Out in the street a violent argument was taking place.

'Torch the place. Burn it down.'

'No, it's bad luck. Leave well alone.'

'Bad luck? All the more reason to burn it down.'

'Mrraow?' A velvety head butted into Schimeon's leg; absent-mindedly he put out one hand to scratch the cat's ears – and then realised.

'Mischkin,' he whispered. 'You little daemon . . .'

'Who'd have thought it?' Baruch said. 'Saved by Jehiel's cats.'

'They're very thin,' Schimeon said, stroking little grey Pischkin, who had slunk back inside to greet them. 'What d'you think they've found to eat around here?'

'*Shul* mice,' said Baruch. 'They were always nibbling the Books of Holy Law. The mice of Arcassanne are not very devout.'

'We can't leave them here. Our friends will return when they realise they've been scared away by a pair of pussycats. Jehiel would have wanted us to take care of them.'

289

'That's all very well,' Baruch said, 'but will they want to come with us?'

Pischkin sat down and began to scratch behind her ear with her back paw.

'And they've got fleas.'

The drone of voices outside rose and fell.

'What's going on?' Baruch said fretfully. 'It's too quiet.'

'I'm not staying here,' the younger of the Hawks said. 'I'm off back to the Tour. Someone's got to alert the Corporal to the situation,' he added, a little shamefacedly. 'He'll send reinforcements.'

'You,' Baruch said, poking him in the ribs with his finger, 'were supposed to protect us. You're not making a very good job of it.'

'I wouldn't go out there, son,' the older Hawk said, looking up from cleaning his nails with a blunt splinter of wood. 'They'll eat you alive.'

The younger Hawk stopped, as though the thought had not occurred to him till that moment. He listened.

'Sounds quiet enough,' he said, opening the door a crack.

'That's what they want you to think,' the older man said with a shrug.

The young Hawk opened the door a little further and slid half of his body outside into the street. After a quick glance around, he slipped out and began to run. Schimeon shut the door after him.

A strange, gargling scream disturbed the silent street.

Schimeon knelt down and put his eye to the keyhole, peering out.

'Stupid young fool. They've caught him. They've got him up against a wall.'

'I told him not to risk his neck,' the remaining Hawk said, shrugging.

'What's going on?' Baruch demanded.

'Ssh!' Schimeon said sharply. He strained to pick out what was being said from the shouts and threats. 'They – they want him to get them into the Tour de la Justice.'

'What?' Tobiah hissed. 'Let that mob near our women – and our children?'

Schimeon straightened up.

'We can't stay here,' he said. 'We've got to stop them.'

*

290

No one even noticed Lia leave the castel; they were all busy in the orchard and the fields, adults and children, desperately working to save what crops and fruit were left after the ravages of the blizzard. There was no point asking anyone to help her search; she must go alone.

She knew she was on a pointless mission. No one could have fallen down the edge of the mountainside and survived a night of such intense cold. But the burden of guilt had been growing steadily heavier; the Hawks had lost their lives searching for her. If she had not run away from Arcassanne, if, if . . .

Yet once she was outside the castel walls Lia felt suddenly free, relieved of all her burdensome responsibilities. The sun-warmed air, clear and fresh as snow-water, had lost all its late-summer drowsiness. She took in deep breathfuls as she walked. It cleansed her of all the sickroom vapours that clung to her; it washed her mind clean of the taint of fever and infection. If she had been forced to stay inside that frowsty room any longer, she would have gone mad –

She sighed. Unlike her mother, she was not good around sick people. She was too impatient to make a good nurse.

She was coming close to the edge of the plateau; somewhere below there must be bodies, torn and broken by the fall.

This is not the time to turn squeamish, girl! she told herself.

She walked the ragged edge of the ravine, forcing herself to gaze down into the narrow valley below. Even without the blinding snow, the stony path here was treacherous, eroded by rain and wind.

She slipped on the loose stones, grabbing at the branches of a hawthorn bush to save herself from plummeting over the edge.

Stones showered down onto the trees beneath.

There came a sudden flapping far below as with raucous cries a flock of carrion crows rose up on ragged black wings.

Grasping at the knotted branches, she leaned slowly out over the edge and gazed down.

A flash of sunlight caught the metallic threads of an embroidered Hawks badge.

And as the crows alighted again, a thick, heaving mass of black feathers, she realised what they were pecking and tearing at with their cruel beaks.

'We'll have no fruit this autumn,' Elon said, hefting his basket on to the table. 'Most of the apples are down. Look.' He picked up a wizened green fruit and cast it down next to the basket. 'What can you do with that? It's not even worth pickling. All the late-cropping fruit has been frozen on the stem – or blown down from the branches.'

'The grapes have shrivelled on the vines,' Jorah said. 'There'll be no wine.'

There was silence around the table as the scholars stared at the frost-blackened fruit.

'I don't understand,' Rahab said in the silence. 'Why has it all gone so wrong?' He picked up one of the hard green apples, weighing it in his hand. 'We call these beings Guardians. So why do they cause such devastation? Why do they harm Tsiyonim and Gentiles alike when they're supposed to protect us?'

'Nothing has gone aright since we were cast out of Tsiyon,' muttered old Lamech.

Rahab was growing weary of hearing the same fatalistic refrain from the Elders. It wasn't an answer to his question; it was merely an excuse.

'I've been trying to make sense of that passage you showed me in the *Sefer Bahir*,' he ventured. 'Perhaps we have misinterpreted the texts? Perhaps we have misunderstood the true purpose of the Guardians?'

'We've spent all our lives studying, and this – this little *tailor* has the impudence to suggest we've not properly interpreted the Holy Law!' spluttered Lamech. 'Listen to me, young man. When you've spent seventy years poring over the holy texts, then you can ask your question.'

It was no more than he deserved, Rahab thought resignedly, for daring to question the scholars' authority.

Malakhi cleared his throat. 'The matter we're supposed to be discussing is our fellow Tsiyonim in Arcassanne. Jorah has proposed that we write again to Comte Aymon, demanding their immediate release.'

'Aymon has seen the power of the amulets,' said Jorah. 'What better time to press our case?'

'So if Aymon refuses to let our people go free, we threaten to raze Arcassanne?' Rahab said.

'Yes,' said Jorah, staring him in the face, unblinking.

'And if Aymon calls our bluff?' Rahab had caught a glimpse of the same fanatical glint in Jorah's eyes that he had seen in Talmai's. 'All he's experienced is two freak storms. If we make our threat, will he believe us? Would *you* in his place?'

'Have you a better suggestion?' Jorah said, his stare stony.

'I think we should wait. At least give Aymon time to respond to the first letter. For all we know, he may have freed our people already.'

'You call yourself Barakiel's Warder and you counsel patience!' Jorah said.

It was a direct challenge.

Just tell yourself he's a difficult customer who needs humouring; he insists he asked for black thread when you made a note he wanted plain . . .

'Why are we divided?' Malakhi asked wearily. 'This issue should unite us, make us strong.'

'How can we be strong when we dither over such important decisions?' Jorah still stared at Rahab. 'There is no place in Tifereth for ditherers. Either you stay here and support our cause – or you leave.'

Jorah's hostile attitude was beginning to make Rahab uneasy. He could not be certain whether the doctor was acting out of still-simmering jealousy or religious zeal.

'Are you questioning my loyalty?' he asked quietly.

'Maybe you've been too long with the Gentiles, Rahab ben Chazael, to see clearly where your loyalties lie.'

Rahab clenched his fists under the table in an effort to control his temper. He could already sense flickers of anger in his mind, lightning-bright. If he lost control he would unleash Barakiel's power on Jorah – and right now, that was a distinctly tempting proposition.

'This is no time to argue,' Malakhi said. 'We must reach agreement on this matter. I propose that we give Aymon another day to respond. If we have heard nothing by the time the first riverboat reaches the Gorge from Arcassanne, then – and only then – do we resort to the threat of Rashiel.'

'No, no,' protested Rahab, 'it won't work. Maybe I have lived too long with the Gentiles – but at least I know the way they think, the way they react. Aymon is a rational, pragmatic man –'

'Rational enough to send armed men against us?' persisted Jorah.

'Not against you – but to find Lia!' Rahab cried in exasperation. 'Why won't you listen? Go question Lord Berengar yourself – he'll tell you. It's all because of Lia. Because she ran away.'

'There! Didn't I say we shouldn't have taken her in?' said Jorah. 'She's brought nothing but trouble.'

'For heaven's sake –' Rahab sagged back in his seat. He had managed to stay alert till now. But the effort of controlling his temper had drained the last of his energy. Suddenly he felt exhausted. His whole body ached for sleep. He could not remember how long it was since he had had a full night's sleep in a proper bed.

'Are you all right, Rahab?' Malakhi said sharply.

'Just tired. Excuse me, Rebh Malakhi. I've said all I had to say.'

He was aware that the scholars were all watching him as he stumbled towards the door, but he no longer cared what they thought. He was too weary to argue any more. The last voice he heard was Jorah's, stiff with self-righteousness.

'Well, and what did you expect, Malakhi? He's a tradesman. He's barely literate. We can't entrust the lives of our people to an illiterate tailor.'

The empty seastrand stretches far out towards the moving silver of the distant sea. The sky is darkening – but lit with fitful flickers of lightning.

Rahab sees a curl of smoke on the horizon; as he watches, the smoke begins to roll in towards the shore.

Suddenly he senses that he is not alone.

Turning, slowly, he sees figures on the sand dunes. Three tall figures on the empty shore, silently watching.

Waiting.

The first of the silent watchers is robed in dark cloud – yet when the flickering brightness of its lightning-pale eyes fixes on Rahab, he is forced to look away.

The second shimmers in a haze of mist-glazed snow.

The third is clothed in dust and flame.

Their silence and their stillness terrify him. There is a purposefulness about their silent vigil. What – or who – are they waiting for?

Rahab gazes out over the sea – and sees the rolling smoke rising from the waves, gathering itself. As it comes closer, it slowly blots out all the daylight, a slow-moving darkness, blacker than a starless night.

Lia sat in the ruined watchtower, hugging her knees to her chest.

Shreds of torn tunic, shreds of torn human flesh . . .

She was not sure how long she had been sitting there amidst the brambles and tangled ivy. She only knew she was not ready to go back yet. She could hear the distant caw of the carrion crows in the ravine. The sound stirred up memories of the birds at their macabre feast. Even now it made her feel sick and faint.

The Hawks had come to rescue her – and their only recompense had been death, a terrifying plunge through a whirl of ice and snow into oblivion.

Gleam of bone, smooth as ivory.

How could she tell Berengar what she had seen?

She would wait a little longer, just a little longer, until she had recovered her self-composure. Until she could brave passing that place again.

Rahab woke. He was drenched in chill sweat, cold as the sea's lapping tide, shivering.

He stumbled out of bed to the window, leaning far out, scanning the sky. It was a brilliant gentian blue, clear as the sheen of fresh-dyed silk; there was not a cloud to be seen. But the sun was well past its midday zenith; he must have slept for several hours.

The dull sense of foreboding still clung to him, a shadowy miasma. He wanted to wash himself clean of its taint.

He went out into the courtyard to draw water from the well. Plunging his hands into the icy water, he splashed his face until the shock made him gasp.

'Feeling more rested now, Rahab? Good, good . . .' Malakhi passed the well, reading as he walked, barely glancing up from the page.

Scholars! Rahab thought, grinning to himself as he shook the water from his hair.

And then he heard the knocking.

Malakhi walked on, seemingly oblivious, engrossed in his reading.

'Do you hear that?' Rahab called. 'Someone's knocking at the gate.'

'I hear nothing.' Malakhi turned round, his eyes glazed, distant.

'One of the children, maybe?'

'They all come and go as they please. They don't bother to knock.'

The knocking came again; faint yet insistent. Rahab went over to the gatehouse and climbed up the stairs to look down from the broken battlements.

'Hallo there!' he called – and found himself staring down into the gold-freckled face of the shepherd boy he had first met days ago on his way up the mountain. But this time the child was not smiling; his face was strained, the blue eyes dark with warning.

'What's wrong?' Rahab shouted down.

'Armed men.' The child's voice was breathless and shrill. 'Coming – this way.'

The brightness of the afternoon seemed to fade.

'How many? And coming from where?'

'Too many. Coming from – the Gorge.' The child turned to run, the sun glinting golden in his hair. 'From – Arcassanne.'

'Wait,' Rahab cried. 'Come in. You'll be safe with us –'

'Safe? With *you*?' the boy cried back over his shoulder as he ran.

Rahab turned to find Malakhi gazing up at him in dismay.

'Armed men?' Malakhi repeated. 'But – but what about our letter? I thought we might have received a reply, I thought we might have entered into negotiations over terms –'

'It's too late for negotiating now,' Rahab said, his voice grim. 'Aymon's sent us his answer. Armed Hawks – a whole troop of them.'

CHAPTER 28

Jaufré d'Orbiel felt the heat of the sun burning the skin at the back of his neck as he watched his men leading their horses up the winding stony track from the shade of the Gorge. It had taken five riverboats to bring the Hawks up the swollen river against the churning current. Now they had reached the head of the track and the path split into two as they emerged from the Gorge at the foot of the mountains. Traces of snow, white as sprinkled salt, still iced the distant, jagged line of peaks.

Jaufré called a halt and summoned Arnault.

'Which way now?'

Arnault squinted up into the sun.

'The path we took goes eastwards, away from the noonday sun.' He looked at Jaufré, frowning into the brightness. 'Talking of sun, Captain, you look as if you've taken a bad dose of it. Remember in Djihan-Djihar you were always telling us to cover up?'

'Just take the lead Arnault,' Jaufré snapped. 'I'm relying on you.'

But as Arnault swung himself up into the saddle, Jaufré surreptitiously passed one hand across his face. His skin felt dry, almost leathery, like old vellum . . . but he had no mirror to check his reflection. He jammed his hat down, curling the brim low over his face. The glare of the sun hurt his eyes and as they rode on, he began to long for evening, for the cool and the night to settle over the mountains.

The Hawks rode on in silence, subdued, grim-faced; Arnault had told them what had happened to their companions-in-arms. Jaufré was in no mood to cheer them out of their gloom. He had preoccupations of his own.

'Odd,' Arnault muttered.

'What's that?' Jaufré had been lost in the dark night of his thoughts.

'We haven't passed a living soul since we left the river. Not even a shepherd. Now doesn't that strike you as odd, Captain?'

297

Jaufré glanced around; the mountain pastures were deserted.

'Word travels fast up here,' he said, shrugging Arnault's concerns aside. 'They're keeping out of our way.'

'Or lying in wait to ambush us,' Arnault said with a twisted smile. 'Keep alert there!' he called brusquely to the men. 'No day-dreaming!'

Jaufré had sent Arnault on ahead to spy out the route. Now Arnault came riding back to the winding column of riders; reins in one hand, using his battered hat to fan his sweat-sheened face.

'There's another fork in the road up ahead, Captain.'

'Well?' Jaufré croaked from a throat dry with heat and dust.

'It's a good place to take a break.'

'Are you Captain, or am I?' demanded Jaufré. 'We'll break when I say.'

'But the horses are tiring. And the men.'

'We've a mission to accomplish. This isn't a pleasure-trip.'

Arnault gave a slow, resigned salute.

'On. Upwards.'

Jaufré heard the mutter of resentment as Arnault gave the order. He scanned the horizon, seeing nothing but the haze of heat veiling the high peaks.

A sound began to resonate within his mind, a strange, dreamlike music that gradually evolved into words.

The words whispered of night, the velvet caress of the dark, the dazzling glitter of the starry canopy that lit the Garden of Perfumed Night . . .

For the first time in weeks without number, his fingers itched to pick up a pen, to capture the fleeting words and images, to celebrate his shadow-lover in verse. And here he was, on horseback, halfway up some damn mountain, miles from pen or paper. He tightened his fingers on the reins, trying to will away the frustration. Why? Why now?

'*It must be accomplished.*'

He glanced round, certain that he had heard the words spoken aloud.

A shadowy figure stood high up on the mountain ridge, taller than mortal man, yet insubstantial as drifting woods-moke against the intense blue of the sky.

'*And now it will be accomplished.*'

He blinked . . . and saw that the figure had gone, a mirage of the stifling midday heat.

The dirt-track behind him was empty; the barren slope, with its lichened rocks and thornbushes, shimmered in the sunhaze.

'Armed men.' Jorah stood, a statue carved of mountain granite, glowering at Rahab across Malakhi's chamber. 'You told us that this Gentile lord I've been tending is a friend. Now comes the evidence of his friendship – a whole troop sent against us.'

'Or sent to look for their missing Lieutenant?' Rahab glowered back. He was determined not to be cowed by Jorah. 'How do we know their intentions are hostile?'

'Malakhi.' Jorah ignored the question, turning instead to Malakhi, who, arms folded, eyes cast pensively down, had not intervened in their argument. 'Don't waste any more time. Authorise the use of the amulets now.'

What was it with Jorah? Rahab clenched his fists behind his back, trying to will away the growing impulse to hit the man.

'Think, Jorah!' he said. 'Rashiel will destroy the castel and leave us homeless. Another snowstorm will bring famine to the whole country. We have to consider the consequences.'

'Barakiel, then.' Jorah said. It was a direct challenge.

'You ask too much of Rahab,' Malakhi said. 'A second summoning could kill him.'

For a moment, it seemed as if the brightly sunlit room grew dark. Rahab blinked.

'Shouldn't we wait to find out who these armed men are, what they want?'

Jorah let out a short, mirthless bark of laughter. 'Wait until our throats are cut?'

Rahab had lost patience with Jorah. He wished Malakhi would take a more dominant role in the argument and silence him. But Malakhi seemed distant, almost unwilling to become involved; unwilling, Rahab suspected, to be forced to take such a difficult decision.

And even as he was still gazing in mute appeal at Malakhi, the room grew dark once more. He glanced out of the window, wondering if clouds had appeared to dull the sun's glare . . .

'Rahab.'

Talmai stood on the threshold, deathly pale, shakily leaning against the doorpost for support.

'Bar Talmai – you should be resting –' began Jorah.

'Can you sense it?' Talmai asked, his eyes fixed on Rahab, ignoring the others. 'The darkness?'

'Darkness? Rahab repeated. 'I – I thought it was clouds – moving across the sun –'

'Clouds?' Malakhi went to the window and gazed out. 'There's not a cloud in the sky. Not even mares' tails.'

'Then what –' And suddenly Rahab understood Talmai's warning.

'What?' demanded Malakhi.

'Lailahel,' Rahab whispered. 'The coming of night. The darkness is coming.'

'Stream ahead!' Arnault called out.

The liquid sound of clear water splashing over stones trickled into the dark labyrinth of Jaufré's thoughts. The dusty dryness of his parched tongue and throat reminded him that his physical body still had human needs, human limitations.

'All stop!' he shouted, raising his hand. The mountain stream was swollen with snow-melt. The Hawks dismounted, hurrying over to plunge their heads and hands into the fast-running water. Jaufré waited, watching as they filled their water-bottles and led the horses to drink further downstream. Only when the last man had drunk his fill did Jaufré go to kneel on the stony side of the stream and lean over the glass-clear water.

The cold shock of the stream-water was like a slap on the face; he gasped as he raised his head, hair dripping down his embroidered Hawks tabard. It was only then, as he knelt over the stream, that he saw, distorted by the fast-moving water, a twisted reflection of his face.

It was not so much the darkness of his sun-seared skin that shocked him, but the worn, wasted look, the hollowed sockets in which his dry eyes burned. He looked ill, burned up with fever.

And yet he felt strong, vigorous, powerful.

Lailahel would protect him. Lailahel would guide him. He was Lailahel's Warder now.

Lia shivered. Glancing up, she saw that the shadows were lengthening. It must be later than she thought; she had left Berengar alone for longer than she had intended.

She stood up, brushing the earth and dead leaves from her skirts. She had not meant to linger so long here. But now she hesitated. Going back meant facing up to the prospect of Berengar's disability.

She saw him limping across the Hall of the Belcastel mansion. His face was drawn, prematurely lined and twisted with pain, his golden hair greying at the temples. She saw them sitting together, awkward, silent, because there was no longer any-thing to say that did not speak of resentment or guilt. There would always be the unspoken accusation that his noble upbringing forbade him to articulate: *I would not be lame now if you had not run away . . .*

And then there was the matter of the Hawks.

She went slowly, reluctantly, to the doorway of the watch-tower. Seven deaths on her conscience. In the burnished light of late afternoon, the plateau shimmered . . .

There were men on horseback coming up the track.

She gripped the rough stone of the tower, feeling it grate against her fingers. The mirage swirled in front of her dazzled eyes.

Afternoon ghosts, returned to haunt her?

And then she realised that the mirage was the clouded dust scuffed up by the horses' hoofs.

A dizzying whirlwind of cloud and snow suddenly swirled through Jaufré's mind: Barakiel, Shalgiel, Rashiel . . .

'Close now, so very close . . .'

His heart beat faster. Above it the amulet burned against his skin, a constant torment.

'Where are they?' he whispered, one hand on the reins, the other sliding to make contact with the amulet. 'Guide me, Lailahel.'

The shadows were lengthening as the Hawks rode on in single file up the narrow track. To their right the mountainside fell away into a sheer-sided ravine. To their left, jagged crags of rocks towered up into the intense blue of the sky.

Ambush country.

The stillness of the barren mountainside was broken only by the clip-clop of the horses' hooves on the rocky path; there was no birdsong, no sultry summer hum of insects. The icy hand of Shalgiel had turned the verdant mountainside to untimely winter, even though the sun still burned in the sky.

Up ahead the track widened . . . and Jaufré caught sight of a ruined watchtower perched on the precipitate edge of the cliff. A plateau lay ahead . . . and there, nestling beneath the peaks, stood the walls and towers of an old castel, its crumbling stones seared by the afternoon sun to tints of ochre and ash.

'Company halt!' he called. 'Arnault – is this the place?'

'Yes, Captain!' Arnault called back. Jaufré could hear sullen resentment in his voice. Somewhere in the deep ravine close by lay the broken bodies of his detachment, unburied. 'Do we attack?'

All that stood between him and the fulfilment of his ambitions were the crumbling walls of the old castel – and a handful of Tsiyonim fanatics. Yet now that the moment had come, he hesitated. They possessed three amulets – and he had only one.

Attack. His hand froze in the act of lifting it to give the command.

Whose will was directing his actions? Was he acting for himself alone? Or was he merely a human puppet in the power of the spirit that possessed him?

'Why do you doubt, Jaufré?' The voice burned in his blood, his brain, dark as midnight fires. *'Fulfil your destiny. I have made you strong, I will protect you. You are my Warder.'*

But . . . afterwards?

'You always wanted to be strong, didn't you, Jaufré? Invulnerable? I have armoured you against life's assaults. No one can touch you whilst you are my Warder.'

'Captain!'

He looked up, blinking, to find Arnault staring at him, eyes narrowed.

'Do we attack? In broad daylight?'

Beyond Arnault, Jaufré's eyes caught a flicker of movement. Someone had come out of the ruins of the watchtower.

A girl.

'Not yet,' he said, pressing his heels into his horse's flank, urging it forward across the plateau.

The girl half-turned as she heard the sudden thunder of horse's hoofs. He saw her face, white with shock, saw her mouth open to scream.

He tugged hard on the reins, bringing his horse to a skidding halt, and leapt down from the saddle, running after her. Lailahel had lent him strength; he covered the rough ground easily.

302

She began to run, but hampered by her skirts, she was slower than he. He lunged out, grabbing hold of her by the wrist, pinning her arms behind her back.

'Let go!' she cried, whipping around, kicking him. 'Let me go!'

'You've caught yourself a mountain cat, Captain!' Arnault called, trotting up.

Her dress was filthy, her dark hair had come loose from its gold-threaded net – but still he recognised her.

'So here you are at last,' he said. He smiled, pleased with his prize. 'Lia Maury.'

Rahab, with Jael clinging tightly to his hand, led Laban and the older girls down the wooden ladder into the castel cellar.

'Ugh,' said Jael with a shudder. 'Big spiders down here. Hairy ones.'

'Light another lantern, Laban,' Rahab said. 'That should keep the spiders at bay.'

'I want to be upstairs with the men', Laban said sullenly.

'We need someone down here to protect the little ones. Someone sensible,' Selima said, handing him the tinder box.

'Are all the children accounted for?' Rahab asked, gazing around at the pale faces peering at him in the gloom.

Only a few weeks ago he had led Thirzah and Iudith down into Baruch's cellar, and now the nightmare was happening again, happening in Tifereth, where he had believed they would be safe. And all because of the amulets . . .

'All here,' Laban said, striking a flame.

'We need someone to keep them amused.' Selima caught Rahab's eye. 'To keep their minds off things . . .?'

'Me?' he said.

'You stay,' Jael insisted, tugging on his hand.

'Yes, Rahab,' Laban said, making for the door, 'and then I can go help defend the castel.'

'You'll stay here,' Selima said, catching hold of him by the collar and hauling him back. 'Because I tell you to.'

'Lia will tell you a story,' Rahab said. 'I'll go fetch her.'

In the courtyard outside, the Tsiyonim were hastily herding the animals into the barn, barricading the outer doors and shutters with benches and tables.

'Has anyone seen Lia?' he asked.

'She's with the Gentile,' someone called.

'What's . . . all the . . . noise?' Berengar asked muzzily as Rahab skidded into his room.

'Where's Lia?' Rahab asked, out of breath. 'They said she was here.'

'Been . . . asleep . . .' Jorah must have drugged him to help alleviate the pain. 'What's . . . going on?'

Rahab gazed down at the wreck of the Hawks' Lieutenant. Should he tell him the truth? Berengar would demand he put his sword in his hand and help him from his bed. In spite of his splinted broken leg, gashed head and cracked ribs, he would insist he should be on guard to defend the castel.

'Are you sure you don't know where Lia is?' Rahab said.

'Gone . . . fetch drink maybe . . .' Berengar's bruised lids closed.

A drink. Had she gone to the well – or to the kitchen? Rahab squeezed through the last gap in the barricaded door and scanned the courtyard. There was no sign of Lia. But a new sound disturbed the clarity of the mountain air, a sound he had not heard since he left the city: the regular rhythm of horses' hoofs trotting in military formation and the jingle of metal links on bridles and harnesses.

And now Rahab became aware of another sound, a distant, dull throb, so deep that he sensed rather than heard its resonance deep in the very core of his being.

The sound stopped him in his tracks. It filled his mind with the dark of winter twilight. It spoke of the coming of everlasting night.

'Is this the place they call Tifereth?' Jaufré d'Orbiel's voice rang out, piercing as a clarion trumpet on the field of battle.

From the battlements, Rahab gazed down on the detachment of Hawks ringed in formation below. His throat tightened with fear. There were too many of them. Even armed with pitchforks and scythes, a handful of elderly scholars and bookish young men would be no match for Jaufré's élite fighting men, all schooled in the art of war in Djihan-Djihar.

'Who is that man?' Malakhi asked.

'Jaufré d'Orbiel, Captain of Aymon's Hawks.' Rahab had not anticipated that the sight of Jaufré d'Orbiel would provoke such a powerful physical reaction. But even the sound of Jaufré's brazen voice evoked memories of fear and hatred that set his stomach churning.

'Open the gates!' Jaufré cried. 'In the name of Aymon of Arcassanne!'

'Why has Aymon sent his soldiers to attack us?' demanded Malakhi. 'We are a peaceful community, scholars and farmers.'

'I have reason to believe you are harbouring a dangerous criminal. A child-murderer,' Jaufré d'Orbiel said. 'Comte Aymon has sent us to arrest him.'

Rahab felt the chill of oncoming night seep through him. Now he understood Jaufré d'Orbiel's tactics – and saw how cleverly they had been outmanoeuvred.

'You are outside Arcassanne's jurisdiction here.'

'We have come to negotiate. You give us Rahab the Tailor – and Aymon will let the Tsiyonim go free from Arcassanne.'

Rahab could sense that, even without moving their heads to look, the attention of the scholars had focused directly on him. Below, the evening sun glinted on unsheathed blades.

'You have a warrant for this man Rahab's arrest?'

'I have even better . . .' Jaufré beckoned. Two of the men came forward, dragging a hooded figure between them. At Jaufré's signal, they removed the hood and blindfold from their prisoner – and Rahab saw a young woman standing blinking dazedly, her dress torn, her dark hair unkempt, unbound about her shoulders.

'Lia,' he whispered.

CHAPTER 29

'Lia,' Rahab said again. 'Oh, Lia . . .'

He had been praying she was safe somewhere in the castel, that all his frantic searching had not been in vain. Instead of relief that she was still alive, he felt a surge of anger. What in God's name had she been playing at to get herself caught? Where had she been all afternoon? What harebrained whim had driven her straight into the arms of Jaufré d'Orbiel?

'Don't bargain with him, Rahab!' Lia's voice carried up to him, shrill with outrage. 'He won't – keep his word –'

'What does this mean, Captain Orbiel?' Malakhi asked, his voice sternly cold. 'Hostage-taking?'

'An assurance of my good faith,' Jaufré d'Orbiel said. 'Give me the tailor. In exchange I will hand over Lia Maury. The others will be released from the Tour de la Justice as soon as we return to Arcassanne.'

Rahab stared unseeing into the misty distance. Now he heard another voice, darkly shimmering behind Orbiel's strident tones. He sensed the presence of a shadowy figure hovering over the distant mountaintops.

'Accede to our demands and you will not be harmed.'

Malakhi hesitated.

'The castel is surrounded!' called Jaufré. 'There's no way you can escape.'

'Then we shall stay where we are.'

'Don't force me to shed innocent blood.'

Rahab glanced uncertainly at Malakhi. What did Jaufré d'Orbiel mean? That he would sacrifice Lia? Or that he would kill indiscriminately to get his hands on the amulets?

'You must allow us time to consider your demands, Captain Orbiel,' Malakhi said.

'You have a quarter-hour to consider. If I have heard nothing from you by then, we shall take the castel by force.'

*

'How do we know?' Jorah stared at Rahab.

'Know what?'

'That we are not harbouring a murderer.' The overt accusation in his eyes froze Rahab to the bone. 'A child-murderer.'

'Oh, please!' Rahab turned away, almost speechless with contempt. 'We haven't the time to waste on this now, we need a plan –'

'What proof can you give us that you are innocent?' Jorah took a step towards him, finger stabbing towards his breast.

Rahab stood his ground, arms folded; he would not let himself be intimidated by Jorah.

'Only my word. And if that's not good enough for you –'

'I say hand him over to Aymon's Hawks. And let them take the Gentiles with them too. Then maybe we'll be left in peace.'

'Peace!' Rahab burst out. 'What makes you think Jaufré d'Orbiel will leave you in peace? I'm his scapegoat, I always have been since this whole sorry business began.'

'Admit it, Malakhi,' Jorah continued, ignoring Rahab, 'nothing has gone right with us in Tifereth since you took in this – this tailor and his Gentile girl. Nothing!'

'Oh, and maybe you've forgotten what we brought with us?' said Rahab. 'The amulets?'

'And what good have they done us?' Jorah still stared at him, his eyes dark, hard as obsidian. 'What's the point in keeping them if we don't use them when our lives are threatened?'

'You can't hand Rahab over to Orbiel,' said Lamech suddenly. 'He hasn't finished mending my coat.'

'We're not talking needlework here,' Jorah said. 'We're talking survival.'

'If we can't live together in harmony here in Tifereth, then there's no hope for us anywhere!' Rahab cried. Why couldn't the scholars see what they were doing? 'This is how it must have been in Tsiyon. Enemies at the Gates of the city – and the Temple Elders arguing with the Warders about petty issues of rank and protocol. Must we go on making the same mistakes again and again?'

A blaze of white light gashed across his sight. He stood, blind, deaf to the arguments around him, caught in a moment beyond time.

The white shore glimmers as the Dark Guardian comes silently walking across the waves, towards the Three who stand waiting on the dunes.

307

The glistening waves turn to ink beneath His shadowy feet. Darkness floods from His cloudy hair.

Slowly the three begin to move towards the oncoming Darkness. Their arms are outstretched in welcome. Slowly they move forwards across the white shore into the embrace of the Night. Their hands meet, clasp tight. Reunited.

And from the heart of their embrace comes a pearl of light, dropping into the pooled darkness like a single drop of water, setting ripples of light slowly spreading outwards.

'Reunited . . .' he murmured. In that one moment's dazzling revelation he realised that he understood the passage in the Second Book of Alevi he had been puzzling over since Lamech showed it to him. It was so simple. And yet the scholars had argued over it for centuries.

'What's that noise?'

Rahab heard Malakhi's voice as if from a great distance away. He shook his head. His sight began to clear. But his tongue was tied and when he tried to speak, to tell the scholars what he had seen, he could only stammer ineffectually. And no one was paying any attention to him, no one had even noticed his brief moment of absence.

'It sounds like . . . like someone chopping wood,' Lamech said, head cocked on one side like a thrush, listening.

'Wood?' Elon went hurrying back up on to the battlements. From high above he let out a strangled cry of rage, pointing, gesticulating wildly.

'What's happening?' Malakhi called.

'My – my trees. They've taken down my best, my oldest cherry, damn them to the seven torments of hell!' Elon was almost incoherent with fury.

'But why? Not for firewood, surely?'

'They're taking off the branches, they're – ah. Ah.' Elon sagged. 'A ram. To batter down our defences.'

'Our quarter-hour is not yet up!' Lamech protested.

'Orbiel is an experienced soldier. He knows how to break a siege.'

Rahab stood silent, still dazzled by the moment of revelation. Why had no one else understood? The Guardians, divided by the petty quarrels and feuds of the Tsiyonim tribes for centuries, desired nothing but to be reunited. Their unity was a symbol of harmony. And Tifereth was the seat of harmony; Lamech had read him the passage in the Book of Alevi –

Only one way . . .

To call on one Guardian to defend them against another would only cause chaos and destruction. They must go forward willingly into the Night, they must give Jaufré d'Orbiel what he had come for: the Guardians would take care of the rest.

He looked around the courtyard, gripped by a sudden apprehension.

'Where's Jorah?' he demanded.

Lamech shrugged.

'Said something about going to lock the door to the Sanctuary.'

Zillaïs's head had begun to throb again, the old, dull throb that warned of an impending attack. The pattern of light from the grilles high in the dungeon wall began to move, to swirl like pale flames. She sat, her head resting against the dungeon wall, the child Thirzah curled asleep beside her in the straw.

Now, why now? She closed her eyes, only to see the swirls of light still flickering in the darkness. Soon the pain would become unbearable. She reached out blindly for her bag of simples, hoping there was a little dried feverfew left to stall the attack. She did not want the women to see her ill; it would not improve their confidence in her as a healer.

The dungeon door clanged open – and a dishevelled young woman was pushed inside. She stood, staring in bemusement at the throng of huddled women.

'Mamma?' she called out tentatively.

'Isn't that your daughter, Chadassah?' said one of the older women. 'Isn't that Michal?'

Chadassah started up.

'Michal! Michal!' she cried, reaching out.

'I'm here, Mamma!' The girl struggled across the crowded floor and Chadassah went towards her, arms open wide, catching her and hugging her close.

'Any news of your father?' Chadassah whispered.

'No news. No news.' Michal kept her face averted.

'You see, a little miracle,' said the older woman who had recognised Michal, nodding her head. 'We mustn't give up hope.'

Chadassah held Michal so that she could look at her, fingers moving to touch her face, pushing the straggling hair back from her forehead.

309

'How have they treated you?' Chadassah cried, voice trembling. 'What's this on your face? Bruises? If they've hurt my girl, I'll kill them –'

'Don't get so excited, Mamma,' Michal said in a dulled voice. 'I'm all right. I'm all right.'

'But your clothes – all torn –'

'What's the matter with Thirzah?' Michal said, dark eyes settling on Zillaïs, who knelt by the child, gently sponging her face. 'And who's this woman?'

Zillaïs straightened up.

'You're not one of us,' Michal said, her voice low and hard. She turned on Chadassah. 'What's she doing to Thirzah, Mamma?'

'I must apologise for my daughter, Dame Maury,' Chadassah said, wiping her eyes on the hem of her apron.

'Your little sister is sick,' Zillaïs said levelly. 'She has a fever.'

'How do we know you're not one of Orbiel's spies?'

'Michal!' Chadassah said sharply.

'After days in this place, how do you know who to trust?' Zillaïs said with a shrug. Her head ached.

'At least we're agreed on that!' said Michal. She was all fierce dark eyes and mussed hair, her whole being charged with a frenetic, desperate energy. 'But listen, Mamma, listen, Auntie Keziah.'

'What do you mean, listen?' Chaddassah said, bewildered.

'Can't you hear? Those voices outside?'

'Quiet, everyone!' Keziah called, her shrill quaver echoing up to the rafters.

Zillaïs, fingers gently pressing on Thirzah's thin wrist, listened too. The child's pulse felt so faint, so irregular; she was sinking deeper into the fever. How was she to break the news to Chadassah? How could she tell her that the little one was seriously ill, that she needed stronger herbs and powders than the Guard had allowed her?

The distant voices were chanting now, chanting rhythmically. The relentless rhythm of their chant seemed to merge with the throbbing in Zillaïs's head. She could not make out the words but she had heard chanting like that before, years before in Tolonada.

'Sounds like people shouting,' Chadassah said.

'The Tour's surrounded. That's why they released me. They've put all the guards on alert.'

'There's a crowd gathering outside the Tour?' Zillaïs knelt up.

'Can't you hear what they're chanting? "Killl them! Kill them!"'

'We came here for protection,' Keziah said. 'What's Comte Aymon doing, allowing these unruly people to threaten us? Baruch was right – he's not a patch on his father, God rest his soul.'

'We've got to protect ourselves,' Michal said. 'We've put up with this for long enough. We've got to fight back.'

'That's very well, dear, but with what?' Keziah said.

Thirzah gave a murmur of irritation and turned restlesly on her little bed of straw.

'What is it?' Chadassah stroked the hair from her daughter's forehead.

'That boy is sad,' she said, almost to herself. 'He wants his mother.'

'What boy, Thirzi?'

She raised herself up and pointed.

'There,' she said crossly, staring into the shadows. 'He's been crying. Why don't you stop, boy? I can't get to sleep.'

'Crying?' Chadassah said puzzled. 'I can't hear anyone crying.'

Zillaïs rose up on her knees, trying to distinguish the child Thirzah was complaining about. For a moment she thought she could hear a faint sound of weeping . . . but then the shouting from outside rose again, drowning it out.

'She's delirious, isn't she?' Chadassah whispered. 'There's no one there.'

Lia watched the Hawks stripping the wood from the cherry tree they had felled, working swiftly, efficiently under Jaufré's vigilant eye.

They had bound her ankles and dumped her ignominiously in the long grass by the horses. She could not even hobble now . . . though she reckoned she could make a good try at jumping, rolling if needs be. There had to be some way she could make good her mistake.

She had no doubt that Jaufré d'Orbiel was mad. Why had Berengar not seen it? Or had they been friends for so long that to admit it would have broken some unspoken, unwritten code of loyalty? But that dangerous, predatory glint in Jaufré's eyes which had so attracted the women of Aymon's court was no

311

longer fascinating; it terrified her. She was not sure what controlled him now ... only that it was as if someone else stared at her from his fevered eyes, someone else animated his emaciated features.

One of the Hawks came hurrying over towards the horses; she looked up and recognised the seamed, weather-burned face of Arnault, Berengar's second-in-command ... whom he believed to be lying dead in the ravine.

'Arnault,' she called in a whisper. 'Arnault!'

He heard her.

'No time to talk, demoiselle,' he said gruffly, rummaging in his saddle bags.

She had to make him listen.

'Berengar is alive. He's in the castel. They've cared for him, bound his wounds. Why are you going to attack the people who rescued him?'

'Alive?' Arnault said slowly.

'You thought him dead, didn't you? And he thought you were dead too. If you attack, what will become of him?'

'Gag her!' Jaufré d'Orbiel had come silently up without her noticing.

'And I believed you had come to rescue me!' she cried. 'You're just using me.'

'I said gag her,' Jaufré repeated. There was a blank darkness in his eyes, an emptiness which chilled her. 'And bind her eyes.'

'She says the Lieutenant is still alive. In the castel.'

'Will you gag her,' Jaufré said, 'or must I do it myself?'

Arnault pulled a scarf from around his neck and knelt down beside Lia. The scarf was none too clean and Lia tried to squirm away as he reached out for her.

'I'm sorry, dem'selle,' he whispered. 'I have to obey orders.'

In the dim light of the *shul*, Schimeon had swept up the broken glass. Baruch was attempting to relight the flame, repeatedly bowing his head as he muttered prayers over the oil and the blackened wick.

'We can't stay here and let them attack the Tour,' said Mandel the Shoemaker. 'We've got to stop them.'

'Agreed!' said Tobiah.

'And if we can't stop them,' said Mandel, 'then at least we'll all die together.'

'Very heroic, Mandel!' said Schimeon. 'You can die if you choose, but my wife and daughters are in the Tour and I'm going to get them out!'

'You think I'd leave my Keziah to die?' Baruch said indignantly.

'There must be another way into the Tour. A secret way,' Schimeon said to the Hawk.

The Hawk shrugged. 'There might be.'

'If you could smuggle us in, we could help defend the Tour.'

The Hawk looked at him scornfully.

'You're wasting your time. You don't stand a chance.'

'Fe!' Schimeon said. 'What's to lose in trying? Who's with me?'

'I am,' said Mandel.

'We're all with you,' said Tobiah.

'And you,' Schimeon said to the Hawk, 'you can stay and look after the pussycats. This is men's work.'

They set to work dismantling the makeshift barricade and cautiously scanned the lane.

'All clear,' Schimeon said, beckoning the others out.

Mandel looked up at the sky.

'Is there another storm brewing? Why has the sky gone so dark?'

'It looks like night,' Tobiah said. 'We'd better hurry.'

'I don't like it,' said Baruch, a shiver in his voice. 'It feels . . . wrong. Like the night the child was killed. Can't you sense it?'

Darkness was fast seeping into the sunlit city like a dark flood, blotting out the light of the sun.

Arcassanne had become a city of eternal night.

The daylight was fading fast. Too fast. Rahab glanced up at the sky as he sped across the courtyard.

Lailahel was coming.

Rahab tugged the Sanctuary door open.

Jorah's hands were on the casket; he was opening the lid –

'Wait!' Rahab cried.

Jorah turned. The sacred flame above his head cast its fiery light on his face.

'I know what you intend,' Rahab said.

'It's too late to stop me now.'

'Don't do it,' Rahab said quietly. 'Jorah, I beg you, don't do it.'

313

A thunderous blow shuddered through the building; the Hawks had begun their attack on the main door of the castel.

'You've fooled Malakhi and the other Elders with your heartbreaking tales of the sack of Galicys. But you haven't fooled me.' Jorah lifted the Barakiel amulet, showing it to him, deliberately taunting him. 'Now that Orbiel has us surrounded, you're going to try to bargain to save your skin by giving him our amulets. Our *birthright*.'

'It would look that way to you, wouldn't it,' Rahab said, teeth clenched with the effort of controlling himself. 'You see everything awry, Jorah. Twisted. You're little better than Orbiel –'

'Deny it. Dare to deny it in the holy Sanctuary – and perjure your soul to all eternity.'

'Oh for heaven's sake, Jorah,' Rahab cried. Jorah was too close to him, thrusting his bearded face into his. If he provoked him much further, the tailor would not be answerable for his actions. 'Must you keep quoting the Prophets at me? Go get ready to use your skills as surgeon and let me do what I have to do.'

He made a grab for the casket. But Jorah was quick, far quicker than he had anticipated, and caught hold of him by the wrist, twisting his arm up behind his back.

'Don't worry, tailor,' Jorah said, teeth bared in a smile. 'One part of your plan will still go ahead.' The grip on his wrist tightened. 'I'm giving you into the custody of Jaufré d'Orbiel. Let him deal with you as he will.'

Pain from the twisted wrist flashed through Rahab's mind, shatter-bright as summer lightning. He heard Jorah give a cry – and the pressure on his wrist suddenly ceased.

Jorah had fallen back and was nursing his hand, face grimacing with pain.

There came another thunderous thud against the main door. The stones of the castel trembled.

Rahab seized the casket and made for the door – only to run straight into Talmai, knocking him over.

'Rahab – stealing the – amulets –' gasped Jorah. 'Stop him!'

Rahab, mind still alive with aftershocks, registered that time was running out, and that in all Tifereth Talmai was the only one capable of stopping him.

'Don't listen to him, Talmai,' Rahab cried. 'Trust me.'

'You've deceived us,' Talmai said. 'Lied to us.'

The walls of the Sanctuary trembled again as the battering ram swung against the door.

'Believe that if you must.' This was not the time to explain his motives; no one would understand. Rahab turned to run.

A blast of ice-cold air froze him where he stood. He saw Talmai's hand outstretched, saw the icy film that had chilled his eyes, legacy of Shalgiel's powers.

'If this is the end,' Talmai said, 'then we must not let the Gentiles cross the threshold of our Sanctuary.'

How could he free himself without injuring Talmai? How could he call on Barakiel to oppose Shalgiel without destroying all their hopes of salvation?

He closed his eyes, concentrating on the ice-shield that surrounded him, willing the energy that crackled in his brain to melt his way out. Water began to drip on to the Sanctuary floor.

Talmai had turned to Jorah, was helping him to sit up, examining his burned palm.

Rahab tried to wriggle his fingers, which had turned blue and numb with cold. The effort was draining his strength; one hand still clutched the casket to his chest; through the other he summoned the last of Barakiel's brightness from his brain.

The icespell turned to water and he plummeted forward, slamming the Sanctuary door shut in Talmai's face.

The passageway was black as Lia's cellar. A dim, louring light filtered down from the high window-slits.

Barakiel, help me.

A tiny shock of blue fire flickered from his fingertips, sizzling into the lock.

He heard Talmai rattle the handle – but the door was locked fast, the metal mechanism jammed, fused together.

'No, Rahab!' Talmai's voice echoed in the Sanctuary. 'Don't betray us! Remember Tsiyon! *Tsiyon!*'

It would take them a minute or two at most to break the lock. Rahab forced his frozen limbs into action, moving off jerkily down the passageway. He had taken longer than he had planned. Maybe he was too late already. The courtyard was murky, as if night fogs had come drifting down from the mountain.

And it was empty. Defenceless.

Where was Malakhi? And Elon?

Their scholarly vows might forbid them to fight – but there were other ways to defend the castel. Were they just going to let

315

Jaufré d'Orbiel's Hawks smash their way inside and massacre everyone?

'It's getting dark,' muttered one of the Hawks as they swung back with the tree-trunk for another blow.

'Not another storm brewing?' Arnault hesitated.

Jaufré saw the unease in his eyes. Arnault had not forgotten the destructive fury of Shalgiel's blizzard.

'*Arnault!*' he said warningly. 'They're relying on you.'

'Come on, lads,' Arnault called, his eyes fixed on the sky. 'One more try and we're in!'

Jaufré glanced up. A shadowy figure hovered high above the castel. Its arms were outstretched, and from its fingertips darkness swirled and spread like a cloud of black smoke.

'Lailahel,' he whispered.

Even as he watched, the figure rose slowly into the air and came drifting towards him, trailing its cloak of darkness from silk-black wings.

'Cloud building fast, Captain.' Arnault said edgily. 'Too fast. This is how it happened before.'

Could no one else see the winged Guardian?

'Shall I give the order to take cover?'

'No!' cried Jaufré. 'The darkness will cover our attack.'

'It'll be too dark to see where we're going!'

'Forward!' Jaufré cried. He could feel Lailahel's dark strength pulsing through his veins.

'Like last time? Straight into the ravine?'

'Follow me!' Jaufré drew his sword, pointing it towards the castel. The steel glinted like a smoky flame in the fast-growing dark. 'Follow my sword!'

The Hawks swung the battering ram at the castel door again, and the ancient wood splintered and broke. One final blow – and the door split asunder.

'Into the castel!' Jaufré cried. Drawn swords flashed in the dimming light as they began to hack through the splintered timbers.

'Good evening, Captain Orbiel,' said a voice from the other side of the broken door, quiet yet insolent. 'I believe you're looking for me.'

CHAPTER 30

'Halt!' Jaufré held up his hand; the Hawks gathered about behind him, swords drawn, edgy, ready to charge.

In the fast-gathering gloom he could not make out the shadowed features of the man who had challenged him, could not even see if he held a weapon. But the amulet began to sing at his breast, a song of unendurable yearning.

'Who are you?' he demanded.

'Don't you know me? You've been looking long enough for me,' came back the calm reply. 'Call off your attack. You stated your terms clearly enough. My life – in exchange for Lia. In exchange for the freedom of the Tsiyonim.'

'Rahab?' Jaufré said, on his guard. The song of the amulet burned more intensely. 'Rahab the Tailor?'

'Rahab ben Chazhael,' the man said.

Jaufré could see the gleam of white teeth in the darkness; the man was smiling. Why would a man giving himself up to his captors smile? Was he insane – or was it a trap?

'Well?' Rahab ben Chazhael asked. 'Where is your hostage?'

Jaufré stared at the tailor. There seemed to be a faint haze of light about him in the darkness . . . and his eyes glimmered, lightning-blue, in his shadowed face.

Barakiel. The voice of the amulet spoke within his mind. *Remember? Storm over Arcassanne?*

'You,' he said, recognising him now. 'I know you.'

'Bring back the girl,' the tailor said quietly, 'and I will give you what you have come for.'

The amulet blazed up fiercely at Jaufré's breast.

'He's just stalling, Captain,' said Arnault. 'Playing for time.'

Arnault's words brought Jaufré back to himself. He became aware of the restlessness of his men, nervy, charged, primed for combat.

'All the time he's keeping you here talking,' Arnault said, 'they're preparing their trap.'

'Let's just kill him,' said one of the Hawks.

'Don't you want to see what I have here, Captain Orbiel?' called the tailor.

Jaufré took a step forward – and sensed the Hawks moving behind him, clustering together, ready to attack. Now he could just make out in the gloom that the tailor was carrying a box. A metal casket.

'It's a trap,' muttered Arnault.

'Stay back,' Jaufré said, rounding on him. 'I know what I'm doing.'

'This is what you have come for, isn't it?' came the tailor's voice again in the darkness.

'Open it,' ordered Jaufré.

The tailor opened the lid of casket . . . and a faint gleam lit his face.

Jaufré felt dizzy with desire: everything he had ever longed for lay within the little casket.

'The amulets,' he said. His voice was low, hoarse with excitement. 'What's to stop me cutting you down where you stand and taking them?'

'You could try,' said the tailor. Jaufré detected a tension underlying the calmness of his voice. Perhaps he was not as self-assured as he wished to appear. 'But I wouldn't advise it. They must be given. Willingly. Not taken by force.'

The fierce song of the Lailahel amulet throbbed through Jaufré's body. One desire obsessed him, one desire drove him. He no longer knew his own will; he knew only the eternal hunger of the Guardian Spirit that possessed him.

'Then give them to me,' he said, sheathing his sword.

'The girl,' Rahab said. He hoped his voice sounded more confident than he felt; he had put all his courage into this.

Jaufré d'Orbiel came slowly towards him out of the darkness.

Rahab took a step back. Behind Orbiel he could see the Hawks clustering together, could see the dim glint of drawn blades. The enormity of the risk he had taken terrified him. Suppose he was wrong – and Jorah was right? Suppose that instead of saving the community, he brought about its destruction?

'Lia Maury,' he said again, quietly insistent.

'Arnault!' Jaufré d'Orbiel's eyes were fixed on the casket. 'Bring the girl here!'

Rahab clutched the casket to him. He did not want Orbiel to

318

see that his hands were shaking. But Orbiel seemed to have preoccupations of his own ... and even by the amulets' faint radiance Rahab could see that his face was terribly altered, emaciated, as though he was being eaten away by some insidious wasting disease. Was this what became of the Guardian Warders? Was this his fate – and Talmai's as well – if they were to call on the Guardians again? Would they too be burned up by elemental forces too powerful for mortal men to control?

And suddenly he felt a terrible kinship between himself and Jaufré d'Orbiel. They were linked, linked by their Wardership, linked through the celestial kinship of their Guardians.

There was a disturbance amongst the Hawks gathered in the gateway and Arnault came pushing through, guiding Lia, his hands on her shoulders, steering her towards Orbiel.

She stumbled and almost fell; Arnault reached out and grabbed her by the arm, roughly jerking her upright. Rahab heard her give a muffled cry of outrage. Even in the darkness he could see that they had blindfolded and gagged her. Dear God, what else had they done? Wild anger surged through him; he wanted to go to her, to reassure her, to hold her –

'Here she is,' Orbiel said. 'Now give me the casket.' He extended his left hand; he still gripped his sword in the right.

'Ungag her first,' Rahab said. He had to be certain.

Jaufré nodded and Arnault pulled the gag from her mouth, the blindfold from her eyes.

'You bastards!' Lia shrieked. 'When Berengar hears of this, you'll pay; he'll have you hung from the walls of the city by –'

If she could still let fly as colourful a mouthful of insults as that, Rahab reckoned she must be all right; he had forgotten she was a sailor's daughter. But it was not safe for her to stay here in the courtyard. When he handed the amulets to Orbiel, there was no telling what would happen. And though his heart ached to have to bid her farewell in this abrupt, perfunctory way, he needed to ensure she was out of danger.

'Lia,' he said, 'go to Berengar.'

'Why?' she said, pausing to draw breath. 'What's going on?'

'Just *go*.'

She must have caught enough of the ragged desperation in his voice to realise the precariousness of the situation. He saw a look of incomprehension pass fleetingly across her face – and then she turned and to his relief, began to hurry across the courtyard.

319

The darkness seemed to intensify, thick black clouds filling the courtyard. Rahab sniffed the air. There was a faint smell of burning. Perhaps the scholars had lit the lamps in the castel . . .

'Now your part of the bargain,' Jaufré d'Orbiel said. His voice was low, breathless, like a man in the grip of passion.

Rahab swallowed. If he was wrong –

He held out the casket. Let Orbiel come to him and take what he so desperately desired. Let him look him directly in the eyes.

'*Stop!*'

A man came hurtling out of the darkness towards Rahab. Rahab saw Jaufré tense, saw the gleam of the unsheathed sword, ready to kill anyone who stood in his way.

'You're giving away our birthright,' the man cried. Rahab recognised Talmai's voice. 'It's not yours to give!'

'Stay back, Talmai,' Rahab said warningly. He felt Barakiel's power tingling in his fingertips. Yet he could not use it against his brother again. To oppose a fellow Warder at the very moment of reconciliation would negate everything. Tifereth would fall, as surely as Tsiyon had fallen centuries ago.

'The fires are lit,' Talmai said. There was a strange, exultant tension in his voice. 'Better the amulets be destroyed with us – than we give them into the hands of a Gentile to use against us.'

Rahab sniffed the air again. The smell of burning was stronger now.

'What have you done?' he said, his voice choked. 'Talmai – what have you done?'

'Better we die by our own hand than by the swords of our enemy,' Talmai said. There was an eerie calmness about him now, an air of resigned acceptance. 'We shall never surrender our Holy Sanctuary. Rather let it be consumed in fire as it was in Tsiyon –'

'Give me the casket,' Orbiel said, coming closer.

'For God's sake, Talmai,' Rahab cried, 'put out the fires!' Where were the other scholars? Why hadn't they stopped Talmai? This was meant to be the moment of transcendence, the revelation that he had glimpsed in his vision. This could have been the turning point –

And now Talmai had ruined it.

'Rahab!' Lia cried from the darkness. 'The castel's on fire! I can't get to Berengar's room!'

'Let the Gentiles burn too,' Talmai said. 'Let them know the terror of the flames. Let them taste their own medicine.'

Rahab became aware of a faint crackling sound.

'Come back to the courtyard, Lia,' he called. 'Come here.'

White-faced, coughing, she appeared out of the rolling smoke.

'Jaufré,' she cried, 'Berengar's in there, he's trapped. If ever your friendship meant anything to you, save him, please save him.'

'Where are the scholars?' Rahab went over to Talmai.

'Give me back the amulets and I'll tell you.' Talmai spoke with unnatural, chill calmness. His eyes glittered in the dark, devoid of emotion, bleak snowfields under a winter's sky.

'What have you done with them, you madman?'

The courtyard was beginning to fill with smoke.

'Captain,' Arnault called, pointing, 'I can see flames. She says the Lieutenant's in there.'

'He can't walk, Jaufré,' Lia said. Tears streamed down her cheeks. 'His leg's broken. He'll suffocate if we don't get him out.'

A commotion began in the barn as the animals locked inside smelt the smoke and began to kick at the doors, in a panic to get out. And from further away, deep within the castel, Rahab caught the distant sound of cries for help.

'Berengar?' Jaufré d'Orbiel repeated. 'Alive?'

'I tried to tell you but you wouldn't listen!' Lia cried. 'Do something – before it's too late!'

'Captain,' Arnault said again, 'we've got to get him out.'

Jaufré nodded. He cleared his throat. 'Hawks!' he barked. 'Get in there – and find Lieutenant Belcastel.'

'Follow me. This way.' Lia set off back into the billowing smoke, the Hawks hurrying after.

'Now, Rahab ben Chazhael,' Jaufré d'Oriel said, 'we had an agreement . . .'

By the flickering light of the burning building, Rahab saw Talmai looming up out of the darkness, the young scholar's face riven with anger.

'Here. Take them; they are yours,' Rahab said to Jaufré d'Orbiel, holding out the open casket. 'Let the Guardians be reunited.'

Jaufré reached into the casket.

'No!' cried Talmai, flinging himself forward, trying to wrest the casket from Rahab's hands.

Jaufré d'Orbiel turned on Talmai. His hand clutched at his breast. Between his clawing fingers Rahab saw the midnight gleam of a fourth amulet.

A figure of towering shadow arose where Jaufré d'Orbiel had been standing, cloudy hair dark as smoke, great sable wings unfurling from broad shoulders.

321

Talmai fell back, one hand upraised, covering his face.

And a soft voice spoke, a voice blacker than midnight.

'My will over yours, Shalgiel. I will not be denied.'

'Talmai!' cried Rahab. 'Don't fight him. If you oppose him, we will all be destroyed.'

'No!' cried Talmai again, but there was an uncertainty now in his voice.

'Remember Galicys,' cried Rahab into the swirling darkness. 'Shaoni –'

Flames, smoke, cries of terror and confusion . . . Rahab reached out in the darkness to Talmai.

'No! *No!*'

'Shaoni. I've come back for you,' Rahab said steadily.

'You let go my hand.' It was no longer the voice of a grown man but that of a frightened child, lost and alone. 'Why did you let go my hand? Why did you leave me on my own?'

'I'm here, Shaoni. I'm here now. I'm not going to lose you a second time.'

He had lost hold of Shaoni's hand once before. He was not going to let it happen again. His hand fumbled in the black of utter night – and caught hold of his brother's, gripping it tightly in his own.

'Shalgiel!' The voice of the Bringer of Night resonated through the courtyard like the sombre tolling of a midnight bell.

'I am here,' Talmai whispered, drawn towards the towering figure of shadow.

'Rashiel!'

'I stand for my mother Zillaïs, Rashiel's Warder.' Lia appeared out of the smoke, her voice uncertain, wavering in the darkness.

'Barakiel!'

And then the sky cracked open and Rahab felt himself lifted up, whirled into the smoke-filled air, rising, drawn into the very core of the darkness –

Lailahel, Bringer of Darkness, steps on to Arcassanne's white shore. He has wandered the earth for years without number, seeking his scattered brothers. Now at last he has found them and they move towards him, their bright faces glimmering in the starless night. Their arms are outstretched in welcome, their hands reach out to take his –

Hands clasped, they rise slowly into the air.

Far, far below lies a walled city, wreathed in dark cloud and gloom.

They skim low over the city walls and the beating of their great wings breaks the clouds, scatters the last shreds of darkness like bonfire

322

cinders, blown away on the wind.

A light gleams faintly in the night, a light that draws them down through the looming cloud-shrouds back towards the world of men.

As they come swooping down, they see that the column of light is made of four intermingled strands; the light-strands ever moving, interchanging, interweaving, a beacon calling them back: the pure, chill white of falling snow, the volatile, electric blue of darting lightning, the fiery glow of spilling lava and the burnished gleam of moon and stars.

A vision of another city glimmers beneath them, a city long since fallen into the dust, a city of light and song, a sacred city, symbol of hope and continuance . . .

Tsiyon.

The starless darkness was fast rolling away, and with it the choking smoke of the fire, revealing the golden glory of a cloudless sunset.

Rahab gazed about him, blinking. He stood, one hand clasping Talmai's, the other Jaufré d'Orbiel's; opposite him, Lia completed the unbroken circle. The courtyard was drenched in golden sunlight, clear and rich as wine.

'There were nine mosaic fishes on the wall of our street, not ten,' Talmai said softly into the golden air. 'Five had blue tails, four had green.'

'Shaoni?' Rahab let out a shout. 'It *is* you.' He didn't know whether to hug his brother – or shake him. 'Come here,' he said. Tears began to stream from his eyes. He was laughing and crying at once as he flung his arms around the young man and hugged him tight.

'Rahab.' Lia's voice brought him back to himself. He turned around, his arm still about Talmai's shoulders, to see she was kneeling beside Jaufré d'Orbiel's prone body. 'What's happened to him?'

He looked down at Orbiel and saw the burned skin, stretched like old leather over the sharp bones of his face. It was the face of a man long dead, a mummified face, animated only by the spirit that still burned faintly in the shadowed eye sockets. A face to inspire terror, Rahab thought, shuddering . . . and pity.

'The amulets,' Jaufré whispered, raising one hand. His voice was barely audible.

All he held was a charred, twisted lump of metal, so burned and fused together that it was impossible to tell it had once been four separate pieces.

323

'Destroyed,' Talmai said in a stricken voice. 'We've destroyed the Covenant.'

Rahab went over to Jaufré and gently took the charred metal from his burned hands, turning it round and round in his fingers. It was still hot to the touch . . . and he could still sense a tremor within, a faint stir of life. He rubbed it, blew, and a few flakes of burnt enamel came off. Beneath the charring and grime he detected a gleam of gold.

'No, not destroyed,' he said, 'but altered. Renewed, maybe.' What was it Lamech had said about forgiveness? 'When the Four Guardians are reunited then Holy Tsiyon will be restored to the children of Tsiyon.'

'But the Guardians –'

'Will always be with us here,' Rahab said, 'in Tifereth. Can't you sense their presence? We could build something – something lasting here.'

A great shout went up from the corner of the courtyard.

'Captain! Captain! Look who we've found!'

Rahab turned around and saw the Hawks triumphantly bearing Berengar with them; their faces were blackened with smuts, their hair singed, but they were smiling, laughing and cheering aloud.

Lia rose to her feet and went running to greet them, excitedly shrieking out Berengar's name.

Rahab turned away. It was too much to expect that all his desires and hopes could be fulfilled. For a few days they had shared a dream – but it had been a dream disconnected from the real world. Lia's past had returned to claim her; hadn't he known in his heart that it would always go this way?

He was only a poor tailor. She would never be his.

The courtyard of the castel filled with people; children ran about excitedly, laughing, skipping and hugging each other.

Yet it seemed to Jaufré that the sound of their laughter was no more than a distant roar, the far-off sound of waves breaking on a darkening shore. No one took any notice of him as he lay where they had left him, head pillowed on his cloak. Maybe they believed him already dead.

'Lailahel,' he whispered.

Through failing eyes he saw the Guardian daemon rise high above him, a pillar of smoke against the sunset.

'Lailahel –'

'I no longer need you. You have accomplished what had to be accomplished. Now the Four are re-united in harmony, in the seat of harmony, in Tifereth.'

The smoke-dark angel no longer inhabited his body, no longer wanted it, ruin that it was.

'Wait –' Jaufré tried to extend his hand in supplication. The effort took almost all his fading strength. His hand? To his horror it looked no more than a blackened, emaciated claw, the flesh shrivelled from the fingers. 'Don't. Don't leave me –' The parched whisper tore his throat. The pain of abandonment was an unimagined agony; as if the very sinews of his heart were being rent asunder. 'Come back. I – I will find you blood, fresh blood to feed upon –'

The air about him crackled. Eyes darker than a starless night stared coldly down into his. He cowered, riven by the chill scorn he saw in them.

'Do you still not understand? There was no blood-sacrifice. We are incorporeal. We have no need of blood – or any other food – to sustain ourselves.'

'B-but the child. Jacou –'

'The child died because of your greed, your pride, your negligence.'

'No!' cried Jaufré, flinching away. 'No, no, no . . .'

Children ran laughing past where he lay, caught up in a wild, hilarious game of catch-as-catch-can. The last, a boy, peeled off from the chase, stopping to gaze down at the dying man.

'What's the matter?' he asked curiously.

'Go away,' Jaufré murmured.

'Don't you know me?' The boy turned his face to Jaufré; it was so dazzlingly bright, it scorched Jaufré's sight. He flung up his claw hands to cover his eyes.

The dazzle of light faded, and through his wasted fingers, Jaufré saw a freckled face grinning at him from beneath an untidy thatch of golden hair.

'J-Jacou?'

'You tricked me,' the angel-child said. 'You offered me food, knowing I was starving, knowing I would not refuse. You drugged me. You gave me no choice. You say you thought only to steal a few drops of my blood – but your carelessness caused my death. You were driven by your own selfish desires.'

Jaufré could not speak; he could only gaze at the boy's radiant face.

'A-atone –' he gasped.

'A few words,' the angel-child said, 'that's all it will take. You know what must be done, what must be said.'

The unearthly beauty of the child's face seared Jaufré to the heart.

'Forgive . . .'

'No, not me!' the child broke into a peal of laughter and went scampering off across the courtyard.

Jaufré tried to raise himself on his elbow. The effort was too great and he sank back to the ground.

Forgive . . .

'There he is, the tailor!' Arnault cried, pointing at Rahab. 'Arrest him.'

Hawks moved across the courtyard, catching hold of Rahab, dragging him back towards where Jaufré lay.

'N . . . no . . .' Jaufré murmured.

'Captain.'

Through the ebbing tide pounding in his ears, he heard someone calling his name. Arnault's face swam in the sunset light above him.

'Captain – what have they done to you?'

'Arnault.' Jaufré plucked at the Lieutenant's sleeve. 'Listen.' Maybe there was no hope of salvation for him – but he had to unburden himself of the terrible weight of guilt pressing on his chest.

'We've caught him. The child-murderer.'

Jaufré looked up and saw Rahab, held by the arms, gazing down at him. He saw the bright shadow of Barakiel in Rahab's face, the last traces of angelic possession.

'You know what must be done . . .'

'Let him go . . .' Jaufré said. His voice rasped in his throat, dry as the rustle of dead leaves. The effort was draining the last of his failing strength. 'He is innocent . . .'

'Captain?' Arnault said again.

Each word lessened the unendurable burden a little.

'I . . . was responsible for the boy Jacou's death . . .' Would they believe him? He could see Arnault glancing at his men, his men looking at each other in confusion. Their hands slowly fell away from Rahab's arms.

'Rahab . . .' The darkness was descending again and this time Jaufré welcomed it; it came rushing in like a black floodtide, rising to drown him. He lifted one hand, beckoning.

'Well?' came Rahab's voice in the darkness.

Jaufré looked up and saw only the glimmer of his eyes, lightning-bright, above him.

'Forgive . . .' he whispered into the fast-flooding darkness.

CHAPTER 31

'Maman!'

Guillemette stopped. Amidst the chaos of shouts and screams in the darkened streets outside the Tour de la Justice, she could hear a child calling. Calling for her. All around her, her supporters swept on through the darkness, heedless. They were battering at the doors with axes and shovels, soon they would break the timbers down.

'Maman! Help me!'

The flaming torch dropped from her hands. That voice, so shrill and terrified – she knew it. It was Jacou's voice. Her child. Her firstborn.

But Jacou was dead. She had buried him days ago. She clutched her head with both hands, trying to black out the sound of his cries.

'No, Maman, no!' The voice pierced straight to her heart, a light, bright arrow.

'Stop!' she cried aloud. No one heard her, no one paid any attention. *'Stop!'* she cried again, straining her throat. Hallucination or no, she had to find out what this meant. But her words were drowned in the cheer that went up as the crowd burst open the doors to the Tour. They had listened to her when she had called for justice, they had followed her on her quest for revenge – why wouldn't they pay attention to her now?

'Let me past!' she shrieked, shouldering her way through, climbing up the steps.

There were Hawks blocking the open doorway, blades drawn. One sprawled face-down on the steps, blood trickling from his head.

'Where is he?' She faced the Hawks, heedless of her own danger. 'Where's my child?'

'Maman!' called the shrill voice again.

'Guillemette.' Someone spoke her name, someone put their arms about her shoulders. She shrugged them off.

'Call off your people!' ordered the foremost of the Hawks. Blood streaked his face, running from a gash in his temple.

'Let me into the Tour,' she said.

'Call them off first!' he replied, trying to staunch the bleeding with his sleeve.

She turned around, facing the crowd. She saw open mouths, contorted with shouting, in the red glare of their torches.

'Stop!' she cried. A few stones thudded on to the steps near her. The shouting, loud as the roar of a stormtide, began to slowly ebb, to subside. 'Wait here. I must do this alone. Wait for me here.'

'*Maman . . .*'

She entered the Tour, following the sound of the child's cries down the damp, narrow corridor.

Guillemette stopped, gazing down. She saw women and children huddled together in the dungeon, staring back at her, their faces pale from days of confinement.

She waded in amongst them, pushing her way through, searching, desperately searching, examining child after child. They endured her frantic investigation silently . . . until one small voice piped up, asking, 'Who's that funny lady looking for?'

She turned. The little girl who had spoken shrank away from her.

'My son,' Guillemette said. 'I've lost my son.'

'Is that him?' the little girl said, pointing. 'He's been waiting. He's been sad.'

Guillemette peered into the shadows. She could see nothing.

'Jacou?' she said uncertainly. There was a sudden dazzle of light in the darkness. In the dazzle, she saw him grinning at her, his freckled face full of mischief and amusement. 'B-but how –'

He beckoned her close. She knelt down, wanting to fling her arms about him, to hug him to her. He leaned forward and kissed her.

'Farewell,' he whispered.

The bright kiss irradiated her mind, her heart; she knelt there unmoving, enchanted by its golden spell.

When the brightness faded, she saw that she was kneeling alone in the darkness of the dungeon. Jacou was gone.

Zillaïs stared at the woman as she knelt alone in the shadows of the dungeon, her arms yearningly outstretched.

328

For a moment, a brief moment, light shimmered about her –
and her worn face was transfigured, lit with brilliance. Then the
light flickered and dimmed.

'He's gone,' announced Thirzah matter-of-factly.

Zillaïs sat up. The blinding ache in her head had disappeared.
She felt clear-headed, cleansed of the accumulated pain of many
years. She felt healed.

'Thirzah,' she said, reaching for the child's wrist. The pulse
was much stronger, her skin felt less hot and sticky and there
was a hint of a sparkle in her eyes.

'That boy isn't sad any more,' Thirzah said, taking her thumb
out of her mouth to point. 'His mother came for him.'

The pinch-faced, ragged woman still knelt in the dust of the
dungeon, hugging her arms to her thin body as though she
were clutching something – or someone – of infinite value.

Zillaïs went to kneel beside the woman.

'Madame,' she said gently. 'Do you feel all right?'

The woman slowly raised her head to look at Zillaïs.

'He was here,' she said, her thin face radiant. 'Did you see
him? My boy? Bright as an angel?'

Zillaïs slowly nodded her head.

Tears streaked the woman's cheeks, glittering like crystals in
the torchlight. She smiled through her tears as she spoke. 'He
hugged me. And do you know what he said?'

'Tell me,' Zillaïs said softly.

'He said – he said, "I have to go now. Don't be sad for me any
more, Maman." And he kissed me. Look. Here.' Slowly she
stroked her hand against her cheek. 'Then he said, "There must
be no more bloodshed. There must be peace now in Arcassanne."'

'Peace,' Zillaïs echoed. She leaned forward and took the
woman's work-worn hands in her own. 'Peace between your
kind and mine.'

'Yes,' the woman said dreamily, pressing Zillaïs's hands in
return. 'That's what he wants. Peace.'

It seemed to Zillaïs that the crowded dungeon had fallen
silent, everyone watching them, listening to their every word.

The woman blinked as though waking from her trance.

'What am I doing here?' she said. 'It's late. My children will be
wanting their supper.' She struggled to her feet and walked
away into the crowd.

CHAPTER 32

Rahab lit the memorial candles and Talmai quietly spoke the traditional words honouring their dead parents. Then they both stood, shoulder to shoulder, heads bowed in the silent Sanctuary whilst the candleflames burned steadily in the darkness.

They would have been so proud to see us here. Here together. Rahab stole a look at his younger brother's face, rapt, attentive . . . and he realised that for this moment he was content, utterly content. When the flames burned down and the light faded then the real work would begin. Somehow he would have to get to know this intense young stranger, to build a bond of trust and affection. It would not be easy. Talmai was still wary of him; it could take a long time to allay the feelings of loss and betrayal that had festered over the long years apart. But Talmai was the only family he had left. He had not spent half his life searching for him to give up on him now.

A distant gale of laughter drifted up from the hall below. The scholars were at dinner, sharing what food they had with the Hawks. It had begun an awkward, silent meal at which neither side seemed wholly comfortable . . . until Elon uncorked a keg of his apple wine and the atmosphere suddenly became much more convivial.

Talmai looked up.

'I promised Malakhi I would return to help –'

'You go on ahead,' Rahab said. He had little appetite for food or conversation. 'I'll join you later.'

Before him on the altar lay the Guardian Amulets, a knot of fused metals: gold, silver, copper and brass, dully gleaming in the lambent glow of the sacred flame.

Here in the Sanctuary he could still sense Their presence. It was as if the shadowy air were charged; a veiled radiance glimmered in the darkness.

'Reunited,' he said, his fingers brushing the metal – and feeling an answering tremor.

Jaufré d'Orbiel's blackened, desiccated face still haunted him. He knew he should despise Jaufré for the ill he had done him . . . but all he felt was a numbed pity. In Jaufré's dying eyes he had seen what his own future might hold. And he kept hearing Malakhi's warning, whispering round and round in his mind:

'Even if They are summoned by a wise man, a good man, they may yet overwhelm him.'

Humankind could not withstand prolonged contact with the Guardians. Every time he had reached out in anger and felt Barakiel's lightning glimmering at the tips of his fingers, he had burned up a little more of his own lifeforce. Now he understood why the Warders of ancient Tsiyon were chosen for their wisdom – it would take a wise man to resist the temptations and pressures that came with such power.

But he – he had not been so wise. Now that the exhilaration had begun to fade, he felt weak, almost as if the blood had thinned in his veins. Even his sight seemed less acute than before – as though a film had coated his eyes. Perhaps after a good night's sleep it would pass . . . for what use was a tailor with failing eyesight?

Someone coughed in the silent Sanctuary; a small, discreet clearing of the throat as though not wishing to startle. Rahab turned and saw that Malakhi had entered the Sanctuary.

'I owe you an apology,' Malakhi said. 'I should have listened to you.'

Rahab shook his head. 'How could you have known? I wasn't so sure myself.'

'But you saved us. It could so easily have ended in . . . in disaster.' Rahab saw Malakhi suppress a shiver. 'Only you heard the voice of the Lord speaking through the words of Alevi the Prophet.'

'Did I?' Rahab had not thought of it quite so literally.

'They'll look to you now.' Malakhi was gazing at the amulets, his face in shadow. 'As leader. They'll come to you for guidance.'

'Me?' Rahab began to laugh – and then realised that Malakhi was in earnest. 'But why me?'

'Not since the days of Alevi have we had a leader, a man who dared risk all for our cause, a man to bring us through the dangers in triumph. The Elders are already proposing making you *Tzaddik.*'

Tzaddik. Rahab felt his face flame; he had not anticipated any such honour or reward.

'You know I have no learning, no scholarship,' he burst out. 'How could an unlearned man like me become your spiritual leader? If any of the Warders is fit for such an honour, it has to be Talmai.'

Malakhi pensively passed one hand over his silvered beard. 'Bar Talmai? There is no doubt that he has the potential to become a leader, a great spiritual leader, maybe. But he is young, inexperienced. Impulsive. Whereas you – you had the vision to see clearly. You did not misuse the powers of your Guardian.'

Rahab shook his head ruefully. Why didn't Malakhi understand? He obviously thought he was being modest, merely making a show of refusing the honour. 'You put it very flatteringly, Malakhi. But I can't claim any kind of spiritual advantage over Talmai. I acted out of fear, out of anger, in Arcassanne. People will go hungry this winter because of Barakiel's coming. I can't claim I'm proud of that.'

'But you can't deny what you have done. You can't just walk away from your people now.' Malakhi came forward, gripping him by the shoulders. 'This might be the moment, Rahab, the moment to call on all our scattered brothers and sisters. The moment to use the power of the Four Guardians and retake Tsiyon for our own.'

'And what do the Books of Law say about that?' Rahab asked, unable to resist posing the question.

Malakhi opened his mouth to reply – and then, seeing the mischievous glint in Rahab's eyes, began to chuckle.

'Ah. You nearly had me there. A sense of humour is a good quality in a *Tzaddik.*' He relaxed his grip on Rahab's shoulders. 'Didn't the great Rebh Issachar save the Tsiyonim in Tolonada a century ago by charming the King with his wit?' And then the laughter faded from his face and his eyes darkened. 'But don't forget what I have said, Rahab. Give this matter serious consideration.'

'Use the Guardians to retake Tsiyon?' Rahab repeated. And then he was staring at a devastated landscape in which a few lone figures crawled between the tumbled ruins of buildings.

Desert sands swirl in gritty eddies under a flame-red sky; grey volcanic dust chokes the air which is bitter with poisonous fumes from lava, spilling red from a raw open wound in the earth. In the fume-

332

*fouled night, the black sky is rent with fitful flickers of lightning – as
snow and ash drift down on to the poisoned earth . . .*

'Rahab?'

Rahab opened his stinging eyes; his mouth burned with the
acrid taste of the volcanic dust.

'What did you see then?' Malakhi demanded.

Rahab tried to blink away the grit and fumes from his sight.

'Terrible things,' he said in a hoarse whisper. 'Oh Malakhi –
isn't it enough that we have restored the Guardians to their
rightful place, here in the Sanctuary? Can't we be content with
that?'

'Maybe for now, it is enough,' Malakhi said, nodding pensively. There was no trace of laughter in his eyes now. 'But in
time others will come, others who may not be as scrupulous as
you, Rahab, others who hear the call to Tsiyon as a call to
battle.'

Rahab did not answer. He felt tired now, so very tired. The
vision had exhausted him; he did not want to think about what
it meant – for him, for Talmai, for the Tsiyonim. Maybe
tomorrow . . . when his head was clearer.

'My boy, you look as if you could do with a good night's
sleep.' Malakhi took him by the arm and led him towards the
door of the Sanctuary. Rahab was too weary to protest; he was
glad to let someone else take charge for a change.

*The beating of Their great wings breaks the clouds, scatters the last
shreds of darkness like bonfire cinders . . .*

Rahab turned on his right side, pulling the cover up over his
head. Whenever he closed his eyes, his mind began to whirl
again with the memory of the Guardians' dizzying flight over
Arcassanne. His body ached with tiredness – but the longed-
for oblivion of sleep eluded him.

White moonlight flooded his chamber. He flung back the
cover. What was the point in fighting it? There would be no
sleep till the moon set.

He rose from his bed and, pulling on his robe over his shirt,
went out into the courtyard.

Tifereth was sleeping; even the animals in the barn and the
tethered goats were quiet. Only the shadow of a cat slunk
silently along the side of the door, stalking unwary barn mice.

Slowly he climbed the weed-grown steps that led to the
battlements.

The moonlight had turned the distant snow-slopes to a shimmer of blue; in the black sky above, the stars glittered with the brittle brilliance of winter ice.

When the vision of Tsiyon had faded – and he had come back to himself in the courtyard below – he had believed that was the end of it. The end of the mystical, cabbalistic union that had afforded them that brief glimpse of eternal Tsiyon, the city beyond time.

But now he kept experiencing little bursts of sensation, little aftershocks that sizzled through his mind. *His* mind? How could he be sure whose mind it was? Every aftershock seemed to stir memories, visions that were not of his remembering . . .

Marble palaces, vast temples, giant winged statues standing sentinel at the four corners of a great Ark of burnished gold and sandalwood . . .

It was as if his mind had been touched by the spirits of countless other Warders, long dead.

And as he stared up at the looming shadow of the encircling mountains, he realised that there was something else . . .

Words.

Rahab – fully aware that he had never penned a line of poetry in his life – was hearing words in his head, words that danced, words that rhymed.

And if there was a dark nocturnal glitter to the words, mirroring the black night sky above his head, he sensed he knew where this gift came from. A last, bizarre legacy from the dying Jaufré d'Orbiel, perhaps . . . or from the poet's dark genius, Lailahel, the Guardian of the Night?

There had to be some way to communicate what he had seen, what he had felt. And these words that danced to their own internal rhythm demanded to be spoken aloud, even to be sung, maybe . . .

He had thought of his life to come in terms of Rahab the Apprentice, Rahab the Tailor . . . but never before Rahab the Poet. The idea enchanted him so much he found he had begun to laugh aloud.

'So what's the joke?' demanded a disgruntled voice below. 'Talking to yourself's the first sign of madness – but laughing to yourself –'

'Lia' he said, surprised.

'The moonlight was too bright,' she said and began to climb the winding stair to join him. 'Brrr. It's chilly out here. Aren't you cold?' She had wrapped a blanket around herself. 'What a beautiful night,' she said softly, gazing up at the stars.

'So you couldn't sleep either?'

'No,' she said, still staring up at the dark sky. 'Look at those stars. And we were up there, so high we could almost reach out and touch them –' She gave a little shiver, pulling the blanket closer. 'Did it really happen, Rahab? Or did we just dream it?'

'Oh, it was real enough,' he said, shivering too.

'Nothing will ever be the same again,' she whispered.

He turned to stare at her. Her eyes burned with a new intensity in a face blanched silverwhite by the moonlight. With her dark hair unbound, released from its net of golden thread, she seemed a creature of moonlight and shadow. Her contact with Rashiel had been so brief . . . but Rahab could see that the Guardian had not left her unmarked: there was a glimmer of elemental fire in her dark eyes. The fire called to him, drew him. She was so close to him their arms were touching, he could see the wisping smoke of her warm breath on the cold black air.

'How can I go back to Arcassanne now?' she said into the night. 'And yet – how can I stay here?'

So close now . . . so close that he had tipped her mouth to his and begun to kiss her, cupping her face in his hands, before he realised what he was doing.

And then he became aware of a third presence, a radiance that glimmered between them in the darkness like the eerie flicker of a distant electric storm in summer.

Rahab slowly let his hands fall away from her face. He could still sense the presence although the radiance had faded.

'What is it?' she said, frowning. 'Rahab – what is it?'

His tongue seemed tied, he could only stare at her, his eyes brimming with love and regret. Was this what it meant to be a Guardian Warder? To be tied, body and soul, to the Guardian to the exclusion of all earthly bonds? How much had he become Barakiel now? Had he given so much of himself to his Guardian that there was so little left to fulfil his own heart's desires?

He tried to reach out to her again, his fingers brushing her shoulders – and a faint veil of starblue light shimmered between them.

Lia let out a little cry, drawing back from him.

'I felt it. I felt it too. What's happening to you, Rahab?'

'I don't know,' he said unhappily. He looked down at his hands, trying to examine them in the moonlight. It seemed as if the very forces that had brought them together were now driving them apart. 'I don't know.'

He heard her sigh.

'Well, I'm not staying out here freezing all night,' she announced, pulling her blanket more tightly around her. It was a brave echo of the old, carefree Lia. 'I'm going back inside.'

'Wait –' Rahab said. He put out his hand to hold her back – and then checked himself, afraid of what he might unwittingly do to her.

'Wait? For what?' she said, her voice sharp as a shard of shattered icicle. 'A lifetime? Or longer?' Then, when he did not, could not, reply, she turned and went back down the steps.

'I wish I knew,' he said into the moonlit night. 'Oh Lia, I wish I knew.'

The rich bass voice of Elon the cantor rolled around the Sanctuary, singing the ancient Psalm of Thanksgiving. There was a triumphant timbre to Elon's voice, the timbre of victory trumpets blazing after battle – and an exultant response as the Tsiyonim sang back the responses.

Lia alone stood silent, staring at the Ark, whilst all around her the others sang on fervently. Stealing a glance at her, Rahab saw tears silently trailing down her cheeks. His own voice faltered. Why was she crying? They had triumphed. They had averted disaster. She was a heroine. They had placed her in a position of honour beside Talmai and Malakhi, before all the men.

Suddenly she was no longer there, she had slipped amongst the congregation and disappeared. Rahab went after her, ignoring the glances and whispering as he wove his way through the scholars. The passageway outside was empty. Which way had she gone? To Berengar's chamber? The thought pained him. That she should go running back to the family that had spurned her for being born Tsiyonim –

And then he spotted her in the courtyard below, standing weeping into the goat pen whilst the goats stared at her curiously, chewing mouthfuls of dry grass.

'Why?' she cried. 'Why humiliate me?'

'Humiliate you?' Rahab said, confused. 'No one meant to humiliate you –'

'Putting me up there in front of everyone. Putting me on show. When I d-don't know the words.'

So this was what it was about. 'They just want to thank you. Nobody cares if you know the words or not.'

'*I* care. Don't you see, Rahab? It matters to me.'

'You can learn.'

'In time, maybe. But it would always be like . . . like playing a part. Play-acting. It would never come naturally.'

'You don't know that.'

'It's easy for you to say.' One of the goats bleated; distractedly, she put out a hand to stroke it. 'And I don't deserve all . . . this. I nearly ruined everything. Getting caught by Jaufré. It could have turned out so differently, we could all be dead –'

He wanted to put his arms around her, to hold her, to comfort her. But a movement across the courtyard caught his eye; Berengar had come out into the courtyard, and was silently watching them.

'There's so much you can do for us, Lia, in Arcassanne,' he ventured, sensing she was still torn between the city life she knew and loved – and the wild, elemental union they had briefly shared in that moment beyond time above Tifereth. 'You could build a bridge between the city and the ghetto,' he was trying to find the right words, 'a-a bridge of understanding. As Lady of Belcastel, you could do so much for the Tsiyonim.'

'Really?' She gave a strange, hard little laugh. 'You have a very diplomatic way of rejecting me, Rahab.'

'Lord Berengar must love you very much,' he said stumblingly.

'Oh, Rahab!' She stamped her foot.

'He came all this way to find you, to fight for you.'

'That's because he's a man of honour. Belcastel honour. He'd have done the same if one of his favourite horses had gone missing. The betrothed, the hunting dogs, the horses, we're all part of the Belcastel chattels.'

'In Arcassanne you told me the wedding was off. Yet still he came looking for you. Doesn't that count for something?'

'Mmm . . .' She was wavering now, his words were beginning to persuade her.

He put out his hand and stroked a loose strand of hair from her face. She caught his hand, holding it against her cheek.

'Don't forget me, Rahab.'

'How could I ever forget you?' He leaned forward and kissed her forehead, catching for one last moment the sweet, tart appleblossom scent of her soft skin. Then he gently withdrew his hand and turned, walking swiftly away, not daring to look back in case his resolve broke.

Lia looked up – and saw Berengar across the courtyard, his face riven with an expression of surprise and bewilderment. How long had he been standing there, watching them?

'It's not what you're thinking,' she said defensively.

The surprise had faded – and was replaced by a look of pain, of dazed, uncomprehending hurt. She hadn't meant to hurt him, she had never meant to hurt him. But she hadn't known until now that he was vulnerable. And the knowledge unnerved her.

'Lia?' Berengar said uncertainly, as if he was not sure it was really Lia Maury he was talking to. 'Lia, what is this?'

'It was a farewell kiss, that was all,' she said, aware her voice was curt with tension.

'That wasn't how it looked.'

He came jerkily towards her, propped on the crutches Elon had carved for him, swinging his broken leg. She saw from the sweat glistening on his face how much the effort cost him and ran towards him.

'It's this, isn't it?' he said between gasps for breath, his face twisted with the effort. 'This – this infirmity. You don't want to marry a lame man.'

'No! That's not what it is –'

'Then what, Lia?' He balanced himself on the crutches. 'And why Rahab? Why my tailor?'

Lia bit her lip. How could she begin to explain to Berengar? He had seen nothing but the flash of blinding light that dispelled the night over Tifereth. If she told him of Guardian Angels and ancient Tsiyonim magic he would never understand; he would think she had lost her reason.

'He saved my life,' she said simply. 'He saved me from the madness in Arcassanne. When your grandmother sent me away from your house, Rahab risked his life to bring me here.'

Now it was his turn to look ashamed.

'She snatched the emerald from around my neck,' Lia said, her hand stealing up to touch the mark where the chain had

338

snapped. 'She told me there would be no wedding.'

'Lia. Lia, I'm so sorry. She treated you shamefully.'

'So,' and she looked him full in the eyes, 'I have no obligation to you or your family, Bera, do I?'

He turned his head away. 'This has all been a terrible misunderstanding,' he said quietly. 'Gran'mère had no right to speak for me. I am Lord of Belcastel – and I chose you.' Forgetting his infirmity, he made to reach out for her and swayed, losing his balance.

She reached out too, catching him by both arms, steadying him. She looked up into his face and saw grim lines etched into the skin around his eyes and mouth, lines of pain and suffering.

'I need you, Lia,' he whispered.

This was Bera, her Bera. It was as if Rashiel's fire had burned away the veils of doubt and confusion from her sight; she saw him clearly now. She saw a good man, an honest man who had come through blizzards to find her.

'I know,' she said, still holding him, her head resting against his chest, feeling the thud of his heart beneath her cheek. 'I know.'

The mountainside resounded to the iron clatter of horses' hoofs as the Hawks slowly made their way back down the steep path away from Tifereth.

They had made a litter on which to carry their new Captain, Berengar de Belcastel.

Rahab stood watching from the battlements.

Last to ride out of the courtyard was Lia Maury. Rahab shook his head in disbelief. She would never cease to amaze him: one moment acting the demure city demoiselle, the next, hitching up her skirts to clamber into the saddle, just as if she were a boy.

She turned to gaze up at the battlements and saw him, waving her hand in farewell. He forced himself to smile as cheerily as he could manage, waving back.

'Farewell, Lia,' he said softly. There was a chill to the morning air, a distinct hint of coming autumn. She had assured him they would commission him to make their wedding clothes . . . but he was not sure he had the heart to do it. It would be hard to be so close to her yet no longer an equal, merely a tradesman.

'You're not going with them?'

He turned and saw Talmai climbing the crumbling stair to join him.

'No.'

'What will you do here in Tifereth?'

'I don't know,' Rahab said, 'I don't know if I'll stay yet.'

'Where will you go?' Talmai's clear eyes gazed back at him.

Rahab shook his head. He was not sure he belonged any-where any more.

'Why not stay here?'

They still had not really talked together. In the days since Jaufré d'Orbiel's death they had somehow contrived to avoid the subject of their shared past, letting any conversation that threatened to touch on painful matters drift away to less contentious topics.

'I don't really fit in here. As you said – I'm no scholar.' Rahab leaned out over the battlements, shading his eyes against the morning sun, watching the cavalcade dwindle into the morning mists.

'You could be,' Talmai said, leaning on the wall next to him. 'If you wanted to.'

'Papa was training me to be a scribe. He was teaching me calligraphy. I was making good progress when . . .' When. He didn't finish the sentence. He didn't need to.

'Did you ever go back to Galicys?' Talmai asked, gazing down the valley.

'No.'

'What happened to you?'

Rahab swallowed. There was a tightness in his throat. So much had happened to him on the road from Galicys; he didn't know where to begin.

'It's a long story. One day I'll tell it to you. But by the time I reached Arcassanne I was sick, starving, like to die. A tailor, Schimeon, took me in. I owe him my life.'

'And that's how you became a tailor's apprentice.'

'He's a good man. He helped me send messages, asking for news of you. He had friends, contacts on the merchant routes. We sent letters, so many letters. But we couldn't trace you. And he was too busy to leave the city; he couldn't spare me for a journey all the way back to Galicys.'

Talmai was silent, worrying at a loose fragment of crumbling stone with his thumbnail.

'You must have wondered why no one came to look for you.'

'I wanted Mama. And Papa. I was sure they'd come back for me. I was so sure. You . . . I thought you were dead. It was

340

years before I came to accept they were dead too.'

'You didn't see.' Rahab closed his eyes, trying to will away the horror of the memory of the wrecked house, the sprawled bodies. 'I didn't want you to see. I wanted to spare you –'

'Maybe you should have let me,' Talmai said, anger flickering in his voice. 'Then I'd have known. For sure. I wouldn't have gone on wishing, dreaming.'

'Maybe I should . . .' Rahab's voice had dried in his throat. It was still too soon to uncover the past. In months to come they might venture back, step by painful step. But not yet. Not yet.

'How dare you! Use my best mixing bowl for your stinking poultices, Doctor Jorah, would you?'

A sudden burst of irate voices down below disturbed the morning's calm. Selima came out of the kitchen, emptying a slop of green slimy mixture on to the grass, sending chickens and ducks scattering. Jorah followed her out, protesting.

'Do you know how long it took to find all the ingredients for that poultice? Lamech's been complaining of rheumatism for weeks –'

'And you can scrub it clean,' she said, planting the bowl in his hands. 'So clean it shines.'

Jorah stood, holding the bowl, scowling after her. After a while, he went over to the well and began to turn the handle.

'A union made in heaven?' Rahab was grateful for the distraction. 'Listen to them! You'd think they'd been married for years.'

'I heard a rumour that she'd taken a liking to you,' Talmai said with a hint of a sly grin.

'All the more reason for me to move on!'

'So where will you go?'

'Back to Arcassanne. I am still in Schimeon's debt. If he's to make a new start, to rebuild the business, he'll need help.'

'Back to the city?' Talmai said. 'But you said –'

'It's too quiet here,' Rahab said, shrugging. 'I'm a city man at heart. This mountain air is too clean for my lungs. I miss the chimney-smoke. I miss the clatter, the bustle, the gossip . . .' Did it sound plausible? Rahab hoped so. How could he tell Talmai the truth? That he needed to put some distance between himself and the influence of the Guardians. He needed to ground himself in the everyday world of Arcassanne, the better to try to understand what had happened here.

341

'I see,' Talmai said. But the frown creasing his smooth forehead told Rahab that his brother did not see.

'You don't get rid of me that easily,' Rahab said. 'I'll be back in Tifereth. If only to see how your translation of the Second Book of Alevi is progressing.'

Rahab reached Arcassanne on the first river-boat of the day, as mists were lifting from the limpid green Aude and the guards were opening the gates.

He stood gazing up at the pepperpot towers, the red-tiled roofs, the doves circling around the rooftops.

He was home.

On the gate a notice had been posted; catching sight of his name, he stopped to read it, peering closely at the bold, black letters:

By order of Comte Aymon of Arcassanne. Let it be known that Rahab ben Chazhael of the Tsiyonim Quarter is not guilty of the crime of which he was unjustly accused. All charges against the said Rahab ben Chazhael have been dropped following the confession made by Jaufré d'Orbiel before witnesses that he did unlawfully cause the death of the boy Jacou.

Belcastel, Captain of the City Guards.

'Thank you,' Rahab said aloud, touching his forehead in salutation towards the Belcastel mansion, nestling high above the River Gate.

Was Lia up there? Or was she back in her father's house in the Merchants' Quarter? He had tried to put her out of his mind. But everywhere he looked, he was reminded of her, every street brought back a memory.

What was the point in wishing? She was betrothed to Berengar. But he'd made her a promise when they said their farewells at Tifereth.

'I'll make you a new wedding gown. Better than the old one. A hundred times better.'

And here he was, ready to keep that promise.

Rahab stood in the charred ruins of the workroom, gazing up at the sky through bare rafters, the rafters beneath which he used to sleep in his leaky garret room.

Why had he expected to find anyone at home? The guards at the Tour de la Justice had told him that all the Tsiyonim had been released days ago. He had come straight here, hoping to find Schimeon.

No one could live in a ruin like this; it would have to be demolished and the whole street rebuilt.

He heard a sound from the back of the house.

'Anyone there?' he called.

Schimeon appeared, picking his way through the fire debris.

'Rahab!' he said. He opened his arms and hugged Rahab till he could hardly breathe. 'What are you doing here? You should be in Tifereth!'

'I've come back,' Rahab said, overwhelmed by the warmth of the greeting. 'I heard you could do with some help.'

'Well, maybe just a little . . .' Schimeon held him at arm's length. 'Let me look at you. The famous Guardian Warder here in my house!'

'How did you hear – ?' Rahab stared at his master in astonishment.

'The family's staying with Zillaïs Maury. Little Thirzah's been very sick.'

'Thirzah sick?' Rahab echoed in alarm.

'But Dame Zillaïs brought her through the crisis. And when Captain Belcastel and Lia Maury came back to Arcassanne last week, there was such a feast to welcome them home! Demoiselle Lia told us of your exploits. Since then, your name has been on everyone's lips in the Quarter.'

'*My* name?'

'My boy, *dear* old Jehiel is dead. We have no scholar to lead us, no priest to guide us. We were going to write to you at Tifereth. To ask you. If you would take his place.'

Rebh Jehiel dead? Rahab could not take in the news.

'I – I don't know what to say.'

'No need to say anything yet!'

'There are plenty of scholars at Tifereth better suited than I. Men of learning.'

'Don't you see, Rahab?' Schimeon said, beaming. 'Learning is a fine thing. But you – you could be a *Tzaddik*. Our first *Tzaddik*. People would respect you. They would listen to what you had to say.'

Rahab sat down on the fire-blackened hearthstone where they used to set the hot irons to cool. A fine film of charred dust came sifting down from the chimney. The taste, the smell of it brought a faint reminder of the vision of devastation he had seen in the Sanctuary in Tifereth. Maybe if he could tell the others what he had foreseen, the devastation could be prevented. Maybe this was what he was meant to do . . .

'But you, master? What will you do for an apprentice?' he said. 'It will take some years to train another to replace me.'

'You could be our first Tailor-*Tzaddik*,' Schimeon said with a little shrug.

Rahab looked up at him – and then began to laugh. The grim vision retreated.

'Rebh Rahab ben Chazhael,' he said, 'Tailor-*Tzaddik* of Arcassanne. I like the sound of that. Yes, I like the sound of that.'